Joanna Vander Vlugt
Dealer's Child ISBN 978-1-9990684-1-7 (Paperback Edition)
Copyright © 2021 Joanna Vander Vlugt/Ozzy Imprint
All rights reserved under International and Pan-American Copyright Conventions.
Manufactured in Canada

Editor: Pip Wallace
Front cover photograph: James Clarke Photos
Book Design by JCVArtstudio

Historical events are mentioned but this is purely a work of fiction, and the characters fictitious. Any similarity to real persons, living or dead, is coincidental and not intended by the author.

First Printing August 2021

Joanna Vander Vlugt & JCVArtStudio: jcvartstudio.net

Other Novels by Joanna Vander Vlugt

The Unravelling

DEALER'S CHILD

Dedication

As a child sitting in my parents' kitchen, I provided a backdrop of clicks on a manual typewriter, typing stories, while my mom cooked meals or knitted. Thank you Mom for encouraging my imagination.

Always in my thoughts.

Forever in my heart.

Love, your *"Number 4 daughter."*

Contents

- Prologue 1
1. Jenga 4
2. Anger Management 17
3. Newspapers 21
4. Oscar - 1968 34
5. Mr. Younghusband 42
6. Red Electric Guitar 50
7. Typewriter 57
8. Valentina 65
9. Gillian with a "G" 77
10. Spider - 1968 92
11. Type "O" 97
12. The Gorge 110
13. Hearing Panel 119
14. Edith 129
15. Selfie Sex Offender 136
16. External Investigation 142
17. Fire 153
18. Family Ties 163
19. Reckoning 169
20. Icing Sugar 174
21. Angel's Counsel 184
22. Dirty Cop 196
23. Never Leave 204
24. Good-Bye 1968 217
25. Office Meeting 225
26. Honey Trap 233
27. 1986 251
28. Hat Trick 256
29. Book Launch 264

30	Terrible Things	270
31	#teamJade	281
32	Dolphin Beach	285
33	Stop Over	296
	Epilogue	306

Author's Note

This book is not a solitary endeavour. I am grateful to the people behind the scenes who answered many questions and provided me with videos and pictures to help me better comprehend tough scenes. Ashley Vander Vlugt, Mom is grateful for your nursing expertise and thank you for inspiring the CPR scene and brainstorming the prologue, *7 Minutes*. Author Carolanne Papoutsis, my critique partner for 20 years, you have seen drafts of this manuscript from the early porridge stages. I am grateful for your suggestions and humour and our many critique sessions in person and over Skype. Pip Wallace, you are a great editor, thinking about book two and how it compares to book one. Identifying writing weaknesses and strengths, asking the tough questions. Susan, Linda and Rose, something must be said about sisterhood if Susan and I enjoy writing about it.

Janet Povey and Ted Beaubier, thank you for educating me about federal drug prosecutions. Nikki Duncan for that accidental meeting in the coffee shop where I learned that Ian is a firefighter. Ian Duncan and Katrina Maki for their firefighter expertise. Ed Vander Vlugt for adding human elements to my character, Adam. Kara Vander Vlugt for always asking about my latest project. Susan Rupertus, lawyer, for checking my legalities. Michelle Dailly and her rabbit Stevie. Susan and Rod Brewer for sharing motorcycle stories over dinner. Lynn Hooper for checking on the makes and models of bikes. Brian Richmond in the U.K. for promoting Canadian indie authors. Dunja Ghag for her strength and inspiration. Mike Sikora for providing the voice of Sergeant Stone in the book trailer and double-checking the police scenes. Jennifer Conklin for the earwig story. Thank you to Karen Kukucha and author Susan Jane Wright, my ARC readers.

The many talented authors I've learned from in the Crime Writers of Canada and Sisters in Crime–Canada West.

Thank you.

Call to Action

The reader is the most important person in the world of publishing. Your support of me has been amazing. I'm issuing a call to action since a few of you, including myself, would like to see this novel made into a movie. If a reader introduces this book to a movie producer and it is optioned for a movie, I will give 10% of the proceeds from this novel being optioned to that reader, once the cheque has cleared. Can Jade and Sage make the big screen?

Prologue

7 MINUTES

Oscar Cooper pushed aside the KFC bucket and wiped his fingers in the napkin Edith gave him.

"Thank you." He crumpled the napkin, tossing it onto the living room table.

"Anything else you want?" Edith asked.

"No." He picked up the shot glass and sipped the last drops of GlenDronach Revival. Drug dealers like him do not grow old. His industry did not include a retirement plan. You were either carried out in a body bag, or buried alive. But by some dumb-ass luck he managed to beat the odds. His partner Archie wasn't so lucky.

Hell's gate was expecting his arrival. Ever since Archie was shot dead, and Genie died a year ago, his life had been on standby. He hoped a bottle of this fine Scotch was waiting upon check-in.

Oscar thumped the shot glass on the scuffed, ring-stained table, his attention diverted to the dialysis machine Edith hooked him up to three times a week. No more. He looked at the retired nurse, her black hair now grey. She used to hate his guts. How dare he fall in love with Genie, her best friend. Genie used to tell him Edith didn't want her hanging around with him. That was the sixties, when everyone wanted to make love and get high. What he would do to step back into 1968 and be with Genie.

Genie. His sweet Genie. At night with the help of his bodyguards, Henri and Bob, he made trips to the cemetery. No chance he and Genie would reunite in the afterlife. He wasn't going to Heaven, or he would have called a priest. Instead, he called Edith with her fentanyl.

Oscar paid Edith well to oversee his kidney dialysis. If she wanted him dead she would have killed him during his first transfusion. She was the only person he trusted to put a needle in his arm. He glanced at her. "Ready?"

Gloves on, Edith nodded. "You know I have a heart condition."

"So don't have a heart attack until after you shoot me up."

Edith frowned. "Always you first, Oscar. Always you first."

Oscar stretched out on the sofa, staring at the water-stained popcorn ceiling. Perfect place for him to die. No one would think twice about a seventy-five-year-old drug dealer dying in this shithole. Some would hold a barn dance and the cops would high-five.

Henri and Bob would arrive in 45 minutes and call the paramedics. He would be front-page news. *Drug Kingpin Oscar Cooper Overdosed*. Steal the thunder from *that* woman.

Edith walked toward him, stubbing her toe on the table leg.

"C'mon, Edith. I need you to be sharp. This is your chance. You can't tell me you haven't fantasized about this."

"I took the Nightingale Pledge. It's not in me to inflict harm."

Oscar rolled up his shirt sleeve. "If I had the strength, I'd do this myself. They're coming for me. You know it. Time for me to go."

Edith fumbled with the syringe. No second chances. No stomach pumps. Straight into the bloodstream. She sighed.

Genie had been right so many years ago. Edith was jealous of Oscar and Genie's love. Genie was her closest friend. Twenty years later when Oscar offered her the job to be a nanny and housekeeper in the Thyme residence and be his spy, she didn't think twice. It meant she would be back in her best friend's life.

His right arm resting across his forehead, Oscar looked at her. "Do not save me. Are we clear?"

Edith nodded, took a deep breath and leaned forward. Her heart hammered in her chest. She brought her hand up. It trembled. She placed her hand holding the syringe against her thigh.

"Come on, Edith," Oscar's deep voice coaxed.

She pricked the needle in his vein and pressed the plunger. The fentanyl oozed down the syringe, disappearing into Oscar's arm.

He smiled.

Seven to fifteen minutes.

Edith stepped back. She dropped the syringe into the bag, then gathered the paper plates and plastic forks and dumped them into the garbage. She opened the door and dropped it outside. She'd take that with her. There could be no indication that a nursing professional had been present. She'd take her gloves off at home. The dialysis machine belonged to Oscar. It would stay here. She grabbed her purse and looked at her patient.

Oscar was out.

Already?

She stepped forward. "Oscar."

He didn't respond.

"Oscar."

Panic rose in her chest. She pressed her fingers against his wrist. No pulse. She stumbled back, knocking over the coffee table. She had killed him.

She had killed Oscar Cooper.

"*Oscar.*" She again felt for a pulse.

Nothing.

No, no, no. She pulled out her Naloxone kit. Her fingers shook as she unzipped the pouch. Three packaged needles with syringes dropped to the floor. She ripped open one package.

Where was the medication bottle? She scrambled across the floor, grabbed the small plastic container and flicked the lid. Three ampoules fell into the shag carpet. She grabbed one ampoule, popped the glass top and stuck in the syringe, drawing in the antidote.

She stumbled over to Oscar and eyed the vein.

"*Do not save me.*"

1 JENGA

*Dr. Emily said my mind was a Jenga game,
and right now the structure was challenged.*

I GASPED AND SAT UPRIGHT IN BED. MY HEART POUNDED. I swallowed and looked around my bedroom. Breathe.

The blankets moved beside me.

"Jade. You all right?" Osmond asked, rolling onto his back, flicking his shoulder-length hair out of his face. The glare from the outside lights slanted through the window, casting shadows on his bare chest.

I picked up my cell. 3:30 a.m. I put it face down. "Bad dream."

"Another dolphin dream?"

I scooted back, adjusting my pillow and leaning against the headboard. "Yes. They were breaching the water, until a man in a yacht started shooting. I … I was trying to save them."

Osmond turned on his side, propping his head on his hand. "Did you?" He ran his hand over my leg.

"Not all of them. Then the man turned the gun on me. It was a dream, Osmond. A bad, bad dream."

"No one's going to hurt you."

Osmond sounded like my therapist, Dr. Emily. I was in counselling. Having found my ex-husband horribly murdered six months ago had done a number on my mental health. Dr.

Emily said we were making progress and close to a breakthrough, but then she accepted a job in Toronto and left me a list of five therapists. I hadn't bothered contacting any of them, putting my breakthrough on hold.

According to Dr. Emily, my Vicodin dependency was masking something from my past. But what? I was tired of digging into my psyche. The more we digged, the more I dreamt about dolphins. Maybe there was a good reason why I couldn't remember chunks of my childhood? Dr. Emily said my mind was a Jenga game, and right now the structure was challenged. If I didn't start filling the gaps, I'd implode.

"Lay down." Osmond patted the mattress next to him. "I'll protect you."

I didn't need protecting. I needed an overhaul. I lay down. Osmond pulled me into him. He fell asleep. I didn't.

Four hours later I put my blue Fluevog shoes, which matched my blue pantsuit, into my backpack. I'd ride my motorcycle into work. A nice reprieve before my sentencing hearing.

"Did you fall back asleep?" Osmond asked, standing in my kitchen, holding a cup of coffee as he read the paper. He tucked his long wavy hair behind his ear. Black shirt, jeans, he had a *presence*.

"Yes," I lied.

"You've been pushing yourself with the opening of the office." Osmond turned a page. "No *God damn* way." His coffee cup came down hard on the kitchen island.

"What's up?" I asked, slipping my phone into my purse.

"Oscar Cooper died," Osmond read. "Drug overdose. Bullshit."

I walked around the kitchen island to see what Osmond was reading. "He was the Island's most notorious drug dealer in the sixties and seventies," I said.

Osmond scratched the stubble on his chin. "Says here he was suffering from kidney failure. Friends found him unconscious. Called the paramedics but it was too late. Fentanyl overdose. *No.*" With a single swoop of his arm the paper flew from the island, scattering across the floor. Osmond paced, pulling back his hair.

"Osmond. He's dead. Chill out."

Osmond braced his hand on the counter, seething. "*Chill out.* He was a monster. He can rot in Hell."

I was overtired and did not have the patience for his theatrics. "You need to get a grip." I slid on my leather coat.

"I need to get a grip?"

"You don't need to raise your voice. You're acting like a temperamental child."

"In the late sixties there was a Mexican drug dealer named Diego Lomas. He ruled the drug trade in Mexico and wanted in on the West Coast action—"

"—What does that have to do with Oscar?"

"Diego disappeared the summer of 1968. No one knows what happened to him. He came up to Canada, visited a supplier and disappeared. Jimmy Hoffa style. There were rumours that Diego was beaten to death with an electric guitar."

I pointed to the newspaper scattered on the floor. "So? I've seen worse."

"Once Diego was out of the picture, Oscar took over the drug trade on the West Coast all the way down to Mexico. He was notorious for having a short fuse and killed whoever ticked him off."

"Who? Oscar or Diego?"

"Both assholes."

"Right now, you're the one with the short fuse."

Osmond looked at me again. His square jawline and stern expression caused many of my friends to think he was always angry. Right now he was vibrating.

"If the drug section hadn't wired Oscar's home, Oscar would never have served time. Oscar Cooper and Archie Malone, his number one. Years later Archie was shot and killed in a drug deal. Nobody knows what happened to Archie's kid. Probably a small-time thug like his old man."

"Osmond. The guy's dead."

"The man sold out his family for money."

"So what? Why are we arguing about dead people?"

Osmond stood silent.

I could see his chest rising and falling. An obituary had set him off and Dr. Emily was worried about *my* structure imploding? Osmond needed help and I did not have the time to talk about this. "I've got provincial court."

"Who are you defending?"

"Lucy Starr. It's her sentencing hearing."

"Why are you defending Victoria's scum-of-the-earth? You're too good for that. You should be at Crown, putting these criminals away."

"Every person in this country is innocent until proven guilty. Every person is entitled to legal representation. That is how our court system works. Now, I've got to go." I pulled open the door. "His Honour 'Convict' Hicks is sentencing Lucy and I can't be late. He already thinks I'm the Anti-Christ."

"You're kicking me out?"

"Yes." I nodded at the door. "I have court."

He grabbed his black leather coat, sliding his arms into the sleeves and slipped on his sunglasses. "Be that way." He stepped on the newspapers he had flung on the floor and jogged down the steps toward his car. I looked at his broad shoulders, his hair flipping back. What was his problem? No, *have a good day, I enjoyed the sex last night, sorry for acting like a jerk.* Not even a peck on the cheek. Things had been tense these last few months. I asked Osmond if everything was all right at the department. He said fine and accused me of being selfish, only thinking about my new practice, not having time for him. Really? If the roles were reversed and a woman had said that, she'd be accused of being 'clingy.'

I looked at the papers, Oscar Cooper's obituary with Osmond's footprint across it. I'd pick that up later. I had to go. I locked up and walked to my Royal Enfield. Focus. Court in an hour. I swung my leg over the bike and pulled on my helmet. I turned the key, kicked the kickstand, then rode out of the parking lot. Fingers crossed His

Honour 'Convict' Hicks was in a good mood and would give my client a light sentence.

In Hicks's courtroom Lucy Starr sat beside me, dressed in a demure beige knit dress held together with Velcro strips. No make-up, long straight blonde hair, she looked innocent ... except, she had a temper.

Lucy was from a long line of Sons of Liberty children, a cult settlement from the early 1900s that had settled in the B.C. interior and were anti-government, anti-establishment, anti-everything. They didn't believe in school and didn't pay taxes. They protested the government and law enforcement by throwing firebombs and holding nude sit-ins. While Lucy's parents served time for various criminal offences, Lucy had the stability of a hacky-sack, bouncing from one foster family to another. I had suggested she dress modestly and maybe Convict Hicks would give her a lenient sentence even though this was her fourth assault charge. She had sat in my office, blinking long lashes over doe-like eyes, nodding in agreement. Yes, she would say she was sorry. Yes, she would say she was suffering from anxiety, because the moon looked cross-eyed at the sun. I didn't care what reason she needed to show remorse, I just needed her to show it.

Lucy had been working as a produce clerk in a local grocery store. One day she lost it and pelted turnips at an elderly customer who complained about the mushy grapes. Valentina Vale, the ad hoc prosecutor, had asked Hicks for the max. Given the snarly mood Hicks was in, Lucy might get it.

The courtroom doors opened and a tall blonde man stepped in and sat in the back row on Valentina's side. Clean cut, he looked at Valentina, nodded, glanced at me and smirked. I recognized him but I couldn't place from where.

"Order in court," the sheriff said.

We stood and His Honour Hicks trudged up the steps to his bench like an overweight pug. He fell into his chair, straightened papers then placed reading glasses on his pushed-in face. "Ms.

Starr, you have been found guilty of assault. This is your third offence."

"Fourth, Your Honour," Valentina interjected. She looked at me and smiled.

"Thank you," His Honour said, jowls flapping. He liked Valentina. Everyone liked Valentina. Rumour had it she texted a naked photo of herself smoking a Pink Kush cannabis roll to the law partner she was seeing at the time. Despite her after hours pleasures, she was a damn good lawyer. She had celebrity status, and the local news station referred to her as their legal expert on any legal situation.

His Honour looked at Lucy. "Your fourth assault while on probation. Do you have anything you wish to say, Ms. Starr?"

Apologize. Grandpa-figured judges did not like sending women to prison.

Lucy remained silent.

I cleared my throat.

"Ms. Starr?" His Honour coaxed.

Lucy sighed.

"I then hereby sentence you to five days incarceration to be served at the Fraser Valley Institute for Women."

"No! I will not be enslaved!" Lucy shouted.

Now you speak!

In Superman-fashion, Lucy ripped open her dress, and stood in bra and panties. "I am the truth. I am purity."

"*Lucy,*" I hissed. "What are you doing?"

"Ms. Thyme. Your client stands half-naked in my court."

No kidding. "Lucy. Get your clothes on."

"I stand neither in false clothes nor false pretenses in this farce labelled justice," she shouted.

"Ms. Thyme—" Hicks bellowed, "—Instruct your client—"

"—You are a *sla-a-a-ve* to your hypocrisy—"

I grabbed her Velcro dress from the desk. "*Clothes.*"

"—You sentence my *purity!*"

"*Clothes.* He'll sentence you to a lot more if you don't put your dress on." I felt like I was singing a Joe Cocker song. The hanging ghosts of the courtroom were splitting a gut on this one.

"Ms. Starr, I hold you in contempt. Sheriffs," Hicks sputtered.

Two female sheriffs arrived. Lucy latched onto the desk leg. "*No*. You can't take me."

One sheriff wrapped her arm around Lucy's waist. The other grabbed her ankles.

Lucy kicked and screamed. The three toppled to the floor, both sheriffs on top of my client.

Do I step in? The screaming, butt-cheeks-flashing, slithering woman on the floor was my client.

The sheriffs stood, glaring at me as they hauled Lucy to her feet. I held out her dress.

One sheriff grabbed it.

Being dragged toward the side door, Lucy's once doe-like eyes fired daggers from her flushed face. "You failed me, Jade. You *failed me*. I will not be shackled into conformity! You soulless pieces of—"

The closing courtroom door silenced her.

We stood.

"Ms. Thyme."

Here it comes.

"Were you aware of your client's antics?"

"No, Your Honour. No idea."

From the corner of my eye I could see Valentina, her fist pressed to her lips, stifling giggles.

"I will not have a mockery made of this court. Ms. Starr's lack of respect will be punished." His Honour Hicks stood.

"Order in court," shouted the last sheriff in the room.

Hicks glared. "Expect a call from the Law Society." His stout pug legs lumbered down the steps from his bench and he disappeared into his chambers.

I sat, feeling sweat around my waist from where my slacks cut in.

Valentina tossed her file in her briefcase. In her poppy red suit, she stepped over. Her flowing dark curls cascaded over her white button-popping blouse. In her early 50s, she didn't look a day over

35. "Jade," she said with her Marlene Dietrich voice. "You're a long way from the pristine offices of Aubischon, Thyme and Bastine. No popping Cristal after today's loss. I thought you were a power hitter. Who are you defending next, Chuckles the Clown?" She flipped her curls over her shoulder and sauntered down the aisle. The blonde man joined her.

I wasn't defending Chuckles the Clown. My clients weren't circus acts ... well ... there was the trapeze artist, but someone needed to defend them, and everyone had a right to counsel. I grabbed my files and followed.

My next client kept his clothes on, thank God. Simon, a 22-year-old waiter, entered a not guilty plea to dine and dash. It was a ridiculous charge. Simon had no prior criminal record, always made his rent and paid his taxes. We would be making another court appearance next week to set his trial date.

Happy that my court appearances were done, I checked my phone and saw a text from my sister, Sage. She wanted to come over with a box of our deceased mother's art. Sage and I were slowly learning that our mother had been an artist in her early twenties. She signed all her pictures *Genie* with an elaborate 'G'. Because of an aneurysm, she had suddenly been taken from us a year ago. I still hadn't returned my father's, Charles's, message from the day before. A text from Osmond buzzed on my phone. *Outside.*

All right. Maybe we could redo the morning.

I zipped into the washroom and changed my Fluevogs for riding boots. I pushed open the heavy courthouse doors, breathing in fresh air and finding Osmond leaning against the metal rail by the bottom step. He brought a cigarette to his lips, tilted his head back, blowing smoke as he laughed at whatever Valentina was telling him. She placed her hand on his arm, looked me up and down, and smirked. The blonde guy with the waxy complexion still stood beside her.

She nodded at Osmond. "Good luck." She linked arms with the blonde man. Where did I know him from? Osmond watched her leave. He straightened and turned to me. His smiled disappeared and I couldn't see his eyes behind his sunglasses. He had something on his mind.

I stepped down the last few steps. "You know Valentina Vale?"

"Where are you parked?"

"You know Valentina?"

He tossed his cigarette on the sidewalk, butting it out with his shoe. "Is that a problem?"

"Didn't say it was. I'm parked there." I pointed to my motorcycle. "What's up?" I asked, stepping along the stone path leading away from the courthouse.

"I have to go."

"Where?"

"I'm being reassigned to Montréal. Undercover. Infiltrate the Black Widows. I leave in a few days. I'll be away for at least a year."

"Really."

"It's not like I can walk up to the gang leader and ask them to please cancel the turf war. I need to establish myself."

"Did you request this reassignment?"

Osmond watched a man lurch into a makeshift shelter in a doorway. "Jesus."

"Don't judge him."

"Jade, don't get all bleeding-heart on me. Cops put their lives on the line to protect citizens like you from strung-out addicts like him."

We reached my motorcycle. "He's not bothering me and you're the one high strung."

I couldn't see his eyes but I felt his disdain. "Then why don't you go sleep with him."

"Why are you acting like such a jerk?"

"I'm a jerk?"

"You're acting like one. When did you request this reassignment?"

"Six months ago."

"After Jules's murder."

"Yes."

"And you decide to tell me now?"

He held his hands out to his sides. "Do not interrogate me."

"I'm not interrogating. You're getting defensive. I want the truth." I shoved my leather bag into the saddlebag. "You couldn't have told me when we were solving Jules's murder. Or after?"

"You had a lot of shit going down."

"I could have handled it."

"Really, like you're handling it now? Still taking Vicodin?"

"I've been clean for six months. This isn't about me. This is about you stringing me along, and I'm calling you out."

"I was the one rubbing your back when you were throwing up. Remember that, Jade? Being dope-sick? Yeah, me. Who was there during the cold sweats? The nausea? Cleaning up your puke and diarrhea because you blacked-out on the toilet?"

"You want a medal? Do not *insinuate*, that you didn't tell me, because it was for *my own good*." I brushed pink cherry blossom petals off my bike seat, swung my leg over and sat.

Osmond stepped forward. "Look, it doesn't have to end this way."

Too late. I fastened my helmet and turned the key. My bike rumbled.

"Jade."

I adjusted my goggles and cranked the throttle. "Clean break, Osmond. Au revoir." I rode out into the traffic. The reflection of Osmond in my side-view mirror grew smaller.

My tears stung. The wind brushed my cheeks. I wanted to speed, but couldn't. Traffic was nasty, ripped up roads and construction was happening everywhere in Victoria. I swerved around potholes and orange-vested traffic control people. Condo high-rises sprouted on every street corner, and crane booms hung like mobiles in the sky.

A car sped past in the fast lane then swung in front, cutting me off. I slowed and hit my horn. *Shoulder check, idiot, and get off your cellphone.* I cruised down Pandora. Cars. Here. There. Engines. *Screw him.* I heard bells ringing and saw the red light on the Johnson Street bridge. The bridge was going up. I geared down. The red and white striped barricade came down. Cars stopped and so did I. A barge horn blared, then slowly the bridge rose to allow the barge passage. I pushed up my goggles and with one gloved hand brushed at my tears.

"Hey darlin'," a man shouted from the car next to me.

Ignore him.

"You ride me like you ride that bike?"

And he thought he was amusing. Screw off.

The bridge lowered. The red and white striped barricade rose and my lane moved. I cruised forward, not before giving the heckler a one-finger salute.

The physicality of crossing the bridge tempered my anger. Come on, Jenga blocks, do not collapse now. I slowed, seeing a yellow and black checkered water taxi glide under the bridge. I made a right turn into The Railyards and after a couple more turns parked my bike in its parking spot.

I dismounted, removed my helmet and grabbed my leather bag. I heard a rattle and reached in, my fingers wrapping around a bottle.

Vicodin.

Not good.

I walked to my condo, weighing the plastic bottle in my hand. I had been clean for six months. The first two weeks had been Hell. I had substituted my addiction with Sage's boxing class. The ritual of slipping my hands into my pink boxing gloves and punching the heavy bag was more than therapeutic. I was beating my demons. I'd step back sweaty and spent, my pink-gloved spaghetti limbs hanging at my sides.

I detoured to the outdoor pavilion jutting over the Gorge, placing the bottle and my helmet on the railing.

Tears escaped. I cursed. I grabbed the Vicodin and looked at it.

He's not worth it. I had been telling myself our relationship was just about sex. Who was I kidding?

I brushed the tears from my cheek when I heard the rumble of a Harley.

Sage's pink Harley, with her doggle-wearing German Shepherd Lizzy in the side car, pulled into guest parking. Sage removed her helmet and Lizzy's doggles. She unfastened Lizzy's harness from the side clip and grabbed the other end of the leash. Lizzy jumped out, and they headed toward me. Long red hair flipping back, long legs, jeans and leather coat, Sage was younger than me but sometimes I felt like the younger sister.

"Hi," I said.

Lizzy's tail wagged. She ran up to me, pawing my leg. I knelt and patted her behind the ears.

"You weren't at boxing," Sage said, hands on hips, "and given the bottle on the railing, I'm guessing you had a crappy day."

I shuffled my feet and looked out at the Gorge Waterway. The yellow water taxi cruised past. "I haven't had any, if that's what you're wondering." I leaned forward and petted Lizzy's fur. Her tail whacked my leg.

"What happened?"

I straightened. "Osmond's leaving in a few days for an undercover assignment back East. He'll be gone for at least a year."

"And you found out today?"

"Yes. He requested the reassignment just after Jules was murdered."

"He knew all this time?"

"He would have told me sooner but he didn't know he'd get it."

"That's crap," Sage said. She waved to the captain navigating the tiny water taxi. She knew everybody.

"I thought—" I cleared my throat "—given what we had gone through after Jules's murder … things would be different. That *he* was different."

"We've all made bad boyfriend choices, and in my case, girlfriend choices. Anything else?"

I pet Lizzy. How did I explain that I felt ashamed? "He … he brought up when I was dope-sick."

Sage crossed her arms. "So to make himself look good, he's

bringing up something to make you feel bad. He's a real piece of work, Jade. You don't need him. Come on—" she tapped my shoulder "—you have a bottle of wine, or two, we can get into."

I nodded.

"We've all done stuff we're not proud of. Don't think twice about him."

I nodded again and told myself, *don't get weepy.* "I have dog treats for Lizzy."

Lizzy's tail whacked me again.

"Chin Chin isn't going to pull another Pink Panther inspired Cato-attack on my dog, is she?"

Lizzy whimpered. I flashed back to my cat, trapesing from the top of the refrigerator, paws outstretched, eyes focused on the unsuspecting Lizzy, who had sat waiting for her dog treat. "Chin Chin's in kitty heaven now."

"Well count us in. What are you going to do with those?"

I picked up the Vicodin bottle, snapped open the lid, and emptied the pills into the Gorge.

Sage looked over the railing then at me. "A few fish are getting stoned tonight."

2 ANGER MANAGEMENT

"And you responded by hitting him with your Transformers lunchbox."

After helping Sage carry in a few of Mom's sketchbooks, I put out a water bowl for Lizzy and grabbed a couple of dog treats. Lizzy sniffed the treats, turned away, and curled up on the rug.

"My dog treats aren't good enough?"

"I think she's in heat," Sage said, pulling tinfoil off a plate. "As soon as she's done, I'm getting her spayed."

"Oh." I looked at Lizzy, her tail covering her nose. "Next time, Lizzy."

"Is there a reason why the paper is splayed across the floor?" Sage asked.

I picked up the pages. Oscar Cooper smiled at me from under Osmond's footprint. "Osmond's temper tantrum. I must say—" I held up the page featuring Oscar in his prime "—you were a handsome man." I folded the paper and tossed it into my recycling bin.

"These are for you." Sage pushed a plate of mini-mousse cakes across the kitchen island. The reason why my clothes felt tighter around the waist.

"These look amazing."

"The bottom layer is a chocolate sponge, white chocolate mousse, a chocolate insert, more white chocolate mousse covered with a mirror glaze. They go well with a bottle of red."

I washed my hands and grabbed a bottle and two wine glasses. Sage took the dessert plate and sat cross-legged on the sofa.

I bit into one and groaned.

"According to my shrink, baking is therapy, a tool to handle my anger management issues."

"Welcome to the club," I muttered. I knew something was up when I visited Sage one Monday night and found Lizzy deserting the kitchen for the comfy sofa, and Sage knocking back a rye and ginger ale as she piped Italian butter-cream rosettes on waxed paper. "When did you start seeing a therapist?"

"Three months ago, when I was charged with beating that pimp. Part of my conditional sentence was counselling."

"What did the pimp do, besides the obvious?"

"He was smacking around one of his girls."

"Do I want to know why you were involved with this?"

"No." Sage reached for a mousse cake. Lizzy circled, and curled up facing the opposite direction. "My shrink has been digging up crap. My anger supposedly stems from Charles wanting to put me in conversion therapy."

Aha. I remembered now. Charles was enraged and embarrassed that the principal had called, wanting to speak about Sage beating up a bully at school, and how had the principal put it, Sage's *condition*. "I remember that."

"Right. That twerp in school had told his friends that I had boobies but I acted like a boy. He wanted me to drop my pants to prove that I didn't have a penis."

"And you responded by hitting him with your Transformers lunchbox."

"That's right."

"You have a right to be angry."

Sage took a deep breath. "Charles took the principal's word over mine."

I squeezed my sister's hand. "So next time, because there will be a next time—" I reached for my wine glass and sipped "—before you hit someone with a lunchbox—"

"—with the pimp it was a Labatt beer can."

"Beer can, call 9-1-1 first."

"*Then* I'll hit him."

I nearly spat out my wine.

"You had no idea Osmond was going back East?"

"Not a clue. The last few months he's been acting strange. The smallest things would set him off, like reading Oscar Cooper's obituary."

"Besides trafficking drugs, Oscar Cooper was a huge art fan," Sage said.

Speaking of which, I glanced at the box of our deceased mother's paintings. Sage and I had purchased our old family home in Uplands from Charles, our father, who didn't want us to call him Father, Dad or Pop. By insisting we call him by his first name, Charles distanced himself from his fatherly responsibilities. It made sitting across from him in board meetings in the old, now collapsed, law firm of Aubischon, Thyme and Bastine much easier.

Sage and I planned to turn the home into a counselling office and rehabilitation centre if we could get the zoning. While Charles bragged about his new house in Cordova Bay by the golf course, Sage and I were left schlepping out coffee makers and out-of-date computer equipment. "Everything's out of the house?" I asked.

"No. That colonial crap called furniture and three old sewing machines are left in the basement. I have more paintings at the condo I'm house-sitting." Sage placed her wine glass on the table and scrolled through her phone. "Here." She passed it to me.

"Mom's art?"

She nodded as she leaned over the sofa arm and patted Lizzy.

I scrolled. "They're beautiful pieces. The flower garden in front of the moon gate is my favourite." I looked closer. "That's not our moon gate. I wonder whose? Why did she stop?"

"Don't know. I like the first picture, *Budgie Outside the Birdcage*."

My cellphone vibrated on the table. I picked it up. VIC PD flashed on the call display. "Hello?"

"Jade."

I recognized the voice but couldn't remember the name. "Yes."

"Sergeant Stone."

What had I done? Didn't Stone get transferred to Tofino? I looked at Sage.

She put her wine glass on the table and mouthed, "Who is it?"

"Hello, Sergeant Stone."

He coughed. "Jade, are you sitting down?"

3 NEWSPAPERS

She rides a Harley and will turn you into roadkill.

I CLUTCHED THE PHONE. "I'M SITTING. WHAT'S WRONG?"
"I regret to inform you that your father was found deceased."
"What?" I uncrossed my legs and sat forward on the sofa. "When? How?"
"Our forensics indicate that he overdosed on cocaine."
I was numb. "Overdosed? Charles?"
"My condolences."
"What is it?" Sage asked.
"Jade, we need you to come to the department and answer a few questions. Or, if you're not up to it, I can attend your residence."
I looked at Lizzy. "I, I have a dog."
"Are you home?"
"Yes."
"Can you get Sage?"
"She's here."
"I'll be there shortly." Sergeant Stone disconnected.
"Jade, what is it?"
I still held my cell to my ear. I looked at Sage. "Charles overdosed."
"Overdosed?" She stared, stunned. "Impossible."
"Sergeant Stone is on his way over."

True to his word, Sergeant Stone, in a grey plaid sports coat and grey slacks, stood in my doorway 20 minutes later. He stepped past me into my condo and I immediately smelled cigarettes, onions and stale beer.

Lizzy growled and barked.

"Lizzy, stop," Sage said.

Lizzy still barked.

"Dogs like me," Stone said, stepping toward Lizzy, hand outstretched.

Lizzy growled.

"She's in heat and the last thing she wants is to be around a male." Sage pulled a treat from a plastic bag in her purse. "Lizzy, sit." She did.

"Coffee?" I asked.

Stone accepted and soon I was handing him a steaming mug. He sat at one end of the kitchen island and Sage sat at the other, with Lizzy staring Stone down.

I leaned against the counter, cup in hand, and listened to Stone tell us Charles hadn't shown up for his early morning tee time. His golf buddy and neighbour, concerned that Charles had fallen and hurt himself, walked over to Charles's Matticks Wood Lane home. He found the front door unlocked and Charles dead on the living room floor.

"When did he die?"

"It is believed in the middle of the night."

I couldn't believe what I was hearing. "He was snorting cocaine?"

"Drug paraphernalia was found in the kitchen. You two will assist in the investigation, unlike Jules's murder." He looked at me.

I wanted to argue that I had solved Jules's murder but I didn't have the energy.

"Thanks to Jade, Jules's murderer was exposed," Sage said.

Stone frowned. "Your father's friends, you know any of them? Could one be his dealer? Any disgruntled, menopausal ex-girlfriends?"

"Excuse me?" I said.

"You know."

"No. I don't know, Sergeant Stone, but please, educate me on how menopausal women are likely to be drug dealers?"

He pinched the bridge of his nose and let out an impatient sigh. "Any of your father's clients dealing coke in exchange for a reduced legal fee?"

"We can't disclose Charles's clients."

"The night he presumably overdosed a neighbour saw a man waiting in a parked SUV two blocks down from your father's residence," Stone said. "This may be a crime of opportunity. I want to know if any items were taken from your father's residence after he overdosed."

Sage sat frozen. Lizzy nudged her hand for another treat. I couldn't remember the last time Sage had seen Charles. Mom's funeral? When Sage and I were in our teens, she argued with Charles a lot. When Sage saw Charles hit Mom, because Mom refused to put Sage in conversion therapy, Sage moved out. She didn't want to be the reason for spousal abuse. When had I last seen him? Six months ago, when he stood in my old office, warning me not to expose the Society. Could the Society be behind his death? A wayward member?

Stone pushed out his chest and looked at Sage. "This is your turf."

"Excuse me?"

"This is the type of gang crap you run with."

"I have no idea what you're talking about."

Stone scoffed. "I'm sure you can find out."

"I'll be damned if I'm reporting back to you."

"I'll arrest you for obstruction."

"Stop, both of you. No one is getting arrested." I dragged my hands through my hair. "Sergeant Stone, if we find anything I'll let you know."

"The forensic team will be finished in a couple of hours. Attend your father's residence and tell me if anything is missing or out of sorts."

I didn't like being ordered around, but that was Sergeant Stone. "Will do."

Stone's cellphone buzzed. He stepped toward the front door.

Lizzy barked.

"Lizzy," Sage said, patting her, not letting go. "I don't like him either," she whispered.

"Stone," Stone said, facing away from us. "Got it." He looked at me. "I'll let them know."

Sage and I exchanged glances.

Stone slipped his phone into an inner coat pocket, more sucking in his gut. "Forensics is done. You can go any time, maybe not now. Tomorrow. You need to process your grief."

I looked at Stone, surprised by his thoughtful comment.

He frowned. "I've been taking sensitivity training. Do you have a key?"

"No," I said.

"I'll contact the constable on duty and instruct him to give you access." Stone flicked a business card on the kitchen island. "Call me, Jade, if you need anything."

I walked over to the door and pulled it open, hearing sirens. The cool air broke up the weighted testosterone. "Good-bye Sergeant."

He stepped out and I closed the door behind him.

I looked at Sage.

We only had each other.

The next morning, Sage and I jumped on our bikes and rode to Charles's home on Matticks Wood Lane, which was next door to the chic Matticks Farm, home to a tea house, art gallery and designer clothing boutiques. If one didn't feel like shopping, the Cordova Bay Golf Course was steps away.

We parked in front of a house with a cedar wood door and blue trim. Exotic shrubs and Japanese maples framed the entrance. No wonder his home had been featured in *Better Homes and Gardens*.

Sage got off her bike and removed her helmet, taking in the garden and interlocking brick. "Have you been here before?"

"Never invited. He sold us the Uplands house, and like an expired restrictive covenant, relinquished us."

"I don't feel so bad. Let's do this." She walked toward the entrance.

"Hello, can I help you?"

We looked back.

An old man pulling a golf bag cart stared at us from the sidewalk. He introduced himself as Charles's golfing buddy and the one who found Charles's body.

"I was expecting to see Valentina," he said.

"Valentina?" I looked at Sage.

"Yes, your father's lady friend."

"Lady friend?" Sage looked at me, arching her brow. "Really? What's Valentina's last name?"

"Vale."

"Valentina Vale?" I repeated.

"Yes. That's it."

"She sounds like a porn star," Sage said under her breath.

"Ms. Vale is something else. She and your father were, you know, close. You should know her, dear. She's a lawyer."

Sage looked at me.

"Yes, yes I do. Thank you. Have a good game." I knocked on the front door.

"What was your name again?" he asked.

"Jade."

Recognition lit his face. "I remember Charles talking about you. You have the silver streak and are straight." He glanced at Sage. "You're—"

"—Not," Sage said.

"Thank you for your help." I again knocked on the door. Where was the constable on duty?

"I have two single sons who could ... you know."

Sage let out a deep breath.

"Sage," I said in a low voice. "He's not worth it."

She stepped back and looked at the man. "No. I don't know."

"Sage, *leave it.*"

He puffed up his chest. Nothing worse than an old rooster. "Straighten things out. Maybe if you put on a dress, you'd stop pretending to be a boy."

Oh my God. We were both wearing jeans and leather jackets.

Sage laughed. "That is so ridiculous it's funny. There's nothing to straighten out."

"Sage. Come on."

"No wonder he was ashamed of you." He pulled his golf bag cart and headed toward the course.

Now she was seething.

"Sage, he's seventy years old."

"So being old gives him the right to be a jerk and pass judgement?"

"No. It doesn't. Rude is rude."

"I'm a good person."

She had tears in her eyes. People's perceptions never bothered her. This had nothing to do with Charles's golf buddy and everything to do with her relationship with Charles, or non-relationship, and mourning the father we never had.

In Charles's eyes, we were noisy beings who messed up his furniture. When we had company, we were instructed to put on a dress and a smile. I was Exhibit A and Sage Exhibit B and then we were whisked to the basement. I really didn't know how I felt. Maybe ... sad. Sad Charles had taken his own life. Sad because I never knew him. Sad because he never wanted to know his daughters. I rubbed Sage's shoulders. "You're more than a good person, you're the coolest person I know. Forget about him."

She swiped tears from her cheeks. "You know Valentina Vale?"

"Unfortunately. Trust me, I don't belong to her fan club."

"Maybe she's left some of her crap behind and we can figure out how involved she was with Charles."

The front door opened and I recognized the constable from my prosecuting days. My assistant Kate used to describe him as a Keanu Reeves lookalike. Sadly, this Keanu hadn't aged well.

"Ms. Thyme." He smiled at Sage and me. "I was watching a golfer 8-putt the ninth hole. Come in." He looked at Sage, who was the same height as him. He smiled. "I'll be out here if you need anything, keep away any nosy neighbours."

Too late.

"Thank you, Constable." Sage walked in.

He stood in the doorway, watching her.

"Ahem," I said.

"Oh, excuse me, Ms. Thyme." He stepped to the side. I swear he was blushing.

I wanted to say, *she rides a Harley and will turn you into roadkill.* Instead I said, "Thank you."

Charles's 2,600-square-foot home smelled of mouthwash, Windex, and leather furniture. A morbid feeling hung from the coffered ceilings. We walked into the elegant living room. I expected to see photos of Valentina on the fireplace mantle, but it was bare. A large bay window overlooked the pond on the ninth hole and had a view of the Strait. Even with a $2 million price tag the home was lifeless.

"It's freezing in here." Sage rubbed her hands over her arms.

The dining room looked sophisticated with a gas fireplace, a second large bay window, and dual globe lanterns over the rectangular table.

"So—" I looked around "—Stone wants to make sure nothing is missing."

"Like we would know, given we were never invited here."

"Let's do our best. You take the kitchen and living room and I'll check the bedroom and bathrooms," I said.

The bedroom I walked into looked to be the master. Plain walls, white bedding with square-print pillows as accents. I pulled open a chest of drawers: socks and underwear, golf shirts, golf shorts.

I heard Sage in the kitchen, running the tap and then a crash.

"Damn it."

"You okay?" I called out, my eyes focused on the desk in the corner.

"I dropped a glass."

I moved over to the desk. Cellphone charger, printer and mouse pad. Old newspaper articles were piled in the corner, beside a glass tumbler and an empty bottle of Jack Daniels. What was Charles researching? I picked up one newspaper article. 1992. I would have been four or five. *The Grizzly Bear Murders*.

"What is he doing with this?" I read how near an old logging road, the bodies of two men had been discovered tied to trees. Forensics determined that the two men had been severely beaten prior to being tied up and then shot in the chest, their bodies ravaged by the wildlife. Authorities believed the murders were drug-related.

"I'd be reaching for the Jack Daniels, too."

I heard Sage sweeping broken glass into a dustpan.

I picked up another article: *Grizzly Bear Murders Unsolved*. The police still had no clues as to who had murdered Jeffrey and Steven Banks. The date printed on the article was a week before Charles's overdose.

Did he know these men? Why the interest in a cold case file from 1992?

I saw a third article. *Legendary Drug Dealer Arrested*. It showed a young and very attractive Oscar Cooper, handcuffed, being directed into a police car. The article outlined Oscar's gangster activities and how, with the assistance of Archie Malone, he had monopolized the province's drug scene.

I picked up another printout. *Oscar Free. Charges Dropped.* "Why were you interested in these?" Did you know Oscar? Who was his defence counsel? I scanned the article and sucked in my breath.

Norman Bastine. *Nox*. My new law partner, the Bastine in Thyme and Bastine. Nox, after counselling and attending AA meetings, had left behind his sardine-slurping ways and cowering behind garbage cans in Fan Tan Alley, and would soon be appearing every Tuesday in remand court as a criminal defence lawyer. In this article he was noted as defence counsel for Oscar

Cooper *and* Archie Malone. Norman, how did you get entangled with these men?

I neatly stacked the print outs and, hands on hips, surveyed Charles's desk. Something wasn't right. Printer. Cellphone charger. Hole-in-one mouse pad.

Where was the laptop?

Where was his cellphone?

I looked closely at the glass-top desk. It was covered in a film of dust except for a rectangular shape where a laptop would be positioned.

I pulled open desk drawers.

No laptop.

I dropped to my hands and knees and looked under the bed.

Golf clubs. No laptop.

Suicide, Sergeant Stone? I don't think so. I picked up the mouse pad and a ripped paper corner fluttered to the floor. I picked it up.

Charlesgolfer1 was written in Charles's handwriting. I snapped a photo of the password with my phone and looked back at the desk.

Laptop and cellphone missing.

I walked out of his bedroom and into the bathroom. A massive clawfoot tub had a wood tray on it with a vase of dead flowers and a bottle of oil. That had to be Valentina's influence. I opened the medicine cabinet: shaving kit, razor, aftershave. If Charles was taking drugs, was Valentina as well? I walked over to a dark oak cabinet, pulled open a drawer and found one black lace nightie and one tiger print. "Sage."

Her steps thunked on the hardwood.

"What?" She leaned against the doorway.

I held up both.

She stepped forward and touched the fabric. "Silk animal print."

"This is wrong."

Her eyebrows furrowed. "What's wrong about it?"

"This—" I shook the nightie "—does not belong with that—" I nodded at the orange Voltaren tube.

Sage laughed. "Well, if you're seventy-plus and have Valentina riding you like a—"

"—Stop. I don't want the visual."

Sage smiled. "What's in this drawer?" She pulled open the second drawer and we saw make-up. Sage picked up a delicate bottle with pink goop in it. "Stunna Lip Paint. Valentina made herself at home, and she obviously likes Rihanna's beauty products." She started to close the drawer, when a bottle of pills rolled forward. There was no prescription label. She stopped then reached in and grabbed the bottle.

"What is it?"

Sage looked at me. "This is street. Charles's or Valentina's?"

I frowned.

"I'll ask around." She took the bottle. "I have something to show you."

I followed her into the kitchen and stood by the long marble island.

She motioned for me to step toward a black garbage bag where beside it, on the floor, was the dustpan filled with glass shards.

"What's that rotten smell?"

"Chicken packaging."

My eyes widened.

Sage opened the garbage bag. "Look inside."

"Do I really have to? I have a history of finding not nice things."

"It's nothing gross."

"It's garbage."

"Just look."

Amongst avocado peels, Saran, and potato skins were picture frames. I glanced at Sage.

"Yeah, see what I see."

I grabbed a towel.

Sage rolled the plastic back and using the towel as a glove, I pulled out the first picture frame. It may have been covered in coffee grounds but there was no mistaking the photo of Charles and Valentina smiling in front of a boat. I looked in the bag. "There are more." I pulled out another picture of Valentina with her arms around Charles's shoulders.

"The fact those are in here," Sage said, "looks like trouble in paradise."

I pulled out one more. The glass was broken and orange juice had stained the photo of Charles and Valentina kissing for a selfie. "When's garbage day?" I squinted at a schedule magnetized to the refrigerator.

Sage stepped back and looked. "Last Thursday. Today's Tuesday. These were tossed recently."

"If we tell the police we found these, they'll say Charles killed himself because he was distraught over his and Valentina's break up. Why else does someone throw photos of their partner in the garbage?" I looked at the photo of Valentina coyly smiling and tossed it back in. "The garbage is perfect."

Sage was about to say something when her attention was diverted by the constable at the front door.

"Excuse me, but Dr. Vlasic is here."

"Dr. Vlasic?" I said.

Sage looked at me. "As in pickles?"

"He's a retired psychiatrist and lives next door. Good man. We've used him to provide expert evidence in some murder trials. He wants to meet you."

We were the unspoken Thyme children and the neighbours were curious. We stepped outside.

In his 70s, an Asian man stood, holding two plants with a case tucked between his arm and torso.

He stepped forward. "Ms. Thyme," he nodded at me then Sage. "My deepest regrets for your loss."

"Thank you," I said. "You knew Charles?"

"Your father let me use his greenhouse. My property is too small."

"What do you grow?" Sage asked.

"Passionflower, orchids, and—" awkwardly he gave me a plant "—and for you—" he gave Sage a matching plant "—the *Maranta leuconeura*. Prayer plant. May it bring you peace."

I looked at the plant. "Thank you, very much, Dr. Vlasic. Did … you see Charles before he died?"

Dr. Vlasic looked at his feet before answering. "The night before. He … told me you would be coming for this and I was to give it to you."

I was about to say, *coming for what*, when Dr. Vlasic held out a thin case, looking me in the eye.

Charles's laptop. I took it. "Yes, Charles wanted me to update his laptop," I lied, knowing the constable on duty would probably report back to Stone.

He discreetly nodded.

"Thank you, Dr. Vlasic. How was Charles? Did he seem depressed? As you can imagine, this has come as quite a surprise. Sage and I are trying to put the pieces together."

"Charles, we talk in the greenhouse. He … was looking forward to sailing again."

"Oh." I glanced at Sage, knowing the photos we saw disposed in the garbage. "Charles and Valentina Vale, his girlfriend, were going sailing."

Dr. Vlasic looked from me to Sage.

"Dr. Vlasic," Sage asked, her voice dropping to a tender pitch, "Was Valentina—"

"—Ms. Vale and Charles broke up," Dr. Vlasic interrupted. "She removed her items from his house."

Not the lingerie.

"And?" Sage coaxed.

"I had been in the greenhouse. Ms. Vale had showed up with two men the night before Charles passed. I thought the men were helping with the move. They argued, shouted, then drove away. No items were taken."

"Have you told this to the police?" I asked.

"Yes."

"Thank you, Dr. Vlasic," Sage said. "For the prayer plant and for keeping an eye on Charles. Did Valentina ever talk to you?"

Dr. Vlasic frowned. "She paid much attention to your father."

He turned and stepped toward the lane.

The most polite and veiled 'no' I had ever heard. I doubt Valentina Vale had a prayer plant from Dr. Vlasic. Give her a cactus. "Dr. Vlasic," I called after him.

He turned.

I stepped toward him. "Do you think—" I looked at the prayer plant then at the psychiatrist's kind face "—you're a psychiatrist." I smiled. "I'm having a hard time believing Charles overdosed."

Dr. Vlasic turned so his back was to the constable. "Charles Thyme did not do drugs."

4 OSCAR - 1968

"I can have dinner with the Dalai Lama."

"Genie, come on," Archie Malone said, as he cupped a match, lighting a cigarette.

Genie slammed the passenger door of Archie's convertible.

"Hey," Archie pointed at his silver Impala, "don't slam the door."

"It's heavy." She adjusted her grip on her painting as she gazed at the stone mansion. When Archie had told her he wanted to introduce her to the owner of The Studio, she hadn't expected this. This dude's pad was outta sight.

"Are you coming?" Archie straightened his Jimi Hendrix-inspired shirt that hung loose over faded jeans. He walked toward the front door.

Genie followed, glancing at a line of convertibles crowding the circular driveway. Cream's *Sunshine of Your Love* blared from a second-floor window. An amazing lime green sports car was parked near the door.

"Wow." Genie stopped. "What type of car?"

Archie smiled. "That's Oscar's Lamborghini."

Genie walked around it. She flicked her red hair over her shoulder and leaned forward to look inside. "It has blue seats!"

"Don't touch it. C'mon."

"What does your friend do besides own The Studio?"

Archie placed his hand on Genie's lower back, guiding her under an archway. "Pharmaceuticals." He blew cigarette smoke away from her.

He must be a pharmacist. Maybe her mom's pharmacist, the nice gentleman who prescribes *Mother's Little Helper.* She adjusted her white headband and straightened the scarf around her neck.

They stepped inside and she immediately smelled pot. Five dudes leaned against the back railing, eying her through a haze. Archie talked to one of them. Genie stood back. John Lennon wasn't the walrus, she was, in her white boots and minidress amongst this crowd of unbuttoned shirts and cutoffs. Girls wearing halter-tops and jeans ran past barefoot.

"Hang loose," Archie said. His friend made the peace sign.

"This way, Genie." Archie steered her toward French doors. In the distance she saw a garden and the ocean.

Two women danced on a living room table.

Archie led her outside onto a patio that reminded her of a field of white mushrooms with its table umbrellas. More people stood, balancing plates, beer and cigarettes.

"Ready?" Archie asked.

"Yes." Then, she heard the opening chorus of The Mamas and the Papas's *Monday, Monday.* She stopped.

"Genie, c'mon."

She propped her picture against a chair leg and started dancing. Others followed.

"Genie, what the hell are you doing?"

"Dancing."

"You're supposed to be hanging with Oscar."

"It's The Mamas and the Papas," she shouted over Dennis Doherty's voice, her arms above her head, hips swaying. She was an awful dancer, but she loved this song.

"You don't make Oscar Cooper wait."

She shouted a lyric at Archie.

Archie looked side-to-side, awkwardly standing amongst

dancing hippies. He shuffled his feet.

Genie smiled.

The song ended and Otis Redding's *(Sittin' On) The Dock of the Bay* played.

Genie picked up her picture. "Okay."

Archie led her to a corner of the patio where a tall man dressed in white pants and a white turtleneck stood holding a drink. She had seen a photo of John Lennon dressed in a similar fashion.

The man butted out his cigarette in an ashtray as he looked Genie up and down and smiled. He glanced at Archie. "Didn't know you were a Mamas and Papas fan."

Archie frowned. "Michelle Phillips is a babe. Hendrix, man, Hendrix. *All Along the Watchtower.* Oscar, meet Genevieve Lapointe. The artist I told you about."

Genie fumbled with her painting.

"Please." Oscar reached for it. "Let me help you. Archie, can you get Genevieve a drink? Can I call you Genevieve?"

Genie blushed. Short blonde hair, high cheekbones, strong jaw and brown eyes, Oscar did not look like the mop-top boys she and Edith hung out with. "What was your question?"

Oscar smiled. "Can I call you Genevieve?"

"What do you drink?" Archie asked.

"Ah—" *what did she drink?* "—wine." *Please don't ask what type.* Archie nodded.

She looked back at Oscar. "Most people call me Genie."

"As in a mystical spirit granting wishes."

"Yes."

"Where's my lamp?"

Genie laughed.

"You like The Mamas and the Papas."

"Who doesn't." She could speak in full sentences, just not now.

"Your work, Genie—" Oscar looked at her painting "—is beautiful."

"Thank you." Where was Archie with that drink? She should have brought Edith. She didn't know what to say. She guessed

Oscar to be about eight years older than her.

"Who are your influences?" he asked.

"John Neville from Nova Scotia. Paul Vanier Beaulieu's work is far out."

"Not Emily Carr?"

"No. Don't tell anybody."

Oscar laughed. "I want to exhibit your art in my gallery."

"That would be cool."

Oscar smiled.

He was so out of her league. "What do you do?"

"I'm a businessman, Genie." He leaned in. "You can't trust anyone over thirty, right?"

Genie laughed. "You're not thirty."

"Shh." His eyes twinkled. "Ah, here's Archie with your wine."

"Oscar, we need to talk," Archie said, handing it over.

"Later, Archie. Genie has given me a beautiful painting. Place it in my office."

Archie took the painting and walked away with it.

Oscar looked at Genie. "Archie is a good business partner, but sometimes, his timing stinks."

Genie smiled. She watched guys and girls dancing on the patio to Sonny and Cher's *I've Got You Babe*. In the corner, girls sat in a circle, passing around a joint.

"How much are you asking for your painting, Genie?" Oscar asked.

"I never thought about a price. I paint because it fulfils me."

"Is nine-hundred dollars suitable fulfilment? I take thirty percent and show your work at my gallery."

"I, ah—"

"—Lay it on me. A thousand and Archie will include framing."

"You like my art that much?"

He leaned in conspiratorially. "I don't like Warhol. Don't tell anybody."

Genie laughed again. She liked this guy.

"So, a thousand dollars per picture and I can pick what I want to show."

"That would be great, Oscar." She sipped her wine. "I can pay down some student loans. The music program I'm in isn't cheap."

"Perfect. Come see my garden, maybe you'll want to paint it." He held out his arm. Genie tucked her arm into his and Oscar led her to a yard of ponds, winding paths and flowerbeds.

"This is wild. What is that?" She pointed to a stone wall with a circular opening.

"That's a Chinese moon gate. It means portal. Every stone tells a different story."

"It's beautiful."

"You are the first person to think so. The rest—" he nodded to the people behind them, "—don't get it."

"I'm not like them. I'm an artist and activist."

Oscar smiled. "What do you plan to do with your activism?"

She smiled. "Well … if the Beatles, four boys from Liverpool, can visit the Maharishi, I can have dinner with the Dalai Lama."

Oscar gulped his drink. "You have big goals, Genie. What would you say to His Holiness?"

"Hello. How are you? We need to talk about the women's liberation movement, racism and peace."

Oscar smiled. He tucked a red curl behind her ear, then picked a purple daisy and placed it in her hair. "Your boyfriend isn't going to like me, Genevieve Lapointe."

"I don't have a boyfriend."

Oscar arched his brow. "Good."

Genie placed her violin and bow in its case and flicked the latches. Finally, after weeks of practice, she had mastered Simon and Garfunkel's *Sound of Silence*. As soon as Edith got home from her nursing class, they'd head to the protest. They had stayed up late making the signs. CIENCIAS. Science. Knowledge. She was the letter "C" and Edith would hold the letter "I". Their friends would make up the remaining letters. They'd march around the university, showing solidarity for the Mexican students slaughtered for protesting the Olympic games in Mexico City. Diego Lomas, the well-known drug dealer, was rumoured to have funneled money into the games. Drug money. She hated that man. He profited off the impoverished backs of the Mexican people, enslaving them into his drug cartel.

Genie leaned the violin case between her floor mattress and beat up dresser. The daisy Oscar had given her two days ago drooped from a Mason jar beside her patchouli incense. The one-room pad she and Edith rented had a bathroom, hot plate and sink. They took turns going to the laundromat. Genie made the peace sign to her Donovan poster as she glided through the bead curtain to her paint easel in the living room. Her painting, *Budgie Outside the Birdcage*, was her rebellion piece which would be shown with five other pieces in Oscar's gallery two weeks from now. Her parents preferred she study music, but that was a drag. She experienced oneness creating art. They didn't get oneness or self-fulfilment, and they didn't like her questioning the status quo. But the more they caged her into a life of mediocrity, the more she rebelled.

Yes, there was a generation gap, and her parents needed to bridge it. Her privileged mother tolerated feminism, having been raised in 1950s doctrine. She'd never forget the time her mother, while sipping a martini, told her, "We don't go into liquor stores; we don't push brooms; we don't work in shops and we don't do other people's laundry." So Genie had grabbed her mother's white bath towel, tie-dyed it yellow, orange and red and turned it into a fringed shirt. Which, with a black marker, she wrote on it, 'death to taxes and conformity.' She was the budgie outside the birdcage.

The apartment door opened and Edith breezed in, humming *Seasons in the Sun*. Her beaded necklaces clicked, swinging from side to side. Wearing a tie-dyed purple t-shirt, and jeans, she flopped onto the mattress, crossing her legs under her.

Genie slipped on her black sandals. "Ready to go?" She checked her light green eyeshadow in the mirror above the kitchen sink and tugged on her halter top. "I have our signs." Genie grabbed the two signs propped behind her easel. "We're meeting the others at the university."

Edith looked at the signs. "Oh."

"The protest. You forgot."

"No. I thought we'd hang with Charles and his friends James and Norman. Check it out—" Edith passed her a card "—Norman made his own business cards."

Genie grabbed the card.

NORMAN BASTINE, CRIMINAL AND CIVIL RIGHTS LAWYER.

She stashed the card in her pocket. "Nice. This is important, Edith. You said after class we'd go to the march."

Edith lit a joint. "Genie, chill. There will be other protests."

"*No*! Hundreds of students were injured, dozens dead in the Tlatelolco Plaza. Whether you're a supporter of the Olympics or not, students have the right to protest without fear of government reprisal."

Edith looked unamused.

"*Edith*! Don't be a hypocrite. Show your support. Their people live in poverty while the government pours millions into these ludicrous games. We have to stand together. You're the letter *I*."

Edith rolled onto her side, propping her head up with her hand. "*I*, a hypocrite? *I'm* not the one dating Oscar Cooper who lives in Cottage Lake and drives fancy sports cars. Who's really the hypocrite, Genie?"

"Oscar wants to show my art, promote my message. He gets me."

Edith inhaled. "He's the establishment, Genie. All he wants is to get in you. Admit it, you're hot for him."

Genie could feel her heartrate rising. She told herself to stay calm. Yes, she wanted to make love with Oscar, preferably while high, but that wasn't the point. "Oscar isn't squashing my freedom or my voice. I see how you look at him, Edith. You're jealous."

Edith pushed herself up. "I'm not jealous."

"You're jealous that Oscar is invested in my art. You're jealous because of his connections. My art is being featured in *Avante*

Garde magazine and I'm making money."

"Is that what this is about?" Edith stood. "Making money, Genie? Your art reflects your soul. You're putting a price tag on your soul. You're selling out to The Man, to *capitalism*. I'm going to be a nurse and help our brothers coming home from Nam, battered, broken. Norman is soon to be a civil rights lawyer and defend those who can't defend themselves. What are you going to do, Genie? Get a pedicure and sip another cocktail like your mother."

Genie swung her sign.

Edith ducked, just missing being nailed in the head.

"*I'm not selling out!*"

Edith stared. "You just about hit me."

"I'm *not* selling out." Genie jammed the signpost against the floor. "Take it back."

Edith was silent.

"*Take it back.*"

"Fine. You're not selling out."

"I believe in peace, civil rights, and feminism. I'll braid my armpit hair if it will bring our brothers home from Nam. But if you know what The Man *thinks*, then you manipulate The Man. With Oscar's help, I can make a difference." Genie paused, realizing she was out of breath. "This—" she held up her *C* sign "—*this* is our voice. Solidarity. The army opened fire on those students."

Edith's brows furrowed and she crossed her arms.

"Now—" Genie took a deep breath, tucked her red hair behind her ears, and held out the *I* "—are you coming to protest, or not?"

Edith grabbed the sign. "I better, before you beat me with the damn thing."

5 MR. YOUNGHUSBAND

"I'm the last person Jade Thyme wants to see."

ADAM'S ARM FLINCHED, HITTING THE HEADBOARD. He groaned and rubbed his eyes. The squeal of tires had woken him from his nightmare. Third night in a row of punk-ass kids drifting their cars. He rolled onto his side. His bed shifted on the fake wood flooring. He was thirty-seven, not seven. Grown men did not have nightmares. Seeing Oscar Cooper the day before he died had tripped him back to *that* visit in the fall of 1992. He reached for the clock radio on the nightstand.

3:00 a.m.

He rolled onto his back. He had a creative writing lecture in the afternoon and needed to sleep. Henri snored on the living room sofa. Bob slept in the guest room. His bodyguards.

The zero on his clock radio clicked, turning over a one.

Why the hell didn't Oscar Cooper have bodyguards on *that* day? He remembered his plastic pumpkin of matchbox cars, sitting in his dad's 1955 black Porsche Speedster, as his dad pulled the Speedster into the long driveway of Mr. Cooper's Schooner Cove beach house.

The trip had been a surprise, given it wasn't his dad's weekend to look after him. He had been watching cartoons, eating

Cheerios when his mom had called *that Godforsaken man*. She had a migraine. Come get his kid. Then she disappeared into her bedroom and closed the door. His dad had picked him up 30 minutes later and told him to bring one toy because they were visiting his boss, Oscar Cooper.

He remembered touching the tree fronds as his father slowly drove over the uneven pavement. One of the few visits he had with his dad. He despised living with his mom, who only talked about ditching the double-wide and taking off to Vegas with her loser boyfriend. Adam never knew if he figured into her crazy plans. Yet, when he changed his last name from Malone, it was her maiden name that he took.

He remembered every detail about that day as if it was yesterday. He wondered if Jade did, too. His dad had parked the Porsche under the shade of a tree. "Take your cars," he had told him. "You can play outside while I talk to Mr. Cooper."

Adam opened the car door, remembering not to hip-check it or his dad would lose his cool. He walked around and stopped. Mr. Cooper's sports car was fluorescent green. "Whoa. Is that—"

"—Yes, that's Mr. Cooper's car. Do not go near it."

Adam lagged behind, eying the gold rims and what looked like black eyelashes around the front headlights.

"Adam, get up here," his dad pointed for him to fall in step beside him.

Adam quickened his pace.

His dad glanced at a convertible BMW, muttered, before stepping up the outside steps and walking to the front door. He placed his hand on Adam's shoulder. "No playing near the cars."

"No sir."

The front door opened and Oscar Cooper stood before them in a white shirt and faded jeans. "This better be damn important, Archie. Hi, Adam."

"Hello, Mr. Cooper," Adam said.

"Is she here?" Archie asked, nodding at the beamer.

Oscar lit a cigarette. "Genie? Yes. She's here with Jade."

"We have a problem," Archie said, hands on hips.

"This can't wait?"

"The Banks brothers, in particular Steven."

Oscar's face turned white.

Adam never wanted to piss off Mr. Cooper.

Oscar looked at him. "Not in front of Adam. The kids can play. We'll go into the office." Oscar poked his head inside. "Jade. Adam's here."

Adam heard a squeal. Girls.

"Adam, you'll play nice. No cutting Jade's hair. I never heard the end of it from Jade's mom."

"We'll play cars, Mr. Cooper."

"Good."

Adam heard running feet. Jade appeared, out of breath. Orange powdered lips, he saw two Cheezies bags in her hand. Her bangs had grown out and didn't look bad. He liked Jade even if she was a girl. She was two years younger than him, in kindergarten, not real school.

"Put your flip-flops on," Oscar said.

Jade slipped her feet into pink flip-flops, trying to keep her balance. Her flip-flops matched her pink jogging pants. Her t-shirt had a picture from *Ducktales*. She looked at Adam. "Hi, Adam. Guess what?"

"What?"

"I get to play with dolphins later," she said, wide-eyed.

"Nice," he said.

"Do not play near the road," Oscar said.

Jade followed Adam. The front door closed and they sat at the cement stairs by the flowerbed, Adam's plastic pumpkin of matchbox cars between them.

"Here." She gave him one Cheezies bag.

He took it. "I get all the Hot Wheels." He dug through the cars and lined up a few. "We need to make a monster mash up. Push that empty flowerpot over."

Jade moved the flowerpot and screamed.

Adam jumped as Jade stomped on earwigs.

"Now you've got bug guts on your flip-flops."

She scraped the bottom of them. "No, I don't."

"Here's how it works." Adam turned the ceramic flowerpot over and placed his cars on it. "Don't step on my Cheezies. We put our cars on the flowerpot like this, and we're gonna see how far we can launch them."

Jade took a green car from inside the pumpkin.

"You can't have that one."

"How come?"

"It's a Hot Wheels. I get all the Hot Wheels."

"But I want it."

"They're my cars."

She pirouetted, her braids fanning out. She bent over and took a red car.

"And not that one." Adam took it from her.

She frowned, jamming her hands on her hips. "What car can I have?"

Adam dug in the pumpkin. "Here." He handed her a pink station wagon. "You can play with this one. Now set up your cars like I have."

"You have three. I have one."

Adam pulled out two more cars.

"I want the green one," she said. "It's like Mr. Cooper's car."

"I'm having the green one."

Jade looked at what he had done and lined up her cars. "And I throw it?"

"You launch it, like this." He showed her. "Whoever gets their car to fly the farthest is the winner. Ready?"

She sat on the step. "I want to play hide-and-seek."

"I don't."

Jade frowned.

"We play cars first then hide-and-seek." He crossed his eyes and stuck out his tongue.

Jade giggled. "Okay. I throw the car."

"You launch it. Watch. Ladies and gentlemen, welcome to monster mash up," Adam said, imitating the sportscasters from Hockey Night in Canada.

Jade giggled again.

Adam smiled, liking his audience even if she was only five. "Will Adam Malone's yellow Ferrari 117 beat Jade Thyme's pink station wagon?"

"Nope," Jade said.

"The crowd goes silent. Get ready, get set—"

Jade sucked in her breath.

"*Go.*"

They launched their cars off the step. Jade's landed on the driveway but Adam's had gone way past hers.

"Hah! I win, and the crowd goes wild." Adam ran and picked up his car.

Jade ran after hers. "Again." She reached for the toy car but accidentally kicked it down the driveway. She ran after it and picked it up when a big car stopped at the end of the driveway. She brushed hair from her face. A man stepped out from the passenger's side.

"Jade, come here," Adam called, walking down the driveway toward her.

The man smiled and kneeled. "Whatcha got there?"

Jade stepped backwards.

"Don't be scared. I'm a friend of your father's."

Adam didn't like this guy. "Come on, Jade."

The man lunged.

Adam grabbed Jade's arm and ran, dragging her.

"You little shit," the man growled.

"*Adam*," Jade cried.

Adam felt a kick to his lower back. He sprawled flat, letting go of Jade's hand. His hands scraped pavement, and he hit his chin. His teeth clicked together.

Jade fell, crying, her hands outstretched in front of her.

The man grabbed her around the waist, lifting her.

"*No*," she screamed.

"*Dad!*" Adam shouted, lunging and tackling the man's legs.

The man kicked him in the stomach. Adam rolled into the fetal position.

The front door flew open. Oscar and Archie ran out.

"*Jade!*" Genie screamed, running after them.

Adam stumbled to his feet, his arm wrapped around his middle. The man was close to the car, propping Jade on his hip like a potato sack. Her chin and forearms bloody, her crying face tore Adam apart as her little hands reached for him.

The man turned, still clutching Jade, and fired his gun.

"Adam *get down*," Archie shouted.

Genie threw herself on Adam, knocking him to the ground, shielding him with her body. "Stay down, Adam." Her body tensed at each shot fired.

Tires squealed and the car sped away.

"Jade," Genie screamed again, lurching to her feet, running after the car. "*Jade!*"

Oscar grabbed her. "I'll get her. Stay here with Adam. Adam, you okay?"

Adam nodded and stood.

"Stay with Genie."

Adam nodded again.

Tears streaked down Genie's cheeks. "You get our girl, Oscar. *You get our girl.*"

"*Archie!*" Oscar ran to his black Kawasaki. He fired up the motorcycle and looked at Genie. "No cops."

Oscar's gun hung from a shoulder holster. He whipped past, a black flash followed by Adam's dad in the Porsche Speedster.

Genie looked at Adam. "You have a bloody lip and scraped hands." She sniffed. "Come on." They walked to the front step.

Adam stopped. "I'm okay, Genie."

She sniffed. "Get you cleaned—" her voice broke.

He didn't like it when girls cried. "I'm … I'm sorry, Genie. I, I tried to get Jade." His voice broke. He rubbed his forearm over his eyes. Boys don't cry.

Genie burst into tears. She looked at Adam and hugged him.

She felt soft and smelled of suntan lotion. Her long red hair tickled his cheek.

"It's not your fault, Adam. It's not your fault." She sniffed. "Let's get you inside, clean up that bloody lip."

"I'd like to wait. Here. If that's okay."

Genie nodded.

They sat on the front step.

Genie gave Adam a tissue for his lip, and sobbing, held one to her nose. She reached around and hugged him again.

"It'll be okay. Mr. Cooper and my dad, they'll bring Jade back. They'll bring her back, Genie."

She brushed her nose with a tissue.

Adam crossed his arms over his knees, his fingers turning the pink station wagon over end-to-end, end-to-end.

The clock radio on Adam's nightstand clicked over a nine. Adam cursed and rubbed his chest. Damn heartburn. He flipped back the covers, swung his legs over the side of the bed and sat.

Oscar had brought Jade back about an hour later, and that was the last time he saw her. Twenty-five years later he found her online. She had been the target of cyberbullying on Twitter when she successfully defended her ex-husband, Jules Cranbury, of second degree murder. Adam couldn't believe she had married the guy. According to her Instagram profile she liked croissants and her favourite bakery was La Roux Patisserie. Under the moniker *husbandyoung* he had subscribed to her legal blog. He thought about contacting her but every logical thread of his being told him that would be a big mistake.

He scratched his five o' clock shadow, then stood and stumbled into the kitchen. He pulled open the refrigerator and squinted at the bright light. Chinese take-out, pizza boxes and beer. He grabbed the Pepto Bismol and chugged a mouthful.

Apple cider vinegar. That's what his assistant Gillian had told him. Apple cider vinegar would cure his heartburn issues. He took a second gulp, wiped his mouth on his forearm and returned the pink bottle to the shelf.

Adam turned.

Henri stood in pajama bottoms like himself, except Henri had a Captain Morgan's rum belly and a Glock aimed at him.

"Henri, it's me for Christ's sake. Oscar hired you two to protect me, not kill me."

Henri lowered the gun. "For an ex-Royal Marine, you should know that sneaking around in a dark house in the middle of the night is a bad idea."

"It's my house." Adam leaned against the counter. Actually it was his and his girlfriend's house, until his girlfriend found a philosophy student more stimulating. The house had been sold. He didn't want to leave, but holding onto it wouldn't bring her back, or the life they had before. *Let it go.*

"Look kid. Before Oscar died, he gave us orders. Protect you, make the delivery, and keep an eye on the girl."

Adam reached for the Tylenol. "I know. I was there."

"You're thinking about tomorrow."

Adam poured water in a glass, thinking about seven hours from now. He threw back the Tylenol.

"It will go fine, Adam."

"Yeah. Right," Adam grumbled. In the glow from the overhead stove light he saw the pink toy station wagon. He picked it up. "I'm the last person Jade Thyme wants to see."

6 RED ELECTRIC GUITAR

*Both men held open their leather coats, exposing
revolvers in shoulder holsters.*

KATE AND I OCCUPIED A SMALL OFFICE LOCATED AT 2 Dragon Alley. The space looked large because of the open floor plan and glass walls. The main reception was white with black accents including the modular furniture and simple overhead lamps. The ten-foot ceilings, exposed brick, and black pipes added to the industrial feel. A local wood carver had created the letters spelling *Thyme and Bastine* behind the reception desk. Today was Norman's first day. He had requested the smallest office, at the back, so he could continue eating sardines and not smell up reception. That's all we needed, a dozen feral cats meowing at our front door. The waiting room was abloom with flowering plants with cards on plastic holders expressing condolences for my loss.

I enjoyed the courtyard and hearing the vocal exercises from the studio across from us. Down the alley was Union Pacific Coffee. The city denied there were underground passages in Chinatown, but my assistant, Kate, and numerous online articles begged to differ. Kate had commandeered our move to this location after the collapse of the old law firm. While scoping out the individual offices and a possible dead file room, she had found an old doorway in a brick wall that led to a stairway and what she called "the dungeon". I had yet to make the trip down there.

My office window open, I heard the vocal instructor, "*do-re-mi-fa-sol-la-ti-do—*", as I read the victim impact statement from the Crown file I was acting on as ad hoc prosecutor. I reached for the yellow highlighter by the prayer plant.

Kind Dr. Vlasic.

He didn't believe Charles had overdosed. I tapped my highlighter against the file, thinking about our conversation three days ago. If Charles didn't overdose then someone administered the cocaine. That meant only one thing ... Charles was murdered.

A knock startled me. I looked up as Kate slipped in, holding a dusty red electric guitar. She closed the frosted glass door.

"Where did you find that?" I asked, standing.

"The dungeon. It's so dusty down there. I need a shower." She blew hair out of her face, then sneezed. "Check it out." She held up the electric guitar. "I found it in the back corner."

I moseyed over and held the neck of it. "Nice guitar. Old. Beautiful ruby red colour. Any idea who it belongs to?"

"No. There are no initials carved anywhere. There's no guitar strap."

"Well, we can't throw it out. We can keep it here for now, unless you want it."

Kate shook her head. "No. I'm going to wash up, but first, my condolences for your loss. Charles Thyme was a well-respected lawyer, and—" she stepped forward and placed a card on my desk "—we got you a card."

"Thank you."

"You have a prayer plant."

Kate knew my success in keeping plants alive. "Yes. Dr. Vlasic, Charles's neighbour, gave one to Sage and me when we saw him. Day three and the plant lives."

"How sweet. Any update on the investigation?"

"The police are treating Charles's death as suicide. Did you know that Charles and Valentina Vale had a thing?"

Kate's eyes nearly popped out of her head. "Vicious Vale? I mean Valentina Vale ... and your father, no."

"Yeah. Anything else?"

"Your ten o' clock initial consult is here."

I propped the guitar in the corner and rolled my chair over to my computer. I clicked the calendar. "Mr. Adam Younghusband. Estate inquiries."

"Yes. About that."

I looked at Kate.

"There are three of them."

"Three Mr. Younghusbands?"

"No. You'll see. *The* Mr. Younghusband, the mystery novelist, has an entourage." She reached for the door.

That Mr. Younghusband. "Okay. Should be interesting."

She opened the door and gestured for Mr. Younghusband et al. to step into my office. I stood, straightening my rust-coloured suit, and walked around my desk when a man dressed in black slacks and a black sports coat and grey t-shirt walked in. Six-two, lean, with medium-length black wavy hair, I guessed him to be in his mid-thirties. Then came the other two. Cue ZZ Top because these men with their sunglasses, t-shirts, jeans, long beards and hair reminded me of the rock trio.

I reached to shake the nicely-dressed man's hand. "Mr. Young—"

"—Spare the introductions, Ms. Thyme," he interrupted. We stared at each other, eye-to-eye. He shifted his gaze to the floor, then gestured for the two men on either side of him to step forward. "For my two friends, are you Jade Charleigh Alexandria Thyme, born June 3, 1987?"

He knew my middle names. "Excuse me?"

He rubbed his jaw. Something flickered in his eyes. Recognition? Irritation? Constipation? "Ms. Thyme, can you show these men your driver's licence?"

I crossed my arms. Even if he was a multi-published author with an easy-listening voice, the audacity of this guy. "I'm not showing you or them anything. This is supposed to be an estate consult."

He leaned forward and tossed an envelope on my desk. It landed with a clunk.

I stepped back. "What is that?"

"Ms. Thyme, if you show Bob and Henri—" he gestured to the men again "—your driver's licence, we will depart."

"What's in the envelope?"

Mr. Younghusband stepped in front of me and I got a whiff of a woodsy cologne. He tipped the envelope and five thumbdrives slid onto the table along with two keys, one long and one short. "Ms. Thyme, show these men your driver's licence," he said in a low tone.

"No."

Mr. Younghusband glared. "No?" He arched one eyebrow, and glanced at my degrees on the wall behind my desk. "Figures you'd be a lawyer."

"What is this about?"

He looked to the man on his left. "Ms. Thyme needs some persuading."

Both men held open their leather coats, exposing revolvers in shoulder holsters.

"Jesus Christ." I stepped behind my desk. "Fine." I grabbed my purse from the drawer. "Here." I held up my driver's licence. My arm shook.

Mr. Younghusband read the information and glanced at me. "You're her."

Bob leaned forward, tipping his sunglasses up. He mouthed the information, then removed his sunglasses and smiled. "You're her."

Who the hell was I supposed to be? Lady Gaga?

Mr. Younghusband looked at the guy on his right. "Are you satisfied? Can we go?"

Bob smiled. "It's an honour meeting you, Jade Thyme." He extended his hand.

I nervously shook it. Now we're friends? The other one, Henri, the quiet one, smiled.

"Adam," said Bob, "our business is done." He smacked Mr. Younghusband on the back. "No hard feelings, hey? Henri's sorry for breaking your coffee machine."

"Espresso machine," Mr. Younghusband corrected.

"Espresso machine. Before we head up island we'll stop at Canadian Tire and get you another one."

"That espresso machine was shipped from Italy."

Bob looked at me.

"I think a Canadian Tire espresso machine would be just fine," I said.

Mr. Younghusband's dark eyes glared. "You're now an expert on espresso machines."

I crossed my arms. "What do you think?"

Bob looked from Adam to me. "Nice to meet you, Jade. My brother and I had orders to get legal confirmation before leaving the package."

"I don't want that." I pointed at the items on my desk.

"We can't take it back," Henri said, with a voice of a giant.

"Take the bloody package," Mr. Younghusband said, still looking at me.

Bob picked up a business card. "You do defence work, eh?"

What carnival show was this? "Yes."

He held up the card. "Could come in handy." He patted Mr. Younghusband on the shoulder. "We didn't use up all the time. Talk to the pretty lady."

I bit my lip.

Henri smiled and waved, and he and Bob left my office.

The door closed.

"What the hell—"

Mr. Younghusband held up his hand. "—Wait."

"Excuse me! This is my—"

"—Ms. Thyme, your composure is much—"

"—My composure!"

"Please."

The clock on my desk ticked. I saw the shape of two men

through the blinds, ambling toward the cafe. "They're gone."

"About time." Mr. Younghusband said, rubbing his forehead.

I walked back to my desk. "You lied about your appointment. What the hell is all this about?"

"It's all there." He looked at me one more time. "You'll never see me again." He walked to the door and was gone.

What the hell was going on? I looked at the five thumbdrives and keys.

"What's up?" Kate asked, standing in the open doorway. "Mr. Younghusband dashed out of here."

"I was going to ask you the same thing." I picked up the thumbdrives. Standard, like the ones I've purchased. "I don't believe Mr. Younghusband was here under his own volition. They left me with these."

Kate took the thumbdrives. "IT can scan them for viruses."

I looked at her. "You're IT."

"I know."

I slid onto my chair, clicking my mouse. I typed 'Adam Younghusband' into the Google search field. "What can we find on you, Mr. Younghusband?"

Kate picked up the keys. "Ah, Jade, this key—" she held up the larger one "—do you know what it says on here?"

"No."

"Lamborghini."

I stopped typing and looked at her. "Why are they giving me keys to a Lamborghini? Is there a body in the trunk?"

"They don't have trunks. That's where the engine is."

"Is this evidence? Maybe, don't touch any of it."

The face of the man who had, moments earlier stood in my office popped up on my computer screen, but this time he was dressed in black robes and wore tabs around his neck.

Kate leaned in. "Is he a lawyer?"

"He was a Clerk Assistant," I said, scrolling as I read the text under his photo. "He was part of the U.K.'s Youth Parliament program."

"No way," Kate said.

"He moved back to Canada—"

"—back? That means he's Canadian."

I scrolled. "Listen to this, he returned home to Vancouver Island and worked in the Legislative Assembly in the Office of the Speaker and the Parliamentary Committees Office. With his parliamentary days behind him, he devotes his to time to being a full-time novelist and sessional lecturer at Royal Roads." I scrolled some more. "His fifth novel is launching this month."

Kate pointed at another photo that had been taken a few years back. "Oh my."

Adam Younghusband stood with two other men. They wore swim shorts and had medals around their necks. Slim with defined abs and shoulders, a tiny part of me felt perverted, creeping on this guy. Only a small part.

"A swimmer's body. Rather delicious. It says he went to the University of Edinburgh," she said.

"What is he doing back here? And why is he involved with Hells Angels types?"

Kate's cellphone rang. She picked it up. "Hello?"

I could hear Sage's excited voice on the other end.

"She's right here." Kate looked at me. "She was with a client."

"What does Sage want?"

Kate pressed her fingers to her lips. "I'll tell her right now. Bye." She looked at me. "You gotta go. Charles's old house, the one you and Sage bought—is on fire."

7 TYPEWRITER

"That's not a message from God."

Dark smoke billowed into the sky three kilometres away.

I cranked the throttle. How could our place be on fire? Sage and I had been cleaning it out since we purchased it from Charles four months ago.

I turned my Royal Enfield right onto Pearl Drive. Now I could smell it, itching in my throat. Cars lined both sides of the street. These cars didn't belong here. Pearl Drive residents had their three to five bay garages.

I parked two blocks away, hung my helmet on the handlebars and ran. I slowed when I saw the City News TV van. *Shit.*

My phone buzzed.

Sage. *Where are you?*

I stopped. *Walking to the house. Where are you?*

By TV van. Talking to Stone.

Coming.

I slunk between cars and teenagers taking selfies with my burning home their backdrop. I saw part of the third floor, a black buttress. I pushed between two people and stood pressed against a barricade.

The Victoria Fire Department sprayed gallons of water on a fire that snapped and flared like a dragon, puffing dark smoke, the flames refusing to be put down.

"Oh my God."

"Jade!" Sage shouted, pushing her way toward me.

"Are you all right?"

"Yes."

"How did this happen?" I asked.

Glass exploded from a window. We ducked.

More shouts.

"I took a load of Mom's belongings home, and I was on my way back when I heard sirens. I pulled over and three firetrucks flew past. It wasn't until I got closer that I realized it was our place." Sage shooked her head.

"What do you think caused it? No one's been living here. Squatters don't come out this far."

"Something in the garage?" Sage asked.

"No," Sergeant Stone said, sucking in his stomach, coming up behind Sage.

Sage rolled her eyes.

"Sergeant Stone."

He looked from me to Sage.

"This—" he waved his cellphone "—started in the corner room. Basement."

"And how do you know this?"

"Twenty-six years on the force, Jade. Your mother was a painter. Any rag soaked in an oil-based stain can spontaneously catch fire."

A constable called Sergeant Stone aside.

"Jade," Sage said under her breath, staring beyond me to my right.

"What?"

"Don't look. Not yet."

"Okay."

"Casually look over your left shoulder to the blonde guy under the maple tree, leaning against the black SUV."

I turned as if looking behind at the spectators as Sage looked at the house. I saw him. "Jeans, leather jacket, blonde hair, stocky, leaning against the passenger side, smirking."

"That's him."

The man looked at me, made a rude gesture, then turned and opened the door to the SUV.

I heard a click.

Sage looked at her cellphone. "Gotcha."

"I've seen him before, but I don't remember where. Send me the photo and I can show Dr. Vlasic. Maybe he'll recognize him."

Sage looked at the house. "This isn't good, Jade. I cleaned out this place. There were no oil-stained rags left in any rooms. I got rid of them first. And you and I know, despite what Stone says, Charles didn't overdose."

Flames roared from windows. I glanced at the structure next door that used to belong to James Aubischon, my father's old law partner. Their homes were the pillars of their stature. A Vancouver investor had purchased the Aubischon residence and was demolishing it for something bigger. Our family home was now engulfed in flames.

Sage looked at me. "Who did Charles piss off?"

I thought of the newspaper articles on his desk. "This isn't retribution for taking down the Society. The Society was dismantled. This ... this is personal."

"There she is," a TV reporter shouted, pointing at me. She barged through spectators, heading in our direction, a camera man behind her.

"I'm getting us a coffee," Sage said.

"Don't leave me with *them*."

"Jade, we'd like to ask a few—"

Sage waved and slipped into the crowd.

"*Sage. Sage,*" I hissed.

The reporter rattled off her name and what cable network she was associated with. The camera man propped a TV camera on his shoulders. The reporter began her rapid-fire questions. Did I believe the fire was an accident? Microphone in my face.

Too early to tell.

Did I believe it was the Society taking retribution?

I had no idea.

Did I believe this fire was connected to Charles's suicide?

No.

Did I believe my life was in danger?

I looked at her, glanced at the large square lens pointed at me. "No."

The reporter continued her spiel about tuning in later for an update on the suspicious fire that destroyed the home of well-respected lawyer, Charles Thyme, who had taken his life two days prior by overdosing on cocaine.

How did she know?

The reporter slithered between people.

"Excuse me." I pushed between the spectators, after her. "Excuse me." I touched her arm.

She swung around. "Don't touch me."

"How did you know Charles overdosed?"

"A reporter never reveals her sources." She turned.

"Hold on."

I reached for her arm again.

"Don't touch the talent," the camera man interjected.

"You're talking about my father. How did you know?"

The reporter frowned. "An anonymous tip."

Anonymous tip?

Two hours later I returned to my office, fielding questions from Kate. Was it determined how the fire was started? Was it arson? Did the police have a suspect? Was anyone hurt? Were there any cute firemen? No, no, no, no, and yes. She confirmed that I had no appointments that afternoon and Norman had his first client, a man charged with impaired driving.

She stepped out of my office and then returned with a candle, a yellow glass bottle, and an eye dropper.

"What are you doing?"

"Please don't take this the wrong way—" she placed the candle by the prayer plant "—but you smell like a bonfire. This—" she squeezed the eye dropper over the candle and immediately I smelled pineapples "—will bring up your spirits. My aesthetician sells this. You're supposed to use two drops in your bath, but—" she looked at me "—desperate times."

I didn't know whether to thank her or be offended.

"And Norman showed up."

"Is he here?"

"Yes. He was hoping to see you."

"Of course."

Kate beckoned Norman from the hallway.

White hair combed back, wearing grey slacks, a white shirt and pink tie, Norman stepped in, holding with both hands a take-out tray with two coffees.

"Norman." I stepped around my desk. "Welcome."

He hesitantly smiled and placed the tray near the candle. He looked at me with sincere blue eyes. "I smell pineapples."

"I supposedly smell like a smoke pit." I fired Kate a look.

She closed the door behind her.

"I heard about the fire," he said. "Charles's home in Uplands."

"Yes. Sage and I actually own that smoking pile of embers."

"Terrible. You've had a lot to cope with."

I nodded.

"My condolences." He rubbed the palms of his hands together.

"Thank you. Please have a seat." I sat in the chair across from him.

With a trembling hand he passed me my coffee. "Kate said if it's not a raspberry truffle mocha, then you take your Americano black."

I laughed and took the cup from him.

He removed the plastic lid from his and sipped. "Your mother, Genie, and I were friends."

"Really?"

He stared at his cup then looked at me. "She was a good artist, but Charles and James didn't notice."

"You did."

He looked at my law degrees behind my desk. "Genie was a whirlwind of sweet mischief. The world was a better place when she was around."

"Aww, thank you, Norman."

He chuckled, shaking his head. "Because of her I got my start in criminal law."

"Really. What type of files?"

"Oh, the usual stuff, trafficking, impaired drivings. Kate said you had a file for me?"

I told him about Simon and the dine and dash charge, and which cog this case was at in the big wheel called justice. "He has no priors. He always pays his rent and taxes and is raising his younger brother. We'll be making another court appearance next week to set his trial date."

"Crown didn't offer a deal?"

"No. They might with you on the file."

"I'll be prepared."

"Is there anything you need? Bookshelves, a chair, any legal texts?"

He thought for a moment. "In the old office, I had a rather worn chair. It was perfect for my back. It didn't come over with the other furniture, did it?"

"Well, let's check." I placed my coffee on the desk. "If it's anywhere it'll be in the dungeon."

We stood.

Norman walked towards the door and stopped. He stared at the red electric guitar.

"Do you like it?" I asked.

He looked at me, startled. "No." He quickly walked out the door.

Strange. I followed him, stopping at Kate's office. She sat at her desk, rubbing her forehead, her phone pressed to her ear.

"Kate," I whispered.

She looked up, frowning.

"The dungeon. Key?"

She reached for a key hanging on a nail and handed it to me. "I did click the submit button. The client has been waiting eight months for a trial date," she said to the person on the other end.

"Sounds serious," Norman said.

I smiled as we walked down the hall and around the corner to the narrow door. I inserted the key, heard a click and then pushed my weight against the door to open it.

Dank air greeted me. I slid my hand over the wall and flicked a light switch. A single bulb hung from the ceiling, providing meagre light. I looked down the stairs that disappeared into darkness. This was a dungeon. "Be careful, Norman." I tried to sound confident, but meanwhile I hoped like hell there was another switch at the bottom. We climbed down the creaky stairs. If we did find Norman's chair, how we were going to get it up these stairs was another thing.

"You all right?" I glanced behind, seeing Norman place both feet on a step before taking another.

"I'm all right," he said, his hands gripping the railing.

"We're just about at the bottom." The stair creaked under my feet. I came to another door that opened into a dark room. I reached around the corner and thankfully found a light switch. Fluorescent lights hummed and flickered. I would never come down here alone.

We stepped inside, making our way around surplus tables, metal filing cabinets, plastic file dividers. In one corner, boxes were stacked on top of each other with BASTINE written on the sides in black marker. I rubbed my cold hands over my silk shirt.

On the far side of the room Norman flipped through a box. "My old files." He pulled out a rolodex and looked at me. "My old rolodex."

"Seriously."

He pulled out a stenographer's chair, the black material worn.

"Norman, we can buy you a new chair."

"No," he said, pushing the chair under the desk. "My old one was perfect. This isn't it."

I stepped around a desk with an odd-shaped suitcase positioned in the middle. I flipped open the lid to find a black manual typewriter with Smith Corona written in the bottom right corner. "This is ancient."

"It's a portable typewriter." Norman smiled. "My sister used to have one. It still has paper in it."

"Does it even work?"

And as if on cue, a letter hammer struck the red and black striped ribbon, printing the letter 'H' on the paper.

Norman and I didn't move.

Another letter hammer tapped the page, printing the letter 'E'.

My heart pounded. "Norman."

"Yes, Jade."

"This is a manual typewriter," I said.

A third hammer struck the page, leaving the letter 'L'.

"And no one's touching it."

I swallowed. "I've been clean for six months, Norman. You're seeing this, right?"

He placed a trembling hand on my arm. "I haven't touched a drop, Jade. I swear."

Then a fourth letter: 'P'. The carriage return pinged and the paper moved up a line.

A colon and open bracket.

The carriage return pinged a second time, the paper moved up and the typing stopped.

I held Norman's arm.

HELP.

:(

"Oh dear God." I flung the typewriter case closed and stepped back. "Norman."

He stared at the typewriter, his rolodex clutched to his chest. "That's not a message from God."

8 VALENTINA

"Every morning we streamed Lao Tzu while practising naked meditation."

We climbed the stairs as fast as Norman could negotiate the 23 steps, stopping to catch our breath.

We stood near the top, Norman leaning against the wall, hands on his knees.

"Norman—" I took a breath "—we tell no one what just happened."

He nodded. "Understood."

We touched knuckles and straightened. "Okay. Ready?"

He nodded.

I opened the door and we stepped out. We walked the long hall and found Kate, standing by the articling student at reception.

Kate looked from me to Norman. "You two okay? You look like you've seen a—"

"—Don't say it," I interrupted.

Kate smiled. "Boo."

I patted Norman's arm. "We'll buy you a new chair, full office suite. Anything you want." Norman headed into his office and closed the door.

"Jade, Valentina Vale wants to meet you," Kate said, loading paper into the printer.

"Oh."

"Tomorrow at four o'clock, the Spiral Cafe. Lucy Starr wants to see you too. I forwarded the email."

I stepped into my office and closed the door. I sat massaging my temples. Mother, if the typewriter is your doing, *not* funny.

I texted Sage. *Vale wants to meet me tomorrow. Spiral Cafe. Free at 4. I need backup.*

Sage responded with fire, lightning, and devil emojis followed by a *yes*.

I chuckled. *Go after we check out fire damage* I texted back. I woke my laptop and read the email from my volatile client, Lucy. She had done her time and had reported to probation as a condition of her release. She was in counselling and attending a reading program. She needed to make amends for her antics in court. Could she see me? I checked my calendar and emailed a date and time.

I sat back in my chair.

I know what I saw. I hadn't touched the typewriter. Norman saw it too. I have been clean for six months. I stood and paced by the red electric guitar. Maybe I should start seeing Dr. Vlasic? He was retired. Would he make an exception for me? I had admitted to my previous therapist that I had continued taking Vicodin when I no longer felt pain from a previous injury. I took responsibility. The ghosts, I thought, were drug induced.

My therapist had said something along the lines of no pain receptors for the Vicodin to bind onto, then Vicodin floats around in the body and provides a euphoric high. Then she looked at me over her glasses and asked what was I trying to mask for wanting that high?

I pressed my fingertips against my desk. What was I masking?

Ghosts?

Depression?

I wasn't depressed.

She had pressed further. My depression could be a side-effect of repressed memories. Something traumatic that had happened when I was a child.

Repressed memories.

Ghosts.

What were the ghosts trying to tell me?

I paced again. This was not good. I could feel it. This was the path that led me to reach for those pills.

Dig deeper, Jade, my therapist had prompted.

During childhood I experienced waves of sadness. But my inner Tinkerbell told me *it's okay. This will pass, and what do I have planned next for Barbie?* For the most part, the sadness did fade. Then I grew up and I no longer had Tink for a life coach.

I marched around my desk and pulled open the bottom drawer, pulling out files, papers, there had to be a bottle. *Somewhere.* I had hidden them all over the place.

Nothing.

I sat in my chair and took deep breaths. "Can I get those memories back?" I had asked.

Yes. Smell, or an incident, could trigger them. They were still there but hiding. I'd talk with Dr. Vlasic. Maybe we could have greenhouse therapy, and any lingering ghosts could bugger off.

The remainder of my day was spent interviewing witnesses and in the evening, I uploaded the five thumbdrives on my laptop and then emailed the uploaded files to my phone. I pressed play and listened to the raspy voice of a dead man.

"Hello ... Jade. I'm Oscar Cooper. I knew your mother."

Stop. Excuse me? Oscar Cooper knew my mother? Did I want to go down this rabbit hole? Was Oscar being truthful? Or was he an obsessed art fan from the sixties who had done one too many acid trips? Given Charles had *supposedly* overdosed and the family home torched, I pressed play.

"You need to know about a few players before I continue with this interview." Scraping of chairs. "These tapes, or audio files or whatever the hell you want to call them, are yours. If you disclose these files to the police, you will bring unwanted attention to you and your sister, Sage."

Stop. He knew Sage and I were sisters. Play.

"Unwanted attention from the cops. From ... men like me. Dangerous men. As a result of my love for your mother—"

Stop.

I pushed my phone across the table. What in God's name was he doing with Mother and what did he want with me? I tapped play.

"My love for your mother."

Stop. No. You're lying. You're an old man just wanting attention. Rewind.

"My love for your mother ... I kept my distance. I run with a rough crowd. I always wanted to keep Genie safe."

Stop. I couldn't do this tonight. I was not ready. Oscar Cooper, you're going to have to wait another day. I was not in the right mindset to listen to this slander.

I tucked in for the night and the nightmares returned. In one dream I played a card game of reasons as to why anyone would torch our family home. Few people knew that Sage and I had purchased it from Charles. When I did fall asleep, I dreamt someone chased me with a hatchet along a cliff and the dolphins trilled below, trying to guide me to safety.

The following morning, my Royal Enfield idled as I waited on the Esquimalt side, as a barge cruised under the bridge, blasting its horn. The bridge lowered. Traffic slowly moved and I moved with it, crossing and turning left onto Fort, a one way street, stopping at many crosswalks and intersecting streets.

I passed Craigdarroch Castle and made another left onto Cadboro Bay Road, passing the fabulous pizza place.

The spectators from yesterday were gone, but there were still cars slowing down, rubber-necking as they drove past. Our family home was a heap of charred wood and rubble, crowned by wispy grey smoke. The only standing structures were brick walls and the porte cochere.

Ash.

Burnt.

I parked and walked up the driveway, seeing exposed brick, and blackened window frames. In the centre was the green armchair. It was as if a bomb had gone off. On one brick wall, what would have been the second floor, if there was still a second floor, a single rectangular mirror hung on the wall. *Mirror, mirror, on the wall, can you tell us who torched it all?*

In the distance I heard a Harley. Sage.

The sound of the engine grew louder. I turned and saw Sage riding down the driveway with Lizzy, wearing doggles, sitting in the sidecar. Sage slowed and parked her bike next to mine. She placed her helmet on the seat and grabbed Lizzy's leash. They walked over.

"I was hoping it would look better in the morning. How are you?" she asked.

"Slept like crap."

"Me too. I can't remember falling asleep."

"How's your girl in heat?"

"Trying to keep the male dogs away. Do you know how many times I've said to a stranger's dog, 'get off her.'"

"How many times has a woman said that to a man?"

"As soon as she's done, she's getting spayed."

I smiled and patted Lizzy's head. "I know, girl. It sucks." I looked at Sage as we slowly walked toward the rubble. "After this, we can meet Valentina Vale."

Sage smiled like a Cheshire cat. "This is going to be fun."

We walked around the blue wire fence that cordoned off the rubble piled inside the foundation. Strewn picture frames amongst piles of toppled bricks; wooden doors jagged and broken; tufts of insulation blew in the grass. We stopped.

"Danger: do not enter," Sage read on a sign. "That was our home. I ... I was cleaning that house out yesterday morning."

We wandered around to the back, stepping over broken chunks of drywall.

Sage cursed. "Who would do this? Any disgruntled criminal

you've defended? Prosecuted?"

"The only person I know is Lucy Starr, and she's doing time for assault with a turnip," I said. We stopped again. The kitchen was the only room that had escaped the flames. I looked up at the cement wall and pointed. "Sage. Look."

Sage followed my gaze.

Spraypainted on the wall was a spider.

"That—" I looked at Sage "—had to be spraypainted—"

"—Last night," she said. "After the fire had been put out. Someone risked being caught, or getting injured, to spray paint a spider."

"That should never have happened," I said. "Our insurance company should have a security guard out here until they assess the situation for insurance purposes."

"I'll deal with them. I'd expect looters but looters don't leave behind artwork."

"We have to be vigilant, Sage. Report anything suspicious, if not to the cops, to each other."

Sage nodded. "I'm asking around. My people."

We walked back to our bikes.

I sat on mine and fastened my helmet. "Ready to meet firecracker Vale?"

"Oh, yeah." She turned the ignition. Her bike rumbled. "Meet you there," she said over her shoulder.

I took off and after a number of turns found myself on Foul Bay Road, then turning right onto Bay Street. Stopping and starting as road crews ripped up the street, I rode over the Bay Street bridge and turned right into Vic West. I parked and saw Sage and Lizzy already sitting at a table outside the Spiral Cafe.

"What does Valentina look like?" Sage asked, as I stepped up and patted Lizzy.

"She's about my height but looks taller because she always wears stilettos. Gorgeous, early-fifties brunette, voluptuous and she's a damn good lawyer. She drives a blue Porsche and practises criminal law."

"Miami blue and, speak of the devil, firecracker Vale has arrived," Sage said, looking over my shoulder.

I turned.

A Miami blue Porsche pulled up to the curb across the street. The entire cafe turned and looked.

Valentina stepped out. Her dark curls bounced with each step. Dressed in a tight black t-shirt that had FIERCE FEMALE written across her chest, she crossed the road in four-inch fluorescent green heels that matched her fluorescent green slim-cut pants.

Tires screeched as cars braked.

Her eyelashes greeted us before she did.

"Charles was sleeping with her," Sage said, under her breath.

And probably Osmond. "Please, I don't want the visual."

Valentina saw us and smiled. She held out her hand. "Jade. Nice to see you outside of court where I've been kicking your ass." She laughed.

Not quite the grieving girlfriend.

Realizing that Sage and I weren't laughing, she became more serious. "I'm sorry about Charles." She air-kissed either side of my cheeks. "You must—" she placed her hand over her heart "—be devastated. I know—" she fanned her face with her white manicured nails as a tear trickled down her cheek "—I am." She sniffed. "Grief. Hitches a ride at its own convenience."

Sage cleared her throat.

"Valentina, this is my sister, Sage."

"Oh. Charles never … never mind." She proffered the same hand but no air kisses.

Sage touched it. "Hi."

Lizzy growled.

"Oh." She looked at Lizzy and pointed as if the dog was an alien. "What's wrong with the muffin?"

Sage glared at me.

"She's in heat," I said. "So, Valentina, I was surprised when my assistant said you wanted to meet. First, do you want a coffee?"

"No." She sat, crossing her legs. "I'm on a Clean."

Sage nearly spat out her coffee. "Really." She coughed. "I'm a personal trainer. This is the first time I've heard of a Clean. Don't you mean cleanse?"

"That's so nineties. It's what my BFF highly recommends. You only eat and drink in small quantities what Mother Earth—" she cupped her palms over her FIERCE FEMALE and looked to the sky "—has provided. Every morning, Dennis, my personal assistant, makes me a natural elixir from apple cider vinegar, honey, the juice of one freshly squeezed orange, cilantro, coconut milk and vanilla. Its purpose is to clean the gastrointestinal tract of any residual toxins from the night before and bring a lightness to the body and soul. That's why Charles—" she batted her long lashes and brushed aside a tear "—Charles's suicide baffles me." Valentina touched my hand. "So sorry. I can stop if this is upsetting."

"No, please go on," Sage said, leaning back in her chair, crossing her legs, petting Lizzy.

Valentina's slightly annoyed glance at Sage didn't escape me.

"Charles and I were reconnecting with nature through diet and spirituality, taking it back to basics. Every morning we streamed Lao Tzu while practising naked meditation. It's clearing the clutter from our minds—" she touched her temples "—which these devices—" she swatted her cell beside mine "—have clogged." She again batted long lashes. "We would smoke a little cannabis to relax and face each day with untethered clarity."

"Charles smoked cannabis?" Sage asked.

"It's been legal since 2018. I'm here, Jade—" she leaned forward and held my hand in hers. I wanted to pull it back but she had a firm grip. "If you need anything, any help with the funeral arrangements, his cremation—"

Cremation?

"—Charles wanted to return to the earth. Ashes to ashes, dust to dust."

She was now quoting the Bible.

"And even if we're combatants in court, we are both humans."

Sage cleared her throat.

"Thank you," I said.

"I heard about the fire at your home." She sat back, tossing long dark curls over her shoulder. "Who would do something like that?"

I picked up my coffee and glanced at Sage over the rim. She had caught it too. Only Sage and I suspected arson.

"Maybe the same person who supplied Charles with cocaine," Sage said.

Valentina pivoted her attention on Sage. "You're not suggesting … Charles … he was always happy when we were together. You're not suggesting—"

"—that you supplied him with a little cocaine in his cannabis?" Sage looked her in the eye.

Valentina tossed her hair over her shoulder again. I was getting whiplash.

"We were happy and I'm aghast–" she sniffed and brushed at more tears "–that you would even suggest such a thing."

"So you gave him this instead?" Sage placed the black bottle of Vicodin we had found in his bathroom on the table.

Valentina fell back in her chair. "No. What is that?"

Valentina was a criminal defence lawyer. She knew *exactly* what that was.

Sage retrieved the bottle and tucked it in her hoodie pocket. "You see Valentina," Sage said, looking over at the Porsche, "what I have a hard time understanding, is that Charles didn't take drugs when he was married to our mother. He hooks up with you and now we're learning that he's smoking pot, snorting coke, and a bottle of Vicodin was found in his home."

Valentina glared. "Maybe if you would have paid attention to Charles, and not deliberately piss him off every chance you had, you'd understand he had demons."

Sage's eyes grew wide and if she had a Labatt beer can …

Valentina shifted her gaze on me. "You took down the Society. Charles was plagued by what he had witnessed." She took a deep breath. "I'm sorry about your home. You have been through a lot, but Charles was happy with me. I didn't give him drugs or suggest drugs. We were on a—"

"—Clean," Sage interjected.

Valentina ignored her. "Your beautiful home. Was there anything salvageable? You grew up there. Memories of your mother?"

What was Valentina fishing for? What had Charles told her? My expression must have said it all because Valentina immediately apologized.

"I'm sorry. The last seven months have been trying. Charles loved your mother."

Liar.

"If anything—" her lashes fluttered as she dabbed at another tear with her index finger "—I felt I never ... measured up."

Sage opened her mouth and I tapped her with my foot under the table. "I think Charles got over our mother's death very well. She's only been dead a year and he was already with you."

"I brought peace." Valentina smiled. "Genie was an amazing violinist, I understand."

Hearing Valentina say our mother's name made my skin crawl.

"I'm tone deaf." She laughed. "Pitch. Isn't that the sticky substance on trees?" She laughed again.

I smiled.

Sage rolled her eyes and patted Lizzy's head, which now rested on her lap.

"Charles said he loved it when your mother played the violin. He only wished she had kept creating art."

"We are just learning that our mother was an artist."

"You don't have any of her work?" Valentina asked.

"No," Sage said. "We don't. Mom's paintings were destroyed in the fire."

I wasn't sure Valentina was convinced.

"I'm so sorry to hear that." Valentina smiled. "Maybe we can go out for dinner. All three of us."

Sage coughed, choking on her coffee.

"Are you okay?" I asked.

She glared again, her eyes watering. She tapped her chest. "Wrong tract."

"Sage and I are still coping—"

Sage coughed louder.

"—with Charles's death."

"I understand. Death is difficult. I'll go two, three days believing I'm okay. Then, I'll be jogging and I'm besot with grief."

Sage cursed under her breath.

"When you are ready." Valentina looked at me. "I must go. Hot yoga. Thank you so much for meeting me during these troubling times. If you need any help, please—" she patted my hand "—call me. I'll contact the Victoria Bar Association and Charles can have the service he so deserves."

And you can land another lawyer? "Thank you, Valentina."

"If you need an extra pair of hands to clean up Charles's house, please call, Jade. Or, if you need something to relax, I can hook you up."

"Valentina, before you go, one question. When did you last see Charles?"

She hesitated and her smile looked a little rigid. "Two nights before his overdose."

Not according to Dr. Vlasic.

"We went out for dinner. Do you want a witness list?"

I had tapped a nerve. This was the Valentina I knew from court. "Which restaurant?"

"Il Terrazzo. I ordered the seafood and Charles had prime rib."

"You two had a good relationship? Charles could be demanding."

Valentina pushed back her chair.

Lizzy stood.

Sage held her collar.

"Charles and I understood each other. Other men, they look at me and think sex. Charles understood *me*."

"So you two hadn't broken up?"

Her eyes widened. Not so FIERCE now.

"No. We had plans to go sailing. Whoever is giving you this

information is a liar." Valentina stood.

"I'm sure it's just gossip in a Starbucks line—up. You know what the legal community is like. I never knew you and Osmond were friends."

"Osmond and I go back a long way."

Really.

"You two are together, right?" Her smile widened.

"No. We broke up."

I could see Sage looking at me. She heard my cold tone. "Enjoy hot yoga," I said, forcing a smile.

Valentina clicked down the sidewalk and crossed the street. She and her fluorescent green legs folded into her Miami blue Porsche, and she pulled out onto the road.

"Jade, I know you say women need to respect each other. How will men ever respect us if we don't—" Sage shook her head "—but that woman is a bitch."

I smiled. "There's something about Valentina Vale that takes me to a new level. How many paintings of Mom's do we have?"

"Three, but I'm not telling her that."

I wondered about Valentina's interest in Mother's paintings. "How long were Valentina and Charles together?"

"Eight months according to Charles's homophobic golf buddy."

"That means Charles started seeing her four months after Mother died and during the shakedown of the Society. Sage ... I believe Charles was murdered."

Sage tapped her stirstick and looked at me from across the table. "I guess we're looking into it."

9 GILLIAN WITH A "G"

"You're hitting on the assistant with poodle hair."

I ARRIVED HOME FROM THE VALENTINA MEETING feeling exhausted. At least Sage had a spin class where she could scream her frustrations at her poor participants.

What did I have? A bottle of Mission Hill Riesling. I plugged in my earbuds and with wine glass in hand, I listened.

"Hello ... Jade. It's Oscar."

Stop. What could this dead drug dealer say that could be so damning? I pressed play.

"Unwanted attention from the cops."

Yes, I know. I fast-forward. "As a result of my love for your mother."

Stop. Rewind.

"My love for your mother."

Skip. I pressed play again. "I always wanted to keep Genie safe."

Stop. I was going to need more wine. I topped up my glass and sipped. Play.

"I met Genie in the spring of 1968 through my business partner, Archie Malone. We were inseparable throughout the summer and fall. Genie was a good artist. There was an honesty in her work, evident in her personality. We hung Genie's art in my galleries in

Victoria and Vancouver. Our Victoria gallery was in Chinatown. It's now a bloody tea house."

I grabbed a scrap of paper and a pencil and made a note, *tea house in Chinatown*.

"Another artist hung in our circle. Darlene Banks. Darlene hated Genie."

Stop. I scribbled *Darlene Banks hated Mom*. "Why?" I said out loud, interviewing this dead man. Play.

"Darlene thought she was a better artist."

I see.

"She expected to be treated like a celebrity, but people wanted to be around your mother. Genie always came to art show openings. Darlene liked the parties. She would get drunk or high, or have a bad trip and make a fool of herself.

"Every piece Genie created was sold. Darlene didn't sell anything. Genie and I fell in love."

Stop. "Seriously?"

Play. "This is before Charles. He was around, but your mother was never interested in him."

Then why marry him?

"Genie would come to the house and paint. There are three art pieces you must know about: Moon Gate Lovers."

Stop. I couldn't write fast enough. Play.

"The painting of my Lamborghini Miura."

Stop. I tipped the envelope and the Lamborghini car key slid onto my coffee table. Tell me I didn't have the keys to Oscar Cooper's Lamborghini? I gulped my glass of white. Play.

Oscar coughed a few times. "I'm tired, Jade. Mr. Younghusband is coming tomorrow. Find the paintings."

You didn't tell me the third? Are there three? More? Come on, Oscar.

"Genie left with them. I made sure of that. Find Genie's paintings. Open the backs. It's all yours. Genie's paintings are priceless." Oscar coughed. "Do not let them fall into Kathy's wretched hands. Darlene spread her hate for Genie to her daughter, Kathy. I lost contact with Kathy when I was incarcerated. Kathy is evil, Jade. Maybe if I handled things better."

He mumbled a few more words then the audio was over. I pulled the earbuds from my ears.

What's the third painting?

The next morning I woke with a white wine headache knocking on my temples. After two Tylenols and a 40-minute run, I jumped on my bike and slowly pulled onto Tyee, noticing a guy in a car following me. I pulled over to the side of the road by a grocery store and waited. The car drove past. The blonde Lundgren-esque driver did not look my way. I was just paranoid. That's all.

Maybe.

I arrived at Sage's gym, an old, converted mechanic's shop. The door open, I heard the heavy rock riff and the voice of Judas Priest singing *You've Got Another Thing Coming*. I stepped inside onto the smooth concrete to see my sister dressed in black shorts and a black sports bra. Her gaze focused in front of her, she heaved a barbell easily stacked with two 40-pound plates and performed a snatch.

I waited until she dropped the barbell, I swear shaking the walls. I stepped around Bosus, battle ropes, a plyometric box and kettlebells. She still didn't see me.

The song slowed.

Sage positioned herself, looked up and screamed. She grabbed the remote hooked onto a fan and turned the volume down. "Jesus Christ, Jade. You scared the hell out of me."

"Do you always leave the gym door open so any creep can wander in?"

"Nobody's coming here except clients," she said, out of breath. "I could easily kill somebody with one of these plates."

"Where are the paintings?"

Sage grabbed the disinfectant bottle and sprayed the barbell, wiping it down. She straightened, grabbing her Gatorade. "Hi Sage. Nice to see you." She gulped the sports drink.

"Hi Sage, nice to see you, where are Mom's paintings? Here?"

"No. At the condo I'm house-sitting."

"Why there?"

"Because I was short on time and wanted to store them somewhere. Why?"

"We have to open the backs of them."

Sage looked at me like I had lost my mind. "Excuse me?"

I quickly explained about listening to Oscar's first audio file. "We also need to find Kathy Banks. Oscar says she's dangerous."

"And why do we need to find this dangerous woman?"

"Because she may be looking for us. Charles had printed articles about the Banks brothers. Oscar Cooper, drug dealer, is warning me about Kathy Banks. There's got to be a connection. "

"Jade, none of this makes sense."

"Help me approach Mr. Younghusband, who delivered me the thumbdrives. He must know more than he's letting on. He must know about Kathy Banks. Then, we can reassess all of this. The thumbdrives and the fire must tie into Charles's murder."

Sage wiped her forehead with a towel. "I have three personal training clients this morning, back-to-back, then I'm instructing a spin class for the UVIC boys' hockey club and then a dentist appointment." She eyed my black pants and blazer. "I'm guessing you have court. Meet you at four at your place?"

"Works for me." We walked to the door and stepped outside. Sage locked up.

"Seriously, Sage, if you're by yourself, that door should be locked."

She waved. "Later."

Wednesdays were known as Disclosure Court, a zoo of guilty pleas for lighter sentences, and I had a few clients entering guilty pleas. I squeezed between bikers and gang members in the Victoria courthouse. A man holding a pillowcase with something in it stood in the corner. I stepped around a woman pushing a baby carriage with a doll in it.

I was supposed to meet Norman's client, who was entering a guilty plea for shoving steaks up his coat sleeve. A crime he had committed numerous times. Norman hadn't shown up at the office. Kate couldn't get ahold of him, so I decided to make a quick appearance on his behalf just in case.

A man stepped in front of me.

"Excuse me," he said, "you look like a nice lady, can you hold Dolly? I'm pleading guilty." He held up a pillowcase with a reptilian shape inside.

"Ah—"

"—You're not allowed snakes in court. Dolly won't hurt you. You could touch her. She feels like a wallet."

"Ah—" *why not.* "Fine." I held the bunched end of the pillowcase, my arm drooped. Dolly was not a light-weight. "What type of snake?"

"Python." The man dashed into the courtroom. I looked at the pillowcase. Dolly shifted and I shuffled over to the side when I saw my client, Simon. "Simon."

"Jade." He stepped over. "I've been looking for you. What do you have there?"

We stepped aside, letting others enter. "Dolly, the python. Long story. What are you doing here? Your trial date is next week."

"A python? Can I see?"

"No." Solicitor-client privilege maybe? "What are you doing here?"

"About that." He glanced around, shoving his hands into his pockets. "I want to plead guilty."

"When did you decide this?" The pillowcase writhed.

"Well. I, I got some legal advice that I can get off with a conditional sentence, I think that's what she said. Get into this reading program thing and do some community work."

"Who gave you this legal advice? I'm your lawyer, Simon."

"It's okay, Jade."

"No, it's not." The pillowcase writhed the other way. *Hang tight, Dolly. Where was her owner?*

"It was a prosecutor. It's cool."

"Let's move over here, away from the door." We stepped to the far corner so others could enter the courtroom. "Who have you been talking to?"

"Ms. Vale."

I wanted to scream *why are you talking to Crown*? I took a deep breath. "You talked to Valentina Vale?"

"Yeah."

"When?"

"This morning. I was hitchhiking into town and she pulled over and gave me a lift. She has this wicked blue Porsche. I couldn't believe my luck. A dude like me being picked up by a hot chick in a Porsche."

My left eye twitched. "And what did you say to Ms. Vale?"

"We just got talkin' and stuff."

"And stuff?" What every lawyer loved to hear. "What did she say? What did you say?"

"She said she was a lawyer. I told her how I knew you and you were my lawyer. You were defending me on this bogus dine and dash charge. She was really nice, and said something about full disclosure, she was a prosecutor and we shouldn't be talking about this, but she was doing disclosure court today, and if I wanted to plead guilty, she could ask the judge for a conditional sentence. I could do stuff like mentoring in a reading program and some community service work stuff. Sounded pretty cool to me."

Valentina had behaved a shade shy of unethical. It is very improper for any Crown to speak to a person with a lawyer. I could report her to the Law Society. "Dammit, Simon, I wish you hadn't talked to her about your case—"

"—Jade, it's okay. I'm cool with pleading guilty."

I looked him eye-to-eye. "You are absolutely certain you want to plead guilty today?"

"Yeah."

"Fine." I pulled open the courtroom door. Valentina clicked toward me in red heels that matched her red suit.

"Jade the doorman, you're so talented. Did your assistant tell you about the plea deal?" She nodded at Simon.

"No. I've just learned."

"I've already spoken to the clerk and Simon's file has been added to the list." She looked at the pillowcase, smirked, and walked into the courtroom. Throttle her with this pillowcase but then I'd feel sorry for Dolly the snake.

Simon stepped in after Valentina. He turned, walking backwards into the courtroom, and smiled. "All good."

I looked from Simon to an outdated picture of Queen Elizabeth hanging behind the bench. A little help here, please, Your Majesty. Snake man approached and retrieved Dolly.

Three of my clients pled guilty and Her Honour issued light sentences. Norman did not show up. I appeared on his behalf and his client was happy with only receiving a fine. Simon's case was the last to be called and he entered a guilty plea and was ordered to pay retribution to the diner as well as 30 hours' community service work.

Five minutes after four, I left the courthouse, pissed off. What the hell was Valentina doing? I dropped my files off at the office and met Sage at my place. We rode our bikes to Hatley Castle, home to Royal Roads University, as well as being the location for a number of sci-fi TV series and movies. We found parking by the Japanese Gardens.

"And why are we here again?" Sage asked, getting off her bike, looking from the beautiful castle to the gardens.

"Mr. Younghusband knows a lot more than he's letting on. Why did Oscar Cooper give him those audio files?"

"Have you listened to them?"

"Yes," I snapped.

Sage looked at me. "You okay?"

I turned onto a mulch path, looking up from the tourist map of the grounds. "Just ... ticked off with a client. This way."

"Nothing you can talk about, right?"

"I don't like being blindsided." I stopped, looking at the entrance to the lush green gardens. We needed to go the opposite way.

"By your client?"

"Yes. It's okay. Legal Aid paid up and the client got his get out jail free card—" my shoes crunched on the stone path "—Mr. Younghusband, according to my Google search, besides being a Clerk Assistant and author, he instructs a course titled *Plotting the Thriller using Plain Language*. We just need to find his department."

"People pay to listen to him talk about plain language? I'd rather find Hugh Jackman and the School for Gifted Children," Sage said, walking beside me. "This place is gorgeous."

"We missed the path. We need to go back a little. How was the dentist?"

"I have uneventful teeth."

I stopped and looked at her.

"That's a good thing."

I nodded and followed a path to a separate building.

Sage trailed after me.

We walked under a stone archway to a set of glass doors. I pulled open one door, holding it for Sage and we stepped in. Compared to the grandeur of the estate, this was the blandest office I had ever seen: cream walls with no pictures, battleship linoleum, wooden desk, and a brown armchair with one saggy cushion.

"Can I help you?"

We turned.

A blonde assistant with curly hair stood out in the drab surroundings. While she typed on her keyboard, a second monitor aired a National Geographic documentary about penguins and gender identity.

"Hi, my name is Jade Thyme. I had a visit from Mr. Younghusband a week ago and—"

The assistant briefly glanced at Sage then at me.

"—he left me items I want to talk to him about. I've tried calling to make an appointment but all I get is voice mail."

The assistant again slid Sage a glance before looking at me. "How about you two have a seat. He may have a few moments before his next lecture."

"Thank you," I said.

"Thank you," Sage repeated.

The assistant stood. She leaned toward Sage. "And your name?"

"Sage Thyme. We're sisters."

"Nice." She smiled.

"I like your penguins," Sage said, pointing at the two stuffed penguins positioned by her telephone.

She pointed at one. "That's Silo and—" she pointed at the other "—that's Roy. They're chinstrap penguins. Silo is my spirit animal."

I looked at my watch.

"Why your spirit animal?"

Seriously, Sage?

"Because Silo has been observed pair-bonding with Roy in the Central Park Zoo. Two male penguins flipper-flapping, ignoring the females."

I frowned. Mr. Younghusband's assistant's spirit animal was a gay male chinstrap penguin? What was I missing?

"Even in the animal kingdom," she said in a sweet voice, "it's okay to be gay and in love."

Sage smiled.

"Mr. Younghusband, right." Her sea-foam suit matched her Kate Spade patent heels that clicked on the linoleum. She knocked on a closed door. A muffled voice called out. She motioned to us one moment and slipped into the office.

I looked at Sage. "You're hitting on the assistant with poodle hair."

"I'm not hitting on anyone." She looked at me all innocent. "I asked about her penguins."

The assistant returned, eyebrows furrowed. She stood in front of Sage. "I'm so sorry," she said, pressing the palms of her hands together. "Mr. Younghusband is extremely busy and asked—"

The office door opened and Mr. Younghusband marched out, gripping a briefcase, a textbook and a bottle of Pepto-Bismal.

"Mr. Younghusband?" I called out.

"Please make an appointment with Gillian, Ms. Thyme."

"Mr. Young—"

He was out the door.

I wasn't going to be brushed off that easy. I ran after him. "Mr. Younghusband, author of five thriller novels and *Plotting the Thriller Using Plain Language*."

He stopped and looked to his left. "You read *Plotting the Thriller*?" He slugged back a mouthful of Pepto.

I hesitated. "Well, actually, no."

He wiped his mouth with the back of his wrist and continued walking, grappling with the textbook and a soft leather briefcase.

"I need to ask you a few questions. Do you need a hand—"

"—I'm fine, thank you."

"Mr. Younghusband," Sage shouted.

"Please set up an appointment with Gillian."

"Can I just run him over with my bike?" Sage grumbled.

"I heard that. I fulfilled my duties, Ms. Thyme," he turned and looked at me, a sullen expression on his face, and for a second I thought I recognized something about this guy. Remove the black-rimmed glasses, take him out of the suit and put him ... nah, it was nothing, chalk it up to creeping him on my office computer.

"I told you." He looked over at the trees then back at me. "I didn't want to see you again." He walked toward another parking lot. "Have a prosperous and good life."

"I believe that is a polite way of saying, screw off," Sage said.

"Why did you start researching Oscar Cooper?" I called.

He unlocked the driver's door of a small vehicle, I couldn't see what kind. His tall frame disappeared. Sage and I heard a rattle, then a *put put put* and a blue-grey square vehicle lurched as it reversed out of a parking spot with Mr. Younghusband hunched over the steering wheel. The gears ground and the Morris Minor stalled.

"Oh my God, he stalled it," Sage said.

After a couple of attempts the Morris Minor came to life and *put put putted* toward the university exit and onto the road, gears grinding.

"What in God's name is he driving?" Sage asked.

"A Morris Minor." I smiled. There was something about Mr. Younghusband that I found intriguing. Maybe it had to do with him brushing me off, or the fact that he didn't feel less of a man driving that car.

Mr. Younghusband's assistant stepped out of the office. She locked the office door, slung her purse over her shoulder and strutted toward her yellow convertible Volkswagen bug. She slid the key in the lock and looked over at Sage and me. "He doesn't really have a class." She placed her hand on her hip. "If you want him to talk, Adam can be found at the Clover Arms Pub drinking a Strongbow."

"Thank you," I said, but Mr. Younghusband's assistant wasn't looking at me.

She dropped her purse in the convertible and meandered over to Sage, writing something on a piece of paper. "Nice bike," she said, her finger trailing over the handlebars.

"Do you ride?" Sage asked.

Gillian tilted her head. "I've never ridden a motorcycle, or even a bicycle. In fact, I don't know much about them—" she tilted her head again "—just that if it sounds like a sewing machine, it must not be very good."

I rolled my eyes.

Sage laughed.

"If you're ever interested in giving me a ride—" she picked up Sage's hand and slid the paper into it, closing her fingers. "—there's my number. Gillian with a G." She took a few steps backwards, looking Sage up and down, then turned and sauntered back to her VW, her sashaying hips demanding attention in her tight-fitting pencil skirt. Her car rattled as it reversed. Gillian with a G then cruised past, firing Sage a sultry look as she toyed with the middle button on her blouse.

I looked at Sage.

"What?" she said. "I didn't do anything."

"I'm looking for the neon sign flashing 'I'm bi and I'm beautiful'. She was really obvious."

Sage laughed as she flipped her long red hair over her shoulder and pulled on her helmet. "Sometimes—" she motioned to her body "—it's nice feeling appreciated. She dresses nicely."

Sage routinely wore boots, tight jeans, t-shirt and a leather jacket. She had legs that went on forever and she could make a paper bag look hot.

"How did she know?"

"Sometimes you do, and sometimes you don't, and *that* can be awkward."

"Has that happened to you? Hitting on a straight girl?"

"Yep."

"What happened?"

"She just about beat the crap out of me. Now—" Sage tucked the phone number in her wallet "—the Clover Arms?"

Gillian with a G did not let us down. Mr. Younghusband sat at the far end of the bar, watching the hockey game. The Canucks had just scored a tie-breaking goal. The bar erupted.

I walked up to the bartender and asked what Mr. Younghusband was drinking. A Strongbow, like Gillian with a G had said. I ordered one for each of us. Sage took hers and I took mine and his. We walked up to Mr. Younghusband. Sage placed her hand on his shoulder as she sat to his left.

He looked from Sage to me. "No." He stood.

"Really, Mr. Younghusband," Sage said, her hand still on his shoulder. "You're not one of those men who ditches a girl after she buys you a drink." Sage slid the bottle toward him.

He took a moment, I'm guessing to rein in his annoyance.

"It's a Strongbow," I said.

He glanced at me. The glasses were gone and he looked even hotter.

"You're stalking and tormenting me," he said, watching the television.

"Stalking and tormenting?" Sage said. "Oh Mr. Younghusband, you haven't seen torment." She patted him on the back. "My sister bought you a Strongbow. Drink it."

He looked at both of us. "This won't work. It may have worked when—"

"—When what?" I asked.

He sat back as if looking for backup. "No matter how much cider or–"

"—Or what?" I leaned my elbow against the bar and fixed him an innocent stare. I was surprised to see him blush. I tapped my bottle to his. "Cheers. For making it out alive with Bob and Henri. Did you replace that Italian cappuccino machine?" I tipped the bottle and sipped.

"Espresso machine."

A server placed a plate of burger and fries in front of him. "The burger's got bacon and—" she nodded at the plate "—I doubled the cheese just for you, Mr. Y."

"My arteries thank you," he said.

My stomach growled.

Sage tapped her bottle with his. "Cheers, Mr. Younghusband. Here's to starting off on the wrong foot."

He picked up his bottle. "I'm so dead." He gulped then put the bottle down. He looked at me a little longer than usual then shifted his gaze to his food. "What do you want?" He bit into the burger.

Your fries. I pulled my notes from my purse and placed them on the bar. "We're trying to find Kathy Banks."

"Bad idea."

"Why?" Sage asked.

He swallowed and picked up a fry. "She is not to be tampered with." He looked at me again. "Have you been listening to the audio, Ms. Thyme?"

Those dark eyes and dark wavy hair. What was it about this guy? "You can call me Jade. Yes, and I have more questions."

"Figures."

"Mr. Younghusband, our house was torched," Sage said. "Burned to the ground."

He paused and looked at Sage. "Arson?"

"We believe so."

He continued eating.

"After the fire was put out, someone spraypainted–" she brought out her phone and pulled up the photo app "—this spider on the cement wall."

He swallowed and picked up Sage's phone.

"You better not have relish on your fingers."

He frowned. "She's got it wrong."

"Excuse me?" I said, looking at Sage.

He put the phone down and ate another fry. "This is the work of Kathy Banks. Darlene's daughter. The one you two need to stay away from."

"And how do you know this?" I asked.

"Research, Jade."

"I've been doing research on Kathy Banks and have found nothing." I slid my notes to him. "I've looked on all social media sites. Nothing. Everyone has some sort of information on the Net. How can Sage and I stay away from her if we don't know what she looks like?"

He bit into the burger.

Damn, his food looked good.

He watched the game as he chewed.

"And," I continued, "why is she spraypainting spiders? She's taunting us."

He swallowed, grabbed a napkin, and wiped mayonnaise from his mouth. "You're clearly not going to let me enjoy my dinner. Kathy is sending a message."

"And that message is?"

He looked at me again and this time didn't look away. "She's found you."

"And I'm supposed to be scared?"

"Yes." He turned his plate so the mound of fries was closer to me and indicated for me to help myself. "They're not Cheezies."

"Do you have ketchup?"

He looked at me like I was an alien.

"I guess not." I took a fry.

He turned the plate toward Sage. "Don't take the biggest fry."

She did. "Why a spider and why should we be scared?"

"On Genie's birthday Oscar bought her a spider necklace encrusted with diamonds and opals worth approximately three thousand dollars. This was in 1968."

"Oscar Cooper gave our mother a three thousand dollar necklace?" I asked.

"Yes. Listen to the files."

"I have been."

"And you've never seen the necklace?" Mr. Younghusband asked.

"No."

"The fire," Sage said quietly. "I got all the pictures out. There might have been a few boxes in the garage and basement, but I can't remember—" Sage flung her hand up in defeat "—it would be a miracle if we found the necklace now."

"Have you seen the necklace?" I asked Adam.

"Oscar drew me a picture of it. Few people knew of the necklace. Oscar, Darlene and—" he hesitated "—his number one, Archie." He swigged his Strongbow.

"Then what Oscar said is true. Darlene spread her hate of Mom to her daughter Kathy, and Kathy is striking back. But why? Sage and I have done nothing to her."

He wiped his fingers on a sanitizer wipe then stood. "Good night. Thank you for the cider" He walked out of the bar.

I took a drink of mine, feeling more stressed. "That was a total waste of time."

"Not necessarily," Sage said.

"Why do you say that?"

"Mr. Y knew mom's name. He knows much more than he's letting on."

"He wasn't exactly forthcoming. It's not like I can subpoena him."

Sage stole another fry. "You'll be hearing from him again."

"Why do you say that?"

"He took your notes."

I looked at the bar. My notes were gone.

10 SPIDER – 1968

"I ain't gonna die."

GENIE SAT ON A BLANKET IN OSCAR'S GARDEN, HER sketchpad propped on her knee, attempting to colour the pond with her pastels.

It wasn't working. She couldn't focus. If Oscar hadn't said they'd have a picnic, she would have packed up her sketchbook and pastels and hitchhiked back to her apartment.

She needed to smoke weed and meditate. She was too anxious. Dr. Martin Luther King Jr. had been assassinated in April. Andy Warhol had been shot in June, and three days later U.S. Attorney General Bobby Kennedy had been assassinated. Genie pressed her hands to the sides of her head. The turmoil. The violence. The poisoning of the environment. The Man's greed was destroying the world. Love. Not hate. Her generation could change the world. But every person trying to make a change was getting beaten or killed. The Chicago 7 weren't trying to incite a riot. They were leading a protest against the war. *The police* pushed the protesters into the glass window of the hotel. *The police* beat them. And then the papers had mentioned that Mexican businessman Diego Lomas was in town. Businessman. Big fat lie. He was a drug dealer and a criminal who terrorized families and used his brother's government influence to suppress witnesses.

It was too much. It was all too much. She couldn't wait for Oscar. She packed up her art supplies. She didn't care if Edith was home. She and Edith had a screaming fight the night before. She was tired of Edith trying to hook her up with Charles Thyme. Oscar never grew up with the same privilege as Charles. Oscar's father had taken off when Oscar was only a month old. It had always been him and his mom. She worked double-shifts, promising Oscar that they would never go hungry. When Oscar became a teenager, he washed cars, mowed lawns, did whatever work possible to make life easier for them. When he got involved in pharmaceutical sales, their life turned around. Unlike Charles, Oscar didn't have a daddy to pay for his education.

"This is where you're hiding."

Genie turned.

Oscar walked toward her. Wearing red striped pants, he unbuttoned his shirt with his right hand as he held a picnic basket in his left.

"How's my birthday girl?"

Genie shrugged her shoulders. "How was your business meeting?"

"Not as cool as hanging with you." He placed his hand on her cheek and kissed her. "Why so sad? It's your birthday. You've been drawing." He nodded to the art pad on her lap.

Genie turned her sketch toward him.

"It looks fabulous."

"My colours aren't blending. My pond looks contaminated by farming chemicals. The flowers droop, probably choked by air pollution and the frogs are dead. My picture might as well be in *Silent Spring*." She placed the art pad on the blanket near her transistor radio.

"Genie, that's the beauty. This is your piece to bring awareness."

She hadn't thought about that.

"It's up to our generation to change the world."

"Fine. Then I won't throw it in the trash."

"You made a daisy chain."

"It's wilting."

He rubbed her shoulders. "Something more is wrong than a wilting daisy chain."

She was silent for a moment, trying to contain her emotion. She didn't want to cry like a weeping teenager. "My father and I had an argument about the Chicago 7. He said the boys deserved every beating. You don't stand up to authority. The police pushed those boys through the glass window and then beat them. The police started the violence. Then I read that Diego Lomas is in town. That scumbag. I hate him—"

"—Genie—"

"—I hate that man, Oscar. I hate seeing him on my TV. I hate hearing him on the radio making excuses for the Tlatelolco Massacre. His smile makes my skin crawl and I want to throw up at the sight of him. I hope he chokes on a margarita and *dies*."

Oscar sat next to her and brushed her hair back.

"Sometimes, Oscar, I get so *angry*. We have to stand up to authority especially when it's in bed with drug dealers like Diego Lomas."

He held her face in his hands. "Change is in the air, Genie. It's coming and your father's scared."

She wasn't convinced.

"I will never let anyone hurt you, or disrespect you. Men like Diego Lomas, he'll get what's coming." He kissed her lips. "Anything else bothering you?"

"Some men came looking for you."

His expression hardened. "Did they say what they wanted?"

"No. They had guns, Oscar. You're okay, right? You're not in trouble. If anything should happen to you-"

"—Genie—"

"—I don't know—"

"—Genie. I'm safe. Archie is always watching my back. Hey, I ain't gonna die. Now, come on. It's your birthday. I've brought you something." He opened the wicker basket and pulled out plates and napkins. He took out a cake box. "Check it out."

Genie opened the lid. She looked at him. "It's a birthday cake. Thank you." She flung her arms around his neck.

Oscar laughed. "Everything's going to be all right, Genie. Your small shoulders can't carry the world's conscience."

She sniffed.

"I have one more thing." He held out a little box.

Genie took it and tugged on the lid. She saw a layer of cotton. She dropped the lid and teased the cotton from the box. She gasped. "Oscar."

"You like it?"

"It's a spider. It's beautiful."

"Let's see it on."

She daintily picked the necklace out of the box. Her fingers trembled. She had never worn jewellery like this.

"The body of the spider is a black opal, the legs are fourteen carat gold, and the diamond is a half carat."

Genie leaned back. "Oscar, I can't wear this."

"You told me you had a spider collection. You don't like it?"

"It's beautiful." Edith could not see this necklace.

"It's your birthday, Genie."

She brushed her thumb over the opal, mesmerized by how the diamonds reflected sunlight. "Help me put it on." Genie handed over the necklace and pulled her hair up.

Oscar placed the necklace around her neck, brushing his hand over her shoulders.

Genie inched around. "How does it look?" She touched the necklace. "I need to be wearing something fancier than a white halter-top and cutoffs."

Oscar eyed the necklace. "It's gorgeous."

She smiled. She cupped his face in her hands and kissed him. She sat back.

Oscar ran his hand through her hair, then with one finger, outlined her face, then her eyebrows.

"What are you doing?"

"Drawing you."

She laughed.

His finger outlined the curve of her lips, then he trailed his finger along her neck. "I'm not as good as you. Should I stop?"

"No."

He trailed his finger over her collarbone then along the chain of the necklace, down between her breasts. He looked at her. "Close your eyes."

She did and felt his lips on hers.

"I . . . want you, Genie."

She wrapped her arms and legs around him as he leaned her back against the blanket.

11 TYPE "O"

He tugged on the zipper of his pants, glancing over his shoulder.

THE KNOCKING ON MY CONDO DOOR STARTLED ME. I removed my glasses, placing them on the charge approval I was doing for Crown.

Ever since the pandemic I had become accustomed to working a few days from home, and still did so. My stainless steel kitchen island made the perfect desk to spread out my work and the coffee pot was at an arm's distance.

I pushed back my stool and stepped over to the door and pulled it open. Mr. Younghusband leaned against the doorframe. He flipped a folded newspaper into my line of vision.

"You're looking for a rental," I said, reading the ad circled in pencil.

He looked at the paper, flipped the page and showed me a photo of a young man in the obituary section.

"Why do I care about the obits? You took my notes."

"Care to join me at the cemetery?"

"You told me you never wanted to see me again and now you're inviting me to the cemetery." I crossed my arms. "Did you make an appointment for this field trip?"

He smiled and waved the newspaper article. "Check out Oscar's new resting place and maybe Victor Banks's, who supposedly died of a drug overdose, according to this poorly written obituary."

"Who's Victor?"

"Kathy Banks's deceased brother. Kathy being the one you are to stay away from."

"The spider graffiti artist."

"That's right," he said.

"And if we find Victor, are we digging up the body?"

"Yes."

My eyes must have popped because he smiled.

"I want to see the gravestone," he said, rubbing his jaw. "I don't believe this ragtag paper."

"A bit macabre for ten o'clock on a Wednesday morning, Mr. Younghusband. And you think I would possibly want to go with you, given how rude you've been?"

"Rude! Me, rude! Your sister would have waterboarded me with my Strongbow if I didn't cooperate."

"You're being a little melodramatic, Mr. Younghusband."

He looked over the Gorge then at me. "Adam. You can call me Adam. I'm here to make … amends."

"By asking me to be your plus one at the cemetery."

He looked at his feet. "Sage could join us. We could grab some grub."

Was he asking me on a breakfast date without asking me on a breakfast date? I held the door open. "I'll text her. See if she's interested." I texted Sage as I walked back inside. Adam followed. I closed my laptop and tidied my files. "We can get her on our way. By the way, how did you find me?"

"You flashed me your driver's licence."

"That's right, after your friends showed me their sidearms." I grabbed my purse, checked the calendar on my phone. Kate hadn't scheduled any appointments. I texted Kate telling her I'd be out a few hours and again texted Sage. *You awake?*

I looked at Adam, who was looking at me, his hands in his pockets. "We'll swing past where she's staying. She's house-sitting

Coco Gin's place."

"That's the name of an actual person?"

"Yes. Sage knew her in school."

"Of course she did."

I locked up and we walked over to the Morris Minor and sat in. It had been restored with grey upholstery and repainted its original blue.

"This is immaculate. What type of Morris Minor?"

Adam shifted from first into second as the car climbed the hill. "Come on," he said, coaxing it. "A 2CV. I inherited it from my mother."

"Oh."

"She passed a long time ago."

"Still sorry to hear."

"She preferred a two-six of gin and gambling her meagre earnings in Vegas. I was raised by my dad."

"What's top speed?"

"Haven't the foggiest, but she can reach eighty-four kilometres an hour, downhill, with the wind."

I laughed.

He glanced at me and smiled.

"Make a left and then pull into that curved driveway. She's in a ground floor condo."

The Morris Minor rat-a-tatted to a stop.

Adam leaned over the steering wheel and looked at the condos. "These are nice. Any available for rent?"

"I have no idea. Sage is just house-sitting for Coco. She'll stay here a few days, then stay a few days at her own place. Be right back." I stepped out of the car and walked along the cement path, passing ferns, enjoying the trickle of water from the water feature. I knocked on the front door. Waited. Come on, Sage. You never sleep in. I knocked again. The door opened. Dressed in a robe, her red hair a tangled mane, Sage leaned against the doorframe, rubbing her temples.

"Late night?" I asked.

"Something like that." She rubbed her eyes. "What's up?"

"You need to check your phone. Adam and I are going for breakfast then to the cemetery. Want to join us?"

She straightened, her eyes wide. "Younghusband. Younghusband is here?" She looked around me. "Where?"

"Adam is in the car."

Her eyes grew wider. "Out front?"

"Yes. He's in the car, waiting. Why are you acting so weird?"

"He can't be here," Sage said, looking over my shoulder.

"Why shouldn't—" the bathroom door opened and a naked Gillian with a G slunk into Sage's bedroom.

"*Oh.*"

"Don't you judge me."

"Oh."

Sage waved me away. "Shoo."

"Shoo? You're telling me to shoo?"

"I'll catch up with you later."

I stepped back. "You couldn't wait until the third date."

She slammed the door.

I turned, dazed, then walked to the car and sat in.

Adam texted a message. "Is Sage joining us?"

"Um … She just got up. She'll join us later."

Adam tucked his phone into his coat pocket. "Right." He turned the key and the car rattled to life.

I looked at him. "Everything okay with you?"

"Gillian's bedridden. She ate something that's not agreeing with her. It's her birthday today. I'm guessing she was out partying last night."

I bit my lip and looked out the passenger window. "All right then. Breakfast and then the cemetery."

We stopped at La Roux Patisserie which served decadent desserts like Paris-Brest and strawberry and lychee cake. Adam placed our order and I found a table. I grabbed the discarded newspapers left behind when the headline of one caught my attention: *Third Victim in Selfie Sex Offender Case*. I read about another woman being cornered behind a convenience store and sexually assaulted. The suspect, a man in his mid-30s, blonde hair, and heavyset, took selfies of himself with his victims. *Sicko.* I tossed the paper onto the next table.

Adam placed a tray with our mugs and croissants on our table and sat, oblivious to the glances from female patrons.

"So, Adam, how does a Clerk Assistant who's served the Senate of Canada, now mystery author, get tangled up up with Oscar Cooper?"

He looked surprised.

"I did my research," I said, before biting into a cheese croissant and savouring its cheesey goodness.

He cleared his throat. "Oscar—" he rubbed his mug with his thumb "—Oscar enjoyed reading my novels while convalescing in prison."

"Not quite the fanbase you envisioned."

He picked up his coffee, sipped, then placed the mug on its saucer. He looked me in the eye. "You're not what I envisioned."

I blushed.

He looked at the display case of treats. "Writers dream of their novels being a *New York Times* Best Seller, not being passed among inmates."

"Consider it a compliment. So Oscar's sprung from jail, how did he get ahold of you?"

He brought his cup to his lips. "You met Bob and Henri."

"He sent them?"

"I'm getting out of my car after meeting my agent, and they pull into my driveway. They forced me into my flat, push me onto a chair and tell me if I cooperate, I'll walk away with a nice chunk of money and two good knees. If I don't cooperate, Henri will convince me otherwise."

"Cooperate?"

"Oscar wanted to meet me."

"Oh. How are Bob and Henri related to Oscar?"

"They're the children of two of Oscar's henchmen. Oscar didn't have long to live. He sent Bob and Henri to pay me a visit and become my new roommates."

"Good Lord."

"One toilet—" Adam tapped a stirstick on the table "—three grown men. One small flat."

"So why did Oscar want to see you? Why the bodyguards?"

"Oscar was concerned about my safety. He still had enemies."

"Your safety? Are you related to him? Why was he protecting you?"

Adam again looked at the display case, his mind elsewhere.

I supposed if Oscar still had enemies, anyone associated with him could be in danger.

"Adam."

He sat forward. "He wanted my assistance writing his memoir. Be his ghost writer, hence the audio files."

"Why didn't he record the audio and save them to the cloud, giving you access? Why did he need you there?"

Adam opened his mouth, paused and smiled. "He didn't trust the cloud. Jade, you don't understand Oscar. He liked an audience. Even at his age, he commanded an audience. And ... I was curious. Once I knew they wouldn't hurt me."

"It was an ego thing for both of you."

Adam shook his head. "Ego for Oscar, not me."

"Oh, come on. Your ego must have swelled knowing legendary drug dealer Oscar Cooper wanted your assistance."

Adam was about to say something then changed his mind. "Oscar took precautions and paid his guards well. I'd be escorted to his house. He would pay for my time, for housing Bob and Henri, and any incidental expenses for the delivery of the thumbdrives and keys to you."

"Why give me the thumbdrives if you're writing his memoir? How do I play into this?"

Adam remained silent, studying my features. "You look like him."

He wasn't listening and had switched topics. "You're not the first to say that."

Adam sat back again. "Really? Others say you look like him?"

"My mother used to say all the time that I looked like my father. I never saw it. Charles had a pointed chin. That's the only thing I can see that's similar. Sage looks more like Mom but I think that's because of the red hair."

Adam sipped his coffee.

"Besides that, why give me the thumbdrives if you're writing his memoir? Why involve me at all?"

"The only person who can answer that is Oscar and he's dead."

I wasn't convinced. There was more Adam wasn't telling me but I'd play along. He was easy on the eyes. "Were you surprised to learn he overdosed?"

Adam stared into his coffee. "Yes."

Why so quiet now, Mr. Younghusband? An upstanding citizen, what's your connection to a drug dealer? I wasn't quite buying the ghost writer story. "So how long have you been in Canada?"

"One year. My fiancée at the time had an internship at UBC."

"Oh."

"She also had a philosophy student."

"*Oh.*"

"I have a flight back to the U.K. in July."

Too bad. We finished our croissants and left the coffee shop, making a quick stop at a florist. We then headed to the cemetery.

Adam parked the Morris Minor next to a black Jeep. He headed toward the front gate and I circled the Jeep. If I didn't know better I would have thought it was—

"—You like Jeeps, Jade?" Adam stood by the entrance.

I walked toward him. "I knew someone who drove a black Jeep. This way. I'd like to visit my mother."

We made our way around plots, keeping our distance from the local deer. "A little further—"

Approximately fifty feet ahead, a man faced a headstone, legs apart. He tugged on the zipper of his pants, glancing over his shoulder. Tell me he wasn't … *urinating.* He was too far away for me to make out his features. All I could tell was that he wore sunglasses.

"Mother is over here." I walked to my right, scooting around Emily Carr's plot.

"Are those flowers for me?" a voice said on my right. I turned and Mom's ghost walked in step beside me.

I stopped. This couldn't be happening. Not again. I wasn't on Vicodin. I was clean. Six months clean.

"It's all right, Jade. Yes. You're really seeing me. You've always seen me. Do you really think *I* would be a drug-induced apparition?"

"Jade, is something wrong?" Adam asked. "You have a rather confused expression on your face."

I pulled my hair back from my face. "I'm ... okay."

Adam smiled and stepped around a headstone.

"Nice to see you. You look different," I said under my breath.

Mother tucked a long strand of red hair behind her ear. "I'm reliving the sixties. I can do that. Pick a decade."

I smiled. "This is Mom's plot." I raised my voice as I knelt and placed a bouquet of pink daisies on the grass.

"They're beautiful. I just wish the man visiting his dead mistress would stop stealing them."

"Really?"

"According to the latest cemetery gossip."

I did a second take, causing me to bump into Adam.

He turned, his hand on my forearm steadying me, and smiled. I could look into those eyes for a very long time. "Sorry," I stepped back.

"Who are you looking for?" Mother asked.

"Victor Banks and Oscar Cooper."

Her ghostly shape dissolved.

"No. Don't you disappear on me."

Adam stepped around graves, reading headstones.

I looked back and Mother reappeared. Her eyes were so sad.

"Oscar's here?" she asked.

"Yes. In fact I have a few questions for you, such as why were you hanging around with him?"

She dissolved a second time.

"*Stop that*," I hissed.

She reappeared on my left. "How did he die?"

"Drug overdose."

She closed her eyes and a tear slipped down her youthful porcelain cheek.

"Are you okay?" The absurdity of my question hit me as soon as I asked it. My mother was dead. A ghost, but still.

"Jade, over here," Adam said, walking toward a headstone.

The man we had seen earlier walked in our direction, taking a drag from his cigarette. Even wearing sunglasses, I felt slammed by the intensity that was Osmond.

"Jade? You all right?" Adam asked.

"Of course, she's fine," Osmond said, his body bumping Adam's arm.

Adam followed. "I wasn't asking—"

Osmond turned. "Listen, asshole—"

Adam moved forward, fist clenched.

"Adam, I'm fine." I stepped between them. "Osmond, what do you want?"

Osmond looked above me. "Sport, give us a moment."

"No," Adam said.

Osmond looked at me. "What are you doing with this prick, Jade?"

Prick? Adam was the prick? I think not. "What does it matter? We're done."

Osmond caressed my arm. "Why are you being like this?"

I pulled my arm away. "Excuse me, we're done."

Osmond clenched my arm and looked at me over his sunglasses.

"Don't touch her," Adam said.

Osmond let go. He stepped back, his breathing ragged. "Jade, you need to let the dead remain dead."

"Or else?" Adam asked.

Osmond looked me straight in the eye. "You've been warned."

He marched toward the parking lot.

I stared after him. What in God's name was going on?

"You know him?" Adam asked.

"Yes. He's a cop. And … an old boyfriend."

"*Him*."

"Leave it. I'm not passing judgement about your ex."

Adam looked in the direction Osmond had come from. He nodded for me to follow.

Pink cherry blossom petals scattered over Oscar's grave and headstone. As peaceful as the image was, I then realized—

"—Jade."

"I see it."

Adam cursed. He looked at the parking lot as Osmond drove away, giving Adam the one-finger salute. "He's an asshole, Jade. Who does something like that?"

I felt sick and sad. We couldn't prove it, but I had no doubt that Osmond had urinated on Oscar Cooper's headstone. "Why does Osmond hate him so much?"

Adam looked at the grave. "You said Osmond is a cop?"

"Yes."

"Oscar was seventy-eight when he died. Osmond would have been a child when Oscar was at the top of his game."

I wondered about Adam's connection. "You're quite forgiving of Oscar Cooper."

"Drug dealer or not, urinating on a man's headstone is unforgiveable."

A pink cherry blossom clung to the 'A' in 'OSCAR.' "What is it with you, Oscar Cooper," I said, "even six feet under, you stir repulsive behaviour in relatively normal individuals?"

"Which audio file are you on?" Adam asked.

"Audio?" Mother asked. "You can hear his voice?"

"I'm on thumbdrive three out of the five you gave me. I do have a full-time job, trials I need to prep for. Plus, it's a little disconcerting having a gangster talk in your ear."

"Disconcerting?" Adam said, shaking his head. "Try having a

hood pulled over your head, being kidnapped, and find yourself in a derelict house, tied to a chair. Oscar Cooper and a woman walk in, a blue tourniquet is tied around your upper arm and the woman shoves a needle into your vein, telling you she's taking a blood sample. Because if you're Type O Negative, you're the lucky bastard who's giving Oscar a kidney."

"And here I thought you were in the O.C. fan club. That would be stressful."

"Stressful? Try bloody terrifying."

"Oscar did have a flare for the dramatic," Mom said.

"And I thought Canadians were polite," he continued.

I bit my lip trying not to smile. "Are you?"

"Am I what?"

"Type O Negative?"

Adam glared. "No."

"You are, dear," Mom said quietly.

"Remind me the purpose of this excursion?" I asked. "We're looking for a grave, right?"

"We're looking for Victor Banks's grave. From Oscar's and my brief conversations," Adam continued, "Oscar wanted reassurance that Darlene Banks was dead. Darlene had two children. She claimed one child was Oscar's, which he adamantly denied." Adam looked to his left. "Darlene and family were buried near a mausoleum which has a statue of a lion—" he looked to his right "—over there."

We walked toward it.

"Is that …" Mother stared at Adam.

"Adam Younghusband. A friend."

"I'm having difficulty locating Victor's death certificate even though the newspaper says he's dead," Adam said.

Mom floated beside me. "A friend?"

"Yes," I whispered.

She stared at Adam.

"You're staring," I whispered.

"Excuse me?" Adam looked at me.

"You can be scary," I nervously laughed. "Not every guy invites a woman to a cemetery."

Adam smiled.

Mother kept staring at him. "What is his name?"

"Adam Younghusband."

Adam stopped and looked at me. "Who are you talking to?"

"No one. I never thought I'd be cruising funeral plots with mystery novelist Adam Younghusband, that's all." I glared at Mother.

Adam continued walking.

"He's a writer?" Mother asked.

I nodded.

Adam stopped a second time, looking at a marker. "That's not right." He continued walking.

"You're not making this easy," I said to Mother, bumping into Adam who had stopped a third time.

"Must you walk into me?"

"Then don't stop."

He held out his hand. "Darlene Banks, 1952 to 2002. Kathy Banks, 1988 to 2015. Strange," Adam said, looking from one plot to the next. "So Kathy died too. Explains why you can't find any information on her."

"So that means Kathy Banks isn't the one who spraypainted the spider on our house."

"Someone spraypainted a spider?" Mother asked.

I nodded.

"Where's Victor's plot?" Adam held up the newspaper article. "It says he's dead. Overdose."

Mom answered. "He's not dead yet."

"What?" I asked.

"Where's his plot?" Adam repeated.

"What did I say, my darling girl?"

"He's not dead yet," I blurted.

Adam looked at me as if I had unlocked the secret to the seven mysteries of the world. "Explains why I can't find a death certificate.

I knew this article—" he held up the folded paper "—was bogus. It's not like you can be haunted by the dead."

Mother sighed.

I looked to my right where she stood.

"What are you looking at?" Adam asked.

"Nothing. Just thinking. Playing a lot of different scenarios in my head. You said Kathy Banks had found me. Well, she couldn't have, because we found her plot. You're looking for her brother, Victor, who's supposed to be dead, but he's not. Maybe it's Victor who torched our home."

"I like this boy," Mother said, circling him.

Adam didn't look convinced. "Near the end, Oscar was heavily medicated. One time he mumbled regrets. Looking after the two girls. I'm sure at that age and in that state some things got confused."

"Why would Oscar care about children unrelated to him?"

Adam looked at Darlene's marker. "The father's not buried with her. Old man Banks."

"He'd be fairly old."

"Something we need to find out." Adam stepped forward.

I was about to say, "Don't step on Mom," but Adam walked right through her. He stopped, then buttoned up his coat and we headed toward the Morris Minor.

12 THE GORGE

"Are you kidding me? I'm not Batman!"

WE MADE TWO MORE STOPS. Adam wanted to finalize a few details about his upcoming book launch that Vale Books was sponsoring. Kate left me a message. Could I stop by the office? It was about Norman.

Adam dropped me off and we agreed to meet in front of Vale Books. I stepped through the front glass door by our suite 2 banner and walked down the hall. Schumann's Opus 102 played from the speakers. I stood in the doorway of Kate's office. No Kate.

I heard the photocopier cranking out copies, and walked toward it, smelling toner. Kate came around the corner.

"There you are," she said, a folded newspaper under her arm.

"What's up?"

She nodded to her office.

We stepped in and she closed the door behind me. This couldn't be good.

She sighed. "I'm worried about Norman."

"I am too. Have you learned anything new?"

"The student told me she saw Norman in the lunchroom. He

mumbled something about promises and time of reckoning and dashed out of here."

I rubbed my forehead. "This isn't good."

"I found this in Norman's office." Kate whipped the folded paper out from under her arm and held it up.

It was the same obituary Osmond had been reading, except the word RECKONING was written in red pencil and Oscar Cooper's photo was circled. "What the hell is so damning about Oscar Cooper dying?"

"I know," Kate said.

"Let's not panic." I tried to convince myself. "I know Norman's had some issues. If we don't get any word from him by the end of the day, I'm calling Vic PD."

"You think that's a good idea? He gets skittish around them."

"We gotta find him, Kate. Whom else do we call? If you can make a list of his file priorities, I'll be back to review them. I already appeared for one of his clients. Right now, I'm meeting Adam Younghusband."

"Ooh. The swimming author."

I headed out the door, almost colliding with an older woman in scrubs. I cut across Fisgard and ducked through Fan Tan Alley, passing shops on either side. I came out on Pandora, swung a right onto Government and walked to Vale Books, that was housed in a neo-classical building and was *the* bookstore to visit whenever tourists came to the city.

Why did Norman take off? Because he witnessed a possessed typewriter?

It had to do with Oscar Cooper's death. I glanced upon a red newspaper box and remembered the newspaper articles on Charles's desk. One article about Oscar had noted Norman as his defence counsel.

"Oh, God."

"You all right?" Adam asked, standing beside me, the breeze making waves with his hair.

"Ah, yes, I'm fine. I talk to myself, you should know that by now.

Ready?"

He smiled and we made our way past a tea shop and hung a left. Adam's gaze was focused on something ahead. "Do you know the two men who look like Dolph Lundgren clones leaning against my car?"

I spotted Adam's Morris Minor and a man leaning against it. "No."

"We're being followed. Time for a different route."

"How do you know?"

"I saw another Dolph clone in the store reflection."

"I'm warning Sage." I called her, relieved when she answered.

"Where are you?" she asked.

"On Government Street. We're being followed. Stay where you are."

"Can you get across the bridge?" she asked. "I can meet you at the dock of the Delta Ocean Pointe Inn."

"Got it."

"Don't hang up. Put your phone on speaker and keep it in your pocket. I'm heading out now."

I slipped the phone in my pocket.

Adam grabbed my hand and we made a left through Bastion Square where artisans had set up booths. A busker stood playing the theme music to the Batman cartoon on his trumpet.

Another man smiled, holding out a moisturizer packet. "Ma'am, free sample."

I'm that wrinkled? "No, thank you."

A clairvoyant with long white hair wearing a purple muumuu with a white sundial print held her hands out as if welcoming me. "Unburden your soul, dear child."

"Not today, thank you." I'm sure a big black spot stained my soul. No one bothered Adam.

We squeezed, single file, between tourists, not saying a word. Adam abruptly stopped as a mother with a stroller cut in front of us. I careened into him.

The child looked at me and screamed. I have that effect on

children.

"This way," he said.

We darted to the right of mom and screaming child, between kiosks, stepping over power cords, maneuvering around storage containers as we made our way to another courtyard. Cobblestones. Space.

Adam detoured, pulling me with him as a garbage truck beeped and reversed.

I looked behind, not wanting to run and draw attention. We saw no one. My heart pounded. I realized Adam and I still held hands. I had no intention of letting go.

Adam looked forward but his eyes scanned the courtyard and alley from side to side.

"I think we're good," I said.

Adam glanced at me. "No, we're not."

"Jade!" Sage's voice rang out from my pocket.

I grabbed my cell, glancing right to left, eying the outdoor murals in the alley. "Heading to the bridge. Meet you on the other side." I slipped my phone back into my pocket.

We were back on Pandora Avenue. The two-lane traffic had a red light. We dashed across the road to a row of parked bicycles. We waited as cyclists cruised down the bicycle lanes. A teenage boy lagged behind. Wearing faded jeans and a grey hoodie, he rode a bike way too small, and dragged his shoes on the road to control his speed. He saw us, turned the front wheel so he stopped. With finger and thumb he pretended to cock a gun and said, "Bang."

Jerk.

He laughed as Adam and I darted across the bike lanes. More cyclists cursed and brakes squealed. We ran down Pandora toward the bridge. My shoes pounded as fast as my pulse as Adam pulled me behind him, snaking around and between couples, who gasped or swore.

We halted at the crosswalk, waiting for the two lanes of traffic to stop so we could cross. Adam and I looked behind. The two men came down the street.

The light changed. We ran across when I heard the warning bells and the horn.

The bridge was going up.

"*Fuck!*"

The first time I heard Adam curse. It rattled me.

The red and white bar came down, preventing traffic and pedestrians from crossing. The cry of seagulls and the idle of waiting cars. No one was going anywhere.

Two more horns.

Adam and I stopped running on the pedestrian walkway.

"How long is this going to take?" he asked.

"The bridge has been under repair, because it could take ten minutes for it to rise and lower. It also depends on the barge."

Adam looked over his shoulder.

Four more guys joined the clones, cornering us.

The bridge steadily rose and I saw the middle yellow line and dotted white lines of the road at a 45 degree angle. We looked either way and on my right I saw a tug pulling a barge with a crane. This was going to take longer than ten minutes.

"Jade." Adam placed both his hands on my shoulders and looked me in the eye. "You have to trust me."

This couldn't be good.

"They're coming."

"I know."

"You know how to swim?"

"*What?*"

"We've got to jump. Quickly. We swing over the railing and land on the bridge's old cement structure below. It's maybe a six-foot drop. We run along the cement, hang a right to the connecting cement strip and jump into the water."

"*Are you kidding me? I'm not Batman!*" And I definitely did not have medals around my neck for swimming.

Adam nodded to our left. "They're surrounding us, whoever the hell *they* are."

The clones were getting closer.

"I would never risk your life, Jade. We can do this. It's our only escape, but we have to do it now before that tug and barge get any closer. We jump toward the middle, not close to the bridge near the rocks."

I looked at Adam.

"Now, Jade. Over the railing."

Jesus Christ. I placed my foot on one of the metal beams. Adam did the same. He climbed over the railing like a monkey.

"Hey, stop. What are you doing?" Pedestrians called out.

"Lady, are you nuts?"

Yes.

Adam dropped and landed on all fours, reminding me of a panther. He looked at me.

I dropped with the grace of a sloth.

He grabbed my hand and we ran side by side on the cement strip. We turned at a right angle and single-file walked along the narrow stretch. My legs trembled. *Don't look at the water. Focus on your feet.* "Adam, there's a flock of seagulls on the next strip."

"They'll fly away."

The next strip of cement came up to my waist. "I can't jump—"

He kneeled, put his hands together and made a step. "Step up."

The barge blasted its horn. I nearly crapped my pants. I put my foot in his hands and he propelled me up onto the cement. The seagulls squawked and flapped, rising in the air, stirring up the smell of bird poop.

Adam propelled himself up and over like a high jumper.

I heard sirens. Someone had called the cops.

"We'll do this together," he shouted, "the water's going to be cold. Do *not* open your mouth." He gripped my hand. "Ready?"

I nodded. Don't cry.

We ran and ... leapt.

Arms flailing, wind pulling my hair from my face, I torpedoed feet first into the Gorge.

Cold.

Murky.

Quiet.
Keep mouth shut.
I kicked and pulled at the water, my arms heavy from my wet clothes. *Pull.* My lungs burned. I'm not drowning in sewage and gasoline.

I broke the surface, gasping, arms beating the water, trying to stay afloat. Hair in my eyes, I couldn't see. I swiped at my wet hair and slipped back under.

Kelp floated above.

Hold breath. Pull.

I kicked and pulled. I broke the surface again and gasped.

Air. Air.

I swiped my bangs again and leaned forward, trying to tread water.

The water crept past my chest to my collarbone. I stretched my neck back.

Under. Air bubbles. Seaweed. *Pull.* I kept sinking closer to the pylons: my limbs heavy and tired, lungs burning, the surface further from my reach.

I ... was drowning.

An arm wrapped under my armpits. Legs kicked under me and I shot to the surface.

I gasped, trying to kick.

Sirens. Shouts.

"I've got you," Adam shouted. His body swam under me, legs kicking. I heard a motor. I couldn't see what was going on. Overcast sky and a line of people on the bridge, pointing.

Adam grabbed something because he stopped swimming and then I caught a glimpse of the yellow and black checkered paint of the water taxi.

"Jade."

Sage.

"Grab the edge," Adam said.

I did and tried to pull myself onto the deck but my arms were rubber. I slipped. Sage grabbed my jacket and hauled me in. I landed on the grey floor, looking at the orange lifejackets tucked under the wooden seats. Thank God.

"You okay?" she asked, her hand on my arm.

Adam toppled onto the floor.

I pushed my hair off my face. "Yes," I sputtered.

Sage looked at the captain. "Go."

The boat's engine kicked in, sounding like bees on steroids. The water taxi cut through the water, passing boats. The captain spoke on a walkie-talkie about swimmers rescued.

Adam sat upright, brushing hair from his face, catching his breath. "You okay?"

"Yes," I said, teeth chattering.

He wrapped his arm around my shoulders and gave me a squeeze. He might as well have been squeezing a sponge.

"Here." Sage removed her coat. "Put this on. Give me your wet one." She pulled a blanket out from under a seat and passed it to Adam.

"Where are we going?" I asked, peeling my wet coat off.

"We can't go to any public dock. The captain—" she nodded at him "—is a friend. He's taking us to the private dock, behind his house. My truck is waiting. We're going to the condo I'm house-sitting. Those guys following you, trust me, there are more of them. They're looking for you, Jade."

I looked through the doorway of the water taxi, gliding through the greenish-blue water.

Adam looked at me, his dark hair wet slicks on his forehead. He picked seaweed from my hair. "I'm sorry."

He had saved me from drowning. "Thank you. M–m–maybe we stick to swimming pools."

He smiled.

I pulled Sage's coat tighter around my body.

"Was jumping into the Gorge your brilliant idea?" she asked Adam.

"We were cornered," he answered.

The water taxi bobbed and Adam and I braced ourselves.

Sage stepped up to the captain and spoke with him.

I rested my head against the cabin wall. I liked staying low, sitting on the floor, looking up at the under side of the bridge as we passed under it. The tug boat and barge were nowhere in sight.

Adam sat back beside me, our shoulders touching.

We passed a Zodiac and two green kayaks.

Sage looked back at us, smiled, then continued talking to the captain.

I dabbed water from my forehead so it wouldn't drip into my eyes. I smelled seaweed. "I need another cellphone."

Adam looked down. He placed his hand on the floor next to mine.

Not looking at each other, our fingers intertwined and we didn't let go.

13 HEARING PANEL

"Sleeping with Gillian, or baking?"

IN LESS THAN FIFTEEN MINUTES WE DISEMBARKED FROM the water taxi. I ducked into my place and grabbed Charles's laptop and dry clothes. In an old truck, Sage drove us back to Coco's condo. Gillian must have left. The building was named Balance, what I needed more of.

I showered and slipped into clean jeans and a sweater. Sage gave Adam a pair of jeans and a t-shirt, not looking him in the eye. She threw our wet clothes into the wash.

A hot chocolate in my hands, I stood at the floor-to-ceiling window in the living room and gazed at the tiled patio and man-made pond surrounded by salal and papyrus. On the far side was a wood walkway that led to an organic bakery and coffee shop. In the pond, beautiful lotus and water lettuce floated on the surface. A blue heron perched in the far corner. Balance.

Nobody would guess that a biker lived here. I heard a rustling and spotted a small rabbit in a cage. "Who are you?"

"That's Walter," Sage said, placing a large mousse cake on the island. "He's a dwarf Himalayan."

Coco had a pet bunny. Walter, the dwarf Himalayan had quite

the pad. Beside his cage, he had a three-storey cardboard home, painted black on the outside with the AC/DC logo. The rabbit looked at me, straw across his furry cheeks, nose wiggling.

I turned to Sage. "What are you doing?"

"Pouring mirror glaze on this cake. It's for Gillian's birthday party."

"Now?"

"I have personal training sessions in the afternoon. It has to be now." She glanced over her shoulder, "Does he *know*?"

"That you slept with his assistant?"

"*Shhh.*"

"No. I said nothing."

The shower stopped.

Sage looked in the direction of the bathroom. "I'm stressed. This ... this ... is a coping mechanism. My shrink's advice."

"Sleeping with Gillian, or baking?"

Sage glared and dropped the wooden spoon on the counter.

The bathroom door opened.

"Act normal," she whispered.

Good Lord. I had been chased by Dolph Lundgren clones and jumped into the Gorge, and she wanted me to act normal.

Adam stepped into the kitchen, clean and wearing the clothes from Sage. Wet dark hair, he looked, well, I stared a little too long. "Have a seat," I said, indicating a stool.

Sage looked at me from under her brows.

"Sage made you a hot chocolate."

"Oh." Adam sat. "Thank you."

"Ah-huh." She poured a thick white liquid into three cups.

"What are you making?"

"A mirror glaze," she said, not looking at him.

"It's for a friend's birthday," I said.

She glared.

"Lucky friend," Adam said.

"I'm sure she's been getting lucky," I said under my breath.

Sage fired me daggers.

Lizzy sat next to Adam, resting her head on his thigh.

"So what the hell were you two doing to get so much attention?" Sage asked, dropping food colouring into one cup.

"We went to the cemetery," I said.

"Someone was watching us—" Adam looked at Lizzy, who only had eyes for him "—and it wasn't this cute dog." He patted her head. Her ears perked up then dropped down.

"And from the cemetery you ended up in the Gorge," she said, dropping orange food colouring in another cup of white liquid.

"I met Adam at Valentina's bookstore," I briefly recapped. "When we left we noticed we were being followed and two goons were waiting for us at Adam's car. We ran toward the bridge to get away when the bridge went up."

Sage braced her hands on the kitchen island. "And you said it was your idea, Adam, to jump into the Gorge?"

"Yes," Adam mumbled.

"Fun first date," Sage said.

Adam blushed.

"You don't think you two could have been just a little paranoid?" she said, pouring a mirror glaze over the first of three cakes.

"No," Adam said, watching Sage. "That's interesting."

"Don't think complimenting my cake is going to earn you brownie points for convincing my sister to jump into the Gorge."

"Sage. It was a tricky situation. I'm fine."

"Really?" Sage said, hands on hips. "You trust this guy?"

Adam looked Sage in the eye. "I would never harm—"

"—you see, Adam—"

Crap. Sage was winding up.

"—my sister is great. Love her to bits, but Jade is very trusting of the men who come into her life, such as that dirtbag, Osmond."

"Sage, stop it," I said under my breath.

"It's all right, Jade," Adam said. "Sage, I will never hurt Jade."

Sage didn't look convinced. "You convinced her to jump into the Gorge!"

"Sage, stop it," I repeated.

"Who's the cake for?" Adam asked.

"Gillian," I piped up.

Sage thunked the pitcher of glaze on the counter. Her sweater caught the cake rack, tilting it. The rack and cake slid sideways toward the floor.

Lizzy licked her lips, mouth open, panting.

Adam grabbed the cake, his fingers digging into the chocolate mousse. "Not today, Lizzy," he said, his sleeves covered in glaze. He looked at Sage. "We don't want Gillian disappointed."

By the expression on Sage's face, I thought she was going to lay an egg. Yeah, the spotlight's on you now.

"Good catch." She held out the cake rack and Adam placed the cake back on it.

Adam stood. "I need to wash my hands."

He disappeared into the bathroom.

Sage again braced her hands against the island and looked at me. "What are you doing?"

"The same thing you're doing," I hissed. "Back off."

"You have to stop being so trusting—"

"—You have glaze in your hair," I interrupted, as Adam walked back into the room.

"I'll wash it out later." Sage stacked the smaller cake on the two larger ones and placed them in a box. "Any idea who the goons were?" she asked, loading up the dishwasher.

"No," Adam said. "But I met Osmond."

Sage looked at me. "Awkward." She looked at her watch. "I've gotta go. You two can stay as long as you want. Don't let Walter out or he'll try to escape."

Adam looked at me. "Who's Walter?"

"The dwarf Himalayan rabbit."

Sage grabbed the cake box. "Jade, I think we're being targeted. I have no idea why. Who did Charles piss off?" She gave Lizzy a pat, slipped her a dog treat and was out the door.

Sage and I had already decided to play it safe and I would stay at Coco's condo. It wasn't wise for me to be alone at my place. She could also alternate living at her own home if I was here. Adam? Hmm. He wasn't staying the night but ... I heard Sage's Harley. Lizzy curled up on her dog bed.

"Where are you with Oscar's audio?" Adam asked.

I recounted what I had learned so far. Archie was Oscar's number one guy. Oscar had met my mom. He loved Mom and her art. He owned the art gallery in Chinatown where downstairs he held great parties with lots of booze and drugs. He was the opium dealer on the island. He knew Darlene was infatuated with him but he only had eyes for Mom.

"Who was in Oscar's circle?" I asked.

Adam looked around and grabbed a pencil from the coffee table "You have paper?"

I turned over a flyer and handed it to him.

He drew a makeshift family tree with Oscar in the middle and my mother linked on the right side. On the left side were the names Archie and Darlene. Adam drew lines coming down from the names. He flipped the page around so I could see it better.

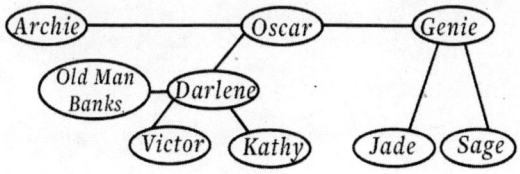

"Darlene—" he tapped her name with the pencil "—claimed Oscar was the father of her children, which is a lie. Oscar ordered a paternity test and Darlene immediately backed down."

"We don't have anything about Darlene's spouse, Old Man Banks."

"Right. Whom we didn't find in the cemetery. Victor, who is

supposed to be dead, doesn't seem to be dead, because we didn't find his plot in the cemetery."

"So, Darlene had Kathy and Victor. You said Kathy had found us, spraypainting spiders on our home. But that's wrong. We saw her plot."

"Oscar thought Victor overdosed but I can't find a death certificate."

"What about Archie?"

"What about him?"

"Could he and Dar—"

"—No," Adam said, cutting me off.

"Okay. Did Archie have any childr—"

"—No."

He cut me off again. "Okay. You all right?"

"Yes."

I moved Sage's prayer plant to a side table to make room and flipped open Charles's laptop. The screen lit up and once again I was prompted for a password. "Crap."

"What?"

"I had a photo of Charles's password on my phone, which is now at the bottom of the Gorge."

"Was his password related to any hobbies? Books?"

I closed my eyes and rubbed my temples, thinking back to the day I was in his office. "Hold on, it was under the mouse-pad which had a photo of a golfer—"

Charlesgolfer1.

I typed the password and the screen flashed to the Windows desktop.

I clicked the files and a list of folders came up. I scrolled.

"That one." Adam pointed to one titled DS. I clicked it open and saw a list of PDF files and JPEGs. "It says Law Society in that PDF name."

I knew what these were. "These are decisions from a hearing panel, when there's a public hearing into a lawyer's conduct." I opened one and scrolled. "Look—" I pointed to the document

"— it's a hearing." I sat back. TV clips, coffee line-up conversations, Tweets, kernels of information. I sat forward. "This is Dennis."

"Dennis who?"

"This is the man who showed up in the courtroom, the guy Sage and I saw at the fire. This is Dennis Sullivan the lawyer."

"He's a lawyer?"

I scrolled. "These paragraphs. Counsel for the Applicant, Valentina Vale. His conduct, criminal conduct, rehabilitative steps, age sixteen involved in gang activity." I kept scrolling. "Charged with fifteen counts of possession for the purposes of trafficking, charged a month later with possession of the proceeds of crime, possession of a firearm, trafficking cocaine."

"Why did Charles have this information?"

"Good question. Valentina defended Dennis."

"Is he still a lawyer?"

I jumped to the end of the document to the decision. "Yes."

"No way."

"'Because of his remorse and rehabilitative efforts,'" I read out loud, "'including his work with various non-profits and a literacy program for offenders.'"

Adam leaned forward. "Click back."

I did and opened a folder named Press. I opened articles about an undercover operation and criminal lawyer Dennis Sullivan being arrested.

"Click back again."

I did.

"That one." Adam pointed to a folder named VV.

"They're pictures." I clicked one. A photo of Valentina at a fundraiser. I clicked on another of her standing next to Dennis, her arm around his shoulders. "Something's not right."

"Why did Charles have all this information on these two?"

"He was building a case," I said.

Adam glanced at me.

I nodded. "Exactly what he was doing."

Adam rubbed his upper lip. "Oscar was positive that Kathy was alive and Victor was dead."

"Hold on. I'm trying a different search engine, and I'm typing Kathy with a 'K' instead of a 'C'. Maybe I'll get better results." I opened another window and Googled Kathy Banks. Sure enough, newspaper articles came up. I clicked on one. "It says here—" I read out loud "—that Kathy died as a result of a police-involved shooting." I looked at Adam.

"Keep reading."

"'The Victoria Police Department executed a search warrant on a suspected crack-house when a known drug kingpin opened fire on officers. One officer was wounded but no officers were killed. The other occupant in the residence, Kathy Banks, who had been sleeping in the next room, was fatally shot.'" I sat back. "Holy crap."

"This doesn't make sense. Oscar was positive the girl was alive."

"Police-involved shooting. I've got an idea." I opened another window and typed in the web address for the Office of the Police Complaint Commissioner. I clicked on the Annual Reports tab. I checked the year of the newspaper article, and then clicked Complaint Summaries and that's where I found it. "They don't provide the deceased's name, but it's a female, police-involved shooting. Look—" I pointed with the mouse "—the circumstances are similar. Except in the Complaint Summary, it says the officers were acting on a reliable tip and the allegations were unsubstantiated."

"The officers aren't named."

"Privacy reasons."

"Oscar was wrong." Adam shook his head. "Tomorrow, I'm calling some friends in the Vital Statistics department. Something doesn't line up."

"I don't see how any of this ties into Charles's death. What type of case were you building, Charles?"

"Valentina Vale had a relationship with Charles. Kathy is dead, from a police-involved shooting." Adam listed the facts on his fingers. "Victor is supposed to be dead from an overdose, but he's not. Valentina's friend Dennis supposedly watched your house burn to the ground and used to traffic drugs, which Valentina successfully defended him on."

I wondered if this had been a case involving Osmond. Sergeant Stone might talk to me. I'd give it a shot. "Charles also wanted to talk to me. I wonder if he found out something tying all of this together." I thought about the newspaper articles on my father's desk. I began typing.

"Now what are you searching?"

"Charles had printed articles." I hit enter. Various headlines were listed in the search results.

Two Men Found Mutilated in Forest.

Adam pulled his stool closer. He pointed to a link. "Click that one."

I did.

Two young men appeared on my computer screen. One man reminded me of someone. Underneath was his name: Jeffrey Banks.

"Look. Jeffrey Banks." I pointed at the screen. "The victim was the father of two and married to Darlene Banks." I looked at Adam. "Bingo. Old Man Banks."

Adam sat back, pulling his hair away from his face.

I tapped the monitor. "This is why we couldn't find a marker for him. There probably wasn't much left of him."

Adam was white.

"What's wrong? Do you know these guys?"

He looked at me. "I've got to go." He stood.

"What's going on?"

He paced, looking for his coat.

"Your coat is still in the dryer."

He rubbed the side of his face then looked at me. " I, um—" he released a deep breath "—I know that man."

"You know a victim of The Grizzly Murders? How?"

"A long time ago, when I was a kid." He stepped forward and cupped my hands. "I'll, um, I'll call you. Lock the door."

Without his coat, he marched out of the condo, slamming the door behind him.

Lizzy lifted her head, circled, then dropped back down in her bed, covering her nose with her tail.

I glanced at grumpy Walter rabbit, who still had a piece of straw in his mouth and glared at me from behind his bars. He kicked straw through the tiny bars before showing me his backside.

What did I say?

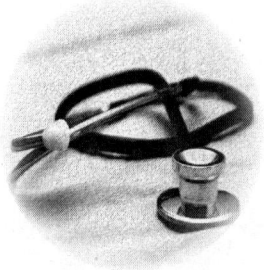

14 EDITH

"I gave him the needle."

Dressed in my black suit and Fluevog shoes, I walked down the courthouse steps. My meeting with the Supreme Court Trial Coordinator had gone well. My next meeting was with Valentina. She wanted to discuss Charles's funeral. I stepped out onto the crosswalk when I was suddenly pulled back as a cyclist sped past in the bike lane.

"They're supposed to stop."

I turned to see who was talking.

Sergeant Stone.

"You can't give him a ticket?" I continued walking.

Stone laughed. "The city's cutting our resources, Ms. Thyme. Fewer boots on the ground. You have a moment?"

I looked at the Sergeant. He shoved his hands into his pockets and looked at the ground. He didn't seem so ... *Stone*. More sensitivity training? "I have time. We can walk. Any more information about Charles's supposed suicide?"

"Actually, yes, but I can't discuss it."

I looked at him.

"When did Detective Reeves tell you he was leaving?"

I stopped walking. A skateboarder swerved around us. "Two weeks ago. Were his prints found at my father's home?"

Stone nodded.

"What was he doing there?"

"He didn't tell you?" Stone asked.

"No. Do you believe Osmond was involved with my father's murder?"

"We're looking into it."

He didn't deny that Charles was murdered.

"What was Osmond's relationship with Valentina Vale?" he asked.

Now, if that wasn't the million-dollar question. "I … I don't know." I felt like we were playing the card game War.

"If he contacts you, let me know." Sergeant Stone stepped away and then stopped. "Oh." He turned. "Ms. Thyme, your client didn't report to her P.O. this morning."

"Which client?"

Stone walked back toward me. "Lucy Starr."

"Lucy was released?"

"Yesterday. Good behaviour. But she failed to report to her Probation Officer."

That wasn't good. Lucy had 24 hours to report to a probation office and have the conditions of her release reviewed. If she didn't report there would be a warrant for her arrest and a charge of breach of probation. "I haven't seen her."

"We have a warrant out for her."

"If she contacts me I'll encourage her to turn herself in."

Stone grunted.

My turn. "What do you know about Kathy Banks?"

"Why are you bringing her up? She was the kid of a low-life drug dealer."

"She was the victim of a police shooting."

"The allegations against the members involved were unsubstantiated. The officers acted accordingly given the circumstances."

"So Kathy Banks was involved in the drug trade?"

"There were rumours that she was involved with a dirty cop. I'll see what I can find out. We can talk about it over dinner."

"No dinner, Sergeant Stone. I'll find Lucy and have her turn herself in. One other thing, any luck finding Norman? I reported him missing a day ago."

Stone shook his head. "We have no leads, Jade. I'll let you know as soon as I hear something."

Stone walked back in the direction we had come, and I walked across the crosswalk and down Fisgard toward Chinatown. I passed the Gate of Harmonious Interest. Tourists smiled and took photos in front of the two lion statues–the guardians protecting Chinatown.

Who was protecting Norman? Oh Norman, why did you run?

A delivery truck beeped as it reversed, and from another truck, palettes of produce were unloaded. Red and orange lanterns dangled across the road, and people sat at outdoor tables talking and drinking coffee. I loved the hustle. I loved the Gate which symbolized growth and peace. The perfect location for my new law office. I turned right onto Dragon Alley and strolled down its narrow corridor to the office. I unlocked the front door, enjoying the trickle of the outside water fountain. I stepped in and locked the door behind me.

Please come home, Norman. Please come home.

There were no articling students around and Kate had taken the afternoon off. I dumped my briefcase on my desk and checked the messages on my phone.

I changed out of my suit into jeans, hanging my blazer behind my office door where my robes hung. I headed out, locking up again, hearing the voice coach practicing *"do-re-mi-fa-sol-la-"*. My bike was parked along the road by Union Pacific Coffee. I strolled past, hearing the coffee grinder, and realized I had forgotten my helmet. I turned back and that's when I saw her. Charles's old housekeeper. The lovely woman who helped get Sage and me to school.

Edith.

She stood, forlorn, clutching Dutch Bakery bags. Shoulders stooped. She saw me, then turned and bustled in the opposite direction.

"Edith, Edith." I ran and grabbed her arm.

A passerby stepped around us.

Tears welled in her eyes.

"Edith, what's wrong?" I hugged her then held her at arm's distance. "Sage and I have been looking for you."

She looked scared. Her eyes grew wide as she looked behind me. "*She's* following me."

I turned. Sage walked toward us.

Edith ran. Her bags twisted and bounced off her legs.

"Edith," Sage and I called. We took off after her.

Edith looked over her shoulder at us.

"Edith, stop," Sage said, ping-ponging against the alley's brick walls, dodging tourists.

Edith collided with the water fountain. She stumbled and her bags flew from her hands. Dinner buns and avocados rolled across the courtyard. Edith wheezed, bracing her hands on her knees.

"Edith," I said, out of breath. "Why so scared? Please. Sit down."

She straightened, her face pale and clammy. Her eyes darted from Sage to me. "I'm sorry." She rubbed her chest.

"For what?" Sage asked. "What could you possibly be sorry for?"

Edith looked at me, her eyes pleading. "I gave him the needle." Her eyes rolled to the back of her head and she fell like a Douglas Fir.

Sage grabbed for her but Edith's body made a sickening thud as she hit pavement.

Someone screamed.

Sage kneeled and tapped Edith's shoulders. "Edith, Edith, are you okay?"

No response.

Sage tossed me her phone. "Call 9-1-1."

Fingers trembling, I dialled.

Sage leaned over Edith's mouth, listening, and held her hand just below Edith's chest, watching.

"9-1-1. Fire, police, ambulance?"

Sage flung off her coat and palm over palm, she began chest compressions. "One, two, three—"

"Ambulance."

"What is your emergency?"

"My friend fell. She's unconscious. Not responding. My sister's doing chest compressions."

"—Seven, eight, nine," Sage said.

"Your location?"

"Fan Tan, no, Dragon Alley, Victoria, B.C.."

"Ten, eleven, twelve." Sage's head bobbed with each compression.

"My sister's doing CPR!" I repeated.

"Is she breathing?"

"Is she breathing?" I asked.

"No," Sage shouted, out of breath.

"No, she's not breathing."

"An ambulance is on its way. You should hear sirens."

"I do." Tears welled in my eyes. I disconnected. A crowd had formed and pushing through it, saying, "Excuse me, excuse me," was Valentina.

She stood next to me and looked at Edith, I could have sworn with distaste. "Valentina, unless you're dropping down in your Versace suit to take over chest compressions from Sage, now is not a good time."

Valentina raised an eyebrow and smiled. "Karma's a bitch."

She walked past, her heels echoing in the alley.

I stared, shocked.

"Twenty, twenty-one, twenty-two."

Sage. I kneeled across from her, palms ready. "I can take over."

She nodded. "At thirty. Twenty-seven, twenty-eight, twenty-nine, thirty." Sage collapsed back.

Palm over palm. "One, two, three–"

"Get back," Sage shouted, stepping back. "A woman's dying here. *Get back.*"

"Six, seven, eight."

The siren was close, really close, then stopped.

Sage held up her coat to give us privacy. "Paramedics are coming."

"Nine, ten, eleven."

I heard the rattle of gurney wheels and two EMT members kneeled beside us. One member took over from me. His gloved hands continued the compressions.

I sat back.

The second attendant asked Sage questions while he unzipped a large blue bag to reveal a defibrillator. He flicked switches.

Edith's head moved from side to side.

Come on, Edith. Come on.

"Hold on." The first attendant held his hand out to the other.

"Edith. Edith. Can you hear me? Edith," the first attendant said.

She moaned. Her eyes fluttered open.

Oh thank God.

"Your friends here—" he nodded at me and Sage "—saved your life."

She mumbled something.

"It's okay, Edith," I said, brushing a pine needle from her curly salt and pepper hair.

Sage wiped a tear from her cheek.

"We're going to take you to the hospital, okay?" the attendant said.

Edith nodded.

The paramedic looked at Sage. "We're taking her to Royal Jubilee."

Sage nodded. "I'll be right behind you."

Edith was lifted onto the stretcher and taken down the alley to the ambulance. Sage picked up the errant avocados, dropping them in a plastic bag. The spectators dispersed.

I flapped my arms at a bird that was making a meal out of one dinner bun. "I'll clean up here and join you."

Sage handed me the bag of avocados. "She was so scared. Scared of me."

I touched Sage's arm. "We'll find out what's going on. You were amazing. We—" my throat tightened and I blinked "—we saved her life."

Sage nodded. "You need to know First Aid and CPR to be a fitness instructor. I've had to resuscitate a middle-aged man during a spin class. Okay, I'll see you at Royal Jubilee." She walked down the alley, slipping on her leather jacket.

I scooped up the last dinner roll, bobbing in the water fountain. Who did you give a needle to?

15 SELFIE SEX OFFENDER

"Why don't you pee on them?"

I WAS A WRECK.
Slept like crap. Edith was still in the hospital in stable condition after suffering a heart attack. She was scheduled for an endocardiogram. I learned that Royal Jubilee was *the hospital* when it came to heart health. I also learned it served good hospital food. Sage and I were not allowed to see her, but being the closest to family, the doctor asked us many questions. Did we know Edith was diabetic? No. Was she a smoker? No. Had she recently suffered any stress or depression? We didn't know. All we knew was that she was a nurse before working as a caretaker, helping our mother.

Sage and I tried to locate her next of kin, but Edith had never married and she had no children. Her one and only sister had passed three years ago. Sage would update me on Edith's progress, given she was noted as the main contact.

That morning I decided to visit the Esquimalt Trailer Park, hoping to find Lucy. I had to do something to get my mind off Edith. Lucy's neighbours were used to her biker lawyer showing up.

I slowed as I rode through construction zones. Road work was being done everywhere in Victoria. I turned into the park and slowed, riding around potholes, a child's discarded hula-hoop. A cat slunk across the road. I parked in front of Lucy's blue and white single-wide and removed my helmet.

I stepped up the two steps and went to knock when I noticed the inside door was open. I pulled open the screen door.

"Lucy?"

Silence.

I stepped in. "Lucy." The screen door clanked behind me.

A fly buzzed and bounced off the far windowpane. I stepped around beer stains on the carpet. Newspapers strewn on the living room table. I picked one up and recognized yesterday's article about the selfie sex offender. Lucy had recently been here. Why had she left her door unlocked?

This didn't feel right. An RCMP homicide detective once told me when a person has that instinct, act on it. He had interviewed countless victims and witnesses who had all started their statements with, "Something didn't feel right."

Did I listen?

No.

A car drove past. I looked in its direction but saw nothing. I tossed the paper on the living room sofa and stepped past the kitchen table where a second fly flitted over breakfast remains.

"Lucy?"

Another car drove past. I walked along the narrow hallway, pushing a thin door open. "Lucy." Clothes strewn on the floor. Suitcases hauled out of closets. Empty hangers dangled on the rod. I turned and saw them on the floor.

Men's sunglasses.

I kneeled and picked them up.

These were Osmond's.

Osmond was an undercover officer in the drug section. I had thought it odd that he had been assigned to Lucy's trivial case. Why the hell had he been here?

Had he threatened her? He didn't need to take off his sunglasses to execute an arrest warrant.

Lucy knew the court system. She knew to report to her P.O. immediately after release. Was Osmond the reason she had made a fast exit?

I moved further down the hall. Where was my client? I pushed open another thin door. Bathroom. Toothpaste spit in the sink. Goopy soap in the soap dish. Medicine cabinet ajar. A few discarded hair pins, old toothbrushes and a hair pick and a bottle of Xanax.

I touched the towel hanging from the shower curtain rod. Damp.

Very damp. I had just missed her.

A car pulled up outside. A door slammed and steps crunched on gravel then ascended the outside stairs.

Lucy.

The trailer's screen door slammed.

"Lucy." I ducked out and into the hall, but it wasn't Lucy who stood at the opposite end of the hall but drug-dealing lawyer, Dennis Sullivan, Valentina's client, the man who had walked into the courtroom during Lucy's sentencing.

Crap.

He smiled then slurped. "Hi Jade. What are you doing here?"

"I'm looking for Lucy, trying to prevent her arrest. What are you doing here, Dennis?"

He said nothing, but kept smiling, taking two steps closer.

Hold your ground.

He braced his forearms against the narrow walls, trapping me. "You're pretty, Jade."

Don't flinch.

Poker face. "Do you know where I can locate Lucy?" I took a few steps toward him, still maintaining a safe distance. "Or, if you could let her know I was looking for her. There's a warrant for her arrest. She didn't report to probation. You're a lawyer. The last thing we want is our clients arrested."

"She said you were crafty."

Poker face.

"Osmond said you were a beautiful bitch." He looked at my breasts.

Osmond?

His phone buzzed.

"You gonna get that? Could be Osmond."

He looked at me then again at my breasts. "I gotta tattoo."

"Have you seen Osmond, Dennis?"

"It's a tattoo of a beautiful woman."

Stay cool. "I need to talk with Osmond. Do you know how I can reach him?"

"It's right here." He rubbed the top of his leg.

Don't look.

"I show you."

"No!"

He undid the button of his pants.

"Dennis, do up your pants. I don't want to see your tattoo."

He looked at me, hurt, then smiled and laughed. He did up the button but the zipper was still flying low.

"Dennis, I'm going. I have a meeting with Mr. Younghusband." I stepped forward when Dennis stuck his hand around my throat and slammed me against the wall.

Osmond's sunglasses slipped from my fingers and clattered on the floor.

"I want to show you my tattoo."

"Dennis, you're hurting me."

He gripped my jaw with his hand and gave me a little shake. "I like you, Jade." He pushed his groin into my pelvis, flattening me against the wall. The creep had an erection. He snorted then licked my throat.

I squirmed and feebly hit his head.

He grabbed my wrist and smacked it against the wall. "Stop it."

"Dennis, let go. You—"

He pressed his forearm against my neck and grabbed my breast.

I gulped. Air.

"I want to show you—" he tugged my shirt from my pants.

"No. Dennis, *stop*."

The walls of the narrow trailer closed. Black splotches. No. I could not pass out. I kicked at his legs. My hand smacked the wall for something. *Anything* to grab.

His phone vibrated.

"Dennis, let go. I'll file a complaint. Law Society."

He angled my head up. "Don't threaten me. Valentina'll get me off." He belched.

A car door slammed and I heard more steps.

Somebody, please.

"Dennis, what the hell are you doing?"

Dennis stepped back.

Osmond stood at the other end of the hall. The bastard smiled and stepped forward. I slid against the wall out of Dennis's reach.

Dennis looked at the floor as if he had been scolded. "You said— "

"—I said nothing," Osmond said. He looked at me. "Where's your boy-puppy now, Jade? Scare him off."

"Looking for these?" I kicked his sunglasses down the hall. "Why don't you pee on them?"

Osmond smirked and scooped them up. "You were warned, Jade." He looked at Dennis, who still stared at the floor. "Dennis, get your cell and do up your pants."

Dennis walked down the hall, head down.

Osmond walked backwards looking at me. "Next time, I won't stop him." He turned and followed Dennis out of the trailer. The screen door slammed. A car engine revved, then tires crunched on gravel as a car pulled away.

I gasped, and my knees buckled. I pressed trembling hands against the wall to keep myself upright. My eyes wet with tears, I lurched forward. The walls leaned to the right then to the left. I stumbled out the trailer.

Fresh air.

Space.

I braced my hands on my knees. You're okay. They're gone. I straightened and with shaky limbs, swung my leg over the seat of my bike.

Breathe.

I want to throw up.

I'm okay. I'm okay.

No, I'm not.

I leaned over to the side and dry heaved.

I sat upright.

You're okay. Few breaths. I pulled on my motorcycle helmet. *C'mon. Routine. Start your bike.*

Turn on the fuel.

Choke on.

Turn ignition.

Kickstart. Nothing.

Again.

Kickstart. Nothing.

Again.

The bike rumbled.

Yes.

I adjusted the choke.

You're going home.

16 EXTERNAL INVESTIGATION

"If Osmond was ever charged for accessory to murder …"

THAT EVENING I STAYED IN THE SHOWER FOR A VERY long time, trying to wash away any traces of Dennis touching my body.

Sage called, saying she was staying the night at Gillian's. She questioned if I was all right. She told me I sounded weird. I told her I was fine and triple-checked the doors.

I needed to tell the police. They would forward charge recommendations to the local Crown Counsel. The local Crown Counsel would forward the charges out of town for fear of bias. Hell, an independent prosecutor might be given the charge approval. Did I want to give a statement? Yes. No. If this went to court, which it would, defence counsel would ask me what I was doing in Lucy's trailer uninvited. Detective Osmond Reeves would no doubt back up Dennis, saying no assault occurred. He had only returned to get his sunglasses, after checking to see if Lucy was there, given there was a warrant for her arrest. Dennis was getting his cell phone after being asked by Lucy to be her new defence counsel. As long as Lucy remained missing, they could fabricate anything. The big question would be, if I had been assaulted why didn't I, a lawyer, go to the police right away?

Because I was ashamed.

Ashamed.

Like every other female who lived with the shame that if she had behaved better, or hadn't done what she did, or had done something to *prevent* the assault it would *not* have happened.

The following morning I sat at my desk, flipping through my *Criminal Code*. Looking up sexual touching. I really needed a raspberry truffle mocha. Kate, seeing me distracted, said she'd grab me one.

I heard voices in the lobby, then Kate's voice, saying 'I'll be right with you.' She stepped into my office, precariously holding a mug and saucer, looking perturbed.

"Thank you so much, Kate."

She placed the mug on my desk and I saw that it sat in a puddle of whipped cream that had cascaded down the side. "It's volcanic."

She groaned. "I told them no whipped cream and they did it anyways. I thought by transferring it over to your regular mug it wouldn't be so messy if I nuked it because it was lukewarm."

"I'm sure it tastes amazing."

Her eyebrows furrowed, she closed my office door and walked back to my desk. "The Vancouver police are here to see you."

"That can't be good."

"Is there anything you need to tell me? Anything I should know? Are you in trouble? You haven't been popping Vicodin, have you? Gambling?"

I smiled. Kate's queries came from a good place. "Haven't touched the stuff in six months and the only gambling I do is the occasional lottery ticket."

"Good."

"I have no idea why VPD are here."

"Okay." Kate eyed me as she opened the door and stepped out.

A few seconds later, two officers dressed in civilian clothes walked in. The female officer had short spiky hair. Her pink earrings matched her necklace that matched her pink scarf and complemented her grey suit. The man wore dark slacks, shirt and tie, and a leather jacket. He reminded me of a Ken doll except with dark hair.

"Good morning," I said, stepping around my desk and holding out my hand. "Jade Thyme."

The officers introduced themselves. They were from VPD's Internal Investigation Section. I sat behind my desk. Inspector Shelly pulled her chair closer. "Ms. Thyme, our condolences on your father's passing."

"Thank you. How can I assist you?"

"Ms. Thyme—"

"—Please call me Jade."

"Jade, we have a few questions regarding Detective Osmond Reeves."

Oh. "Yes."

The male Sergeant glanced at Inspector Shelly and sat forward in his chair. "When was the last time you had contact with Detective Reeves?" he asked, his voice deep.

Wasn't expecting that question. *Yesterday.* "Oh, well—" I let out a deep breath "—um, yesterday." Only answer the question, do not offer anymore.

Inspector Shelly scribbled notes in a notebook. "Yesterday? Whereabouts?"

I cleared my throat. "Ah, I was visiting my client, Lucy Starr." I smiled. "Trying to find her so she can turn herself in and not get arrested. He had stopped by."

Inspector Shelly looked at me. "Why would he be there?"

"I, I was wondering the same thing."

Inspector Shelly tapped her pen. "You didn't ask."

"No. I've been a bit distracted." *Do not offer any more information.* "A family friend had a heart attack the day before."

"You do ad hoc Crown Counsel work?" the Sergeant asked,

leaning his elbows on his knees.

"Yes."

"Are you under contract to do any federal drug prosecutions?"

"Not at the moment."

"So you have never prosecuted a drug trial?"

"No. I have prosecuted individuals who are known drug traffickers for *Criminal Code* offences, such as assault or kidnapping, but never have I prosecuted anyone for trafficking." Just answer their questions, offer nothing more.

"When did you first meet Osmond?" Inspector Shelly asked.

"We knew each other in college, but if you're asking recently, it was about six months ago when Jules Cranbury was murdered. Osmond showed up in my courtroom."

"You two have stayed in contact since Jules's murder?"

"Yes."

"What type of relationship do you and Osmond have?" Inspector Shelly looked me in the eye. "Are you friends? More than friends? Friends with benefits? A couple?"

I found this question odd and rather personal but I would play along. "We were more than friends."

"You said were?" the dark-haired Sergeant said.

I sighed. "We're no longer together, Sergeant. We split up. Osmond, and I'm sure you already know this, was assigned to infiltrate a biker gang in Montréal. He told me he would be gone for at least a year."

Both the Sergeant and Inspector scribbled in their notebooks.

Good Lord. What was this about?

"When did you hear of his reassignment?" Inspector Shelly asked.

I thought back. "Whatever day Oscar Cooper's obituary was in the paper. That afternoon he told me he was leaving for an assignment in Montréal. I'm sure you're aware of that."

"Not before?"

"No."

"Was that the last time you saw Detective Reeves, Jade?" She repeated the question.

"No. I told you yesterday. May I ask, what this questioning is about?"

Both investigators remained silent.

"Inspector, Sergeant, I understand you can't provide me with details, but—"

"—Has Osmond ever assaulted you, Jade?" Inspector Shelly looked me in the eye.

"No."

"He's never raised a hand?"

"No."

"And if he had, would you tell us?"

I thought about Dennis Sullivan and Osmond watching, as if my assault was a spectator sport. "Yes."

Inspector Shelly sat back and crossed her legs. "We are conducting an investigation into Detective Reeves's conduct. The Office of the Police Complaint Commissioner has issued an Order for an External Investigation. We have reason to believe Detective Reeves has committed numerous counts of discreditable conduct, and we're trying to establish a timeline."

Discreditable conduct. The category for very serious offences. "What is he alleged to have done?"

Both investigators stared at me.

"I will not discuss any of what you tell me with anyone. Consider this office under the Cone of Silence."

Inspector Shelly looked confused.

Didn't she ever watch *Get Smart* reruns as a child?

"If Osmond was ever charged for accessory to murder would you be willing to act as Crown witness?"

Holy shit. Osmond. The man who had given Dennis permission to assault me *next time*.

"Jade?"

"Ah, yes."

"We believe he was involved in some capacity. So you would act as a Crown witness?"

"Yes. His defence counsel would—" I couldn't believe I was saying this "—would discredit me, allege that I was a witness for the Crown out of spite for a failed relationship."

"We'll jump that fence when we get to it. The time you said Osmond walked into your courtroom, when you were defending Jules Cranbury, ties into the flight times of him returning from Montréal the prior day. Did he discuss any of his work with you?"

"No."

"Did you ever meet any of Osmond's friends or family?"

"No."

"You didn't find that odd?" the Inspector asked.

"I didn't give it much thought until you brought it up. We are both busy people."

The Sergeant pulled a photograph from his notebook and passed it across the desk to me. "Have you ever seen the man on the right?"

My heart dropped. Dennis Sullivan. The creep from yesterday. The same man Sage and I saw watching the fire. "This is Dennis Sullivan. He's a lawyer. Or was. I'm not certain if he's still practising."

"You know him?" the Sergeant asked.

He's big and strong but doesn't know it. He has no sense of right or wrong and he's a sex offender.

I explained about going to Lucy's trailer to get her to turn herself in and Dennis showing up with Osmond. I had my chance to acknowledge what would be a count of sexual interference under the *Criminal Code*. And even though I knew better, I remained silent.

The Sergeant looked me in the eye. "Do you know that Dennis Sullivan is a person of interest in a number of sex assaults?"

I felt sick. *Say something.*

"Sadly—" Inspector Shelly took out another photo "—none of his victims want to provide a statement. Why do you think Osmond was at Lucy Starr's trailer?"

"I told you, I don't know."

The Inspector sat back and looked at me. "Jade, you are a smart, successful lawyer. I find it hard to believe that you didn't ask your ex-boyfriend why he was showing up at your client's residence."

"I had other things on my mind."

The Inspector checked her notes. "Your friend who suffered a heart attack the day before."

"Yes. Edith. She's at Royal Jubilee. My sister Sage and I performed CPR before ERT showed up."

"How's your friend doing? She going to be okay?"

"We don't know."

The Inspector slid a photo across my desk.

My heart dropped again. It was a photo of Dennis Sullivan and Osmond, talking and drinking beers. "Osmond could be working undercover. That's his job in the drug section."

"Very true," the Sergeant said, "except this photo was taken," he turned the photo over, "two days ago in Vancouver."

"Jade, we believe you have nothing to do with Osmond's activities," Inspector Shelly said.

Me! Activities.

"Osmond's not the first police officer to turn and he won't be the last," the Inspector said.

Turn.

"The money offered from the other side is lucrative. Osmond owns a house in Vancouver and drives a McLaren. How can he afford that on a detective's wage? We all know money laundering has inflated the Vancouver housing market, and we believe Osmond is involved in a money laundering scheme. We want to find out with whom."

This news was too much. Arms crossed, I was shutting down. Compartmentalizing. "I'm sorry, I can't see how I can be of assistance."

Inspector Shelly put down her pen and took off her glasses. She looked me in the eye. "Jade, why am I getting the feeling that you're holding something back?"

Don't answer that.

The Inspector rubbed her eyes. "You know, Jade, I joined the police department in 1984. There weren't many female officers in the force at that time. I have witnessed a lot of things in and outside the department. I can retire in five months. And as uncomfortable and as embarrassing as it may be for you disclosing your relationship with Osmond, it is nothing in comparison to the embarrassment the Victoria Police Department is going to face when the findings of our investigation go public. You can also fathom the cross-examination Osmond's defence counsel will put me through at his public hearing."

The dark-haired Sergeant smiled. "Nobody despises a bad cop more than a good cop. There are good people at Vic PD. The Chief requested the external investigation from the Office of the Police Complaint Commissioner. The Chief will have to answer questions from the media, while Osmond hides behind his defence counsel. Can you tell us of any conversations or strange occurrences that happened while you and Osmond were together? You are the only connection we have to him."

I sat back in my chair and told them of the day Osmond walked into my courtroom, of his assistance during Jules's murder investigation. I scrolled through the calendar on my phone, confirming dates and times when he was in town. Everything, including how I found it odd that a detective of his expertise had been assigned to Lucy's assault case. I stuck to the facts and stopped there. "Lucy's missing," I said.

"We are aware of that," Inspector Shelly said, closing her notebook. "Thank you, Jade."

The Sergeant took back the photo of Dennis and Osmond. "Jade, both these men are dangerous."

No kidding. "Have you questioned Valentina Vale?"

Inspector Shelly and the Sergeant exchanged glances, which told me they had, and Valentina hadn't been so forthcoming.

"She has acted on Dennis's behalf," I said.

"When Osmond gets in contact with you—" the Sergeant said, standing "—and we believe he will, we strongly encourage you to call the police—" the Sergeant slipped his business card onto my desk "—and please, for your own safety and the safety of your family, stay away from him."

I took the Sergeant's card and walked him and the Inspector to the lobby, where Adam leaned against the counter talking to Kate.

He straightened when he saw the officers and looked at me. His expression saying, 'Are you all right?'

Inspector Shelly stopped. "Excuse me, are you the author, Adam Younghusband?"

Adam smiled. "Yes, I am."

And the Inspector was off. "I have read every mystery novel in your Alfred Wright series. God, if I had known you'd be here, I would have brought my latest copy for you to sign."

"Well—"

Inspector Shelly interrupted him. "Can I give you a little constructive criticism from your number one fan?"

Adam opened his mouth to speak but the Inspector continued. "Wright's love interest, Heather, she needs to eat. We never see her eat. Maybe throw her a bun or two, or have her slop some spaghetti on her dress."

We laughed.

"I hope I haven't offended," Inspector Shelly said.

"Not in the least. Spaghetti, I'm sure I can work that in with the next set of rewrites. If you have a business card, I can send you an autographed proof of the next book, or reach out if I need a beta reader."

Inspector Shelly's eyes widened, and if she wasn't in love with Adam Younghusband before, she was now. "That would be fabulous." She handed Adam a card. "If you need any technical information, I would be more than happy to help."

"Thank you," he said.

The Inspector and the Sergeant left.

Adam looked at me. "Do you have a moment?"

I nodded to my office and he followed. Adam closed the door. He stepped forward and held out a cellphone. "I owe you one."

I smiled. "Thank you."

"Everything okay?"

"Yes."

"Does this have to do with that cop, your old boyfriend?"

"Yes." I forced a smile. "But all's good. I'm safe."

Adam didn't look convinced.

"So what did you want to talk about?"

"The other day, when I dashed." He rubbed his chin. "When I was a kid … I witnessed a friend get kidnapped."

"That's horrible. Did your friend get found?"

"Yes. It all worked out. She—" he looked at me "—she's doing well." Adam slipped his hands into his pockets. "Really well. The men who abducted her were the victims of the Grizzly Bear Murders."

"From the newspaper article."

"Yes."

"So the guys who kidnapped your friend got murdered? You need to tell the police, or at least your friend. She must be wondering. Or does she know?"

"The police were never involved and the men, well, you saw, they were fed to the grizzlies."

"Then how did your friend get rescued?"

Adam looked at the framed law degrees behind my desk. "Her father was very powerful."

"So—"

"—He got her back. Besides, she's doing really well. Why bring back that pain?"

"Closure. Are you still in contact with her?"

Adam looked dejected. "I don't think she knows I exist."

I stepped up to him and rubbed his arm. "You really should tell her."

Adam looked at me. "Jade."

"Yes."

"You're … you're—"

"—Jade." Kate poked her head into my office. What now? "This better not be about another fire!"

Kate's eye widened.

"Oh, God."

"Sage," Kate said. "Her house. Fire."

17 FIRE

"You're evil and a coward, and I hate you!"

WEARING AN EXTRA HELMET I HAD IN THE OFFICE, Adam sat on the back of my bike, holding onto my waist as I maneuvered the Royal Enfield through back streets, weaving around cars, pedestrians, slowing, accelerating. *Get out of my way.* I recognized Sage pulling out from behind a car and accelerating, riding the yellow line.

Jesus, Sage. You're going to get yourself killed.

A car in the oncoming lane. Sage swerved back into our lane. She made a right and opened it up on a deserted farm road. I did the same. We whipped past cars. I slowed, turning onto another back road. Adam leaned into the turn with me, then we were off, the fields on our right a smear of green. Soon, Adam and I pulled into the driveway of Sage's house. I braked.

Firetrucks. Cars. Firefighters.

That smell—smoke.

Sage dropped her helmet and ran toward her burning house.

Adam got off the bike.

"Sage!" I shouted, running after her.

Dark smoke billowed from broken windows. Flames crackled.

Sage, with cat-like reflexes, dodged a firefighter.

"*Sage.*"

Another firefighter grabbed her around the waist, lifting her, as she kicked and screamed. "*No.*"

"You can't go in there," the firefighter shouted, wrestling her back.

"My dog," she cried, beating his hands. "My dog."

Lizzy.

"Her dog?" I heard the terror in my voice. "Have you seen her dog. A German Shepherd."

Please, God.

An explosion. We crouched, shielding our heads with our arms, backs to the building.

Sage turned, eyes pleading, mascara-tears streaming her cheeks. "*Please*, my dog."

"Your dog," the firefighter said.

Sage nodded.

"This way."

His arm over her shoulder, he spoke in low tones as they walked.

Adam and I followed, walking behind a firetruck and over to a make-shift tent. The firefighter smiled and pulled back a flap.

A MotoCityDoll, with soot on her face and long dark hair in a ponytail, petted Lizzy.

"*Lizzy.*" Sage dropped to her knees. Her arms engulfed Lizzy as she pressed her face into the dog's fur. Lizzy rested her head and front paws on Sage's shoulders. Sage's body shook as she sobbed.

I wiped tears from my eyes, smiling as Lizzy's nose sniffed Sage's hair.

Sage looked at the biker. "Did you get her out?"

The biker leaned forward, scratching Lizzy's fur. "I was working out in the gym and smelled smoke, then heard her barking."

Sage sat back, still hugging Lizzy. "I'm so sorry, Lizzy. I'm so sorry I didn't take you on the bike."

"A window had blown out. With another Doll's help, we ran in. I leaned to pick her up but she jumped into my arms."

Sage hugged Lizzy, who licked the tears on her cheeks.

"Thank you," I said. "For everything."

The biker stood and smiled.

"Thank you," Sage said, not leaving Lizzy's side. "How can I repay you?"

The biker rubbed the back of Lizzy's neck. She looked at Sage. "Sage, that fire wasn't an accident. Somebody set it. And whoever did, knew your dog was inside. Who does something like that?"

"A sicko," Adam said, stepping forward, kneeling and petting Lizzy's head. "Did you see anyone around the house?"

"No. I have to go. I'll check back in. The Dolls will look into this." She opened the flap and disappeared.

I looked at Sage as she pet Lizzy's fur.

"I am so sorry, Lizzy," Sage said. "I'm so sorry. Nobody will ever scare you or attempt to hurt you again. I promise." She sniffed, wiping her nose with her sleeve. She looked at me. "Whoever did this—" her voice broke. "I'm going to hunt them down and beat them."

I kneeled beside my sister. "Then when you're done, it's my turn."

Sage smiled. She sat on the ground, pulling Lizzy onto her lap, hugging her. "I'm so sorry, girl. So sorry."

I patted Sage on the shoulder. "I'm going to see if I can find anything out."

Sage nodded.

"I'll come with you," Adam said.

I opened the flap of the tent, watching the chaos, when I saw him.

Sitting.

On *my* bike.

Arms crossed, Dennis Sullivan watched Sage's home burn, a stupid grin on his face.

"*Asshole.*"

I walked out of the tent.

"Jade, don't—"

"—kill him? Not yet," I said.

"Jade—"

A firefighter pulled Adam aside.

I marched toward Dennis, swooping up Sage's bike helmet from the ground.

Dennis saw me and smirked.

"*Get off.*"

"I want to show you my tattoo."

I clenched my hand around the helmet's mouthguard. I'll knock that tattoo into next year.

Dennis swung his leg over the seat and stepped back.

"You started this fire."

"No, I didn't."

Liar.

"I was riding. I pulled over to the side of the road because I heard sirens like Valentina told me."

"Then Valentina is the pyromaniac," I concluded.

"That's not nice. Valentina says you stole from her."

"Excuse me?"

"Was Sage inside?" He tried to look around me. "Her dog okay?"

I swung.

"Jade." Adam grabbed my arm, then placed his hands on my shoulders, looking me in the eye. "Not now."

"Mr. Younghusband."

"Dennis, you need to leave," Adam said, glancing over his shoulder.

"Is the dog okay?"

I lunged.

Adam held me back. "*Not now,*" he said quietly.

"I hate him," I said, under my breath.

"Mr. Younghusband, we're having a book reading, are you coming? You can bring Jade."

My heart pounded.

Adam shook his head no, then turned to face Dennis. "You need to leave. Now."

Dennis looked hurt. "Valentina was right. You're a stuck-up *bitch*, Jade. Valentina said you stole from her. You're evil and a coward, and I *hate you!*"

Adam nailed him with a quick upper cut to the jaw.

Dennis's head snapped back.

Adam grabbed Dennis's arm and escorted him toward the crowd. "I told you to leave, Dennis."

A woman gasped.

Dennis lunged out of Adam's grip, holding his chin. "You hit me."

Another woman stepped aside.

Dennis glared at Adam then at me. He rubbed his chin and walked down the street where cars were parked on either side of the road.

"My apologies you had to witness that altercation," Adam said, smiling at the people who had gathered. "My friend—" he indicated me "—was rudely insulted by that man, and her dog just about got killed in the fire."

"Aw," a spectator said.

"Is the dog all right?" another person asked.

"Yes, the dog is okay." Adam waved and walked back to me.

We heard a squeal of tires and a black SUV sped past.

"You all right?" Adam asked, slinging his arm around my shoulders and walking me away from the crowd.

"Somebody tried to kill Lizzy," I sniffed. "I think it was Dennis. He either started the fire, or helped. He was watching when our house was torched. This fire was deliberate. He's a desperate scum-sucking creep who's tied to Valentina, and—" I let out a deep breath.

"—*and?*" Adam coaxed.

And he molested me.

I turned and looked at the flames and smoke. "Lizzy could have—"

"—Lizzy is safe now." Adam brushed my hair back from my face. "Anything else going on, Jade?"

Tell him. "We should check on Sage?"

"Did Dennis hurt you?"

"Dennis takes his orders from Valentina. They're in this together."

Adam wasn't buying my deflection but he didn't push. "What did you allegedly steal from Valentina?"

"I don't know. But I'm going to find out."

Her home now only embers, Sage, Lizzy and I returned to Coco's condo. Adam had a lecture to instruct at Royal Roads but he promised to swing by. It was at the condo that we received a visit from Sergeant Stone.

"Sage, how are you doing?" he asked.

"Lizzy's safe," Sage said, patting her dog. "I've lost all my belongings but … that crap is replaceable. Lizzy isn't. That's all that matters." She didn't look at Stone but kept petting Lizzy.

"Do you want anything, Sergeant Stone?" I asked. "Wine. Coffee."

"Do you have anything stronger?"

"Yeah. Aviation Gin. Crown Royal."

"Crown Royal. I've finished my shift."

Sage looked surprised, so was I. We were having a drink with Sergeant Stone. No reason to believe he didn't like knocking back a rye. I grabbed the bottle and filled three Disney shot glasses. I slid them theirs. "I don't believe this is a 'cheers' kind of moment."

Sage looked from her glass to mine. "You gave me Donald Duck."

"Yeah, so?"

"Why do I get the duck and you get Minnie?"

I swapped shot glasses. "Better?"

She threw back her shot as did Stone.

He tapped his glass on the counter. "So Sage, who have you pissed off?"

"Excuse me?" she said.

"You ride with a rough crowd."

"My crowd wouldn't hurt a dog or burn a house down. It was

my crowd, the MotoCityDolls, who were the first beating down flames. It was a MotoCityDoll who rescued my dog. So don't tell me it was my crowd!"

"Again, who did you *two*," Stone repeated, "piss off?"

"We're trying to figure that out," I said. "This has something to do with Charles's murder."

Stone stared at the shot glass. He looked from Sage to me. "In 1968 your mother had a relationship with Oscar Cooper."

"I know," I said.

Sage pulled up a stool. "You didn't tell me."

"I've been going through some old files," Stone continued. "The cops were called a few times to Oscar's residence. He was the dealer on the island. Why your mother hooked up with him—"

"—is not for us to judge," I interrupted.

Stone frowned. "Oscar loved her art. You can't choose your fans. They started seeing a lot of each other. What your mom, Genie, didn't know, or what she didn't want to know, is that he was laundering money and dealing opium. He had an art gallery in Chinatown. Hugely popular. Nobody suspected that your mother's beautiful paintings, framed with thick frames, made the perfect spot to stash money and opium."

"Jesus." Sage grabbed the Crown Royal and poured another round. "She must have eventually found out."

"Yes. Because that's when they broke up. Darlene Banks was another artist who hung out with them. As soon as your mother ditched Oscar, Darlene clung onto him. But that didn't last. Darlene had two kids with another low-life drug dealer known as Old Man Banks. His name was actually Steven Banks. He had a brother, Jeffrey, who was basically his driver."

"They were the victims of The Grizzly Bear Murders," I added.

Sage looked at me. "Grizzly murders?"

"I'll fill you in later."

"Yes. After Steven and Jeffrey's murders, Darlene took off with the kids to the Caymans or some island," Stone continued. "Darlene returned to Victoria when Kathy and Victor were in their teens."

"Victor is still alive, and Kathy died in a police shooting."

"Yes." Stone pushed his Goofy glass across the counter.

"Victor could be master-minding the fires," Sage said, topping up his glass.

Stone threw the rye back. "What I'm about to tell you cannot be repeated."

"We won't say a word," I said.

"Kathy followed in her father's footsteps. Steven Banks dealed with Oscar, Kathy was small time. She was nothing like Oscar or her father, but she hung out with the same crowd.

"The drug squad was trying to find a crack-house. They had reasonable grounds to believe that a small-time dealer was selling drugs and guns from his home. They couldn't pin down the location, until one drug squad member got an idea."

Stone looked at both of us. "Make a deal with Crown. Oscar's sentence could be reduced if he gave us information on Victoria's drug scene."

"Did Oscar agree?"

"Yes."

"Seriously?" Sage questioned. "Giving up one of his own?"

"Oscar was old. He was on dialysis. Maybe he hoped to see Jesus. But Oscar, being Oscar, had conditions. Private cell, better food, private gym time. The man had so much respect in the slammer that no one ever thought that Oscar would snitch. A deal was made. Nobody knew of the arrangement."

"Did you find the location of the crack-house?" I asked.

"Yes. Oscar tipped us off and told us when a new shipment of guns was arriving. The drug squad raided the guy's home. Of course there was gunfire. ERT was called in."

"ERT?" Sage asked.

"Emergency Response Team," I said. "Our version of SWAT."

Sage nodded.

"The dealer was taken out," Stone continued, "and … so was Kathy."

"That would have repercussions," I said.

Stone nodded. "Gang members, civilians, were upset about her death. When the story broke, the headline was *Police-Involved Shooting, Bystander Killed*. What the papers didn't report was that Kathy had just snorted two lines of coke when the raid happened. Officers told her to stay down but she didn't and was caught in the cross-fire. She died instantly. Multiple gunshot wounds to the chest."

"I read in the police commissioner's Annual Report the allegations against the officer were unsubstantiated. It was the dealer's shot to the heart that killed her, not the police officer's."

"That's correct."

"Holy crap," Sage said.

Stone looked from Sage to me. "Darlene committed suicide and Oscar stopped cooperating with us."

I leaned forward, rubbing my temples. "Imagine the guilt knowing you provided information to the police that resulted in your girlfriend's daughter being killed. Yes, it can be argued that Kathy hung with a bad crowd, but still, your actions directly resulted in another person's death."

Stone grunted. "He's lucky one of his rivals didn't shoot her in a McDonalds' drive-thru. It's the life they lead, Jade. Oscar Cooper was not a nice man."

I didn't dare mention that I was listening to Oscar's memoir on my cellphone.

"Men like Oscar, people romanticize them. Before Oscar was incarcerated, it was rumoured that he uncovered a plot to kill Archie by a rival gang. Did you ever hear of the Fraser River Six?"

"Yes," Sage said. "But weren't they all killed?"

"Yes. Oscar had them shot dead while they were ordering their Big Macs."

I choked on my rye. I wheezed.

Sage patted my back. "All right?"

"Yes," I croaked.

Stone turned to me. "You would be prosecuting a man like Oscar for five counts of murder if you were Crown Counsel back then."

I leaned forward. "And if I had defended Oscar, I would have got him off in front of a jury." Stone and I could go all day with this argument.

Stone stood and held up his shot glass. "Thank you." He looked from Sage to me. "We'll be investigating this arson along with the other one. This is retribution for something. This is *personal*."

I crossed my arms. "So you now believe the other fire was arson?"

Stone frowned. "We got an anonymous tip."

Sage and I looked at each other.

"You two need to look at the sequence of events. Oscar died. The same day your father, Charles, was found dead of a cocaine overdose. When did the shit slide sideways? Call it old cop's intuition, but this has to do with Genie and Oscar."

18 FAMILY TIES

I was suffocating.

AFTER SERGEANT STONE LEFT, SAGE SHOWERED THEN took off on her bike to see Gillian. Not wanting to smell of smoke, I showered and threw my clothes in the wash. Wearing blue sweatpants and a hoodie, I lowered all the blinds, activated the security system, and settled on the sofa with a glass of wine and a bowl of microwave popcorn. I threw back a few popcorn kernels when I noticed Walter the dwarf Himalayan rabbit, straw in his mouth, staring at me from his cage. I stepped up to him.

"I'm not supposed to let you out."

He wiggled his nose.

"You're a flight risk."

He lapped around his cage, kicking up wood chips, and stood at the door.

"You have a rattle and a green stuffed frog. Play with them."

He picked up the rattle with his teeth and flung it.

"Really? Fine." I opened the little gate and hopped out.

I sat on the carpet, leaning against the sofa, smiling as Walter hopped to his shoebox house and nibbled last night's menu of carrot and parsley.

Earbuds in, I pressed play and listened to the final audio file, hoping to uncover how a drug dealer had messed up people's lives and how did Oscar know me.

Oscar sounded tired but his voice livened up as he talked about his humble beginnings and being raised by his mother. His father had deserted his mother as soon as he found out she was pregnant.

During those times, being a single mom was considered disgraceful. Why couldn't she keep her man? Or, she must be a "loose woman." Oscar was labelled a bastard.

I stopped the recording and gulped my wine. It annoyed me that mother and child were ostracized while the gigolo father gallivanted around.

I continued listening. Oscar's mom took Oscar to school and then worked as a waitress in a restaurant. Oscar would walk home, do homework then his paper route, while his mom worked a second job as a cocktail waitress.

Oscar and his mother had a good relationship. Her love got him through the tough years of being bullied in elementary school. In grade eight he shot up to six feet and was not one to be picked on. He kept delivering papers and, because of his good looks, bored housewives tipped generously, and offered the teenage Oscar more than just tea and cookies.

During one paper delivery to an affluent household, Oscar was pitched a business opportunity: add one more rolled newspaper, containing a package, to his route. Oscar was paid the same money his mother made at the cocktail bar. Good at this job and discreet, when his mom was diagnosed with cancer, Oscar's money paid for her painkillers. When her pain got too much, Oscar was paid with opium. That was how 14-year-old Oscar Cooper was introduced to drug trafficking and easy money.

I pressed pause and rubbed my forehead. Walter hopped to where I sat. Should I keep going? Walter? He nudged his head under my hand and I petted his soft fur. "You want love like the rest of us." I pressed play.

"Jade, I loved your mother."

Stop. I was getting used to that. I pressed play again.

"We broke up in the fall of 1968. We didn't see each other until 1986."

A year before I was born.

"If you believe in numerology, there must be something significant with those numbers, 1968 then 1986. Turbulent times in 1968. Martin Luther King and Robert Kennedy were assassinated. Andy Warhol was shot. The violence bothered Genie. I bought her a spider necklace for her birthday. She loved it but wouldn't wear it in front of her friends. They claimed it bound her to hypocrisy and the will of the white man. Bullshit."

I pressed stop.

The spider spraypainted on the back wall of our house. Somebody knew about Mom's necklace. Somebody knew Oscar had given it to her. Who? Charles? Likely. Did he tell Valentina?

Why would Valentina want it? It wasn't hers. She never knew my mother. Why want a necklace of your boyfriend's dead wife?

Greed.

"What do you think, Walter?"

The rabbit licked my fingers.

I grabbed a handful of popcorn and pressed play.

"I'm dying, Jade. If I have any chance of staying out of Hell and reuniting with Genie, I need to come clean."

I sipped my wine.

"I convinced myself that we could make it work. Dealer and artist. I'd keep my business separate from Genie. Initially I wanted Genie's paintings to launder money and smuggle opium. But something changed ... I changed. I didn't want to taint Genie's art with my drugs. We used Darlene's paintings. She was more than happy. I thought it could work until Diego Lomas came to town."

Stop.

Did I want to hear more? Was I prepared for what I might learn? My finger hovered. I pressed play.

"Diego Lomas was Mexico's number one drug dealer. He heard about me and my opium. He wanted in. He came to Victoria and visited the gallery. We were in the basement where the backs of paintings were lined with opium and cash and framed. I gave him a sample.

"The problem was that Darlene hadn't created any new work. So Archie grabbed two of Genie's paintings and lined and framed them. I was pissed because Archie had used Genie's painting of my Lamborghini, Diego's favourite.

"Our boys were supposed to be watching the door, instead they were watching the Olympics hosted by Mexico City. The first games televised in colour. Genie showed up unexpectedly. The boys didn't notice her and she came downstairs when we were packing Diego's shipment. Diego was a disgusting man. He believed he owned everyone. Genie hated him, and I didn't want her around him.

"The asshole started harassing her. I told Genie to wait upstairs when Diego backhanded her."

Pause.

I grabbed more popcorn. *And?*

"I lost it."

I stopped chewing.

"I grabbed the first thing I saw. Darlene's red electric guitar. I swung that guitar like a baseball bat and crushed Diego's skull. I still remember the sound."

Red electric guitar.

I thought of the one Kate had found in the dungeon. Tell me the murder weapon used to kill Diego Lomas was not displayed in my office? "Ah shit," I said, sitting back.

"Ah, shit," Oscar said. There was the sound of a chair leg scraping against a floor. "In twenty seconds I had killed Diego Lomas. We were stunned. Then Diego's boys reached for their guns and Archie shot them." Oscar made the sound of gunshots.

"I grabbed Genie and her paintings and led her to the tunnel under the gallery. I told her to never come back. I didn't want her work tied to a crime scene. If anyone, police, Diego's boys, knew that Genie had witnessed Diego's murder, she would be hauled in for questioning or killed. Or both. I had sealed our fate. She would never be safe with me."

I gulped my wine and grabbed more popcorn.

"The next time I saw Genie was 1986. She was performing with the Vancouver Symphony Orchestra. She didn't know I was there until later. Charles was out of town. I met up with Genie that night in her dressing room."

Oh.

A long pause. I petted Walter.

"At first she didn't want to see to me. We talked. A lot. I was sad she wasn't creating art anymore."

I wonder why, Oscar?

"Genie had poured her creativity into her music."

Another long pause.

"We left her dressing room and went to her hotel room."

I popped a popcorn kernel in my mouth and reached for my wine glass.

And?

"We made love."

I froze. Wine glass inches from my lips.

"Nine months later you were born."

I couldn't move.

"I don't know any other way to say this, Jade. I'm your father."

My wine glass slipped from my fingers.

Oscar said other things but I wasn't comprehending anymore. Secret. No one know. Protect me. Protect Genie. Photos. Genie mailed him photos. Kept an eye on me. Paid for Sage's braces. Loved both girls. I ripped the earbuds from my ears.

I picked up the wine glass and, hand shaking, placed it on the table. I grabbed a towel and dabbed the red stain on the carpet, wiping in the tears that dropped from my cheeks.

Walter sniffed the stain.

I couldn't do this.

I sniffed.

I couldn't … do this … this … anymore.

I grabbed Walter and put him in his cage. I backed up, stumbling around the room. I paced between the sofa and the kitchen island. I couldn't do this. I might as well be in Walter's cage. Oscar. Mom. The lies. I was suffocating. I slipped on my shoes and coat, grabbed my keys and marched out of the condo.

19 RECKONING

"Do you remember? That day?"

I WALKED 2.5 KILOMETRES INTO THE CITY.
Numb.

At some point the clouds opened and released a downpour. I must have flipped up my hood but my hair still hung in wet ribbons around my face.

I didn't know where I was going. I didn't know where I was from. If anyone had asked my name, I would have said, "I don't know." I waited with others in a pack as the Johnson Street bridge lowered. The guard rail went up and people crossed. I hesitated. Who was I leaving behind? Jade Thyme? What truths waited on the other side? I stepped slow, purposeful. The wind pushed back. Not so easy.

I walked along the inner harbour.

Sticks and stones may break my bones but names will never hurt me.

Who was I?
Jade Thyme?
Jade Cooper?
Sage.
She was my sister.

No, *half sister.*
No.
She was my sister.

My real father supposedly loved me but could never be in my life. Sage's father, Charles, despised her and had been in her life.

I leaned against a stone wall. No wonder Charles never wanted anything to do with us. In his eyes, Sage was an abomination. And I, well, I was never his kid.

My phone buzzed in my hand.

I wanted to throw it in the harbour.

Text. Adam. *What are you doing?*

I snorted. Having a nervous breakdown. I turned around, realizing I stood across from The Empress Hotel. I wiped the raindrops from the screen and typed, *standing across the street. Outside The Empress.* Send.

A couple, arm in arm, laughed as they stumbled past.

Five guys lurched in my direction. I turned and faced the inner harbour.

My phone buzzed again.

Adam. *Be there in ten.*

I looked at the water, the light from the boats reflected in the ripples. The Legislature was lit up, outdoing the stars. *Where are you now, Mom? I could really do with an explanation. You couldn't have told me yourself? I had to hear it from a drug dealer.*

I pressed my fist to my lips and blinked. I was sad for her. Sad for what she had given up to protect me. Angry at her for falling in love with *him.* Wishing she had told me herself. Wishing that she was still around so I could talk to her. Wishing I could tell her that despite everything ... I loved her.

"Jade."

I turned.

Adam stood, the collar up on his coat.

"Did you know?" I demanded.

"You've been listening to the audio files."

"Did you know?"

"Yes."

"But you didn't tell me!"

"Would you have believed me? Or would you have thrown the thumbdrives at me and told me to fuck off?"

Possibly.

"A total stranger approaches you and says you're—" he stepped closer and lowered his voice "—Oscar Cooper's daughter."

I looked over the harbour. "Did Oscar pay you to protect me? Is there another part to this arrangement? Because Goddammit, now's the time to come clean, Adam."

"My part was to deliver the audio files and the keys. The thought of hanging around with Oscar Cooper's daughter scared the hell out of me."

The *burden* of that name, Cooper. I braced my hands against the wall, vibrating. "Adam, you are not helping. I'm flying without landing gear right now. I need something real. *Real.*"

He leaned against the wall, facing me. He looked at the water. "I was seven. You were five. We used to play matchbox cars."

Images of me clicked in my brain like a PowerPoint presentation but it was out of order. Running. The steps. The pumpkin of cars. Running. A little boy grabbing my hand. Running.

Adam.

I looked at him.

"You were the only girl who liked cars. You were the only girl who laughed at my jokes. Do you remember? That day?"

"There ... were men. They took—"

"You." Adam looked at the harbour again. "They pulled into the driveway. One guy went after you, but I grabbed your hand and we ran." Adam's voice broke. He looked over at The Empress.

"Steven Banks. He kicked you," I said.

"I let go and he grabbed you. You reached for me, knees bloody, crying, as he turned and ran with you to the car. Oscar and Dad went after him and the driver. Oscar brought you back on his motorcycle."

Adam cursed under his breath. He turned, hands braced on the stone wall, staring over the harbour. "I have played that day over and over. If I hadn't let go … if I hadn't let go, you wouldn't have been taken and your mom would still have visited Oscar. We could still have played cars. But after that day, you and your mom never came back."

I brushed tears from my cheeks.

"For years—" his voice broke "—I thought it was my fault."

I shook my head. "No."

"If we hadn't played cars. Those men would never have kidnapped you."

"Adam—"

"—Younghusband—" he jammed his hands in his coat pocket "—Younghusband is my mother's maiden name. My real name is Adam Malone. My father was Archie, Oscar's number one.

"I've known all along that you were Oscar's daughter." Adam let out a deep breath. "I believed if I told you I was Archie Malone's kid, *that kid* who let go, you'd hate me." He leaned his forearms on the wall, exhausted. I rubbed my hand across his shoulder blades.

"I wondered what happened to those men. My dad didn't come back with Oscar and you. I wondered if Dad was alive or dead. Oscar told me Dad had to take care of a few things. When Dad returned, he didn't look at me but went straight into the bathroom to wash up. There was blood on his clothes." Adam rubbed his forehead. "I knew then. Things had changed." He straightened. "I need a drink."

"Me too."

He looked me in the eye. "I'm sorry."

I held onto his arm. "It wasn't your fault."

I stepped forward, as did he, and we embraced. The drawbridge protecting my anxiety was pulled back up. No invasion tonight my friends.

Adam kissed the top of my head.

I breathed in the scent of his coat.

"Jade, we were dealt a bad deal."

"I know. This is going to get ugly, Adam. Our fathers murdered

those men … and somebody knows."
He tightened his embrace. "And, they're coming after you."

20 ICING SUGAR

*"Because it won't look suspicious, you digging a hole
and burying ... icing sugar."*

We walked across the street to The Empress and found a corner table at The Q-Bar, the hotel's lounge styled with mauve Art Deco inspired decor. I sat in a lime green chair; colourful art portraits of various queens hung behind the bar.

Adam ordered a plate of the black raspberry and perry oysters and a rum and Coke. I ordered a Concord, a signature cocktail, made with Casamigos mezcal and Giffard creme de violette. It was a beautiful lilac-coloured drink topped with egg white foam.

I asked what had happened after that horrible day and learned that two months later, Adam's mother no longer wanted custody.

"I lived in Victoria with my dad until I was thirteen," he said, picking up a shell, and sucking back an oyster. He wiped his mouth. "I asked him once about those men, and he gave me a warning backed up with threats of the strap if I ever brought it up again. I wasn't to talk to anyone about what I saw, who I was with or say anything about that afternoon. Not to Mom, not to a school counsellor, not to my dorky friends. No one. That afternoon was to disappear into a black hole and I was to forget about you."

"That's a big secret for a child," I said.

Adam finished his drink. "Especially when the bodies were found and every newspaper in the country wrote about it."

"You told no one?"

Adam nodded. "I became a little shit at school."

"No wonder."

"There was a really bad night at home. I was in grade eight and had the flu. I was upstairs. A man visited Dad. They got into a bad fight. Furniture breaking. I can't remember the reason. All I heard was the crashing. Dad kept a revolver in his nightstand. Loaded. I grabbed it."

I held an oyster shell in mid air. "What happened?"

"I stumbled downstairs into the kitchen and pointed the revolver at the man pummeling Dad. I told him to stop or I would blow his brains out."

"And?"

"He stopped. Dad was really messed up. Broken nose. Black eye. Both the man and Dad told me to put the gun down."

"Did you?"

"No bloody way. I was fixated on that man. I wanted to pull the trigger so bad."

"What happened?"

"I didn't know Oscar had arrived. He stepped into the kitchen and I nearly blew his head off."

I set the oyster on my plate. "Oh Jesus."

"Oscar walked up to me. My hands were shaking and I was still pointing the gun."

Adam swirled his glass, stirring up rum-fueled memories.

"Oscar told me to lower my arms. I did. He removed the gun from my hand. He then walked up to the man and pressed the muzzle against his forehead."

"Oh, God."

"He saved me, Jade. His prints were on the gun and if anyone was going to jail for murder, it would be Oscar, not me."

I reached for my cocktail glass. Empty. "Then what happened?"

"He told the man that if he ever said a word about what

happened, or came back to this house again, or hurt Archie or me, Oscar would find him and take him to the woods. The man took off. Dad cleaned himself up. Oscar told me to take a Tylenol and a shot of rye and go to bed."

"But you didn't."

"Hell no. I sat at the top of the stairs and listened to them. He and Dad argued. Dad didn't want to do it at first, but Oscar convinced him to send me to live with my aunt—"

"—In the U.K.," I interrupted.

"Yes. Oscar said if I stayed, I'd either end up like him, in juvy or dead."

"You were trying to protect your father, Adam."

Adam looked at me. "I wanted to kill that man and I just about did. Dad sent me away. I hated him for it."

"Did you ever see your father again?"

"No. I wrote a few letters but I got nothing in return. On my birthdays, my aunt would give me money from overseas. And at Christmas there was usually this ridiculously expensive toy under the tree from the Canadian Santa."

I smiled. "He wanted you to have a future."

"Yeah. He set up an education account for me when I came of age." Adam smiled. "So I joined the Royal Marines."

I laughed.

Adam looked at me for a long time, his gaze interrupted by the server who took away the discarded oyster shells.

"You took your mother's maiden name."

"Dad's idea, so no one would know who I really was."

I leaned back in my chair. "If you did that, then why couldn't the arsonist have done the same?"

"Who do you think changed their name?"

"Valentina."

"You believe Valentina Vale is—"

"—somebody else. She had ulterior motives for hooking up with Charles. Children of fraudsters change their names. What about the children of those men, the victims of the Grizzly Bear

Murders? What if one of their children is still alive?"

"That child could be anybody."

"Exactly."

"What's the connection to Valentina?" Adam asked.

"Maybe she defended them, or prosecuted them, or maybe they attended her remedial reading program."

"You're accusing Valentina of orchestrating your father's murder. For what reason? Your father's money? She's wealthier than him."

"With Valentina, it has to be personal. What could Charles or I have that she wants? It has to be more than the necklace."

The server returned and Adam took care of the bill. He walked me back to Coco's condo. He waited, hands in his coat pockets as I unlocked the door. I wanted to invite him in. I wanted to escape for a couple of hours into sexual bliss, where time stood still. But I didn't want to screw this up. Instead, he smiled and waved as I slowly closed the door.

The next morning, Sage returned from Gillian's and took Lizzy for a morning run. I fed Walter bunny kibble then sat in a lounge chair on the patio, gazing into the pond, sipping my Jabba Java raspberry truffle mocha.

Waiting.

Sage didn't know.

She knew I had spilled red wine on the carpet, which I later cleaned with doggie odour-resistant cleaner under Lizzy's and Walter's supervision. Sage didn't know the reason for the mishap.

"We're back," Sage said. She bustled around in the kitchen, opening, closing cabinets, telling Lizzy to sit then, "Good girl."

She joined me on the patio, sitting on the other chaise lounge. Wearing Lycra pants and a black-strap Lycra top, her shoulders and arms glistened. Beads of sweat on her temples and her hair pulled in a ponytail, she gulped from a Gatorade bottle. Lizzy lay by her feet.

"Good run?"

Sage twisted the cap on. "Excellent. This girl—" she patted Lizzy's head "—is the best running partner." She looked at me.

"What's up with you? You look tired."

"I was up late listening to the recordings."

"The reason for the spilled wine."

"We need to talk."

"Shoot."

How do I tell her? With Sage, straight up. "Sage—" I looked at her and glanced away.

"Spit it out. This better not have anything to do with Gillian."

"Hell no. I like Gillian. I like seeing you happy."

"Then what is it? You and Adam had sex on the sofa and Walter had to cover his eyes."

I wish. "No. Charles ... is not my real father."

Sage's mouth dropped open. "Say what?"

"Charles Thyme is not my real father."

"Then who the hell is?"

I looked at my mocha. Was it too early to add Baileys? Or what about that small bottle of espresso vodka in the cupboard? "Oscar Cooper."

The colour drained from her face. "What are you talking about? You haven't been—"

"—I haven't taken anything. I can get the audio and you can listen yourself. Oscar and Mom knew each other way back. They broke up and didn't see each other until September of 1986."

"How do you know he's telling the truth? That he's not messing with you?"

"Because he also admitted to murdering Diego Lomas with an electric guitar."

I didn't think Sage could get more pale.

"Mom witnessed it. She was twenty, twenty-one. That's why they broke up. They never saw each other until after she performed with the Vancouver Symphony Orchestra. Oscar visited her after her performance. Charles was out of town and that's when—"

"—Stop." Sage patted Lizzy's head. "Am I still Charles Thyme's daughter?"

Her voice sounded distant, like when she was a child and

something bothered her.

"Yes."

She kept patting Lizzy's head. "How do you know?"

"The last time Mom saw Oscar was in 1992 when the Banks brothers tried to kidnap me—"

"—Kidnap you?!"

"Yes. The memories, they're fragmented. I'll remember one thing and then another memory will pop up like a hand puppet, shouting 'remember this traumatic incident when you were five.' I was five when the Banks brothers attempted to kidnap me. Mom never saw Oscar after that. Sage, nothing changes between us. We're still sisters."

"Half-sisters," she said quietly.

I sat at the edge of the chaise lounge and shook her knee. "Look at me."

She looked up, her eyes tearful.

"We're sisters and don't you ever think otherwise. Remember when you were seven and left the harmonica outside? Who helped you wash your mouth out after you tried playing it, not knowing it had become infested with earwigs?"

Sage squirmed. "You did."

"That's right. You were hysterical. I don't blame you."

She brushed a tear aside and squeezed my hand. "You told me that if an earwig had made it into my stomach, my stomach acids would blast it like the Imperial Army's Death Star in Star Wars."

"Exactly. And then what did we do?"

"We walked to the Dairy Queen and you bought me a chocolate-dipped cone."

"That's right. Which three hours later caused you to have severe stomach cramps, because we didn't know you were lactose intolerant."

Sage looked at me. "Anyone else know about these files?"

"Adam."

Sage nodded. "That's why all this shit's happening, Jade. Someone knows Oscar Cooper is your real father. Many people would be thrilled to seek revenge on Oscar's only surviving child."

I brought my knee up and propped my elbow on it. Sage was right. The repercussions not only on my career, my real father being a drug dealer, but also … my life.

"If Oscar's enemies get wind of the audio, that he wanted Adam to write his memoir, a tell-all, they don't know what Oscar may have spilled. Oscar donated to charities. He was in powerful social and political circles. He knew people in power and that's why he was able to get away with what he did. If you're a stinking rich CEO of a tech company and Oscar's memoir comes out, you don't want any connection to it."

Once again I felt my Jenga supports teetering.

Sage patted my shoulder. "Sadly, my dear sister, Oscar may have come clean of his sins, but intentionally or unintentionally, he has made you a target."

I had been in shock learning that Oscar Cooper was my father. Oscar admitted to killing Diego Lomas. Others in the drug world would want to know what Oscar admitted, or whom he implicated.

"Have you listened to all the audio files?" Sage asked.

"Yes. Oscar mentions Mom's paintings. Do you have them, or were they destroyed in the fires?"

"I have three of them."

"Where?"

"Here. Why?"

"I want to check the backs."

"What about you?" Sage asked. "Do you have any paintings?"

"A few. Mother didn't keep an inventory. There could be more out there. Oscar wanted me to find all of them, but—" I threw my hands up in the air "—God knows how many are out there."

"Follow me. They're inside." Sage stood and Lizzy and I followed. "I was planning on taking them to my place, but kept forgetting. Thank God," Sage said, as she slid three flat boxes out from beside her art desk. I flipped the lid open and Sage and I saw a bright image of a redhead playing an electric guitar, sitting on a blue shiitake mushroom inside a psychedelic shell.

A lump formed in my throat when I saw Mother's signature on the bottom. "Why the hell did she stop creating art?" I picked up the framed picture. Heavy. "Hold this, please." I stood and grabbed two knives from the kitchen drawer.

"What are you doing?"

I kneeled. "Taking off this frame. Back up, Lizzy," I said, as Lizzy sniffed my hand holding the knife.

Sage pulled Lizzy back.

I undid the screws, pulled the back off and removed a cardboard sheet. There was a cushy plastic layer. I looked at Sage.

"Is that what I think it is?" she asked.

"Let's find out." With the sharp knife I slit the plastic and pulled the two sides apart. "Holy crap." I picked out one clear plastic-wrapped bundle.

Sage held Lizzy, who strained her neck, sniffing. "Hundred dollar bills." She looked at the back of the painting. "That's a fourteen by eighteen-inch wide frame." She rubbed her forehead.

Lizzy sniffed the bundle of cash in my hand from corner to corner.

"What do you smell on that, Lizzy? Heroin? Opium?"

"Do you think Mom knew?" Sage asked.

"I have no idea. I have never seen these paintings hung in the house. You found them in the basement, right?"

"Right."

We pushed the picture to the side and Sage pulled out the second one. It was a painting of a black 1955 Porsche Roadster.

"I want this one," she said.

We unscrewed the back, cut the plastic and found more bills.

"How many bills do you think are in a bundle?" Sage asked.

I counted the number of bundles and thought of how many bills the debit machine could take. Fifty bills max. These bundles were the thickness of four cellphones stacked on top of each other, four bundles across and eight bundles in length. "There could be anywhere from ten to thirty thousand dollars cash lining the back of this one frame."

"I feel lightheaded. Shall we see what's behind picture number three?" She slid it out and handed it to me.

It was a painting of a pool and garden in India. Beautiful. I had the frame off within seconds, slit the plastic and saw a puff of white powder.

Lizzy strained under Sage's hold.

"No, no, Lizzy." I pulled the plastic apart and saw not cash, but packets of white powder. "If that's not icing sugar, we have just committed an offence under section six of the *Controlled Drugs and Substances Act*." I dropped the knife and pressed my hands to my face.

"What's section six of the *Controlled Drugs and Substances Act*?"

"No person shall possess a substance blah blah blah and we definitely have more than one kilogram of a substance."

"And given how Lizzy is sniffing the plastic, I don't think this is for making royal icing."

"We are sitting on roughly thirty thousand in cash and who knows the street value of whatever this is. Does opium have an expiration date? Opium is more of a brown colour. Cocaine?" I waved my hand over the picture. "I have no way of getting this tested. What am I supposed to do? Walk into the police department and say, hey, how's your day going? Do you mind testing this packet of white powder that I found behind one of my mother's paintings and tell me what it is? And if it is what I think it is, guess what, there's plenty more." I rubbed my forehead. I could feel the headache, a light throb by my right temple.

"Jade, this is my kind of problem."

I stared at my sister. "You stash drugs?"

"No. Just let me think for a minute. You can't make this decision because then you'll be implicated. My people can help. No questions asked."

"The more people who know about this, the bigger our chances of discovery." Jesus. I sounded like a criminal.

"Bigger chances of *my* discovery. You're not going to be there. I've got this."

Sage pulled the powder packets out of the back of the picture. "You are going to put the frames back on these pictures, including the two with the money stashed behind them."

"And what are you doing with the—"

"—*Icing sugar*?" Sage looked at me. "I'm going to Mom and Charles's old house, our torched house."

"Why?"

"To bury the icing sugar."

"Sage, that's not the greatest idea."

Sage reached for her gym bag and dragged it over. "No one will know. We don't know what this stuff really is." She tossed out sweaty gear and dropped in the icing sugar packets. "Who are the legal owners of that house?"

"We are."

"Before then."

"Da—" I just about said it. "Charles."

"He never thought I'd amount to anything and he's dead. For all we know this could have been his icing sugar. Reasonable doubt."

Sage sounded like a lawyer. "Because it won't look suspicious, you digging a hole and burying … *icing sugar*."

"Better than a body," she said.

"Now you're scaring me."

"I don't want you anywhere near—"

"—the icing sugar," we said together.

21 ANGEL'S COUNSEL

"She's here. You can see her. The garden ghost."

I HAD TO DO SOMETHING WHILE SAGE WAS DOING HER confectionary disposal. I decided to go to Charles's place in Cordova Bay and see if I could find the spider necklace.

I parked my Royal Enfield at the curb and glanced at Charles's pristine home. I wondered about the type of halfway house in which Oscar had spent his dying days.

Charles had died here.

Suicide.

My ass.

I hung my bike helmet off the handlebars and walked toward the front door. Charles Thyme may not have been my father, but he had been my guardian. Stone had given me Charles's house key, which I fingered on my keyring. I unlocked the door and stepped in.

I stood on the Italian tiles in the foyer. Lifeless. I pulled open the white doors leading into the living room. The large sofas and armchairs, the white fluffy area rug. I was a voyeur, no biological connection to the man who had lived here. I had been the intruder in his life. Did he know? Was that the reason he never wanted me to call him Dad?

In his bedroom I stopped and looked again at the desk. Everything was the same except ... not. Cellphone charger, printer and mouse pad. Check. Glass tumbler and empty bottle of Jack Daniels.

Jack Daniels. I'd take a swig, too, if I had been reading the newspaper articles, which ... were gone.

Who took them?

Who had a key?

Valentina.

That little bitch. What are you hiding?

Now, I was determined. Could there be anything left here that I had missed, and hopefully she had missed? I pulled open the closet and saw a billion ties hanging from a sagging tie rack. Sage and I would have to deal with all this. Not just ties, but his belongings. I pushed suits from one side of the closet to the other. No incriminating phone number scribbled on a piece of paper in a coat pocket. No secret door. Not even a safe. I opened dresser drawers, pushed around socks and underwear. Another drawer, golf shorts neatly folded, and the next drawer contained, golf shirts and sandwiched between a Ralph Lauren and a Versace Medusa Polo shirt, I felt an envelope.

I grabbed it and pulled out a private investigator's report. I flipped the page over. Charles had hired a P.I. to follow Valentina.

Not all sunshine and lollipops in their relationship. I sat on the floor, leaning against the bed.

There was a photo of Dennis Sullivan with Valentina when they were teenagers, leaning against each other. Steven and Jeffrey Banks stood beside them. There was another picture of them. They must have been around 10, sitting in a two-seater toy car. Between them kneeled another little girl and written in Charles's handwriting was the name 'Kathy Banks'. This sweet little girl would grow up and get shot in a drug raid. The daughter of Steven Banks, the victim of the Grizzly Bear Murders. Someone with a pencil had circled Dennis and Kathy's faces. What's special about them? Are they related? I studied the photo.

He's not dead yet, Mother had said in the graveyard, when Adam and I were looking for Victor Banks's plot.

Adam and I sitting in The Q-Bar and Adam confirming that he had taken on his mother's maiden name.

I looked at Dennis Sullivan.

Dennis, Dennis, Dennis. Who are you? Kathy's brother? Did you change your name from Victor Banks to Dennis Sullivan? Valentina defended you before the Law Society. You were all friends. If you and Kathy are Steven Banks's children, who are you Valentina?

I spread the pages out in a row on the carpet and took photos. I tucked them back into the envelope and replaced the envelope in Charles's dresser drawer.

I checked another dresser with zero results. I moved into the bathroom, its walls lined with white subway tiles. The shower was as big as my first apartment. Unlike my apartment, this shower had disco lighting and a stereo system.

Nice.

"Charles could listen to Vivaldi's *Four Seasons* while lathering up."

I spun around.

Mother sat legs crossed on the *throne*.

"Dear God, Mother. Can you please give me a little warning next time?"

"Like this?"

Water sprinkled from the rain shower.

I crossed my arms, smiling, and leaned against the shower door. "What are you doing here?"

"I could ask you the same."

"I'm looking for your spider necklace."

"Have you found it?"

"No. I think it was in the house. You wouldn't happen to remember where you left it? Any insider information you wish to share with your daughter?"

"I put it somewhere safe."

"That being?"

A sad look ghosted Mother's face, which I'd have thought impossible given she was a ghost. "I can't remember. I hid it a long time ago. You've checked the house?"

"Yes, which by the way, someone torched. People are after us, Sage and me. I thought it had to do with ... Charles's death, but Charles has nothing to do with it. He was collateral damage. He couldn't provide useful information so he was discarded. This, whatever this is, has to do with Oscar Cooper. The man you loved. My father."

"You know."

"It would have been nice to have learned from you."

"Oscar was scared for our safety. I was scared. It was best if no one knew, but still people found out. You were a targeted kidnapping." Mom looked at me. "Do you remember—"

"—being kidnapped? I have images of a man walking toward me. Running. I remember Adam being there."

"He's the man you've been spending time with."

"Yes. Oscar hired him to find me and give me what's turning into an audiobook. Why would Oscar do that?"

"Oscar and I had a deal. He would never contact you while he still had air in his lungs."

"He had someone else contact me after he was dead."

Mother shook her head. "Oscar could have anything except fatherhood. You always want what you can't have.

"We foolishly thought we could keep you a secret. But that day when you were taken, those men ... the rage and sorrow I felt was like nothing I had felt before. Oscar wasn't the only person who wanted them dead."

"So he killed them—"

"—to send a message. I told Oscar he would never see you, or me, again. I would not risk some other thug kidnapping you, or Sage, or worse, killing you two out of revenge."

"How did he take it?"

"He wasn't angry at me. He was angry that he couldn't protect you. That was the tipping point. Because after that incident, if anyone crossed him, he'd kill them. No second chance to go after his family."

"Did Charles know?"

"Eventually."

"So you had an affair?"

Mother uncrossed her leg and crossed the other. "Yes."

Neither she nor I said anything for a moment.

"Oscar was always good to me, Jade, and he was good to you and Sage. He paid for a lot of things."

"He was a drug dealer."

"He was a rough diamond. I loved one facet of that diamond."

"He was a drug dealer. My real father was a *drug dealer*. What were you thinking falling in love with *him*?"

"Jade."

I recognized that tone of *back off*.

"He was not a good boyfriend choice," she agreed. "Yes, I'm guilty of adultery. Yes, I saw what I wanted to see. But do I regret any time I spent with him? No. Why? Because I got you." She brushed a tear.

I felt guilty. I had made my mother, a ghost, cry. I sat on the edge of the tub. "I'm sorry."

"I can imagine it was quite the surprise."

"So why are you here?"

"I need your help, darling."

"Excuse me? You're in Heaven—you are, right?"

"Sort of."

"Sort of?"

"Well, Remedial—" she rolled her eyes and stood, floating over to the mirror. She touched her fingers to her cheeks. "I'm trying to get Oscar into Heaven and I need your help."

"*Excuse me?* Shouldn't you be trying to get yourself out of Remedial, whatever the hell that means."

"God's not listening."

"Why are you in Remedial?"

"You're a lawyer. Help me negotiate with Him."

"Why are you in Remedial?" I repeated.

Mother looked at her feet then at the shower. "It's a long story. Besides, I'm working on getting myself out. Nobody likes me there."

"Well, what did you do?"

"*Nothing.*"

There was that tone again. Mother had most definitely done *something*.

She brushed a strand of hair back. "Tell me," she said, her voice calmer, "how to make a case before God. I don't expect Oscar to be in the Best Behaviour category, but there's room in Remedial since the politician got bumped back to earth."

I was gobsmacked.

"Jade, say something. You're an excellent lawyer from what I've heard through the heavenly grapevine."

"Yes. But … because of *Oscar*, Sage and I are in this mess. Because of people he either killed or beat, or God-knows-what, tied to a tree, someone killed Charles, your husband, and made it look like an overdose and is trying to kill Sage and me. And then Oscar leaves these audio files because he wants to write a memoir, and you want me to prepare a case on Oscar's behalf before *God*."

"Yes."

I wanted to say Oscar could rot in Hell but didn't. I rubbed my eyes. "I can't believe this. I'm now angel's counsel."

"It has a nice ring to it."

I heard a tinkle of bells.

I glared.

Mother smiled. "Better than being the devil's advocate."

I groaned. "So—" I couldn't believe I was having this conversation "—speaking of Hell and damnation, the supernatural, is Oscar haunting Norman's typewriter?"

"Oscar's haunting Norman's old typewriter?"

"Someone or something is and it scared the hell out of Norman. He's gone. I can see you, why can't I see Oscar, and what is possessing the typewriter?"

"Well, I'm no expert but because Oscar has one foot in Hell, he's dealing with different protocols. Maybe a hellish MOU. I understand it's very bureaucratic down there. A lot of red tape."

I laughed, and I was about to ask if it was bureaucratic in Heaven when I heard a thump outside. Mother and I looked at each other. I walked into the living room, and through the French doors saw Dr. Vlasic moving around in the greenhouse.

"The funny man," Mother said.

I looked at her.

"He whispers to the orchids."

How did she know? "You haven't been tormenting him?"

"No. He's very forgetful and forgets to water some plants, so sometimes I'll slide a flowerpot that needs watering across the workbench."

Oh dear. The poor man. "Stay here, please. I'd like a conversation with him without moving plants."

Mother frowned.

I stepped outside and walked along the dirt path that twisted between trees and birdhouses toward the white framed greenhouse with a stone foundation. Dr. Vlasic moved around, muttering, holding a yellow watering can, testing the soil of various tomato plants. The greenhouse door open, I still knocked. "Dr. Vlasic."

He jumped, dropping the watering can.

Oh Mother. You *have* tormented him.

"Oh. Oh. Ms. Thyme. I—" he stepped forward and picked up the watering can.

"—It's nice to see you, Dr. Vlasic. May I come in? Am I interrupting?"

Relief showed on his face. "No. Please." He looked around and pulled up a wobbly stool. He brushed off dirt and indicated for me to sit. "Would you like some tea? Oolong." He held up his tea cup.

"No thank you. This is a beautiful greenhouse," I said, looking around as I sat.

Dr. Vlasic drank from his cup. "Generous of your father to let me use it."

Except Charles is not my father. "Dr. Vlasic, I was hoping I could ask you some questions."

"Yes, yes." He turned to what looked like a strawberry plant. He looked back at me again, maybe confirming that I was human and not a ghost, before trimming long shoots.

"What do you know about Valentina Vale?"

He clipped a stalk. "Oh no."

"He's not supposed to prune that."

I spun around and saw Mother hovering in the rafters.

"*Mother*," I hissed.

She put her finger to her lips to *shh* me.

Really! "Ahem, Dr. Vlasic, let me be more specific. Did Valentina and Charles seem happy? Did they argue?"

He clipped at the plant. "Valentina … she is purposeful."

"Meaning Charles was a means to an end?"

"Charles was very in love with Valentina. Valentina was not in love with Charles."

"I see." *So Valentina wielded the power in their relationship.*

"Valentina has goals. She—" he looked at the hummingbird feeder hanging outside "—Valentina is the Rufous hummingbird."

I smiled. "Really, how so?"

"Rufous hummingbird, beautiful but the bully of all hummingbirds. Chases other hummingbirds from a feeder. Resilient. Can fly for miles."

"So who was Valentina chasing away?"

"No one." Dr. Vlasic turned to me. "Charles was a wealthy man. Valentina came to feed." He turned back to his plant. "Valentina has a foundation. She wanted Charles to donate."

"To the reading program?"

"Yes. Charles refused."

"Why?"

"One day Valentina had Detective Reeves over."

My heart flipped. "Oh."

"Charles returned from golfing and he caught her giving Detective Reeves a duffel bag."

"Really."

"Valentina and your father had a big fight. It wasn't their first. Valentina left. Charles saw me here. He came out and sat where you are, drinking his Jack Daniels."

"He didn't trust her?"

"He told me he had hired a private detective. That Valentina was dangerous, and not who she pretended to be."

"When was this?"

"A month before he died."

"He kept seeing her?"

"Of course he did," Mother answered.

"He said he had no choice."

"Everyone has a choice," Mother and I said together.

"Ms. Thyme, Charles was concerned about his safety and yours."

"Did Charles indicate who Valentina really was?"

"He said, and I didn't comprehend, but he said, good thing Genie dead." Dr. Vlasic turned. "Her past—" he waved the pruning sheers "—coming back to haunt, or something like that."

I looked at Mother, who even for a ghost, looked paler.

Mother floated from the rafters. "How old is Valentina?" she asked me.

"Valentina is eighteen years older than me. Dr. Vlasic, if I have any more questions, can I stop by?"

Dr. Vlasic looked around. "She's here. You can see her. The garden ghost."

I smiled. "It's only you and me, Dr. Vlasic."

The greenhouse door slammed.

I jumped.

Mother was gone.

Dr. Vlasic looked at me. "Can you ask her to stop moving the plants?"

I smiled and said good-bye. I rode to the burnt house to check on Sage. My bike parked, I walked around the blue wire fence toward the back. A squirrel darted, stopped, looked at me, chirped a warning and disappeared into the shrubs. I glanced at the shell of a home–one of Tolkien's Two Towers.

I ducked maple tree branches and tromped around pink azalea shrubs. If desolate had a smell this was it.

I made my way toward the moon gate and saw Sage in the distance, tying Charles's small boat to the dock. She walked toward me.

"I thought you were digging?" I said.

"More like dumping. I'm not telling you anything else. The icing sugar is taken care of."

"I feel like we're having a conversation in the White House. Where's Lizzy?"

"She wasn't well. She wouldn't eat her kibble and her stomach gurgled non-stop. I made her white rice. I figured let her rest while I take care of this. Any luck at Charles's finding the necklace?"

"No." I stepped beside Sage. "I spoke with Dr. Vlasic."

"And?"

"Charles had hired a detective to look into Valentina, and he had told Dr. Vlasic that Mom's past had finally caught up to her. Charles was worried about our safety."

"More likely your safety." Sage looked to her left.

"What's wrong?"

"I thought I heard a car."

"I heard nothing. It's this place. Did you find the necklace? Anything? Anything at all?"

"No," Sage said, kicking burnt embers. "A lot of ash and soot. The necklace must be here but I doubt we'll find it." Sage pulled back fencing so we could step through.

"But you still want to take a quick look."

"Yes. Before this place is demolished."

I saw the ash on her slacks. "We shouldn't be wandering through here."

"I know," she said, pushing open the back door. "There've been squatters. I saw potato chip bags and beer bottles in what was the living room. One fraction of this home wasn't touched by the fire, but there's smoke damage. This used to be the kitchen."

A creepy feeling came over me as I looked at the blackened stove and charred kitchen cabinets. Ash covered the floor. "Sage, we should go."

"A quick look. Where else could the necklace be?" She pulled open drawers. "People are torching our property, threatening us. Why? There has to be more of a reason than you being Oscar's daughter."

As strange as that sounded, I was getting used to the idea. Right now, though, Sage was obviously stressed and not thinking logically. "Sage, I doubt Mother hid the necklace in the kitchen."

"What did Oscar do—" Sage said, opening cupboards "—to make someone want to get back at you? All because of a necklace? I don't think so."

"Do you want to see my tattoo?"

Sage and I spun around.

Dennis Sullivan stood.

"You're trespassing, Dennis. You need to go," I ordered.

He stepped forward. "Why? What are you two doing?"

"Nothing," I said. "You need to leave. Now." I pulled out my phone.

Dennis pulled out a gun and aimed it at Sage. "Put the phone down, Jade." He moved closer to us.

I slid my phone into my pants pocket, hoping I had dialled 911. "There's no need for the gun, Dennis. What do you want?"

Dennis stepped toward Sage. "I like you. I send you pictures on Instagram."

Sage stood still.

"You're pretty." He reached to touch her when Sage batted his hand.

Dennis grabbed her wrist and yanked her against him, the gun muzzle against her temple.

"Dennis," I said, my voice dropping a pitch, "let her go."

"You have to see my tattoo."

"I don't want to see your stupid tattoo," Sage gasped.

I stepped closer. "Dennis, get out."

"No," he shouted. "Sage is going to see my tattoo."

"I don't want to see it. Now *let go*."

He pressed the gun muzzle under her jaw. "It's of you."

I felt sick.

Sage bit his wrist.

He screamed and hit her on the back of the head with the gun.

I tackled him, drilling my shoulder into his mid-section, sprawling us onto the floor. His gun slid out of reach.

Sage scrambled from under him and grabbed a chair.

I lurched to my feet, finding myself looking down the barrel of a gun. I looked up.

Osmond.

"Sage, put the chair down," Osmond said, staring at me. "Or Jade's going to get hurt."

I heard the clatter of a chair behind me.

"Dennis." Osmond kicked Dennis's gun across the floor.

Dennis grabbed it and stood.

Osmond nodded at Sage.

Dennis drilled his fist into Sage's face. She spun, dropping to the floor, nose bleeding.

"Stop it. Let her go," I said.

Osmond grabbed me by my coat and slammed me back against the wall. "Like you've got a say in this."

Dennis stepped over Sage, turned her over and backhanded her.

"Stop hitting her."

He smiled at me then grabbed Sage's wrists and dragged her out of the room.

22 Dirty Cop

"Women aren't the only ones who can weaponize sex."

"STOP HIM!"

Osmond tightened his grip. "Shut up."

I gasped. "Os—"

"—I said, shut it." He again banged my body against the wall. My head throbbed. I stared at him. Not understanding, wanting him to stop Dennis. I heard a crash from the other room.

"Where's the money? The audio files? The paintings. Give it to me and Deranged Dennis leaves Sage alone."

"I don't have—"

Osmond's eyes narrowed and he again banged me against the wall. "Not the right answer, Jade."

"*No*," Sage yelled from the other room.

"Tell me what you know and I'll stop Dennis from raping your sister."

I squirmed. "We only have cash. *Cash*. The back of the pictures. That's it," I pleaded. "I'll give it to you. Let Sage go."

"That's not all Oscar left you."

Sage screamed.

"Stop him!" I kicked against the wall and tried to swing at Osmond.

He stepped back, letting me go, then backhanded me. My body twisted. I hit the kitchen cupboard, and slid to the floor. I pushed myself to my hands and knees. I heard another scream.

Osmond grabbed me around the waist and rammed me against the wall, my face pressed against it, my ears ringing. "Tell me." He turned me around, his hand gripping my throat. "Where is it?"

I gulped. "You're ... choking—"

He flung me toward the kitchen table. I grabbed onto the edge but still fell to the floor.

"Do you really think I came back into your life because I *liked* you?"

I crawled, following the blood splatters on the tile, sensing him behind me. "I'll give it to you." Blood dripped from my nose. "All of it. Sage's house. Let Sage go."

Osmond stepped in front of me and kneeled. I scrambled backwards.

"It's called a honey trap for a reason, Jade. Find a pathetic woman starved for a little attention." He pushed aside the upturned table. "Show her some affection, screw her and she'll tell you anything."

"You can have all of it."

His cell vibrated.

"Women aren't the only ones who can weaponize sex. Rogue cop, fighting the bad guys, sleeping with the successful lawyer, like a romance novel." He grabbed my coat collar. "I had you eating out of my hand."

I scooped handfuls of ash. "Eat *this*." I mashed my hands into his eyes.

He screamed, covering his face with his hands, and stumbled toward the sink.

I ran down the hall.

Sage.

I stopped at a doorway where I saw Sage, face down on a charred pool table, hands tied behind her back, her leggings and underwear around her ankles.

Dennis stood behind her, undoing his belt. "... I'll show you my tat—"

Noooo. Armchair. Fireplace. Firepoker. I lunged, grabbed and swung. I heard the snap as the firepoker struck Dennis behind the right knee.

He screamed and dropped.

I swung again, this time hitting him in the shoulder. He screamed again, wide-eyed.

I stepped back, lost my balance and crashed against the pool table, pulling Sage over onto the floor with me.

"*Sage!*" She lay, eyes open but unfocused.

I stumbled to my feet and moved toward Dennis lying on the floor. I raised the firepoker above my head.

"Stop."

Osmond again had his gun pointed at me, his eyes bloodshot, streaks of wet ash on his face.

I clutched the firepoker.

"Put it down."

This firepoker was my only defence.

"Dennis, get up." Osmond kicked his foot. "Drop it, Jade."

I stepped forward, vibrating, clutching the firepoker like a baseball bat. "*No.*" My voice came out raw, like an injured animal. "You hurt me." I swung the poker.

Osmond and Dennis stepped back.

"You hurt my sister."

I swung again. "You come near us and I'll take your God damn head off."

Osmond's eyes widened. His hand wavered. "Dennis, we gotta go. Bikers."

Dennis struggled to his feet. Blood soaked through his pantleg. He staggered and glared at me.

Osmond lowered his gun. "If I don't find what I'm looking for, I'm coming for you and he'll kill her dog." He stepped backwards then turned and took off after Dennis.

I wanted to kill him.

"Jade."

Sage.

I dropped the firepoker and pulled Sage upright. "Hey," I cradled her head in my hands. "You with me? Come on, girl."

She moaned, her head hanging forward. She pulled her leggings up and leaned against the pool table.

She had a cut on the side of her head, a bleeding nose and a split lip.

"Sage." I did up the buttons on her shirt. "Hey, talk to me. Come on, girl."

"I'm here." Her fingers trembled as she touched the cut over her temple. "He hit me. Something hard. I saw black."

"We gotta get out of here."

"Help coming?" She rubbed her wrists.

I stopped for a second, remembering what Osmond had said. "I think so." I slipped my shoulder under her arm and grabbed the firepoker. "One step at a time, and God help anyone who comes close to us." We lumbered down the hall and out the back door.

I heard bikes and looked up to see Bob and Henri. A passenger sat behind Henri. The bikes stopped, the passenger jumped off and ran toward us, undoing their helmet. Adam. I dropped the firepoker.

"Jade. Sage. Dear God." He stepped back, giving us space. He ran his hands through his hair. "I'll call an ambulance?"

"I'm fine," Sage croaked.

"Jade. Sage," Bob said. "I'm so sorry."

"Not your fault," Sage said. "A couple of Band Aids and a little gin."

Henri rubbed his face. "We are very sorry, Miss Thyme. Your father'd kill us if he saw what happened. We failed him. We failed you."

My father.

What else did Oscar Cooper leave you? Osmond had asked.

"How did you find us?" I asked as we walked toward our bikes.

"You pocket dialled me," Adam said, looking sheepish. "I heard. I tried getting here as soon as I could, bringing reinforcements. I ... I activated the GPS on your phone before I gave it to you."

Sage looked at him. "Thank you."

"I wish I was quicker."

"We need to go home," she said, pulling away from me, sitting on her bike.

"Sage, you can't ride," I said.

"Like hell I can't." She grimaced as she pulled on her motorcycle helmet. She looked at me, tears in her eyes. "We have to get home before Dennis kills Lizzy."

We clambered onto our bikes. Engines rumbled, we followed Sage, taking back roads and shortcuts.

We arrived at the condo. Sage lumbered inside. I followed with Adam on my heels.

Inside, Lizzy sat up in her bed. Sage dropped to her knees and hugged her. She motioned for Bob and Henri to come forward. They talked in low voices.

"I wish you had told me where you were going," Adam said, standing next to me.

"I just returned to our old home."

Adam looked at my cheek. "Who did that to you?"

"Osmond." Where was that gin?

"The asshole at the cemetery?"

Bob stepped away from Sage, who still hugged Lizzy as she quietly spoke to her.

I couldn't look at Henri or Adam.

"The man the police warned you about at your office," Adam said.

"Yes."

"We've got to report this," Adam said, voice raised.

"No cops," Henri said.

Bob took out a box of dog treats and gave it to Sage. He then stepped out onto the patio and made a phone call.

Adam looked from Henri to Bob. "So what are you going to do?

Give him a pair of cement shoes?" Adam asked.

Henri smiled. "That's old school. No cops."

Sage gave Lizzy treat after treat. Lizzy rested her head on her thighs. Sage leaned forward, patting her head. "Thank you, Lizzy." She sniffed. "Momma's had a rough day."

Bob walked back in and kneeled beside her, patting Lizzy. "I called her. She said they'll be here soon."

Sage nodded.

Who was she?

"Sage, we escort the Dolls off the island, make sure no one bothers them."

"Bob, that's kind of you, but the Dolls don't need an escort."

"Sage. We want to help."

"Fine," she said.

"Excuse me." I walked to the bathroom, closed the door, and locked it. My hands gripped the glass circular sink basin. Keep it together. I slowly looked at my reflection. Dark blood stains on my shirt, bruising on my neck and dried blood under my nose. One cheek was the colour of a ripe avocado. The woman staring back at me was a scared shadow. Not a confident lawyer. I turned on the taps, splashing water on my face, trying to wash away shame, choking back tears.

Honey trap.

I pressed my face into a towel. Keep it together. Sage had it worse. It all could have been much worse. I fished around in my purse and found a bottle of Tylenol. I popped the lid and shook out Vicodin.

"Jade, are you okay?" Sage called through the door.

"Yes." I dumped the Vicodin back into the bottle and dropped it in my purse. I opened the door and looked at my sister's bruised face. "I need Tylenol."

"I have some. Come on." I followed her into the kitchen and she gave me two which I chased with the gin. Sage, Bob and Henri talked about something but I wasn't listening. Adam stood across from me. I could feel him looking at me, but I couldn't look at him.

We heard the rumble. Bikes. Lots of them.

"Who's here?" I asked.

"Friends," Sage said, clipping on Lizzy's leash. She grabbed the doggles and opened the door. She and Lizzy stepped outside followed by Bob and Henri.

I stepped forward when Adam put his hand on my arm. "Don't … say anything right now."

He rubbed my arm. "If you need anything …"

I nodded and we stepped outside.

The MotoCityDolls, Sage's motorcycle gang, rode side by side. They had saved me once before when I was looking into my ex-husband's murder. Now, they were saving Lizzy. They pulled into the circular drive in front of the condo, causing a lot of head turns. One biker, dresssed in a blue jean jacket and jeans covered with black chaps, had a sidecar and stopped before Sage and Lizzy. She turned off the engine and flipped up the visor. "Sage. You tell me the son-of-a-bitch who did that to you?"

This biker with the pretty blue eyes was obviously the *she,* Bob had called. I detected a French accent.

"In time. Thank you for coming, Coco."

This was Coco? I remembered her having braids, braces and Barbies.

"This is Lizzy," Coco said, leaning over the sidecar, petting her with her leather-gloved hand. Lizzy's tail whacked Sage's leg.

"You ride with me, Lizzy, ici." Coco patted the sidecar.

Lizzy jumped in.

"She knows French," Coco said.

Sage knelt and slipped doggles over Lizzy's eyes. "You get to go for a bike ride, Lizzy." She gave Coco the leash which she clicked into the safety catch on her side.

Lizzy pawed Sage's arm, as if to say, come on, get in.

Sage sniffed. "No. I can't go with you, girl." Her voice broke. She sniffed again.

Lizzy pawed her arm a second time.

"You silly dog," Sage said, wiping her cheeks with her sleeve.

"You'll be safe this way." She rubbed the dog's neck with one hand, then slid her hands around the dog's jowls, looking her in the eye. "I promise. I'll come get you when this is done. Momma's gotta take care of some bad people."

Lizzy whimpered.

I brushed tears from my cheeks. Adam rubbed my shoulder.

Sage stood and stepped back. "Bob and Henri want to be on the ride."

Bob and Henri were already seated on their bikes.

"It's all good, Sage," Coco said, petting Lizzy. "Lizzy will have a good time with my dog, Neville. I feed Lizzy pastries."

Sage nodded. "If anything happens to me—" she swallowed.

"Arrête ça."

Stop it.

"No. If anything happens to me, or Jade, or if I get arrested—"

Arrested?

"—the Dolls and I, we look after Lizzy and then we kill the son-of-a-bitch who hurt you. No witnesses." Coco brushed her gloved hands together, as if brushing away dust.

Sage stepped forward and hugged Lizzy. "No chasing squirrels." She stepped back.

"You need help, telephone. The Dolls. We got your back."

"I will."

Coco started the Harley, flicked down her visor, and slowly turned, following the bikers ahead of her. Lizzy sat like a seasoned passenger. She looked back at Sage.

Sage bit her lip, blinked a few times and blotted tears with her coat sleeves.

Four more bikers, two by two, rode into formation behind them.

"She'll be safe, Sage," I said, stepping up beside her. "Smart thing to do."

Sage braced her hands on her hips, not looking at me. "I'm going to kill Dennis Sullivan." She turned and walked into the condo.

23 NEVER LEAVE

His power lives through me.

MY JENGA BLOCKS BROKEN, THE NEXT morning I called in sick. I asked Kate if an articling student could appear with my latest shoplifting client at her first appearance. Kate said yes and told me to get better. She had it covered.

My forearms braced on my thighs, I sat outside at the picnic table of Coco's condo. Lost in thought, I stared at the water lilies in the pond.

I threw a pebble. It made a tiny splash. I felt Mother's presence next to me. "Where were you when we needed you the most?"

Mother linked her fingers and leaned forward. "I was putting my face in front of Sage's to soften that awful man's blows." Mom tapped my knee. "You need to watch out for her? She's very angry."

"I wonder why."

"You were so strong, Jade."

"Strong? *Strong*? Sage and I were beaten up and—" sexually assaulted "—I don't think *strong* is a commendation I'm proud of at the moment."

Mother was silent.

"I've never felt so much *rage*. I … I wanted … to beat Dennis.

Beat him. All because of Oscar. The man you loved."

Mother didn't say anything for a moment, then she looked at me. "Even dead Oscar is feared. Somebody is trying to destroy his legacy. What Dennis and Osmond did, they own that, not Oscar."

"His *legacy*? *I'm* his *legacy*. His power lives through me." I rubbed my face, wincing at the tender area. "Osmond knows I'm his daughter."

"Osmond is an evil man."

"And Oscar wasn't?"

"Unlike you with Osmond, I didn't have this foolish notion that I could change him. I saw good in him and—" Mother hesitated.

"And?"

Mother looked at the pond. "How's the grumpy rabbit?"

"Walter's fine. Don't change the subject, and I never thought I could change Osmond."

Mother looked at me then quickly looked away. "I … killed … him."

"What are you talking about? Killed who?"

Her gaze. She was no longer earth's child, but Heaven's remedial resident, yet at this moment she was in another place, another time.

"I got so angry." She looked at me, eyes wide. "That rage you speak about." She gazed at the goldfish. "He thought he could boss anyone around. Oscar. Archie. Me. We were pawns to him. To be kicked and spat upon. He hit me. I snapped."

"Who hit you?"

She looked me in the eye. "Diego Lomas."

Oh.

My.

God.

"The electric guitar was right there. I didn't think twice. I grabbed it and swung. Oscar and Archie were stunned. Archie saw Diego's boys reach for their guns and he took them out. One shot." She made the shape of a gun with her finger and thumb. "Ping. Ping." Each of them. Oscar covered it up. Sent me away. He started the rumour so no one would suspect me."

It was my turn to stare at the goldfish.

"Oscar went to all lengths to protect me. To protect you and Sage. Trust me, when Osmond's time comes ... Oscar will be waiting."

I stared at Mother.

She looked at her hands. "I understand if you're ... ashamed of me."

I wanted to wrap my arms around her shoulders but she was a ghost. "I'm not ashamed of you. I could never be ashamed of you. Who was there when you killed Diego?"

"Archie, Adam's father. Diego's men were in the room. Archie shot them. There were two men upstairs. I don't know what happened to them. I'm presuming they would have come downstairs having heard the gun shots. Archie took care of them. Jade, this is what Oscar and I didn't want to happen. Someone finding out about you."

"Well," I said, "it's happening." I shivered. I heard footsteps crunching on the gravel and quickly looked over my shoulder.

Adam.

"I like him," Mother said. "He was a sweet boy."

"He's returning to the U.K."

Mom pulled the hair back from my face. "We'll see about that."

Adam sat beside me, where Mother had sat. "If I'm the last person you want to see right now, I'll leave."

"You can stay."

He leaned forward. "I wish you had told me where you were going, or what you were doing."

"What does it matter? You had my GPS synced to your phone."

"I should have told you. I'm not stalking you."

"No. You're tracking me."

"That GPS told me where you were yesterday. Men tried once to kidnap you. I wasn't going to let that happen again."

"I'm not your responsibility."

"For Christ's sake, Jade!"

I looked at him with a raised eyebrow.

He let out a tense breath. "God knows what could have

happened yesterday if Bob, Henri and I hadn't shown up."

"I'm grateful for your help, but this isn't your problem and I'm not awarding medals."

"I don't want a medal. I want you safe. I'm as much a part—"

"—No! You're not. I'm not your responsibility. Your responsibility ended when you dropped those damn thumbdrives on my desk."

"Oscar Cooper thought differently."

"Adam, you can't fix this … you can't protect me. You can't reverse what Oscar started."

He looked me in the eye.

The sliding door opened. Sage stood, her cellphone pressed to her ear. "You two need a time out?"

"We're fine," we said, and turned away.

"Yeah, right."

"Who are you calling?" I asked.

Her face had the same avocado tint as mine. "The insurance company. I'm on hold. Don't scare the fish." She stepped inside and closed the sliding door.

Adam rubbed his hand over his face. "I have sat in a Beirut cafe with bullet-pocked walls, waiting to meet with an informant. Yet, I can't keep you safe in Victoria."

What the hell was he doing in Beirut?

"Ludicrous," he grumbled.

I jammed my hands into the pockets of my hoodie. "My kidnapping thirty-odd years ago wasn't your fault."

"Jade, Oscar didn't—"

"—Didn't what?"

"He didn't want any harm coming to you after he was dead."

"So he kidnaps you, puts my life on your conscience, because you haven't already been living with guilt, and practically takes your kidney. Nice man. If he loved me, he should have taken his secret to the grave, like Mother did, instead of only thinking about his *redemption*. Maybe he should have thought about that thirty years ago. Or, even better, if he wanted to protect me, then tell me who the hell is doing this?"

Adam was silent.

I paced.

"He wasn't certain who was coming after him. He was dying. Not of good health."

"Do not defend him."

"I can't walk away, Jade. I shook hands with the dealer, and ... I really like the dealer's child."

"Well, that dealer, my father—" *keep the secret, protect Mother* "—that dealer ... Oscar ... killed Diego Lomas and your father knew."

"How do you know this?"

"I just do. Did Archie ever speak of—"

"—No. He told me very little. So, do Dennis and Osmond know? How are they connected?"

"I don't know, but I'm going to find out." I rubbed my eyes, and winced where I had the bruise. "Osmond will kill you, Adam, if you get in his way. I like you ... a lot, and I can't handle anything happening to you."

A vulnerable expression passed over his face and I knew he was looking at the bruise across my cheek and the green tinge under my eye.

"Not if I paste him into the pavement first."

I looked away.

"I'm not leaving you, Jade."

That's what Osmond had said. My eyes moistened with tears. I could remain tough as long as I remained angry.

"I hate what that asshole did to you, but even more, I hate that I wasn't there to stop him."

I stared at the fish. Sage said I was too trusting.

"I am not Osmond, Jade."

"I've been asking myself how could I have been so blind about him? What warning signs did I not see? What did I choose not to see because I wanted to believe that someone could—" *love me.*

Honey trap.

Adam rubbed my back.

I released a jagged breath.

"You're asking the wrong questions."

I looked at him.

"You should be asking, 'How could that brute have hurt you?' What man hits a woman?"

I released another tense breath. "What man points a gun at his ex-girlfriend?"

Adam's face hardened. "He pointed a gun at you?"

I was quiet.

Adam looked at the pond, his breaths short. "What does this asshole look like again?"

I showed him a photo of Osmond that I still had on my phone.

"Send it to me."

I texted him the photo. "If this gets out, Adam, if the Internal Investigation Section catch him and he has a public hearing, which he will because he has nothing to lose, and it gets out that we were involved, my reputation, my career … I'm ruined."

Adam wrapped his arms around my shoulders and kissed the top of my head. "None of this is getting out."

I sat back and looked at him. I reached into my hoodie pocket and pulled out the Tylenol bottle.

"You're giving me Tylenol?"

"No. What's inside isn't Tylenol … it's Vicodin." I held the bottle out to him.

He took it. "You're stronger than you think."

I unclenched my hand and in my palm were three more. "I came too close."

He held out his hand and I dropped the pills into his palm.

"I'm getting you and Sage some old school protection."

"Old school?"

"Yes. Stow away your espresso machines."

For the first time in the last twenty-four hours, I smiled. "Bob and Henri?"

Adam nodded.

"Well, the day after tomorrow, Sage and I are going to the

Vancouver to find Lucy. A warrant is out for her arrest. I've been talking with Lucy's sister, and she thinks Lucy is working in an art gallery over there."

"I'm coming with you."

"We're taking our bikes. I don't think your Morris Minor can keep up."

"I won't be driving the Morris. What time are you leaving?"

"Nine a.m. ferry, so be here at seven-thirty. We'll be in rush hour traffic."

"I'll be here." Adam slid his hand through my hair. "I want to take you somewhere."

I didn't want to go anywhere, not with this shiner, but reluctantly agreed.

Sage was inside still on her phone, talking to someone about our trip. I wrote a note that we were going out. She nodded and waved.

We climbed into the Morris.

"Where are we going?"

The car struggled to life. "Chinatown."

"Can you be a little more specific?"

Adam hesitated. "Oscar's art gallery which is now a tea shop."

"Oh."

"You should see it." Adam turned the steering wheel and pulled the Morris Minor onto Tyee Road. "I've been in the archives, researching old Victoria maps. I came across one map that showed Victoria during the late sixties. Oscar's art gallery was prominently noted. From my research, he was quite the self-possessed man."

Self-possessed? "What do you mean?"

"He presented himself well. The cops didn't touch him because he donated big dollars to many charities. He was a money launderer before his time and an incredible business man."

"And I'm supposed to be proud?"

"No. But maybe see the whole man."

We drove across the bridge and made a left onto Wharf and found a spot on Fisgard. Adam parallel parked.

"Ready," Adam said, stepping out of the car.

I did the same.

Adam flipped up his coat collar, slipped his hands into his pockets and held out his elbow.

I held onto it.

We made a right onto Government Street, walked half a block, passing red lanterns, and stopped outside the white and red awning of the Silk Road Tea Store.

"This is it?" I asked.

Adam pulled open the door. A bell tinkled. "After you."

I stepped in. My shoes echoed on the hardwood. The cream shelves contained large metal cannisters labelled *chocolate hug herbal tea*, *lullaby wellness* and *waterfall oolong*. Black tables displayed teacups. A long black tasting bar with stools lined the opposite wall. At the far end, exposed brick. The tea shop was internationally known and written about in the *New York Times*. In the second wing, beauty products lined the shelves.

"May I help you?"

I looked over my shoulder and a tall woman with short dark hair and wearing a black mini skirt with a matching jacket strolled up to us.

Adam held out his hand. "I made an appointment with the owner. My name is Adam Younghusband."

The lady's eyes lit up. "You were talking with me. Nice to meet you." She shook Adam's hand. "You were interested in the history of the building."

"Very much so."

"Follow me, and I'll show you downstairs."

I might as well have been invisible. She walked toward one end of the tea shop. I had no clue how we were getting to the basement.

We stopped at a door.

"The stairs on the other side of this door are narrow—" the owner said, yanking on the sticking door "—so please watch your step."

Adam slouched as we followed her in.

The stairwell was dark and I thought another dungeon, like the one at the office. I was in an updated version of *The Lion, the Witch and the Wardrobe* as we descended into Middle-earth.

"Not only do we sell tea upstairs, but downstairs is our spa," she said in a subdued tone. "Mr. Younghusband, you mentioned that you are researching businesses from the late sixties."

"Yes, my partner and I are conducting research for my upcoming novel," Adam said, placing his arm around my shoulders.

The owner looked at me, and with a flick of a glance, eyed my bruised face.

"Motorcycle accident," I lied.

She nodded. "This building—" she lowered her voice, causing me to lean in "—was once owned by the infamous Oscar Cooper. He was supposedly quite the womanizer and drug dealer."

Fact or gossip? God, I was defending him. "Really?" I feigned surprise.

Adam smiled.

"The upstairs was Oscar's art gallery. He had works from Seattle-based artists, Maritime artists, and there was performance art, too. You weren't anybody until you were invited to a showing at Oscar's gallery. Writers held book launches and poetry readings." Her eyes swooped over Adam. "Mr. Younghusband, we would be honoured if you hosted a book reading here."

"I'm sure something can be arranged."

The owner smiled.

"I never knew Oscar Cooper had such a passion for the arts," I lied.

"Oh, he did. His mother loved art and she had a positive influence on his life. Here, downstairs, is where he held private parties. Supposedly opium was one of the condiments, then later cocaine."

So that's what Sage had disposed of—cocaine?

"Some of these walls are original to the art gallery. I can only imagine what nefarious activities took place. Over this way—" she walked toward a large room that might as well have been snatched from an Austin Powers movie, "—is our lounge, where patrons can relax and enjoy one of our looseleaf teas while waiting for their treatment. The lounge hasn't changed since 1968 when it was owned by Oscar. Tea?"

"Yes, please," Adam said.

The manager poured tea into two teacups and passed one to Adam and then to me.

"This is our Angel Water tea."

"Thank you."

Adam looked around. "This building hasn't been affected by the road construction and the addition of bike lanes?"

"We have been fortunate," the owner said. "Except for this small opening where the brick is crumbling." She walked over to the exposed brick wall. "Trying to find a contractor to patch up the brick work in this construction boom is ridiculous." The owner's cell vibrated. She removed it from her pocket and frowned. "Excuse me, I'm needed upstairs. Please feel free to explore."

"Thank you," Adam said.

The owner walked past, stopped and looked at me. "I forgot to mention. If you believe in ghosts—"

I nearly spat out my Angel Water.

"—it is rumoured that the shop is haunted. One masseuse hates working the late shift, because one night she saw a female ghost." The owner headed upstairs. The door above shut and a tomb-like silence descended on us. Adam and I looked at each other.

"Any dibs on the ghost?" he asked.

"No clue." *Mother*. I walked toward the orange and green floral-print sofa in the lounge. I thought about the parties that took place after hours. Did Mother partake in any of them?

"Yes, I did," she said, flitting in front of me.

I smiled. *Thank you for joining us*. I walked between the sofa and table. I placed my hand against the bricks. Hard, cold. Did they listen to the Rolling Stones down here?

"Of course." Mother flitted past again, making me dizzy.

"This—" I looked around "—is a large room. It makes me

wonder if this is where they framed the pictures and padded them."

"Bingo," Mother said.

She didn't seem her usual ghost self.

"Or, if they did all that here," Adam said, his voice fading as he walked down the hall to one massage room.

Mother lingered, furrowing her forehead.

"Why aren't you comfortable here? It's warmer than the cemetery."

She looked at the ground, then at the sofa. "This is not a good place."

"It was Oscar's gallery."

She shivered, still looking at the corner of the room by the sofa.

I followed her gaze. She saw the past but I saw a table displaying tea bags and cups and saucers. I looked back at her. *This is where she killed him.*

She looked at me with tears in her eyes.

"According to a local historian," Adam said, stepping back into the room, "there is a tunnel that leads to a private dock. The tunnel has been closed in, walled behind bricks."

I walked toward the far brick wall. "Probably this one. The one that had to be repaired."

I felt Mother beside me again, arms hanging by her sides. "Are you okay?" I whispered.

Her hand touched the bricks. "It all happened here. Our escape."

"Our?"

"Dear Norman was with me."

No way.

"Oscar gave me my three pictures, grabbed my wrist and led us down the tunnel."

"A great escape route." Adam stood beside me, resting his arm across my shoulders. "There's only one entrance on the first floor. Jade?"

"Yes," I said, stepping out of my thoughts and touching the brick work.

"And if they had a look out," Adam continued, "they could

quietly carry on their business downstairs and nobody would be the wiser."

"Or if certain individuals wanted to visit Oscar unnoticed—"

Adam's eyes grew wide. "Like Diego Lomas."

A teacup crashed on the floor.

I jumped.

Adam and I kneeled and picked up glass shards, placing them on a saucer.

"They could use the tunnel," Adam said, looking at the brick wall.

I nodded. "Why do ghosts haunt certain locations?"

"Restless spirit, unresolved issues. Usually it means the ghost is not at peace."

Mother *definitely* wasn't *at peace*.

Adam placed the last glass shard on the saucer and placed the saucer on the table.

I stepped away from him and looked at a photograph on the wall. A woman with long blonde hair, wearing bell-bottom pants and a paisley blouse, played a red electric guitar. The very same guitar in my office.

"Far out," Adam said from across the room.

I walked over.

He stood in front of a framed black and white photograph. A man leaned against a brick wall, arms crossed, a cigarette between the 'V' his two fingers made, smiling. Tall, blonde with high cheekbones and dark eyes, he carried himself with confidence and was gorgeous in a rugged Swedish way.

"Oscar," I said.

Adam looked at me.

Something came over me. Mother and I placed our hands on the brick, near his picture. The man I had been listening to, whose bourbon-drinking, cigarette-smoking voice I heard in my head, looked at me from 1968. Emotion tightened in my throat. I blamed it on fatigue. "He was handsome," I whispered.

"Yes," Mother said. "Yes, he was." She sucked in her breath and faced the centre of the room.

"What's wrong?" I said under my breath.

Her eyes grew wide. "Oh my."

I glanced at her.

"He's beckoning."

"Who's beckoning?"

"Saint Peter. Edith is at the gates." Mother smiled. "I finally have company in Remedial."

24 GOOD-BYE 1968

"You have to go. Tonight. Go to Haight-Ashbury."

G ENIE GEARED DOWN GOVERNMENT STREET.
"Genie, I don't think this is a good idea," Norman said, his hand braced against the inside door of the Volkswagen bug as she turned a corner.

"Norman, you worry too much. Oscar is a great guy." She was tired of everyone accusing him of being a drug dealer. She knew he dealt pot, and most likely the pot they smoked. So what was the big deal? "I promised Oscar, actually Archie, a painting."

Oscar's gallery was on the edge of Chinatown and would be coming up soon. She pulled over to the right, turned off Wharf and onto Herald. She had made a wrong turn. No worry. She would cut through Dragon Alley and Chinatown to get to the gallery. She parked when Steppenwolf's *Magic Carpet Ride* played on the radio. Damn. She turned up the volume and she and Norman bopped their heads in time with the beat, singing to each other. The song ended. She and Norman laughed and she turned the car off. She grabbed her picture. "I'll be right back."

Norman opened the car door. "I'm coming with you."

She placed her hand on his wrist. "Really. Just hang here. I'll be ten, fifteen minutes."

Norman glanced around the neighbourhood. "Genie, I don't—"

"—Hey—" she playfully tugged on the wood peace symbol that hung from his leather necklace "—peace out, man. Everything's cool." She stepped out of the bug and slammed the door.

Her thongs made a flapping sound against the pavement as she ran up the street and ducked into Dragon Alley.

"Hey sister," a guy called, "what's the rush?"

She was late. When Archie had called wanting a painting for an out-of-town buyer, she was ecstatic and promised to drop one off earlier in the day. But she had forgotten about the peace march and now she was behind. She could have used a magic carpet ride.

Red lanterns, a red dragon statue, she saw the Gate of Harmonious Interest and turned left.

Oscar's gallery. She slowed, feeling sweat soak into her blouse. She tugged on her jeans, took a deep breath and pulled open the front door.

Two guys she didn't recognize stood around a TV watching the Olympics in Mexico City. She didn't give a damn if it was the first time the Olympics were being broadcast in colour. The colour of blood as far as she was concerned. The TV went fuzzy and one man adjusted the rabbit ears.

She slipped into the next room, past Darlene's abstract paintings, pulled on a tiny door and descended the narrow stairs into the basement. She heard the Rolling Stones's *(I Can't Get No) Satisfaction*, and smelled cigars. Oscar's, then Archie's, voice, floated up the stairs, then another man's. She stepped into the party room and stopped. Oscar and Archie stood around a large table where Archie lined the back of a picture with wads of cash.

Archie saw her first. "Shit."

A goon with slicked-back hair, strumming Darlene's unplugged red electric guitar, dropped the guitar and pulled out a gun, aiming it at her. Another goon did the same.

"Hey, hey," Oscar said, stepping in front of her, his hand out.

"Guns down. It's all right. Genie's my friend." Oscar spun around. "Genie, what are you doing here?"

"I owe you a painting. I told Archie I would drop it off today."

Oscar glared at Archie. "Give me the painting and go. I'll call you later."

"What's going on? Are you okay?"

"Go. *Now*."

"Oscar. Who is this?" A man stepped forward.

Genie's heart dropped. She recognized him from newspaper articles. He was shorter than she expected. Stocky.

Diego Lomas.

"Genie has to go," Oscar said, grabbing her hand and moving toward the stairs.

"Why the rush, Oscar? It's not often I meet the artist of my paintings, especially a beautiful artist like this." He extended his hand to Genie. "My name is Diego Lomas."

No way in hell she was going to shake it.

"Diego, Genie has to go." Oscar pulled on her arm.

"You painted this beautiful picture?" With his cigar, he motioned to the picture on the table as he placed his arm around Genie's shoulders, walking her toward the table.

His breath smelled of alcohol. Her heart pounded. She tried to make sense of what was going on. What was Oscar doing with Diego Lomas?

"She doesn't speak," Diego joked.

His goons laughed.

Archie looked apprehensively at Oscar.

Oscar stepped forward. "Diego, Genie has—"

"—Genie," Diego interrupted, "is going to tell me about her beautiful painting." He squeezed Genie's shoulder. "Or what is it you say, cat get your tongue." He smiled, rubbing his hand over her back as he puffed on his cigar.

"Don't touch me."

"Ah." Diego laughed. "The mouse squeaked."

The goons laughed.

Oscar stepped toward the table. "Diego—"

The second goon aimed his gun at Oscar. "Stand back."

"Genie needs to tell me about her beautiful picture." Diego touched her hair, sniffing it. "Only I say when people come and go."

Oscar's hands formed fists. "Genie, there's dinner in the kitchen. Diego and I won't be long."

Genie stepped away when Diego's hand grasped her upper arm and pulled her beside him. "The painter with the red hair is going nowhere."

"She's hungry," Oscar said.

"She can eat after I tell her why I like her paintings." He squeezed her arm as he pulled her toward the table, her picture in the middle.

Her heart echoed in her chest. This imbecile needed to let her go.

"I like your paintings, Genie," he stepped away from her, slipping a knife from his belt, "for their beauty and their purpose. Like you, Genie, you have beauty and purpose." He stabbed the knife into the canvas and sliced.

"*No!*" Genie shouted. "What are you doing? You animal."

Powder packets poofed open like a teddy bear popping its stuffing.

Oscar took a step when the goon cocked his gun.

Diego turned. "Animal? Animal? You call me an animal." He slapped her, sprawling her over the sofa. She grabbed the upholstered arm.

"*Genie!*" Oscar shouted. "Diego, get your men and get the—"

"Stand back," the goon said.

Genie gasped, her hand pressed against her cheek. Her temples pounded. She swallowed. Tasted blood.

Rage.

"You need to teach your woman respect, Oscar," Diego spat.

Red. She gripped the neck of the red electric guitar.

"You defend this stupid bitch," he continued.

She carefully stood and swung.

Diego's eyes grew wide, his cigar dropped from his mouth, and the electric guitar cracked his head. He spun and dropped, his body made a slapping sound as it hit the concrete. Blood pooled around his head. Eyes lifeless.

Archie fired a shot.

Oscar grabbed the goon's wrist, spun him around and broke his neck. The goon's body slid to the floor.

Genie dropped the guitar and bolted.

"*Genie*," Oscar shouted.

She ran down the hall, yanked open a door and found a room full of plywood and plastic.

Oscar grabbed her arm and pulled her into him, pressing her against his chest. "Genie, I'm so sorry. He shouldn't have hit you. Nobody hits you."

He pushed her hair back from her face. "Please forgive me."

Eyes wide, she pulled away from him. "He's dead."

"I know. I know."

"They're all dead."

"I'll deal with it. You've got to get out of here. Your paintings. Follow me." He grabbed her hand, leading her back to the room.

She cringed, hearing more shots upstairs.

"Don't look at the bodies. Archie and I will take care of them." He led her around a corner to a small door. He grabbed three of her paintings and quickly wrapped them in plastic.

Footsteps thumped down the stairs. Oscar pulled out his gun, aiming it at the stairwell.

Archie burst through, flinging Norman toward the table.

Norman hit his nose. He grabbed onto the edge, stopping himself from slipping. He looked at Genie, his nose bloody.

"I found this idiot upstairs," Archie said, his gun pointed at him.

"Norman's my friend!" Genie shouted. "What did you do to him?"

"Genie ... I'm okay." He rubbed his shirt sleeve on his face.

"Oscar," Archie said, his tone stern, "he's—" he waved his gun at Norman "—a witness."

Norman's face turned white. Blood on his shirt. He had lost his peace necklace.

Oscar paced, cursing.

"Oscar," Archie said again, "you know he's a *witness*."

"Archie, stop," Oscar said.

Genie looked from Archie to Oscar. "What is he talking about, Oscar?"

"Genie, please," Oscar said. "You shouldn't have come here."

"What is that supposed to mean?" Genie demanded.

Oscar stepped around one dead guard and looked at Norman. Archie nodded.

"Please," Norman said. "I saw nothing. I was waiting in the car and I got worried about Genie."

Archie placed the muzzle of his gun against Norman's temple.

"Oscar, stop him!" Genie pleaded.

Oscar leaned his hands against the table and looked Norman in the eye. "You have one chance to convince me why I should trust you."

Norman swallowed. "Hear me out. I'm not armed." Sweat trickled over his face.

Genie sniffed. "Norman."

"It's okay, Genie." He looked at Oscar. "I'm reaching for my wallet, and I'm pulling out a card." He held up the card before placing it on the table. "My name, phone number, address. Business card. I'm a lawyer. I'll watch over Genie, and I will forever be at your service."

Oscar stepped forward. He picked up the card, looked at it, looked at Norman. "Lower your gun, Archie."

Norman breathed.

In five minutes their lives had changed. Bile gathered in Genie's throat. She swallowed once, then twice. She couldn't throw up. Not now.

Oscar tapped the card on the table. "You'll be my lawyer from this day on."

"Yes. Absolutely." Norman nodded.

"I'm *not* asking."

"Understood."

"All right, Norman Bastine," Oscar crossed his arms, "what have you witnessed?"

Norman looked from Archie to Oscar. "Witnessed?"

"That's right," Archie said. "Witnessed."

"Well—" Norman wiped sweat from his forehead "—if I were your defence lawyer and you told me that your friend, here, pulled his gun and shot the two guards upstairs, killing them, well, then, I would say your friend was acting in self-defence. The police report would show that the men were armed, had drawn their weapons, and were uninvited guests."

Oscar smiled. He tucked the card into his shirt pocket. "Norman Bastine, as my lawyer, I instruct you to take Genie down this tunnel—" Oscar pointed "—and get the hell out of Victoria."

"Yes." Norman stepped over a body.

"*Now.*"

Norman grabbed Genie's arm, and led her toward the tunnel door.

Genie saw the red electric guitar on the floor.

"Oscar, cops—"

"*—Shut up*, Archie."

Oscar stepped up to Genie, opened the door and, crouching, slipped through, pulling her after him. She felt a draft. "I don't want your paintings, or your name tainted by this. Do you hear that, Norman?"

"Yes," Norman said.

Genie clutched her paintings to her chest. They felt heavy. "Where are we?" It was much cooler where they stood.

"We're in a tunnel. It'll lead you to Store Street. You've got to leave. Don't come back."

He wasn't talking about just tonight. He meant forever. "I'll … I'll never see—"

"—You can't stay here. His people." He pointed toward the open door. "They can't know you were here." His hands caressed her hair and he hugged her. "I love you, Genie," he whispered in her ear.

"You have to go."

"Come with us."

Oscar pulled out his wallet and placed a wad of cash in her hand.

"I don't want your money. I want you, Oscar. The two of us. We go. We start over. We change the world."

"No," his voice cracked. He closed her fingers around the cash." He slapped another wad into Norman's hand. "Your retainer."

"Understood."

"You have to go. Tonight. Go to Haight-Ashbury. Get out of the country."

"You can't stay here," Genie said. "They'll kill you."

"I won't give them the chance. Go." His voice was harsh, pushing her away. "Get out of here. Don't ever come back."

She saw his sorrow. "I've ruined everything." She brushed the tears from her cheeks.

"Come on, Genie." Norman coaxed, holding her arm, leading her down the tunnel.

She rubbed her cheek against her shoulder, blotting tears. She gulped and lurched. She looked back at Oscar's black silhouette in the doorway, before he closed the door.

25 OFFICE MEETING

I collapsed against the door, pounding on it with my fists.

WE CHANGED OUR PLANS.
We didn't go over to Vancouver as originally planned to look for Lucy. Sage and I spent the day making funeral arrangements for Edith and trying to find out if she had any next-of-kin.

We were both distraught, and we dealt with our grief in our own way. Sage spent a lot of time with Gillian. I did what I always do. Poured myself into my work.

Kate was at a professional development workshop at the Victoria Conference Centre, and the articling student was on vacation. And Norman ... he was nowhere to be found.

I had the office to myself, and I paced from one end to the other, my arms crossed, stopping short of the door to the dungeon and the possessed typewriter. I abruptly turned and paced from the back to the front.

People were dying around me. Charles's murder was made to

look like an overdose. Edith had said she'd given him a needle. I couldn't believe she had killed Charles. Besides, Charles had supposedly died from cocaine. Oscar overdosed from injecting fentanyl.

I stopped.

While still alive, Mother had once told me that they all knew each other: Mother, Edith, Charles and Norman. Edith had gone to school to become a nurse. They all must have known Oscar, too.

For all the dealers who wanted Oscar dead, had Edith given him a lethal dose of fentanyl?

I stood, stunned, in the doorway of Norman's small office. *You couldn't just get high and make love, could you? You all had to get messed up with Oscar Cooper.*

I stepped in. Pens and pencils neatly arranged to the right side of his blotter. Simon's file in the middle. Clock in one corner of the desk and his rolodex in the opposite corner, beside his daytimer. Old school. I swung the rolodex around and flipped through cards, recognizing some names. I stopped at the C card, seeing COOPER, Oscar and numerous phone numbers.

Charles was looking into Oscar's past. Everything stems from you, Oscar.

In his daytimer Norman had an appointment two weeks prior with Charles. What were you going to tell him, Charles? I glanced at the file on Norman's desk and thought about the box of files in the dungeon.

I marched out of his office, grabbed the key from Kate's desk and unlocked the dungeon door. I pushed it open, flicked the light switch and looked down the narrow cement stairs that led into darkness.

Crap.

I slowly made my way down, my hand gripping the cold railing, smelling cement. I hated this place. Hated it. I reached the bottom, flung open the door and flicked on the lights.

The overhead fluorescents buzzed. I propped the door open with a chair and walked around tables toward the three file boxes.

The portable typewriter was still there on the table at the end of the room.

It's okay.

The cover is closed.

I pulled off the lid of one box and flipped through dusty files, sneezing. The date range on the box lid said, 2000 – onwards. A few motor vehicle accident cases, civil forfeitures. Norman did everything.

I moved that box to the side. The second box was labeled COOPER 1 OF 2. Now we're getting somewhere. I pulled off that lid and the first file was from 1994. Drug trafficking. Oscar was found not guilty. On the left-hand side was the account for services rendered. Fifteen thousand. Oscar, you were definitely good for business. I put that file aside and grabbed another and sat on the table. I really shouldn't be doing this, reading Norman's file without permission from his client.

"Well," I muttered, "his client is dead." I flipped a page and that's when I heard the ping of a carriage return.

I froze and the hairs on my arms stood on end.

You heard nothing. Nothing. I glanced at the typewriter. It still had its cover on. I flipped a page of yellow foolscap notes. I'm over-reacting because of this stupid room. Norman had written *1975 to 1992*. The name *Diego and Szonja Lomas* was circled and underneath the word *daughter* with a question mark.

Lower on the page was *Dennis* circled. Arrows shot from his name.

Gangs when a teenager.

Adopted, graduated Law School.

Off the rails when adoptive mother died.

Half sister Kathy Banks?

I flipped the page and a card fell out. I popped off the table and picked it up. The card was yellow around the edges and what I guessed to be Courier font. Norman's name with his phone number and address. It must have been his first business card. I tucked the card back in the file and put that file to the side, when I saw the brown folder labelled *Banks brothers, 1992.*

The year I was kidnapped. I grabbed it.

Newspaper articles slipped out about the grizzly bear murder of Steven Banks and his brother.

Norman had more notes.

Dennis, son of one Banks brother.

Kathy the other.

Cousins.

Did Dennis want revenge because he knew Oscar was behind the grizzly bear murders? I flipped pages back and saw the name again.

Diego and Szonja Lomas.

How did any of this tie into them?

The fluorescents hummed louder.

That was it. I was taking the box upstairs. I tossed both files in, pushed down the lid, grabbed the box by the side cut-out handles and turned.

The typewriter was positioned on the table. Keys exposed. I could see HELP and the sad face.

Nope, not scared. I stepped around the table, when the carriage return pinged. I stopped. A finger might as well have trailed down my spine. The lid had been closed when I walked into the room.

Tap.

I closed my eyes.

Tap.

I placed the box on the table and looked at the typewriter twenty feet away from me.

Tap.

I pressed my hands to my face and walked around the table toward it.

The carriage return pinged twice and the paper moved up two lines.

"Oh, dear God." I stepped back, bumping into the table behind me.

HI J

It knew my name began with the letter J. I pulled my hair back from my face. What did I do? "I'm clean, I'm clean, I'm clean. I haven't touched a drug in six months. I'm clean."

Colon. Closed bracket.

:)

"Screw off."

Colon. Open bracket.

:(

"What do you want? Why are you doing this?"

The letter hammers hit the paper with machine-gun rapidity. I couldn't see what was being typed. The carriage return pinged and the hammers jammed.

I stepped forward, and fingers trembling, flicked back each individual hammer. One tapped my finger.

"Stop it." I saw what was typed.

COMINGKILLYOUDEAD

"Who?"

Eight quick taps.

THECHILD

Which child? I leaned back against the table "Who … are … you?"

Five slow taps. The carriage return pinged.

I stepped forward.

OSCAR

The lights flicked off. The door at the top of the stairs slammed shut. I jumped. The lock clicked.

No. I lurched around the table, tripping over the chair I had used to prop the door open. I stumbled up the steps. "*Hey, hey!*" I gasped, halfway up, clutching the railing. I hauled myself up the remaining steps, my thighs burning. I collapsed against the door, pounding on it with my fists. "Let me out!" I gasped. "Hey!" I pounded on the door. "I'm stuck in here."

"Jade?"

Kate.

"Yes." I hammered on the door with my palm. "Open the door."

The lock clicked and the door opened to reveal Kate and light. "What are you doing in the dungeon?"

I pushed past her and collapsed on the sofa.

She looked down the stairs. "You like dark creepy places?"

"No."

Calm down. It's all right. It's all right. You're fine. Fine. I marched into my office, pulled open the bottom drawer, grabbed my empty coffee mug, pulled out the bottle of Baileys and poured. I tossed it back. Poured more and tossed it back.

I held onto the back of my chair.

Kate stepped in. She looked at the Baileys then me. "Are you okay?"

"I was looking at Norman's old files. Trying to understand why he disappeared. Old client." I looked at Kate.

"Jade, you're white, like—"

"—Don't say it."

"Okay. Sickly white. Sickly."

"Thank you."

"I don't mean to dump on you, but Lucy Starr just walked in."

I looked at her, still breathing hard.

"Lucy. There's a warrant for her arrest, yes, yes—" my brain had the capacity of baked meringues right now "—ten minutes, give me ten minutes."

"Yeah. Sure." Kate turned toward the door. "Are you sure you're okay? You have a bruise—"

"Bike accident." I smiled. My assistant didn't look convinced. "Can you ... can you, not now, when you have a moment—"

"—You want me to get the file you were looking at?"

I nodded. "And the three boxes."

"Not a problem." Kate closed the door behind her.

I told myself to pull it together. Not a good impression having a bottle on my desk and a coffee mug. I placed both in my bottom drawer. I sat and told myself to breathe. One breath in, hold for two, breath out. Repeat.

A light tap on the door. That wasn't ten minutes.

Kate poked her head in. "Lucy is here to see you." She pushed opened the door and Lucy sauntered in. She had traded in the beige knit dress for a lime green mini, and the Velcro strips had been upgraded to a rhinestone-laced bodice. Her white bolero jacket matched mile-high white boots. Blonde hair cut stylishly short, I wouldn't have recognized her on the street.

Wow. I stood. "Lucy. How are you?"

She flopped down in the chair across from me, crossing her legs. "I'm here to make amends." She admired her lime green nails.

"Oh." I sat back down.

She rolled her eyes. "Valentina says I need to make amends for how I behaved in court."

"Valentina. Did Valentina tell you there's also a warrant for your arrest for not showing up at your probation office?"

"Yes. And I've made amends. I showed up with Valentina, she was duty-counsel, I think that's what you call it, and she had a word with the Crown."

"Really."

She leaned forward on my desk. "Yes. Valentina got me a job."

And a new wardrobe. "That's great. Where?"

"The Mountain Coastal Gallery and Resort. I'm one of seven art tour associates."

"What does an art tour associate do?"

"I show people around the gallery and provide them with information about the art pieces."

"Sounds like a good job. Valentina has been very helpful." And she's taking advantage of vulnerable people.

"And I'm in Valentina's reading program."

The reading program. "Is there anything I can help you with, Lucy?"

She stared, blinking her long lashes over doe-like eyes. "Is he hiding?"

"Who hiding?"

"Your partner, the old guy."

"Why would you ask that?"

She shrugged and cast a glance upwards.

Underneath all the flash, where was my turnip-throwing client? There was more to this visit than *make amends*. "Lucy, is everything okay? This is quite the transformation."

She stared, gnawing on her bottom lip. "I'm back in Van tomorrow."

"For the new job."

She rubbed her forehead and that's when I noticed the bruising on her arm and the needle marks. If I said anything, she would run. "Lucy, do you have a phone number I can call you at so Kate can keep our files up to date?"

She rattled off her number which I scribbled down.

"Jade?"

"Yes."

"Did he pound you?" she asked, looking at my face.

I looked at the notepad then at her arm. "Yes. Osmond Reeves did this to me. Your turn."

She grabbed a pen and the notepad. She wrote quickly. "If—" she blinked back tears.

"Lucy, what is going on?"

She abruptly stood, knocking over Dr. Vlasic's prayer plant. "Sorry."

"Lucy." I wanted to grab her arm but didn't.

"I gotta go." She tapped the notepad with the pen. "If … anything should happen, that's my sister, and those—" she pointed at the five names she had written down "—those are the other girls." Bloodshot eyes, she swiped at the tears on her cheek. "And, yes."

Osmond, you bastard.

"Lucy."

She dashed, and by the time I got to the front door, Lucy was gone.

26 HONEY TRAP

"She won't think twice about killing you."

"HE'S LATE."

"I'm sure Adam will be here soon. A little patience, Sage." I tapped my boot against the step, loosening mud. *Come on, Adam.*

Sage paced between her bike and mine. "He better not show up in that Morris Minor. I'm not adjusting our road trip to suit him. You know I wanted to go to Vancouver two days ago."

Yes. Sage wanted to clear her head and escape to the big city. I wanted to go to Vancouver to find Lucy. I had to do something to help my client. If, I, a professional, felt intimidated reporting my assault to the police, there was no way Lucy would report her assault by a police officer to the police. Then there was Sage. "You okay?" I asked her.

"I'm fine."

Like hell she was. Since the assault, Sage kept saying she was fine, but I knew she wasn't. She had zero patience for *anybody*. If she had grumpy Walter's rattle she'd fling it.

I wanted to talk about the assault. Dennis. What he had done to her and what he had done to me. Sage wasn't alone, but every time I brought it up, Sage decoyed or stormed out of the condo. Trauma cannot be stuffed in a cardboard box and tucked in the back of a closet. Sooner or later the lid will flip open.

Sage pulled on her helmet and walked to the end of the driveway. She struck a pose, her legs slightly apart, hands on hips, looking in both directions.

"I'm sure he'll—"

"—Screw it." She marched back to her bike. "I'm not—" she swung her leg over the seat "—waiting for him."

Then we heard it. A bike engine rumbling, getting louder.

Sage looked at me.

A black bike with a tall rider swung into the cobblestone loop in front of the condo.

"No way." Sage said in disbelief. "That's a—"

"—Ducati," I said, smiling. *Well, well.*

The Ducati idled next to Sage's bike and sure enough Adam flipped up the visor of his helmet. He looked ... *hot*.

"Road work, I had to detour and the bridge went up. We have a ferry to catch." He flipped down the visor and pulled out of the driveway.

I scrambled onto my bike.

Sage pulled out after him and I followed, grinning like an idiot. I was going to enjoy this road trip.

We arrived at the ferry terminal, boarded and remained on the car deck. I questioned Adam about his bike, learning that Ducati tires are more angled, meaning Adam could lean much further to each side. I gave him and Sage the low-down on Lucy.

"You think she's in trouble. What type of trouble?" Sage asked.

"You have a Labatt beer can around? That kind of trouble."

"Someone's pounding on her?"

"Someone's doing something and she's scared."

When the ferry docked in Tsawwassen, we rode to Ladner and stopped at a local hole-in-the-wall restaurant that made amazing fish and chips.

"Lucy told me that she's working at a small art gallery as an art tour associate. She's one of seven. Valentina got her the job." I placed my phone on the table.

Sage leaned back in the booth, popping a fry into her mouth. "How can that be a bad thing?"

"Maybe she's being forced to offer more than tours." Adam pushed his basket of fries aside. "You said she's one of seven, and she gave you names and phone numbers of the others."

"Yes."

Sage looked at me. "So who's she hanging with that she's not only worried about herself but the other girls?"

"That's what I want to know."

"Right." Adam pulled his Pepto from his pocket, slung a mouthful, and returned it. He zipped up his jacket. "Shall we push off?"

Sage stared at him, shook her head and exited the restaurant.

We rode into Vancouver. Sage checked us into the Marriot and stayed behind in the hotel room. Adam and I walked to Coal Harbour, passing the 2010 Olympic cauldron. Dodging tourists, we made our way down the steps and to the walkway. We found the art gallery. Adam waited outside while I stepped in and approached the front desk clerk and asked for Lucy.

The clerk rolled her eyes. "Who's not looking for her?"

"Excuse me?"

"She's supposed to work today but is a no show. I'm supposed to be at a bachelorette party in Whistler. Instead, I'm covering for *her*."

"Oh. So other people are looking for Lucy?"

"Yeah. One dude was big. Like not fat, but tall. Blonde hair. Weird skin."

"Plastic-like?"

"Yeah."

Dennis.

"The other guy, he was hot. Shoulder-length hair, tall, moody. Pour me a cup of him."

Osmond. I wanted to tell her the personality didn't match the packaging. "And when was this?"

"Um, yesterday, I think."

"Thank you." I turned to leave.

"And then there were the weird guys."

I stopped at the door. "Weird guys?"

"Yeah, Dolph Lundgren wannabes. Claimed they were extras from a movie set."

Oh God. "Thank you. You've been very helpful. If Lucy contacts you—" I walked to the counter and slipped her my business card "—please tell her, I just want to talk."

The clerk took my card, looked at it, then at me. "She's in trouble, isn't she?"

"Not if I can talk to her. Thank you." I stepped outside.

Adam turned, hands in pockets. "Not here?"

"She hasn't showed for her last two shifts. It sounds like Osmond, Dennis and the goons are looking for her."

"*Christ*. Contact her sister?"

"No. She wasn't too pleased to talk the first time I called. She said this was typical Lucy behaviour, get a decent job, make good money then not show up. I could bugger off. I'm worried, Adam."

"The police."

"I don't have a lot to go on. I'm not family. Bruised arm and she didn't show up for work. She reported to her P.O."

We walked back the way we came, passing yachts and expensively-clad joggers. A seaplane growled in the blue sky. We turned the corner and sitting on a bench, smoking a cigarette was Simon—my dine and dash, guilty-pleading client. "Simon." I walked toward him.

He glanced at me, looked at his phone, then did a second take. "Jade." He smiled and stood, looking like he had stepped from the pages of GQ. The boy cleaned up well.

"Simon. How are you?"

"Good."

"What's that written on your jacket?"

He pulled on his jacket so I could see the logo on the pocket.

"You work for the Mountain Coastal Gallery and Resort."

"I'm a chauffeur. Valentina got me the job."

"Really."

"What are you doing in Van, Jade? Court?"

"I'm looking for a client. Lucy Starr. A petite—" I held my hand chest height "—blonde who was also in Valentina's reading group."

Simon frowned, then realization dawned on his face. "*That* Lucy. She works in the gallery."

"Do you know where she is?"

Simon looked at his shoes. "If I see Lucy, I'll tell her to contact you."

Adam stepped forward. "Buy you a pint?"

"Who are you? A cop?"

"Simon, this is—" *the man I want to sleep with, despite the fact he's returning to the U.K.* "—my friend, Adam Younghusband."

"The author," Simon said. "I like your books." He held out his hand and Adam shook it.

"Still interested in a pint?" Adam asked.

"Yeah." Simon smiled.

"Lead the way," Adam said, as if sensing Simon's hesitation.

Simon led us toward a side street.

Adam winked.

We didn't walk far and were soon seated in a poorly-lit bar that had a stripper pole and three TVs mounted to the wall, broadcasting hockey, soccer and baseball. We slid into a small booth with a sticky worn table. Adam and Simon sat on the outside edge. Adam ordered two pints of whatever was on tap and I ordered a Diet Coke.

Adam groaned, his attention on the TV. "Liverpool got scored on."

"The man likes his soccer," Simon said.

"So how was Valentina's reading program? I've heard good things about it."

Simon opened his mouth then shut it as the server dropped coasters in front of us. She placed a pint in front of him, then

Adam, and thunked a bowl of nuts in the centre. "On the house."

She turned.

"Excuse me—"

She was gone.

Adam looked at me. "She forgot your drink."

Figures.

Simon flagged her down.

"What can I get you, sweet-cheeks?"

"My friend—"

She looked at me.

"—ordered a Diet Coke," Adam said.

"Did you, dear?"

Don't dear me. "Yes."

"Be right back."

"Thank you." I turned to Simon. "So how was Valentina's reading program?"

He sipped his pint then sat back.

Silence.

"Simon?"

He looked at me.

"So tell me about the reading program?"

He hunched over his beer. "It's all above board."

"But?" Adam said, sitting back, stretching out his legs.

Simon looked at Adam. "For those who want to earn additional credits, there are odd jobs to teach responsibility."

This didn't sound above board.

"Doing what?" Adam asked.

"Delivering books to the participants in the reading program."

"Except?" I prodded.

Simon drank some of his pint. "The pages of the books are glued together and inside is a cut out compartment."

"What's Valentina moving?" I asked.

"It's not literature," Adam muttered.

Simon sipped again. He glanced over his shoulders before leaning in over his pint. If he could, I'm sure he'd slip under the foam of his beer.

"What's Valentina moving?" I asked, lowering my voice.

"You didn't hear this from me—" he sighed, gulped a mouthful, looked sheepishly at me, then Adam "—fentanyl, cocaine."

"Bloody hell," Adam said.

Exactly what I was thinking. I now understood Simon's nerves.

Simon threw back another gulp and wiped his mouth on his sleeve. "Don't worry, Adam. I haven't seen any of your books being used."

Adam frowned.

"Not just anyone is chosen to be Valentina's book mule," Simon continued. "She picks those she doesn't believe can be reformed. I have no idea why she picked me."

Because Simon is cute and Valentina probably has much bigger plans for him.

"How many participants in the program?"

"About fifty. We all met the first night. That was a Tuesday. On the Thursday, we were divided up. Half of us attended book club on Tuesday and the other half on Thursday. Lucy and I were in the Thursday group."

"You wouldn't be able to give me names of participants in your Thursday night session."

"Hell no. We only went by first names. Valentina said last names were a sign of possession. We were equals."

Of course they were. Why else separate the sheep from the goats. "Are you still in the program?"

"No. On the last day, Valentina gave us a party. No booze. She called us individually into her office and gave us a parting gift."

"A book?" Adam asked.

Simon smiled. "Yes. *The Young Entrepreneur*, and inside was a hundred-dollar bill. She said she would help us start over, and that an entrepreneur is an individual who takes on greater than normal financial risks." Simon gulped his pint, which led me to believe that the good stuff was coming.

"Did Valentina offer you a job?" I asked.

Simon sat back, blinking. "You still don't have your Diet Coke."

Deflection. I smiled. "Simon?"

"She can be very persuasive, Jade."

"Oh, I imagine she can. She's powerful, beautiful, sexy."

Simon's face turned red. He cleared his throat and didn't look me in the eye. "I felt proud of myself. I finished the reading program."

"And you should feel proud," I said.

"And she was dressed really nice. I think it was a red dress."

It was definitely a red dress if he still remembered.

"And she was sitting on the desk, and I was in the chair and she leaned over and handed me a book."

"And a chauffeur's job?"

Simon's ears turned red.

Oh, maybe something more.

"I didn't want to spoil her success rate."

Success rate at what? Valentina used sex to control men. Honey trap. "What does she want you to do?"

"Deliver books and pick up clients and bring them to the gallery."

"Who are your clients?" I persisted.

"People like you and Adam."

"Like us?" I looked at Adam.

"Lawyers, teachers, housewives. I don't know the people. I've been given an SUV. I get the books, a list of addresses, and I deliver to the address. And if I show I'm responsible and do a good job, I'm given bonuses like nice clothes, or a month's rent, or a nice car to lease. And if I'm really good, my brother's also given a bonus."

It took an evil and manipulative person to use an individual's weakness and family members to snare them into corrupt practices.

"Is Lucy doing the same thing as you?" Adam asked.

"No. Lucy isn't delivering books. Valentina likes her though. She and her team were waiting for her when she walked out of jail. Valentina took Lucy shopping for clothes. A starter package so she could turn her life around."

"How do you know this?"

"I was their driver."

"And what did Lucy have to do in return?"

"Work at the art gallery. She'd greet patrons and give private tours." Simon gulped his pint.

"And you know this because you were the driver?"

"Right." He gulped again.

Adam pulled out his phone and flashed a photo of Dennis. "Have you seen him?"

"Yeah. He's in Valentina's security team."

"And this guy?"

"Osmond."

My heart thumped. "What does he do?"

"He's head of security. He also books the private tours for the gallery."

"And you know this because you're the driver," Adam repeated.

Simon nodded.

I had to get Simon to reveal Valentina's clientele. "So what does that involve, Simon? Who do you pick up?"

"I'm not supposed to discuss the clients. We signed a confidentiality agreement."

You signed your soul to the devil, that's what you did. I wasn't giving up. I tapped the coaster my Diet Coke was supposed to sit on. "I don't need names. These must be affluent Vancouverites who can afford private tours of the art gallery."

"Yeah. And out of—" Simon cleared his throat. He looked uncomfortable, casting quick glances over his shoulder.

"—Out of town clients?" I asked.

Simon stared into his mug.

Now he was clamming up.

"Simon, you're telling us this information because Lucy's disappearance bothers you."

He released an anxious breath and ran his hands through his hair.

"It's Lucy," Adam said. "You're worried about Lucy. You know she's only eighteen."

Simon squirmed. "That means she's an adult."

Lucy was far from an adult. "You drove her somewhere or with someone," I prompted.

He looked at Adam. "I—" he hunched over his mug again "—I picked up an art dealer from the harbour where he had moored his yacht. I took him to the art gallery. Lucy gave him a tour."

"And?" I coaxed.

"Valentina texted me. I was to take Lucy to his hotel."

"Did you?"

"Yes."

"When was this?" I asked.

"Two days ago."

"Have you seen the art dealer since?"

"No. I asked Valentina about him and she said Osmond drove him back to his yacht. The dealer wanted to tour the island on his helicopter."

"And Lucy?"

"Valentina said Lucy had a cold and she wasn't taking any risks given the pandemic, and Lucy not getting vaccinated. She told Lucy to self-isolate for fourteen days."

Oh dear God. I reached over and touched Simon's wrist. "You did the right thing telling us. I think you're right. I think Lucy is in trouble. Adam and I will try to find her. But you, Simon, you've got to get away from backstabbing, double-crossing Valentina—" *And stop thinking with your penis.* "She won't think twice about killing you, or your brother, if you don't suit her needs."

"Sage?"

"Yeah," she said, tugging on the backpack's zipper.

I hesitated as I packed my belongings. We had a good night in the pub, joking and grilling Adam about the royal family, and if it was soccer, or really football.

"What is it?"

"Dennis Sullivan—"

"—I'm not talking about—"

"—He assaulted me too."

Sage froze. "What did you say?" she asked, not looking at me.

I repeated myself and without taking a breath, told her about the assault at Lucy's trailer and Osmond showing up.

Sage sat at the edge of the bed, looking at me.

"My assault wasn't anywhere near as terrible as yours—"

"—don't you say that. You don't know what that asshole would have done if that other asshole Osmond hadn't stepped in. Abuse should not be compared or graded." She placed her hand on my knee and gave it a little shake. "Are you okay?"

I nodded, choking back tears.

"No, you're not." She sat on my bed, hugging my shoulders.

"We need to go to the police," I said.

"No, we don't."

A pounding on the door interrupted us.

"Jade, it's important."

Adam.

I looked at Sage as I walked across the room to the door. I checked the peep-hole then opened the door. "What's up?"

Adam marched in. "Turn on the TV."

Sage clicked the remote and the set hummed to life.

"Channel 52," Adam said, pacing, hands in his pockets.

"That's local," Sage said, clicking.

"Right."

"What is—" then I saw Lucy's photo behind the news anchor on the screen.

"In the early morning hours, VPD were called to the Downtown Eastside where a young woman's body was found."

"Oh my God." I pressed my hands to my cheeks.

Sage looked at me.

"The woman has been identified as Lucy Starr. She was last seen leaving the Mountain Coastal Gallery and Resort two nights ago around nine p.m. The young woman is the latest victim of the city's opioid crisis, having overdosed on fentanyl—"

"No." I held my hair back from my face.

"It is believed she was in the Downtown Eastside to purchase more of the opioid that has been killing many—"

"Did Lucy do drugs?" Sage asked.

"No," I whispered.

Adam still paced.

"The police are asking for the public's assistance in locating this man, Simon Labelle, who is alleged to have been involved with the deceased."

Simon's face popped on the screen.

"Simon, what have you gotten yourself into?" I said.

"Citizens are encouraged to contact their local police if they see this man, who is considered a person of interest.

"On April fourteenth, the Provincial Health Officer declared a state of emergency in the number of opioid overdose deaths. In the last five years, we have seen a fifty percent price jump in the housing market, which the Attorney General alleges is connected with money laundering—"

"Turn it off," I said. I sat on the edge of the bed.

Sage dropped the remote on the mattress. "I guarantee you, Osmond or that prick Dennis took care of her."

I didn't know what to do. Adam and I had spoken to Simon the day before. He knew nothing of Lucy's whereabouts. Was he lying?

"You think he killed her?" Adam asked, standing in front of me. "He was your client. You know him better than any of us."

"Simon's not a murderer. You saw him."

"He was also looking over his shoulder the entire time."

"I think he's in over his head."

Adam looked me in the eye.

I looked away. Lucy had come from a dysfunctional home, and our broken red-tape justice system had failed her. "I failed her."

"Jade, this isn't your fault," Sage said.

She kneeled and held my hands in hers. "We're gonna go home, rest, and figure this shit out. All right?"

I nodded.

After checking out and fueling up the bikes, we were on the road. Sage rode in front, Adam on my left, as we made our way toward the Tsawwassen ferry terminal. I thought about what had happened over the last few weeks.

Charles died from a suspected cocaine overdose, shortly after that our family home was torched. Adam gave me Oscar's audio files. Adam and I were chased. Sage's home was torched. Then Sage and I were attacked by Osmond and Dennis. Lucy supposedly overdosed. Simon was MIA. The one person connected to Charles, Lucy and Simon: Valentina, and behind her, Dennis and Osmond.

I geared down as we approached a corner, passing majestic mountains on my right. Ever since that day, when Osmond had read Oscar's obituary, nothing had been the same.

We accelerated on the flat.

Why did Osmond lie?

Why was Osmond mixed up with Dennis?

Why had Osmond assaulted me?

I geared down again and came to a stop, my bike idling next to Adam's. He looked my way and gave me a thumbs-up. I reciprocated.

He's not staying. He's heading back to the U.K..

The light turned green. We accelerated. Sage took off, leaving a sizable gap between us.

If Charles wasn't the golden goose, then who?

Me.

Why?

I was Oscar Cooper's daughter.

A black SUV came up fast behind Adam and me. Jerk.

It pulled into the oncoming lane and sped past. Another car came in the opposite direction, and the SUV swung back into our lane.

Adam and I looked at each other, then Adam took off, his Ducati having twice the cc as my Royal Enfield.

I geared into fifth, the trees on the side of the road a green blur.

The SUV grew smaller, as well as Adam.

Sage.

The break light flashed on Adam's bike.

I saw the hairpin turn.

Sage's Harley flipped end over end, disappearing over the embankment, followed by Sage, tucked in a ball.

No.

The SUV disappeared around the corner.

I slowed, parked and ran. "Sage! Sage!" I scurried over boulders, hearing Adam's footsteps behind me. I saw her bike, mangled pieces of metal sprayed over the edge of the cliff.

"*Sage!*" I screamed, looking around at the evergreens.

"Over there." Adam pointed.

Sage lay prone on a narrow dirt path.

"Sage!" I ran.

She didn't move.

"Sage." I dropped to my knees and gently shook her shoulder. "Sage, get up." I heard my panic. "Get up."

Her arm moved under her body.

Adam stepped beside me. "You shouldn't—"

"—*Sage.*"

She groaned. Her helmet moved from side to side. She dragged her knee and arms up under her, pushing herself up on her elbows.

"That's a girl, that's it. You can move."

She kneeled on one knee and removed her battered helmet.

"*Fuuck.*"

"Are you all right?" Adam asked, holding out his hand.

Sage looked at the ground.

"Sage." I tried to look into her eyes. "Look at me."

"Yeah, yeah. I'm fine. Stop shouting. That jerk. In the SUV."

"Did he hit you?" I asked.

"He tried to. I had sped up to create space, but that corner. I looked in my rear-view mirror just as my front tire hit the soft shoulder—"

"—and you and your bike flipped."

Sage nodded then winced.

"We need to get you to a hospital," Adam said.

"No." She slowly stood, pushing aside his helping hand. She looked at the surrounding trees.

"Your bike's destroyed, but you can get another. The important thing is you're—" my voice caught "—you're okay."

She stepped and looked in the other direction.

"What are you looking for?"

"I saw her."

"Who?"

She looked at the cliff and treetops approximately five steps away. She turned and looked behind her, then at the bent foliage behind me, her eyes glossy. "Mom. She stopped me from rolling off the cliff."

My eyes teared up.

Sage stepped gingerly along the path.

"We need to call the cops," Adam said, following her.

"No cops," Sage said.

I heard the crunching of tires on gravel. We looked at each other.

The black SUV parked on the edge of the road where Sage had gone over. A door opened and slammed shut. Footsteps.

Dennis stood above us on the embankment. He looked at Sage.

Adam scaled the path.

Dennis jumped into the SUV and skidded onto the road. Adam was on his bike, spraying pebbles.

Sage looked at me. "I'm going to kill Dennis."

"You're not killing anyone," I said, out of breath. "We're calling the police."

"No, we're not."

"Sage."

She looked at me.

"You're not killing him."

Her eyes narrowed. "Fine. I'm cutting off his testicles and shoving them down his throat."

"You're not cutting off his testicles, because who would look after Lizzy when you're in jail?"

She thought for a moment.

We heard a bike and saw Adam park on the shoulder. He got off and jogged down to where we stood.

"Slick moves there, Ace, but I take it you didn't catch him." Sage said.

Adam pulled off his helmet. The wind played with his hair. "He's an asshole, Sage, I'm not denying that. Yet, Dennis is not worth risking my life to bring him in. He'll get what's coming to him. For what he did to you—" Adam then looked at me "—and for whatever he did to Jade."

Sage and I remained silent.

"Right. I'll call for a tow."

"To tow what? An exhaust pipe! A gas tank? No tow. No cops. I'll call my people." Sage pulled out her cell, the screen now shattered. "I need a bike."

"You can't ride," I said.

Sage cursed again, jabbing her finger over her phone, which I gathered had been destroyed in her crash. She threw it over the embankment. "I need your phone."

"No. You're not getting on another bike until you've seen a doctor."

"I'm *fine*."

"No you're *not*. I'm not letting you ride—"

"—*You're* not *letting me* ride? Don't pull that older sister crap on me."

"Ladies," Adam said.

"Stay out of this," we both snapped.

Adam stepped back, hands in the air.

"You either get on the back of my bike—" I pointed "—or the back of Adam's. *Pick*."

"I'm not getting on a Ducati." She limped past me then Adam, heading toward our bikes.

I looked at Adam. "That settles it. She's doubling with me."

Adam watched Sage hobble up the path. "Sometimes, Jade, your sister scares me."

I smiled. "She likes you ... I think."

"She *tolerates* me."

"Imagine if she didn't like you."

The rest of our ride was uneventful. We were first on the ferry, bikers always are. Leaning against the rail on the outside deck, Adam guzzled Pepto-Bismol as we admired the coastline. Sage borrowed my phone and disappeared inside.

The ferry arrived on time. Sage doubled on the back of my bike, and we rode back to Coco's condo. We pulled into a parking spot only to see the front door fling open and Gillian run out.

"*Baby*." Gillian's arms whipped around Sage's neck. "I was so worried about you, so worried." Her voice broke.

"I'm all right," Sage said, wincing.

Gillian pulled back and planted a long kiss on Sage's lips.

I placed my helmet on my seat, feeling a little jealous of what Sage had.

"You know," Adam said, walking over to my bike, "last week when Gillian told me she met this amazing hot girl, I didn't realize it was your sister."

I smiled and looked at Gillian and Sage, arms around each other's waist, talking. Gillian gently touched Sage's bruised face. "I'm happy for them."

Adam followed my gaze. He touched my chin with his index finger and thumb, then ran his hand through my hair. "Sage was lucky this time. We were all lucky this time."

"I know."

Gillian helped Sage inside the condo.

"They're still out there: Dennis, Osmond, Valentina." I looked Adam in the eye. "I'm tired of this, Adam."

"Bring the fight into your corner."

I nodded.

"If you want," he said, super casual, "I've moved out of the house, and I'm staying at The Empress. You could come over and look through my files. Work out motives?"

An adult study date. We both knew where this could lead. "I'm tired, Adam."

He tried to hide his disappointment.

"But ... I'm in. That'd be great."

27 1986

I'm a far cry from flip-flops, cutoffs and halter-tops.

GENIE SET HER WINE GLASS ON THE DRESSING ROOM table. She had received a standing ovation for tonight's performance. Even the first cellist applauded. The audience loved Vivaldi's classics and capping the concert with the *Four Seasons* was the cherry on the cake. While the rest of the orchestra went out for drinks, she wanted to spend her birthday at home. She pushed back her chair and slipped out of her green silk dress and into a white blouse and pleated checkered slacks. She slid on her favourite long camel coat with its wide lapels, untucking her hair. She didn't look like Danish supermodel Renée Simonsen, but she loved the model's clothes.

A knock. "Mrs. Thyme? Security."

Genie pulled open the dressing room door just as the security guard said, "You have a visitor."

Her heart dropped.

Oscar.

He smiled. In one hand he had a box and in the other a bouquet of roses. "Hi, Genie."

The security guard looked from Oscar to Genie. "Is everything all right, Mrs. Thyme?"

"Yes," she said, not looking at the guard. Wider across the chest, white shirt, dark sports coat, Oscar looked impeccable, of course. His blonde hair was longer in the front but short on the sides. "I know this man." She held open the door.

Oscar stepped in and she closed it behind him. She let out a deep breath and turned. "What are you doing here?"

"Business. I saw in the paper that musician Genevieve Thyme was holding an AIDS benefit concert at the Orpheum. I had to see the beautiful violinist with the long red hair."

She crossed her arms.

"You look like a model."

His compliment fell flat. She thought of the sleepless nights when she lay awake, rehearsing what she would say if she ever saw him again. She couldn't remember a damn thing.

"I brought you—" he flipped open the box lid "—a birthday cupcake."

Genie took the box. "Thank you." She put the box on the table.

He held out the bouquet. She took it and placed it by the box.

"I've been following your career."

"So you're stalking me."

"Not at all."

"It must be more difficult laundering money in a violin case than in the backs of paintings."

"You'd be surprised."

She glared.

"Bad joke. Too soon." He slid his hands into his pockets. "Still painting?"

"Haven't touched a brush since 1968."

Oscar looked at the floor. "I'm very sorry about that. I should have stopped Diego sooner. I handled the situation poorly."

She propped her hands on her hips. "*You handled the situation poorly?* You used my art to launder drug money. And then ... and then I killed—"

"—*I* killed Diego Lomas with an electric guitar," Oscar interrupted. "Archie shot his guards. Do not, Genie, tell anyone what went down. Diego had a family, wife, one or two kids. No one can know."

She glanced at him. He was still sexy, insatiable, Oscar.

"I would do anything to change the past, Genie. I ... I didn't want to lose you. More of Diego's boys could have shown up, hell, his brother was in the government. We could have had the entire Mexican army at our door. I was trying to save your life."

She was silent.

"Charles Thyme is the last person I thought you'd marry."

"You told us to go to Haight-Ashbury, so Norman and I did. Charles tagged along."

"How was it?"

"How was what?"

"Haight-Ashbury?"

"Awful. Charles did a lot of LSD. Every time I did, I had a bad trip. I kept hallucinating about you and bashing people's heads in with red electric guitars. To this day I'm Lady Macbeth and I can't look at red paint without thinking *blood*!"

"On the bright side, you didn't bash my head in."

"Are you trying to be funny, Oscar, because it's not working."

He was silent.

Genie frowned. "So why are you here? A bigger reason than wanting to hash out the sixties and bring me cake and flowers?"

He pulled an envelope from his coat pocket and placed it on the table by the cake. "If anything should happen to me, my future wife gets it all."

"It's called danger pay," Genie said.

"I want you to have this." He tapped the envelope. "It's a State of Title Certificate for the property in Schooner Cove and a few other items. Whatever's on the property is yours. Don't tell anyone about this." He tapped the envelope again. "Not even Charles."

"I don't want your money."

"It's not money, Genie. I don't want you hating me, and I don't want you at another man's mercy. This ... is an out. Should you ever need it."

She shoved her hands into her coat pockets. "I don't hate you. I never hated you. I only—" *loved you.* She felt her throat tighten. She looked away.

Oscar stepped forward. "Where's Charles?"

"Toronto. He's a speaker at a law conference, and … when he's not lecturing, he's screwing his Madonna-esque secretary, who I guarantee you is not Like a Virgin."

"And you?"

"What about me?"

"If you're not creating art—"

"—I lose myself in my music. Or, I do aerobics."

"Aerobics?"

"Yes." She rolled her eyes sheepishly. "I saw *Flashdance*. Everyone wants to look like Jennifer Beals."

Oscar chuckled. "You're going to add the water thing to your performance?"

"No. Don't be silly. What about you? You're engaged."

"Yes." He sighed. "Business is booming. We provide party favours to the rich."

"I can imagine."

"Any kids?"

"No," Genie said. "Charles, well, it's complicated."

Oscar nodded.

"Archie still with you?"

"Yes. You really haven't created any art?"

"I'm part of the establishment, Oscar. Look at me. I'm a far cry from flip-flops, cutoffs and halter-tops. I've become the person I despised."

"I believe the word is *yuppie*."

"You had a chance, Oscar, to leave it behind. You could have come away with me."

"You don't know how much I wanted to."

"But the drug money was too good an offer to refuse."

"Genie, you can't walk away from my industry. You're carried out in a body bag or buried alive. You deserved more than a life on the run with me."

"We were both naive. I better let you go." She stepped forward, reaching for the door handle. "Your future wife is probably wondering where you are."

Oscar stepped forward at the same time she did. His hand caressed hers. They looked at each other, then wrapped their arms around the other. Genie breathed in his cologne. "I've missed you," she whispered. "I hear on the news of a shooting and I wonder if I'm going to hear your name as one of the deceased."

He held her face in his hands. "Hey, I ain't gonna die." His thumbs traced her eyebrows and he kissed her. Genie slipped her hands through his hair. He groaned and pulled back, leaning his forehead against hers. "I should go."

She nodded.

They didn't move.

"We were going to change the world, Oscar."

He brushed her hair back from her face.

"Don't leave," she said. "Not yet."

He twined a red curl around his finger and looked her in the eye. "Lock the door."

28 HAT TRICK

Canadian model overdoses in Vancouver hotel room.

Dressed in flannel pajama pants and tank top, I stumbled from the bedroom and into the living room. A digital 3:15 glowed from the hotel room's microwave. I sat on the sofa, bringing my knee up under my chin and flipped through Adam's scribbled notes.

The word 'consequence' jumped out at the top of one page and an arrow pointed to Charles's name. I yawned and rubbed my temple.

Dennis's name was written on the side. He was a lawyer until he was caught siphoning money from his trust account to support his coke habit. Valentina had been his lawyer during his discipline hearing.

How was Osmond involved with Dennis and Valentina? He didn't wake up one morning and decide to become a bad cop.

Mom's past coming back to haunt her, those were Dr. Vlasic's words. Mom was single for a short time before she married Charles. What could she have done to make someone seek revenge?

I picked up a newspaper article from 1968. The photographer had captured Mom protesting, waving a placard with the letter "C" on it. I squinted. Was that a young Edith next to her?

Above her photo, the headline, '*Students Protest Oppression in Mexico*'. I tapped the article, maybe there was something here. I put that article to the side.

I flipped open Adam's folder of newspaper clippings: the Grizzly Bear Murders; the Diego Lomas "missing" article; *Targeted Hit in Canada?*; then memorial service of Diego Lomas 10 years after his disappearance.

"There you are." Adam leaned against the wall, his arms crossed in front of his bare chest. His pajama pants hung loose on his hips. "I rolled over to hug you but the bed was empty."

We had spent the evening working crime theories before we worked ourselves into his bed. "I couldn't sleep. Hamster brain."

He walked to the refrigerator. "Do you want anything? Cold Chinese food, a cupcake, me."

"No thank you to the Chinese food and cupcake. A serving of you is not off the table. You did promise me a hat trick."

He smiled, before chugging juice from the jug. He walked over and sat beside me, rubbing his eyes. "Still trying to connect the dots?" He pivoted his file, picking up articles.

"We're going about this wrong. Each name. Each incident is a puzzle piece but we're jamming the wrong pieces together."

"You've got your mom's protesting article to the side."

"Yes. Who was the leader of Mexico in 1968?"

"I have it here." He picked up an article. "Ferdinand Lomas. Diego's brother."

"You have a lot of articles about Diego Lomas and the Mexican government."

"Oscar wanted to know everything about Diego and his family. He died before I could ask him why."

I picked up a pencil, flipped a page over and drew a circle and put Mom's name in the centre. "Dr. Vlasic said that Mother's past had come back to haunt her. Who was in Mom's past? Oscar." I printed his name and drew a circle around it. "Charles." I wrote his name and circled it. "They are connected through Mom." I drew a line connecting the circles. "Now ... Valentina." I wrote her name and circled it. "We know she's involved in coercion, drugs, possibly human trafficking, but we can't prove it. We don't have reasonable and probable grounds to get a search warrant. She was involved with Charles."

"In 1968 your mom, Charles and Oscar were in their twenties. Valentina wasn't born until 1969."

"Good point." I tapped my pencil. "So how's she connected to Mother?"

"Who were the people who attended the gallery?"

"According to the owner of the Silk Road Tea Store, wealthy people. Performers. Artists, celebrities. The gallery was referred to as The Studio. The place to be on a Saturday night."

Adam rubbed his eyebrows. "If Oscar's running drugs out of there, it was more than your law-abiding citizen showing up on a Saturday night."

I looked at Adam.

"What?" he asked.

I flipped through the newspaper articles. "Oscar wanted me to know of my past, so I could be protected." I spread out the newspaper articles starting with Mom protesting; the Grizzly murders and suspicion that they were retaliation murders; Oscar's arrest then release. Articles about Oscar donating to a police charity, to a politician's campaign. Charles's overdose. "What if my kidnapping was a consequence like Charles's murder?"

"A consequence of what?"

Mom's past. I picked up the article of Mom protesting.

"Jade?"

I had it. The answer. I could feel it. I needed to let the pieces click. If only Mother could tell me. Or had she? She wanted to plead her case before God. She was in Remedial. Why? What had Mother done to be placed in Remedial?

Think.

"She told me at Coco's condo."

Adam arched an eyebrow. "Who told you what?"

I killed Mexico's number one drug trafficker. Diego Lomas.

I sucked in my breath. I wrote Diego Lomas and circled his name, drawing lines to Mom's and Oscar's names. "She witnessed Oscar murder Diego Lomas," I lied, keeping Mother's secret.

Adam's eyes widened. "Are you serious?"

"Yes. This has got to be it. Her past coming back to haunt her."

"Diego Lomas disappeared. Nobody knows any—"

"—Mom did. She said—"

"—*She*?"

Whoops. "I meant Oscar's tapes. Archie, your dad, was there. Two men upstairs. Diego. His men downstairs were killed by—"

"—My father." Adam cursed.

"There were two guards upstairs watching the summer games. Who were the two guards?"

Adam scrambled through the articles in the folder. "In this one, it says 'Diego Lomas, a Mexican businessman, and his four colleagues did not return to Mexico City. Authorities are stumped how a prominent businessman and his colleagues could vanish in Canada, a peaceful nation. Some speculate that the businessmen met their fate on an unscheduled hunting trip. Their rented Chevrolet Blazer was found near a popular hunting area in B.C.'s wilderness. Others believe it was an outside hit. Many countries are watching this investigation, especially the Mexican government.'"

"Does it say anything more?"

"Yes." Adam continued reading. "'Diego's brother, a cabinet secretary close to the President, is demanding an independent investigation by Mexico's National Guard into his brother's disappearance and possible murder. The Canadian government has expressed its condolences to the Lomas family and pledge full disclosure of the RCMP findings. Diego is survived by his wife, Szonja Lomas, who is five months pregnant with their first child.'"

My head snapped around. "Diego had a child?"

Adam looked at me, realization dawning on his face. He flipped through more articles in his file then pulled out another one. "Ten years after the disappearance of Diego Lomas, the Lomas family held a memorial service to honour the Mexican entrepreneur and father, whose disappearance caused mass speculation and international conspiracy theories. Diego Lomas disappeared during a business trip to Canada. An investigation was conducted by the RCMP but was closed with no further evidence, much to the fury of the Lomas family. The cabinet secretary Lomas was later gunned down in his home three months before Mexico's national election.'"

"International scandal. Well, that rules the brother out."

"'Diego Lomas is survived by his wife, former model Szonja Lomas, and their ten-year-old daughter Alexy Lomas, seen clutching—'" Adam looked at the print out "'—her mother's hand.'"

I leaned over. *The child* was what Oscar had typed. *This ten-year-old child.* I thought of Norman's files and handwritten notes. "There she is. Norman was right all along." I tapped the image of a young girl, her face looking away from the camera. "Diego had a daughter. When was this article written?"

Adam looked at the bottom of the page. "1979."

"She would be around fifty now. What's the daughter's name again?"

"Alexy Lomas. You think she's Valentina?"

I shivered. "Yes."

Adam slid that article into the line-up and flipped open his laptop. "One way to find out. You said fifty?"

"Yes. She looks incredible for her age," I grumbled.

Adam gave me a second glance. "Not as good as you." His fingers tapped over the keyboard. "Valentina would need to apply for Canadian citizenship."

"Unless she was Canadian."

"You think Szonja was Canadian? That's an Eastern European name."

"Why Canada then? Why would Diego come to Canada to do business when his next door neighbour is the U.S.? There had to be a connection worth the trip. If Szonja had family here, why not during a family visit, work out a drug deal? Write off the expenses. Heck, if he purchased property up here, it would be a great way to launder money."

Adam continued typing. "Go through the mother. She wouldn't have anything to hide." Adam typed 'Szonja Lomas model'. "Look at this—" he pointed to the screen "—Canadian model Szonja Taragos announced her engagement to Mexican businessman Diego Lomas. The two plan to marry in the Notre-Dame de Quebec Basilica-Cathedral. The Hungarian beauty was one of thousands of Hungarians who immigrated to Canada during the 1956 Hungarian Revolution."

"Knew it. Okay, now their daughter."

Adam rubbed his hands together before typing in Szonja's name 'child/daughter' and a list of hits came up. He pointed to the screen. "Birth announcement. Szonja Lomas, married to Mexican businessman Diego Lomas, gives birth to a healthy baby girl, Alexy Valencia Lomas."

Adam let out a deep breath. "Where are you now, Szonja?" he typed in her name again and scanned the hits, and I saw it.

Canadian model overdoses in Vancouver hotel room. "Oh crap." I pointed.

Adam clicked on the article. "*Shit,*" he muttered. "When did this happen? Christmas of 1992. Szonja overdosed on alcohol and painkillers, leaving behind her twenty-three-year-old-daughter, Alexy Valencia Lomas."

"Alexy would be an orphan."

"She's gotta be Valentina," Adam said.

"You think she changed her name? Now what are you doing?"

Adam opened another window. "Valentina's Instagram page. People put too much crap on the internet." After a few clicks he found it. He scrolled past photos of Valentina standing with her colleagues before the B.C. Supreme Court bench; photos from an office Christmas party; cats, cats, cats and more cats.

"She must have a photo of when she was called to the bar, even if it's old. Who would be standing beside her?"

Adam scrolled further.

"There." A man and a woman, lawyers I recognized, stood on

either side of her. "No parents. Scroll up."

Adam did.

"Stop." I pointed to a photo of a young woman modeling a black mini-skirt and white turtleneck and knee-high boots. The woman was gorgeous. Written in the Instagram caption were the words, *Always in my heart. Luv Alex.*

"This—" I tapped his screen "—is a photo of a photo of Szonja Lomas."

"What's the date?"

We looked.

Adam hovered the mouse over the post. "May 10, 1992."

I Googled it on my phone and looked at Adam. "Mother's Day. Valentina is Szonja and Diego Lomas's daughter."

Adam dragged his hand over his mouth. "Bloody hell."

"Valentina changed her name from Alexy Valencia to just Valentina. It all makes sense. She must know that Oscar killed her father. How, I have no idea, and she's seeking revenge—"

"—on you," Adam said.

I patted his knee. "How did she meet Dennis? That's the next question."

Adam stared at the screen.

"Say something, Adam."

"She knows Oscar killed her father. Then she knows that my father must have been involved. She's been very accommodating with the book launch."

"Maybe she wants you to write her biography. A tell-all about what really happened to her father."

Adam rolled his eyes.

"And if you don't, she'll kill you."

"Oscar was no saint, but Diego Lomas, he murdered families."

"Adam, they were both bad men. It's a matter of whose family you're connected to. Do you think Valentina was working you over to get to me?"

"Oscar must have been suspicious of Valentina." Adam stood and paced. "That's why he had me dig up the articles on Diego

Lomas."

I looked at the article about Szonja Lomas's overdose. 1992.

"Adam, what if Szonja knew."

"Knew what?"

I lined up the articles again. "What if Szonja suspected Oscar had killed Diego, and what if she arranged for the Banks brothers to kidnap me? And it all goes wrong. The Banks brothers are murdered. What if she told Valentina what happened and then Szonja committed suicide. What if Valentina is finishing off what her mother started?"

Adam's face lost all colour. "The book launch is tomorrow. How am I going to protect you from Diego Lomas's daughter, who is hellbent on revenge?"

"That's not your responsibility."

"Tell that to a dead Oscar Cooper."

"Adam," I stood, his pacing unsettling, "Valentina—"

"—She's coming for you," he interrupted. The concern on his face triggered my panic. "She'll make your murder look like a suicide, like she did with your father and with Lucy. We go to the cops."

"No cops."

"You sound like Oscar," he said.

"The cops are already in her pocket."

"Who does she have?"

"Osmond, that we know of."

Adam cursed and walked over to the window.

Fatigue settling in, I rubbed my eyes. "Valentina's going to be at the launch. We bring her into my corner. Who do we have in our pocket?"

Adam looked over his shoulder at me, looking pretty darn sexy. "My number one fan."

"Who?"

"Inspector Shelly of the VPD's Internal Investigation Section."

29 BOOK LAUNCH

" ... I felt like a voyeur, eavesdropping on his character's conversations."

THE ROUNDHOUSE IN VIC WEST MADE AN EXCELLENT venue for Adam's book launch. Large banners, featuring either an image of Adam, or his book, hung on the exposed brick walls. High ceilings. Purple and white lights, the same colour as the book's title, shone on the jazz band.

Servers dressed in black brought in silver trays of appetizers from the outside food truck, placing them on bistro-style tables.

I stood by the bar. A few attendees still wore masks, including Inspector Shelly, who stood in the opposite corner near the washrooms, reading her autographed copy. At Adam's request, she gladly attended the launch as a fan and off-duty police officer. The Sergeant, who I'd met alongside Inspector Shelly, was here as well.

I strolled toward the spiral tower of books at the signing table. The room filled and chairs were occupied. I spotted Adam at the other end of the room, leaning forward, a glass of red wine in his hand, listening to an elderly man in a suit. I walked toward him.

Adam looked up, winked, not missing a beat of the elderly man's conversation.

The man looked at me, looked at Adam, patted Adam on the shoulder and excused himself.

"Hello," Adam said, his eyes doing a quick sweep of my black knee-high boots, black skirt and grey sleeveless blouse. His black framed glasses gave him a sexy, intelligent look.

"You have an incredible turnout and the place looks spectacular."

"The 6 by 5 banners are a little over-the-top," he gestured.

I laughed.

"I think I saw Simon," he said.

"Simon? My client, Simon?"

"Yes. I think it was him. I alerted Inspector Shelly."

"He's my client. I can't ditch him."

"He sold out Valentina for a pint. A very low threshold, his loyalty. He'll sell you out, Jade."

I felt conflicted. "He's still my client." I gazed over the crowd. "Have you seen Valentina?" I asked, trying to change the subject.

"Yes. Outside, yelling at some poor sod on her phone. You okay?"

"Yes. Let's enjoy your moment," I said, stepping back.

Adam grabbed my hand, pulling me toward him.

Could this be it? When he tells me he's not returning to the U.K.?

"About London."

This was it. Stay calm. "Yes."

"I've, um—" he looked at the floor then at me "—I decided—"

"—There you are!" Gillian said, rushing toward us, delicately holding a pastry.

Are you kidding me?

Adam let go of my hand.

"Am I interrupting—"

"—No. Not at all," Adam said.

I wanted to smack him with his book. And even though I liked Gillian a lot, I wanted to drop her into the punchbowl. *Yes, you are interrupting.*

"It's time?" Adam asked.

"Yes." She nodded. "If you could take your seat by the podium, and have you tried these almond thingies?" She held up the pastry. "They're blinking delicious."

Adam headed over to the stage.

Gillian looked at me. "I was interrupting, wasn't I?"

"My glare was that obvious?"

She nodded. "I think you topped Valentina."

I patted Gillian's shoulder. "You've organized a killer launch."

She beamed. "You really should try these."

Sage, dressed in black pants tucked into thigh-high boots and a black silk shirt, walked her tall frame over to Gillian. Her long red hair glistened and the application of extra foundation hid any bruising from her toss from the motorcycle. She slipped her arm around Gillian's waist.

"Taste this," Gillian said, holding up the pastry.

I headed to my chair, squeezing past people, stepping over feet like I used to as a kid in church. I sat.

I looked over my shoulder.

Inspector Shelly sat in the back row, and on the opposite side of the room sat the Sergeant. I hoped there were many plainclothes officers in the audience.

I heard the clicking of heels, turned, and Valentina in a wicked strapless red dress sauntered to the front, casting a seething glance my way. I gathered my coat around me.

I looked to my right. Sergeant Stone stepped over feet much like I had as he made his way toward the empty seat beside me.

"Jade." He nodded, smelling of rain and disappearing in the folds of his trench coat.

"Good evening," Valentina said into the microphone, her deep voice grabbing everyone's attention. "Thank you for coming. It's invigorating to see so many Adam Younghusband fans."

The audience clapped.

Valentina nodded and smiled. "That's right. Let's show the talented Adam Younghusband some love."

The audience clapped harder.

Adam frowned.

"I am honoured we can launch Adam's novel, *Gangster Child*, at the Roundhouse." Valentina faced Adam.

Adam found me in the audience and nodded.

Valentina flipped her hair over her shoulder. "I was drawn to Adam's characters in his debut novel, *Sin and Sacrifice*. When I began reading *Gangster Child* I was amazed by Adam's depiction of crime scenes and his accuracy of police investigations. While reading the dialogue between a reformed mob boss and the protagonist—" Valentina stopped for effect "—I felt like a voyeur, eavesdropping on his character's conversations. One would almost believe Adam had first-hand knowledge."

He did.

The audience laughed.

Adam cleared his throat.

"Crap," whispered Sergeant Stone. He reached into his pocket and pulled out his cell. "Excuse me." He stood and shuffled out of the row.

"The character transformation, the discreet dropping of clues are masterfully executed in Adam's chic prose." Valentina eyed the audience. She had us, well not me, in the palm of her hand. "The motives and faults of real characters who do not have the good fortune of being born into good families."

She could say that again.

"Through the protagonist we learn that we have to kill a part of ourselves to become the person we are destined to be, and the villain's journey as an orphan ... his sacrifice, so he could destroy those who judged him, tore ... at my soul." She placed her hand over her cleavage.

Diego Lomas's daughter.

Alexy.

Orphan.

"The protagonist's self-realization that we can thrive despite life's casualties is a reminder to us all—" Valentina looked directly at me and arched an eyebrow "—the strong ... will survive."

I heard a shuffle, the scrape of chair legs. The lady to my left moved her chair over.

"Without further ado, ladies and gentlemen, it's with great

pleasure I introduce to you, Adam Younghusband." Valentina turned, and clapped as we did.

Adam walked to the podium. He dropped a sheet of paper, picked it up and placed it on the podium. He braced his hands on either side. He nodded at Valentina.

"Good evening," he said, leaning toward the microphone. "Thank you, Valentina, for your eloquent praise. You're a tough act to follow."

The audience laughed but Adam didn't. He wasn't joking.

"And thank you Gillian, my assistant, for organizing this event." He cleared his throat. "I'm supposed to enlighten you about writing this novel. Any writer will tell you, a well-written story is put together with front bits, back bits and sections. We butcher the English language to create prose so it effortlessly flows from the pages into the reader's imagination, where we hope to grab and hold that individual hostage for however many pages." Adam stepped back, rubbing his hands. "We then hand over our magnum opus to our editor, who rips it apart and points out the gristle and tells us where to trim the fat, and asks us to stop making up words."

The audience chuckled.

Orphan.

I thought of the photo of Dennis and Valentina with Steven and Jeffrey Banks. They had been murdered by Oscar and Archie. Steven's wife, Darlene, overdosed, and his daughter was killed in a police shooting. Nobody knows what had happened to his son, who could very well be Dennis Sullivan.

"I relied on archetypes, in particular the archetype of the orphan," Adam said. "A character who has unmet needs and desires and treads a tragic line between good and evil.

"Carl Jung loosely used the term 'orphan' as one who has experienced abandonment. In *Gangster Child*, the villain is trying to prove that he is just as good as our protagonist."

Adam stopped.

Someone in the audience coughed.

Adam looked at me. The realization dawning for us both. Valentina Vale. Life imitating art. She wanted my life.

"Yes." He cleared his throat and looked at his notes. "My apologies, I've lost my place." He flipped pages and continued, then he reached for his book, his hands shaking and read, his voice captivating. He finished his reading, leaving us, of course, at a cliffhanger. Applause erupted.

I looked at Valentina, who smiled smugly.

Adam thanked everyone for coming. "Enjoy the evening. Try the pastries, according to my assistant, they're blinking good."

"They are," Gillian's voice rang out from the back.

The audience laughed and clapped again.

Adam stepped back. Valentina glided up to the podium. "Adam will now be signing copies of his book."

The jazz band struck up a rendition of *In the Mood*. The audience was on its feet. A line up formed at the book signing table.

I couldn't stop this. If I gave Valentina the pictures, the money, and Mom's necklace, it still wouldn't be enough. She wanted my life, which in her eyes looked perfect. She was determined to kill everyone around me. Her envy festered into jealousy which festered into hate. She'd regard herself the winner. After a month or two, she'd realize she may have my possessions, but she still wasn't me. She would kill me, eliminate the reminder of the life she could not have because unbeknown to her, my mother had killed her father.

I had been so deep in thought that I didn't notice the person who had sat next to me. I felt a tap on my shoulder. I turned.

"Hey Jade."

30 TERRIBLE THINGS

Adam tackled Osmond, driving him into the cupboards.

"SIMON! YOU'RE ALIVE. I WAS WORRIED ABOUT YOU."
He looked at his hands.

"Are you okay? You're looking good." He did look good. Sports coat, clean jeans, white shirt.

"I ran. The cops think I killed her. I didn't, Jade. I've been calling in anonymous tips," he whispered.

"Simon, you've got to turn yourself in."

"I know." He scanned the room.

"Is there anything you can think of, conversations, text messages, photos, notes, anything that might incriminate Valentina and not you?"

He scratched the stubble on his jaw. "Well, yeah, maybe, it's not much."

"Tell me, you never know."

He glanced around.

A woman moved from the front of the book signing table. Adam reached for a book, stopping mid-reach as he saw me and Simon. A man stepped in front, blocking his view.

"Can we—" he nervously looked around "—talk outside? I don't want Valentina seeing me."

"Yeah." I picked up my coat.

"Thanks Jade. I want to turn myself in if you'd still be my lawyer."

"Of course."

We slipped past attendees and headed to the side door. Simon gestured for me to go first. I did.

"This way," he said. "Just on the other side of that party bus. The smokers don't go there."

Clutching Adam's hardcover book, I took a step and hesitated. Maybe we should stay inside.

"This is perfect," he said, walking in front of me, "no one can hear us by the wood stairs." He stepped around the bus and stopped.

I followed. "What do you want to tell me?"

"There was this night—" he nervously looked around "—when Valentina wanted to see me. New instructions."

"You mentioned that the other day."

Simon looked at me. "Jade."

"What?"

"I'm sorry."

The bus door opened and a Lundgren clone, followed by Osmond and Dennis stepped out.

I bolted but Osmond grabbed my arm and pulled me into a chokehold.

"Let go of me," I clawed at his arm. "*Let go*."

"Not so fast, Jade," Osmond said.

I glared at Simon. "Are you in on this?"

He stared at the ground.

"*Look* at me. I trusted you."

Valentina sauntered around the bus and stood next to Simon. She patted his shoulder. "Good boy, Simon. You've just earned your little brother's college tuition."

Simon looked at me. "I'm—"

"—Off you go, Simon," Valentina ordered. "Your job is done."

Simon hesitated.

"Simon," Valentina said. "You know what happened to Lucy when she defied me."

Simon walked away, his head down.

"*You worthless piece of—*"

"—Shut up," Valentina said, her hand clutching my jaw. "Shut—" she shook my head "—the fuck up." She nodded at Osmond. "Take her inside."

"*No.*" I grabbed the doorway of the bus. Useless. Osmond dragged me up the carpeted steps.

Dennis smiled.

"No. You *asshole.*" I squirmed.

The Lundgren clone sat in the driver's seat.

Osmond threw me onto the floor. I landed face down on the purple carpet. I scrambled forward, smelling the leather of the stretch sofa. Large blacked-out windows, I could see out but no one could see in. I spun around when Osmond pasted me against the window.

"If you don't behave, your boyfriend writer," Osmond whispered, "gets into a bad fight with the security guard behind him, who works for us. Hope he can still write another novel. And Sage, Dennis is a dog pulling at a leash to get at her."

Valentina walked toward me, a wine glass in her hand.

"What do you want?" I asked.

Osmond let go and I dropped onto the leather sofa.

Valentina leaned forward, looking me in the eye, then backhanded me across the face, knocking me onto the carpet.

I rolled onto my back.

"Osmond, hold my wine glass." She straddled my body, grabbed my shirt and hit me again.

My face pressed into the carpet, nose bleeding. I didn't move.

"Wine." She held out her hand and Osmond handed back the glass. "Get us out of here."

Osmond's steps retreated then the bus engine rumbled. I didn't move as we pulled out of Esquimalt. Jaw sore, my cheek stung. Let her think she won. I kept my eyes closed, trying to figure out where we were going.

Valentina kicked me in the side. "*Pathetic.*"

The leather sofa winced under her weight. The bus made a number of turns and stops, then slowed as it climbed up an incline and stopped. The engine turned off.

Footsteps. Osmond's? Dennis? Where was Dennis?

"Wake her up," Valentina said.

Ice was dumped on my head. I jolted, sputtering, pushing wet hair out of my eyes.

"Let's go." Osmond hauled me to my feet and we exited the bus, walking down a driveway and up steps to a desolate house. He pushed me onto a chair at a kitchen table. The house was in darkness except for the overhead stove light.

"You know where we are, Jade?" Valentina asked, leaning against the kitchen table.

"No."

Osmond took Adam's book from my hands and tossed it on the table. He yanked my arms behind me and tied my hands together.

"We're sitting in the house where your father, Oscar, spent his dying days. But you should know that."

"I didn't."

Valentina walked around the table. "Liar." She slapped me.

I would have fallen off the chair if Osmond hadn't grabbed it. Leaning sideways, my blood dripped on the floor. My nose. I sat upright.

"We looked everywhere for his hideout and found it the day after the asshole died. If I had a dick I'd piss on his grave."

"Osmond did it for you."

Valentina hit me again and grabbed my chin, staring me in the eye. "You look like him." She shook my chin. "And you ... *disgust* ... me." She spat on my cheek and straightened.

I was *angry*. Shortened breaths, my chest rising and falling.

"We had bets on whether you'd save him."

"Save him?"

"You were his blood. Probably the only one who could have donated a kidney. But you didn't."

I could have saved Oscar. He chose to die rather than expose me as his child.

"Oscar killed my father." She crossed her arms. "Do you know who my father was?"

"A low-life criminal."

She hit me again.

Jesus. Stop asking me questions if you don't like the answers.

She hit me on the other side.

"I would slit your throat right now, but I want Adam to see your pain and remember that pain for the rest of his life."

I heard footsteps on the stairs outside, shuffling, then the kitchen door opened and Dennis walked in, one arm in a sling, dragging an unconscious Adam by the wrist. He let go and Adam dropped, a heap on the floor.

"Get him up," Valentina said.

Adam groaned. Osmond and Dennis picked him up and positioned him on the chair across from mine.

Swollen black eye, bloody nose, Adam looked at me. "We make quite the pair."

Osmond punched him, knocking him off the chair. "Did I say you could talk?"

Adam mumbled something.

Osmond punched him again.

"Stop it!" I shouted.

Adam was propped up in his chair.

"Tie him," Valentina ordered.

Osmond tied Adam's hands behind his back.

Valentina strolled around and slid up on the table, facing him. "I like you, Adam." She crossed her legs. "This—" she waggled her finger "—doesn't have to end this way. Bloody. Beaten. How's your hand? My Lundgren goon didn't break it, did he? It's your bitch girlfriend I want." Valentina pointed at me. "I figured your dad, Archie, was just following orders, and with Oscar Cooper as a boss, you didn't cross him or he'd feed you to the bears. Right?"

Adam looked at me, then at Valentina. "My dad tied Steven Banks to the tree ... my dad shot Diego."

Adam was lying to save me.

Valentina nodded at Osmond.

Osmond hit him.

"Stop it!" I shouted again, sitting forward, pulling at the twine that bound my wrists.

"Adam, Adam, Adam." Valentina slipped around the table. "Lawyers don't like being lied to. Oscar thought he had gotten away with beating my father with an electric guitar. He didn't stop trying to protect Jade's bitch mother."

Valentina believed Oscar had killed her father.

"She—" Valentina pointed at me "—had everything. The big house, a family." She walked toward me. "Do you know what happened after my father was killed?"

I didn't answer.

"His rivals killed Diego's brother and then they were going to kill us. They burned down our home. Mom and I barely escaped Mexico."

"What happened to Diego is *not* my fault," I said.

Valentina backhanded me. "Wrong answer."

She paced around the table. "But you sure benefited, didn't you, Jade. Dennis and his sister Kathy grew up without a father, because Oscar took care of Old Man Banks. After Darlene died, Dennis and Kathy were put up for adoption, but I found them. Then Oscar rats out to the cops and Dennis's sister is shot in a drug bust. It didn't take much to get Dennis to join my team. We changed his name from Victor Banks to Dennis Sullivan and put our plan into motion."

My cheeks tingled and my head pounded.

"Now you're quiet." She lunged and, with her hands around my neck, knocked my chair backwards onto the floor. She punched me once, then twice.

"Valentina." Osmond pulled her off. "Not until she gives us what we want." He propped up my chair.

"Get out of my way!" Valentina screamed, pushing Osmond. "You," she pointed at me, "your pure existence robbed me of the life

I deserved, which Oscar stripped from me. You had a loving family. You had everything. I've been waiting a long time, Jade Thyme. A long time. Plotting, bringing Dennis and Osmond into my plan—" she hit me "—watching—" she hit me again "—as you took down The Society and reaped—" she motioned her hands in the air "—the praise bestowed upon you like a superhero." She hit me again.

The room spun and grew dark around the edges. My face felt like it had been popped with a baseball.

"Valentina, stop."

Adam.

"You want Oscar's Lambo. I'll tell you. Let Jade go."

Adam didn't know where it was.

Valentina straightened her dress. "I don't negotiate, Adam."

I looked at Osmond, leaning on the kitchen table, arms crossed, looking at me. "You bastard," I mumbled, my lip fat and bleeding, saliva running down my chin.

Valentina smiled. "He worked you over while I worked over Charles. Trying to find out where the hell everything was, the pictures, the necklace, the cash. But Charles knew nothing."

"You killed him."

"He asked questions about Dennis and me. He hired a *detective*. When Oscar died, it was open season. Your protection was gone. Now, I want the keys to the Lamborghini, the money, the necklace. Where are they?"

My wrist and fingers cramped as I tugged on the last bit of twine. "Sage's house, which you burned to the ground. And no matter what you steal from me, you will never be me."

Valentina leaned forward. "It was never about being you, Jade," she whispered. "Look at you. Bloodied nose and lip. Black eye. You look like shit." She twined a strand of my hair around her finger. "I'm taking from you what was taken from me. For the longest time I felt locked out of my own life. Standing outside, banging on the glass, banging to be let in. I had two options. Kill myself, or kill you. I'm still standing." She snapped her fingers at Dennis. "Give me your phone."

Dennis lumbered forward and handed it to her.

She held it up. "Smile for Sage, darlin'."

I looked at the floor.

She clicked and handed the phone back to Dennis. "Show Sage and tell that dyke that if she doesn't cooperate, I'm killing her sister."

Dennis nodded. He looked at me, then at Valentina.

"What?" Valentina asked.

"Can I?"

She looked at me and smiled. "Quickly, we don't have much time."

Dennis smiled. He leaned forward and touched my cheek.

I pulled away, but he held my head in his hands.

"It's okay, Jade. I come back with the goods—" he ran his hand down my throat "—and then I can show you my tattoo." He rubbed his hands over my breasts, kneading. "I'll ask really nice and maybe Valentina will video tape."

I glared at Osmond.

He smiled.

I ... hate ... you.

Dennis rubbed his genitals. "Then I can sell the video on the Net."

"Go, Dennis. Now," Valentina ordered.

He lumbered out of the kitchen.

I looked at Osmond again, sitting with his back to Adam. I looked at Adam. He looked like he wanted to kill somebody.

I looked at Valentina. Did I dare make her lose it? If it gave us an opening to get out of here? The twine was loose around my wrists.

"You got something you want to tell me, Jade?"

Valentina stood, so damn cocky. I glanced at Adam. He looked like a cat ready to pounce.

"Oscar didn't kill your drug-dealing daddy."

"Really?" she scoffed. She propped her hands on her hips. Hands stained with my blood. "Then who the hell did?"

"My *mother*."

Her eyes grew wide.

The twine binding my wrists slipped to the floor. I lunged just as Valentina did, swinging my leg and kicking her in the crotch.

She buckled, gasping, legs crossed.

Osmond grabbed for me but Adam sprung onto the table, swept his leg up and kicked Osmond in the head, knocking him backwards. Osmond dropped to the ground. Adam jumped on top of him, fist raised.

Valentina screamed and lunged, toppling us onto the floor. She grabbed my hair and banged my forehead against the lino.

Pain shot from temple to temple.

She pulled my head up again and banged it against the floor. Spots. My vision blackened.

"Get ... up."

Through bloody strands of hair, I saw the masculine hand on the floor and Oscar, as he looked in his prime, kneeling before me, as if counting down a boxing match.

"*Fight*." He pounded his fist on the floor.

Valentina grabbed my hair again, pulling me up. I threw my weight against her, drilling my elbow into her face. She fell backwards.

Adam tackled Osmond, driving him into the cupboards.

I scrambled upright.

Valentina lurched toward me, swinging a broken wine bottle. I jumped back, colliding with the table, stumbling over a metal stool. I grabbed it and swung, knocking the wine bottle from her hand. I swung again. She ducked and tackled me around the waist, driving me against the gas oven. Arms flailing, I hit the knobs.

She clawed me.

I grabbed her hair, kneed her under the chin and flung her like a dishrag to the floor.

Teetering, she kneeled on one knee.

Finish you off, *bitch*. I grabbed Adam's hardcover book and with both hands, swung it up the side of her head. She dropped and didn't move.

Panting, I let go of the book.

Adam landed on his back on the floor with Osmond in a chokehold on top of him. Osmond gasped, and pulled on his arm, his legs kicking. Adam flipped him over, laying on top, squeezing. Osmond flailed, then lay motionless.

Adam clambered off, his shirt shredded and bloodstained. "Jade." He sniffed. He grabbed my hand. "Gas." His eyes glanced over the room. "C'mon. Gotta get out of here." He grabbed me around the waist and we lumbered to the door.

Dennis's cellphone was on the floor. He had forgotten it. I scooped it up and saw spots. Adam half-dragged, half-carried me over the stoop. "C'mon, Jade, c'mon." We lurched across the street, partially hidden by a shrub. He pressed me against his chest, hugging me with one arm. "You okay?"

"Not so tight. My face hurts."

He loosened his grip. "Are you okay?"

I nodded. Scared to say anything for fear of crying.

"I am so sorry—" his voice broke "—for not stopping Dennis, for not stopping—"

"—It's—"

"—We were outnumbered. I wanted them to forget I was there. I'm going to pulverize that creep—"

Brakes squealed.

We looked and a black SUV swerved into the driveway. Dennis clambered out and ran toward the house.

"Now's my chance."

"Adam, no." I held him back.

Dennis had returned for his cellphone, which I had in my pocket.

He yanked open the screen door and stopped. "Valentina. Osmond. No!" He ran in.

"Jade, I'm—"

"—Adam, look."

He followed my gaze.

Oscar strolled down the side of the house, smoking a cigarette.

He walked up the steps and hesitated as if sensing we were there. He took a final drag, pulled open the screen door, and tossed his cigarette into the house.

Flames plumed up the walls and around the doorframe.

Oscar walked in.

31 #TEAMJADE

"...if you think my book sucks, tell me instead of using it to bash someone's face in."

Adam and I slunk behind the people gathered on the sidewalks watching the fire. Firefighters spilled out of two firetrucks.

Two blocks away, Adam called Gillian, holding his phone away from his ear as she shrieked, "*Where are you?*"

Fifteen minutes later, Gillian's Volkswagen careened around the corner. Sage sat in the passenger seat, gripping the dash with one hand and pointing at us with the other as Adam waved them down.

I was happy to see my sister.

The Volkswagen squealed to a stop and Sage was out before Gillian had turned off the motor.

"Jade." She ran toward me and scooped me into a suffocating hug. "Don't ever leave without telling anyone where you're going." Her voice broke. She stepped back, her hands still cupping my shoulders. "Are you okay?"

"Careful." I winced.

"Who did this to you? I'm going to beat the crap out of them. Valentina? Dennis?" Her face paled. "*Osmond?*"

"Valentina and I had a few rounds." I glanced at Adam as Gillian stepped beside him.

"Valentina, Osmond and Dennis are in the fire up the street," Adam said. "They're not going to make it."

Sage looked at him. "Say no more."

"Adam needs to go to the hospital," I said. "Your hand's broken, isn't it?"

He nodded. "Dennis was a prick when he loaded me into the SUV."

"You're pretty messed up too, Jade," Sage said.

We hustled into the Volkswagen and headed to Royal Jubilee Hospital. The emergency room doctor set Adam's wrist in a cast, and told him since it was a clean break it should quickly heal. He then asked Adam to autograph his copy of *Gangster Child*.

Another doctor stitched up the gash above my eyebrow. My nose was surprisingly not broken.

On our way out, we saw a local news story about a house fire in James Bay and the three occupants inside having died from smoke inhalation and severe burns. Their identities would be confirmed using dental records. Although not official, the police suspected the home stored flammable and dangerous substances that were used in the arsons that had occurred a few weeks ago. The public's assistance was requested in identifying two people seen leaving the blaze. Adam and I looked at each other and walked out of emergency only to be greeted by Inspector Shelly and the Sergeant. We were wanted for questioning.

I learned that when Adam saw Simon and I exit the Roundhouse, he bolted from the signing table, leaving a stunned line-up, which ultimately made for a great news story and skyrocketing book sales as well as a Facebook fan page. What Adam's fans didn't know was that once outside, another Lundgren clone had clotheslined him. Gillian saw Dennis and Simon stuff Adam into the back of the SUV when she had gone outside to get another batch of almond thingies. Gillian told Sage, who had already been looking for me. Inspector Shelly and Sergeant Stone were already searching for us and an all points bulletin was issued for the abduction of Jade Thyme and Adam Younghusband.

In separate rooms, Sergeant Stone questioned me and another sergeant questioned Adam. Stone nearly fell off his chair when I told him Valentina had kidnapped me. I told him the truth as much as possible. For motive, I said Valentina had an unhealthy jealousy of me and my success. I did not mention Valentina's lineage, and I definitely did not mention mine. Sergeant Stone sat back in the chair, closing his notebook, and tapped his pencil.

"Anything else you want to tell me, Jade?"

I looked at my hands. I suspected Stone wondered if Oscar was my father but I was not going to admit it. I would throw him other fish. I reached into my pocket and pulled out Dennis Sullivan's phone. I pushed it across the table. "That's Dennis Sullivan's phone. He forgot it at the house."

Sergeant Stone sat forward and using his pencil, pulled the phone toward him. He looked at me. "Why are you giving me this evidence?"

"Because there may be photos on it ... of his sex assault victims."

Sergeant Stone flipped open a fresh page in his notebook. "Why do you think that?"

I looked him in the eye, and I could sense his anticipation that I was going to deliver him something big. "Because I was one of his victims." My eyes welled with tears. I wouldn't bring up Sage's assault. That was her business.

Stone pushed aside his notebook. "Do you want another coffee?"

"Yes, please."

"I'll get you one. It's going to be a long night."

I nodded.

He returned with a coffee and I told him what happened in Lucy's trailer. Two and a half hours later, I stepped out of the interview room. Adam, battered in his ripped shirt and sports coat, sat at the end of a long line of chairs. He stood and walked over to me.

"You okay?"

I nodded.

He brushed my hair back from my face. "We take our weary, beaten bodies back to the hotel?"

"That would be nice."

He wrapped his arm around my shoulders and we walked toward the front door. "Next time, Jade, if you think my book sucks, tell me instead of using it to bash someone's face in."

32 DOLPHIN BEACH

"You wouldn't be the first Cooper."

F ORTY-EIGHT HOURS LATER, WE STOOD IN THE DRIVE-way of Coco's condo. Coco handed Sage Lizzy's leash. Sage kneeled and rubbed Lizzy's fur, receiving a licked face while Lizzy's tail beat against the sidecar.
"What have you been feeding Lizzy?" Gillian asked.
Sage looked at Coco. "She's looking a little round, Coco."
Coco tisked. "I thought it was the baguette."
Sage smiled. "You were feeding Lizzy baguettes?"
"She liked it."
"I could imagine."
"But, it was not the baguette."
"The escargot?" Adam asked.
I chuckled.
"Non. See, my dog Neville, he—" she looked from Sage to me "—how should I say, he make love to Lizzy."
We laughed.

"What can I do? It's nature."

"I'm remembering that line," Adam said under his breath.

I poked him in the ribs.

"Coco—" Sage smiled, her hands held out to her sides "—I trust you with my dog, and she comes back expecting."

Coco laughed.

Sage wrapped her arms around Lizzy's neck. "You're going to have puppies, Lizzy. Beautiful puppies."

"What type of dog is Neville?" Adam asked.

"Bernese Mountain dog."

Big puppies. "I'll take one of Lizzy's puppies," I said.

Adam slung his arm around my shoulders. "So will I."

I looked at him. "You're heading back to the U.K."

"I've been offered a professor's position at Royal Roads."

"You're staying?"

He kissed my temple. "This island sucks you in. I might be Coco's neighbour in one of these condos."

"I go," Coco said, rolling her bike forward. "The Dolls and I have a ride. Stay as long as you want, Sage. Oh, the skinny man."

"What skinny man?" Sage asked.

"Valentina's gopher."

"Simon," I guessed.

Coco nodded. "Word is, cops arrested him. Held him overnight so he can make a first, a first—" Coco snapped her fingers.

"—First appearance," I said.

"That's it. He didn't make it."

I stepped forward. "What do you mean, 'he didn't make it'?"

"When he was escorted to the courthouse, he had a bad accident in the sheriff's van. Got into a fight with another prisoner. He's alive but in a coma." Coco started the engine. She smiled, waved, then pulled out of the parking lot.

Sage, Gillian and Lizzy headed toward the condo. Sage turned. "You two coming?"

"We're examining Mom's paintings, trying to figure out where Oscar hid the Lamborghini."

"Good luck."

"You don't want to join us?"

Sage tried to act cool but I saw the hint of a smile.

"What's up?"

Gillian slipped her arm around Sage's waist. "Sage, is getting another tattoo."

"Really! Of what?"

"Roy and Silo!" Gillian said, smiling ear-to-ear.

I looked at Sage. *Roy and Silo?*

She looked sheepish.

Adam chuckled. "The two gay chinstrap penguins."

"Well, well." I smiled. "That's taking your relationship to a new level. Make sure they do a good job."

Sage waved.

Adam and I walked past the pond and along the gravel path by Fol Epi Bakery. "I wonder how that happened? Simon getting attacked."

"Not a bloody clue," Adam said, as we turned onto the Galloping Goose Trail.

I glanced at him. "Says the man who still hasn't explained why he was meeting an informant in Beirut."

A smile tugged at the corners of Adam's mouth but he remained silent.

At my place, we pulled out the box of framed pictures, and sitting on the floor, sipping wine, we admired Mother's art.

Adam held up one canvas. "This is my favourite," he said, looking at the Lamborghini.

"It was based off the photo Mom had taken when the Lambo was parked in front of Oscar's home."

Adam frowned. "Really."

"Yes. Why? What's wrong?"

"The background."

"What about it?"

Adam held the picture at arm's length. He pulled out his phone and Googled Willowbrook Manor, Oscar's place. He pinched the screen and dragged, magnifying the image. "This—" he nodded toward the canvas "—isn't the manor."

"Why do you say that?"

He turned the picture toward me. "This car may have been in Oscar's driveway at Willowbrook but that gazebo, that barn, that's not Oscar's place."

Mother had property. Had she been hiding Oscar's Lamborghini all this time?

"Where's your mother's property?" he asked.

"Dolphin Beach in Schooner Cove."

"Who owns the property now?"

"Sage and me."

"Have you ever been there?"

"Once or twice during the winter. There's not much there except an old, locked shack that I never had the keys—"

I looked at the living room table and the keys Adam had given me weeks ago. I looked at Adam. "Road trip?"

In a matter of minutes we were in Adam's Morris Minor heading up island, leaving Victoria behind. The Morris struggled on the incline going over the Malahat but we eventually made it. Two hours later we drove past Fairwinds Golf Course and found ourselves on Dolphin Drive. The beach flirted through the tree branches, and the waves sparkled from the sun. "This—"

"—This what?"

"Slow down. This—" I looked out the side window; if I was a child, I'd put my hands against the glass. "This is where the dolphins play."

Adam smiled. He slowed and we made a sharp turn. He flicked the signal light and turned left into a driveway, stopping before a padlocked gate. "I don't see security cameras or Rottweilers," he said, looking up through the front windshield.

I stared past the cedar tree boughs at the water. "I'd pretend that I swam with the dolphins." Keys in hand, I stepped out. Birds twittered. The waves lapped. I slipped a key into the padlock and turned. Nothing. I tried another key. The lock clicked open. I pushed open the gate. Adam drove in. I closed the gate after him and sat back in the car.

My hand braced on the dash, the Morris Minor dipped and jolted over potholes. The drooping cedar boughs dragged over its roof.

"There." I pointed to the left.

Adam pulled up in front of a cottage and parked. We stepped out. I turned around, breathing in the fresh ocean air. Maple trees and isolation. A rush of a memory, of me, giggling, running, hands out pretending to be a plane. I squinted at the sunshine peeking through maple leaves. "I wonder if this was where they'd meet up."

We walked around a tiny cottage with its sagging shutters and peeling paint. I saw the barn. "Adam." I walked toward it, noticing footprints in the mud. "Someone's been here."

The barrel of a rifle poked out from the side of the barn, then a hunched man with cracked John Lennon glasses and dirty clothes crept into view.

"Jade." Adam stepped in front of me.

"It's okay, Adam. I know him." I stepped forward. "Norman. It's me, Jade."

The rifle wavered. "Jade."

"Valentina, Dennis and Osmond are dead."

"The house fire," he said.

"Yes. And this—" I held my hand out toward Adam "—is my friend, Adam Younghusband. He's an author."

Adam waved. "Nice to meet you from this end of a rifle."

Norman eyed him as he lowered the rifle. "You look like someone I once knew."

"Really?" Adam smiled. "I hope he was a decent chap."

"No," Norman said. "He held a gun to my head."

"Oh."

Norman shifted his gaze to me. "The Lambo is in the barn."

"Adam, can you give us a moment?"

Adam stepped back to the driver's side of the Morris Minor.

"Norman, let's catch up," I said, walking toward him.

He leaned his rifle against the barn. "I know him from somewhere."

"C'mon, let's sit under this cherry blossom tree."

Norman shuffled after me. We plunked ourselves down on the bluff, admiring Dolphin Beach below. Norman took out a kerchief and cleaned his glasses.

"We've missed you, Norman. We were worried."

"I deserted you. I'm sorry, Jade." With trembling fingers he slipped on his glasses.

"Are you doing all right? Need anything? You're staying in the cottage, right?"

"I hope that's okay. Genie said I could crash here whenever I wanted."

"Absolutely. Do you need any food, water—" *medication.*

Norman again pulled out his kerchief and wiped his eyes. "He had me on retainer. He trusted me. He once told me that the day he died, there would be hell to pay, and I was to watch out for his interests."

"So when you read Oscar's obituary—"

"—I knew I had to protect the Lambo. Oscar would have wanted that."

"Oh, Norman." He had interpreted 'interests' as Oscar's lime green Lamborghini. "Well, you did a good job. It's still here. Valentina didn't get it."

Norman wiped his blue eyes again, and I realized he was mourning. "We're old, Jade. Oscar, me. We didn't have a chance against Valentina, especially with Dennis and Osmond as her henchmen."

"She can throw a mean punch," I said.

"Oscar knew she was onto him, but he kept calling her Alexy. I didn't make the connection, or I would have warned you. He couldn't hand over the thumbdrives himself. He was ill. If he was seen near you, he'd make you a target."

I glanced over at the Morris Minor where Adam was texting. *So he made a younger, more capable man be his messenger. Someone who would care.*

"Oscar, your father, he ... he became my friend. I was his last hope to keep him out of jail. He'd stroll into my office and say, 'My freedom's in your hands, Norman. I like you, so don't fuck this up.' My apologies for the language."

I chuckled. "That's okay."

"I was always a little concerned what might happen if he was ever found guilty, or held on a show cause hearing. If you were on team Oscar, he treated you like family. If you pissed him off ... he fed you to the bears."

I shook my head. "Is that why you never told me he was my real father?"

Norman poked the ground with a stick. "Jade, I suspected. But I shared Genie's fear. If anyone found out the truth, you, or Genie, could be killed. I stepped over a dead man in Oscar's studio. I saw what the Society did. I kept my thoughts to myself, to protect myself and to protect you, Sage and Genie. Oscar's retainer, bought my silence."

I rubbed Norman's shoulder. "Oh, Norman."

"Now, they're all gone. Genie, Charles, Edith, Oscar."

"You've got me. I'm not going anywhere. I'm your family, Norman, and wait until you meet Sage. She rides a Harley."

"She rides a Harley?"

I nodded.

"Oscar would approve. He liked bikes. He'd take Genie on rides. She'd have the biggest smile. Everyone loved Genie. But she only loved Oscar. I don't know if she knew the extent of what Oscar was doing. I sure wasn't going to bring it up. Times we'd come here and she'd vent, yell and scream. Then when she was done, we'd listen to The Mamas and the Papas, get high and see what pictures we saw in the clouds.

"I prepared the conveyancing documents when Oscar wanted to give her the property. She was a garden fairy."

A cherry blossom floated, resting on Norman's shoulder.

She was my *Tink*. What I searched for while using Vicodin.

"She married Charles out of convenience. He offered her safety and protection."

I patted his shoulder. "Well, you're not alone, Norman. You have me."

He nodded.

"You can stay here as long as you want. Promise me though, that you'll come back to the office? Or do I have to put you on retainer?"

Norman smiled. "You wouldn't be the first Cooper to have me on retainer."

I laughed.

"I'll come back, but Jade ... can the red electric guitar be put in the dungeon?"

"Absolutely." I stood. "I'm going to check out my new car." I walked to the barn. Adam joined me.

"Everything all right?" he asked.

"Yes. He just needs a little time. He was close to Oscar. Now, let's check out this car." I tried one key, nothing. I tried the second, no luck.

"The next one," Adam said.

I tried it, heard a click and looked at Adam.

He smiled.

I removed the lock, flipped the latch, and Adam and I pulled open the creaking barn doors.

The outdoor sunshine blazed inside, revealing a car covered by a blue tarp.

I saw the excitement in Adam's eyes.

Without saying a word, we walked to opposite sides and pulled up on the tarp, exposing a bull emblem and lime green paint.

"This is it," Adam said.

My heart beat faster. We pulled the tarp back, exposing the black grill and what looked like eyelashes around the headlights. "Oh ... my God."

Shiny fluorescent green paint, a sleek body design and black tires, the Lamborghini was like a hidden jewel in the dilapidated barn. We tossed the tarp on the ground.

"Holy shit," Adam muttered. He stepped back, taking it all in. He looked at me from across the hood. "Did you see the gold? On the rims?"

I nodded. "It's—"

"—Absolutely amazing." He looked the car up and down and walked around the front. "The last time I saw this car was the day you were kidnapped."

"How do I unlock the driver's door?"

Adam came over to my side and opened the door, which swept upwards. "Suicide doors."

Blue leather interior.

"Have a seat," he gestured.

I sat in. Adam closed the driver's door, darted around and sat in the passenger seat. "Does it start?"

"My feet don't reach the pedals."

We maneuvered the seat forward. I inserted the key, pressed in the clutch and brake and turned the key. The car rumbled.

"Aha!"

"You have the emergency brake up, give her some gas."

I did. The engine roared. Surprised, I pulled my feet off the pedals. The Lambo lurched and stalled.

I removed the key. "I can't believe I did that. I know how to drive a stick."

"You've inherited a savvy sportscar, Jade," Adam said, his hand caressing the dash. "If it wasn't himself, Oscar paid someone to take good care of her.

"1968. What a year. Ferruccio Lamborghini was only twenty-two when he designed the Miura. It has flaws but it's a masterpiece in design. V12 rear engine turned sideways. The doors, when opened, are to look like the horns of a bull. Only 761 Miuras were made and you own one of them."

"This car was ahead of its time."

"Absolutely," Adam said. "And it's more than *just* a car. If you're into pop culture, the late Eddie Van Halen has this engine revving in his song *Panama*."

"How much is it worth?"

"The Miura was considered one of the first super cars. You're looking at six-hundred and fifty thousand pounds which converts to–" Adam whistled "–one million and sixty thousand Canadian dollars."

I gripped the steering wheel with both hands. "This, this—"

"—Lamborghini, yes."

I looked at the console and seats. "Anything in the glove box?"

Adam tried to open it. "Locked."

I gave him the keys. He unlocked the glove box and smiled.

"What?" I leaned against his shoulder, trying to get a better view. Adam took out a narrow plastic box and gave it to me.

It trembled in my hands.

"Open it."

I wedged the lid off. Mother's spider necklace sparkled as if saying, *about time*.

"What everyone's been after." He brushed my hair back. "It'll look nice on you."

The necklace snaked between my fingers. The history behind these jewels. My phone buzzed in my pocket.

"Are you getting that?"

"No."

My phone buzzed again.

He kissed my temple. "It could be important." He sat back in the passenger seat, looked at the glove box and reached forward.

I put Mother's necklace back in its box. I glanced at my phone. Sergeant Stone. He could leave a message.

Adam pulled four wads of cash from the glove box.

"That's drug money," I said. "You, Norman and Sage know that Oscar was my father. Valentina, Osmond and Dennis knew but they're dead."

"Bob and Henri have sworn allegiance to you and—" Adam hesitated "—me."

I looked at Adam.

"Archie, supposedly treated their fathers very well." He held up a wad of cash. "What are you going to do with this?"

The cedar boughs swayed. Maple leaves skirted across the dirt.

"If I turn the money in everyone will find out I'm Oscar Cooper's daughter. The police will question me. They'll want to know where I found the cash. If I don't turn in the money, I'm in possession of crime proceeds. I'm risking my career."

"So," Adam said slowly, "what are you going to do?"

I gripped the steering wheel with both hands. "I'm keeping the damn car."

Adam smiled.

The sun came out from behind a cloud and lit the driveway.

Adam waved the wad of fifties. "And the cash?"

Norman still sat under the cherry blossom tree.

"It goes back in the glove box. One day, you never know, Norman might need it."

33 STOP OVER

"Screw your Highway to Heaven. There isn't one."

Adam came back to my place. We celebrated finding the Lamborghini with wine, jazz and pizza. We reminisced about the times we played together. He stayed the night and I got my hat trick.

The next morning he stood inside my front door, flipping up his coat collar. "Tonight, dinner at Il Terrazzo?"

"Italian food sounds wonderful."

He leaned over and kissed my neck under my ear. "I'll text you later."

I waved as he stepped out, closing the door behind him. Still dressed in my blue pajamas, and holding my cup of cold coffee, I trudged into the kitchen. I placed my cup on the island and pulled open the refrigerator door. Leftover pizza. I flipped the lid, took out a slice and bit into it. I hip-checked the refrigerator door closed, and found myself face-to-face with Oscar.

The pizza muffled my scream.

Oscar grinned. "Jade."

I swallowed without chewing. "You and Mom are going to give me a heart attack."

"You like the Miura?"

"Yes. Thank you."

"Adam treating you with respect?"

"Yes. How long have you been here?"

"Not long."

Oh, good.

"You took quite a beating."

"I'm sore. Very sore. Tylenol. That's all I'm taking. Tylenol. Nothing addicting. I'm clean. I've been clean for six, no, seven months now." I hardly knew this man, my father, but I babbled like a child. "Granted, seeing a ghost possess a typewriter nearly put me over the edge."

He smiled. "Stay clean, Jade."

"So why can I see you now? Why aren't you possessing my laptop or cell phone?"

"Want me to?"

"No!"

Oscar crossed his arms as he leaned back against the kitchen island. "I made a Hell of a good deal."

"Bad dad joke."

He laughed. "If I killed two people, Hell would release its hold on me."

"You killed three, Valentina, Osmond and Dennis."

"I'm good at what I do."

"So why can I see you, but Mom can't?"

"You're human, like a stopover. She's not."

"You're not trying to get into Heaven?"

"No, but there is Remedial, and that's where I need you to do something for me."

I brought my mug to my lips. "It's a little late to give you a kidney."

He chuckled.

"As long as it's not negotiations with God."

Oscar smiled. "Genie's been to see you."

"She pops in and out."

"I want you to reunite me with her."

I sputtered and placed my mug down. "Excuse me—" I wheezed "—I thought you said—"

By the level stare Oscar gave me, I had heard correctly.

"Jesus." I pulled out a red stool and sat. "When did I become a medium?" I took another bite of my pizza, chewing but not tasting.

"You're not. You're a—"

"—Stop over," I said, mouth full.

"Genie and I are on different planes."

"Figuratively, or—" I swallowed "—do we need to talk with Boeing?"

"Have you always been this cheeky? Where's the little girl who wanted to swim with dolphins?"

"She grew up and became a lawyer."

Oscar smiled. "A damn good one, I understand. Our spirits aren't connecting, Genie and me."

"Mom mentioned something like that," I said, taking another bite.

"I hope you'll take this seriously. You can communicate with both of us, so you can bring us together."

I sipped my coffee. Cold. I grabbed it, stood, and placed it in the microwave. "And just how am I—" I pushed 10 seconds "—to accomplish this? Can you at least give me some sort of template?" Start.

I turned.

Oscar smiled. "You're smart. You'll figure it out."

The microwave pinged and Oscar was gone.

The next morning after getting myself a raspberry truffle mocha and Kate a chai latte, I called Kate into my office and sheepishly asked if she believed in ghosts.

"Absolutely. My aunt summoned a ghost after Thanksgiving dinner."

"Recently?" I asked, my mocha midway to my mouth.

"No. When I was a child. But—" Kate pointed her finger to make the point "–she made the table rise from the floor and the gravy boat tip, staining mom's honeycomb Damask tablecloth. Mom wasn't pleased."

Logical Thanksgiving tradition after saying Grace, eating too much turkey, and having a few glasses of wine with the pumpkin pie. "Can ghosts be reunited?"

Kate nodded. "Absolutely. Haven't you watched *Ghost Chasers* on Amazon?"

My expression must have given away my answer.

"Obviously not," Kate said. "I'll make inquiries." She leaned forward. "And Jade, I promise *absolute discretion*."

I really was losing my mind. Asking my assistant how to reunite ghosts.

At the end of the day, Kate delivered. "You have a minute?" she asked, popping her head into my office.

"Yes." I sat forward and put aside the Report to Crown Counsel I had been reading.

"So—" she sat, eyes wide, her hands clasped on her lap. She reminded me of Tinkerbell. "The parties to this rendezvous-"

"—Yes."

"—Must follow the Law of Common Occurrence."

"You're serious."

"Once summoned, they need to converge on common ground, and a common object must be used to bind their souls. They can only be brought together by a person common to them both. Right now, the ghosts are likely spiralling around each other on separate planes. They need to come together on the same journey."

That's what Oscar said. "That's it? I don't need to count back thirteen days from the next full moon or anything like that? Or recite an incantation?"

Kate glared. "You're mocking me."

"No, no. I appreciate this information very much. It just seems so easy."

"Do you have experience summoning ghosts?" Kate asked.

"Ah, no ... it's not on my CV."

"One other element must be present."

Now she was going to tell me I needed a pig's hoof, or something more vile, like the eye of newt from *Macbeth*.

"A strong common emotion experienced by all, which is also connected to the common object, must be present."

That might be difficult. How did one know what emotion? I barely remembered the little time I spent with Oscar. "Okay. So, how do you know if it works? The celestial reunion. Do you hear a heavenly rendition of Peaches & Herb's *Reunited*?"

Kate frowned. "You're mocking me."

"No, no, well, it's not you. I come from a background of evidence and facts. I value your advice."

"There isn't a light show. Harps won't be striking up the soundtrack to Star Wars. You'll know when it *doesn't* work, because the two souls will see each other but not be able to communicate, which I think is worse."

"Kate, thank you. I really appreciate this information. Please take the rest of the afternoon off."

"Jade, it's closing time."

"Oh. Take off early tomorrow."

She smiled, stood and walked to the door. She stopped and looked back. "I hope your souls are reunited."

I smiled. "Me too."

That night I explained everything to Adam. He agreed that the best location would be Oscar's old art gallery, The Studio. He contacted the owner of the tea shop and agreed to a book signing in exchange for an unchaperoned research visit. The shop owner was more than happy to accede to our request.

The following Saturday, we descended the dark stairs of the Silk Road Tea Store and stood in the basement amongst the 1968 furniture.

Adam looked around and shivered. "Common ground."

We felt it. Nerves. Would it work? Were we crazy? Should we check the classifieds for a coupon for psychiatric services?

I walked over to the brick wall and placed my hand against it, then traced the grout lines with my fingers. "I'm going to try," I whispered to any ghost listening. I kneeled and placed my backpack on the floor and unzipped it. I pulled out Mother's spider necklace. The diamonds winked in the light.

"Your common object," Adam said, kneeling beside me. He looked from the necklace to me. I rubbed my thumb over the spider's body. "Please work," I whispered.

"I've been looking for that necklace."

I spun around.

Mother stood over my shoulder.

"She's here," Adam said, looking around.

"You and Sage always played dress-up in my clothes and jewellery."

"Good to see you," I said. "How's it going with God?"

"He's deliberating."

"That's good."

"What are you doing with my necklace, Jade?"

I cleared my throat and looked at Adam.

"She's talking to you," he said. "By the look on your face I'd say she's talking to you. Does she like me? She near me?" He looked side-to-side.

I smiled. "What am I doing with this?" The necklace dangled from my fingers. "I'm going to clear a highway to heaven." I spread the necklace on the floor into a circle.

"That was a Michael Landon TV series. Why the hell are you doing that?"

"It's important."

"So is eliminating greenhouse gases but that's not happening soon."

"All okay?" Adam asked.

"She doesn't want me using her necklace," I whispered.

"Adam Malone, yes, I knew he wasn't returning to the U.K."

"She sees you," I said quietly.

Adam blushed.

Mother smiled. "Please tell him, Jade, that he was a very sweet boy. He consoled me more than I consoled him on that awful day."

"I'll tell him." I looked at Adam and repeated her words.

Adam turned a deeper red.

Mother crossed her arms. "Now. I want my necklace."

"You can't have it."

"Oscar gave me that necklace."

"Yes. I know."

"Why bring it out if you're not giving it to me?"

I couldn't believe we were having this argument. "It's for my Highway to Heaven. You wanted this. The reunion with Oscar."

"There is no Highway to Heaven."

"Okay, airstrip? Is that better? Or how about *Staircase to Heaven*? No? Not a Led Zeppelin fan?"

Her eyes grew wide. She was pissed.

Adam tapped my shoulder. "Ah, Jade."

I looked up. Oscar stood in the corner. I looked at Mother. She couldn't see him.

Oscar stepped out from the dark corner.

"I see him," I said.

Oscar smiled.

I motioned for him to come over.

"Now what are you doing?" Mother demanded.

"She wants her necklace," I said.

Oscar chuckled. "She's giving you grief."

"A little."

"Who are you talking to?" Mother asked.

I looked at Oscar. "Hold on." I pulled out my phone, hit play, and The Mamas and the Papas's *Monday, Monday* played. I set my phone on the ground and looked at Mother.

She stared at me, tears in her eyes, and I wondered if she was reliving 1968.

I looked at Oscar. "You better know what to do, because I sure don't."

He winked.

I stepped back beside Adam, both of us transfixed.

"Really, Jade." Mother glided over to the necklace. "What type of hocus-pocus game are you playing?" She leaned over and touched the necklace but couldn't pick it up because Oscar had his hand on it.

Mother looked at me, questioning.

"Genie," Oscar said. Mother looked away from me and by the expression on her face, I knew she could see him.

"I can see her now," Adam whispered.

"Don't let go, Genie," Oscar said, smiling.

Mother did not take her eyes off Oscar.

"You ready for a ride?" Oscar asked.

"She's not answering. Something's not right." I looked at the necklace. A golden light did not glow from it. The ceiling didn't open and a great light shine down from the heavens. Instead, the diamond spider wiggled its legs and kicked the gold chain. It crawled up and over mother's wrist, leaving a trail of gold dust over her fingers. It then crawled over Oscar's hand, leaving another trail of gold dust. The spider crawled over the chain and tucked itself into its original position as if going for a nap. A sheet of glass might as well have been between Oscar and Mother. They stared at each other but couldn't communicate.

"It didn't work." My voice broke.

"Common ground, common object," Adam rattled off, "common person, common *emotion*." He looked at me. "You are not emotionally attached to the necklace."

"What are you saying?"

"Oscar gave the necklace to Genie because he loved her. She accepted it because she loved him. That's *their* emotion. Not yours."

I looked at Oscar and Mother, seeing the forlorn expressions on their faces, placing flat palms against each other but still separated. "What do I do? I can't leave them like this."

Adam reached into his pocket. "I don't know if it will work."

His fingers uncurled.

The pink station wagon matchbox car.

You can play with this one, his six-year-old voice echoed in my ears.

Adam wiped his eyes. "It has all our emotions."

I took it like I had when I was five. I stepped toward Oscar and Genie and placed the station wagon on the floor. I pushed it through the gold circular trail that had been Mother's necklace.

Mother stared at me with the pain she must have experienced on the day I was kidnapped.

"No!" Oscar shouted.

Fear lodged in my chest and spread like ice through my veins. I was helpless. Small and totally helpless. I couldn't breathe.

"*Jade!*" Mother shouted, falling forward, landing in Oscar's arms. She looked at him. A tear trickled over her cheek, and she and Oscar embraced.

I fell backwards.

They stood, reached for me, but I was the one on the different plane. Mother mouthed, 'thank you.' Oscar nodded, then they walked through the bricks and disappeared, leaving behind blue and fuchsia-coloured smoke.

"Jade, it worked." Adam hugged my shoulders and kissed me.

I looked at where I had placed the necklace. A circle of diamonds, gold, and blue and fushcia-dust sprinkled the floor. I felt gutted.

He squeezed my shoulders again. "You did it."

"They're gone."

"It worked, Jade. They're together."

I nodded, but selfishly, felt sad. "Will I ... will I ever see her again? See him?"

"They're at peace."

I wiped my eyes and grabbed my purse, dumping coins out.

"What are you doing?"

I picked up a few tiny diamonds, dropping them in my purse. I brushed as best I could the gold, blue and purple dust into my palm.

"What are you doing, Jade?"

"It's—" I looked at Adam "—it's not breadcrumbs, but I have to. Just in case." I wiped my cheeks. "Just in case Oscar and Mother need a stopover."

EPILOGUE

FALL 1992, 10:20 AM

OSCAR STOOD, HIS ARMS AT HIS SIDE, STILL GRIPPING the gun that was pointed toward the ground. He looked at the two men. One was dead, the other would be soon.

"What do you want me to do with them?" Archie asked.

"Worthless pieces of shit." Oscar kicked one man's foot.

The man, his face bloodied and swollen, groaned.

"When are you assholes going to learn," Oscar kneeled beside him. "I ain't gonna die. And hurting my family, I'm gonna snuff you out." He stood and kicked the man in the ribs. He looked at Archie. "I'm taking Jade home and hoping like hell she never remembers this day. Tie them up. Put them in the trunk. Move the cars to the side of the road. Wait for me." Oscar looked at Archie. "We're sending a message. Do not *fuck* with Oscar Cooper or his family, or he will kill you."

Archie nodded and grabbed one man's wrist, dragging him to the side of the logging road.

Oscar slipped his gun into its shoulder holster and walked toward the kidnapper's Oldsmobile. "Jade," he said softly. "Jade, it's Oscar. Everything's okay. I'll take you home to Mom and Adam."

He didn't see Jade in the front seat. *Shit.* He pulled open the driver's door. No one. He pulled open the back door. On the far side, curled up like a wood bug was his little girl.

Oscar kneeled. "Jade."

She looked up. Her chin quivered.

Her tear-stained face wrenched his heart. Never again would anyone terrorize his family. He choked back the lump in his throat. "The bad men are gone. All gone." He so much wanted to say

Daddy's gonna take you home, but knew he couldn't. "I'm gonna take you home to your Mom and Adam, all right?"

She crawled up onto the seat.

Oscar held out his hand. Jade took it. He scooped her up, propping her small body on his hip. Her tiny arms wrapped around his neck and she rested her head against his chest.

"Where are the bad men?"

Daddy tied them up for the bears. "Adam's dad is making sure they never take a little girl or boy again," he said, walking toward his motorcycle. "We're going home. You can play in the backyard with Adam. That sound good to you?"

Jade nodded.

"I need you to be a big girl, and sit nicely on the back of my bike. Can you do that?"

"Yeah."

"I'll ride very slow, but you must hold onto me and not let go. You promise?"

"I promise."

"Good. Never let go, Jade."

About the Author

Joanna Vander Vlugt is an author and illustrator. As a teenager, she drew charcoal portraits and wrote mysteries. Under the pseudonym J.C. Szasz, her short mysteries *Egyptian Queen* and *The Parrot and Wild Mushroom Stuffing* were published in Crime Writers of Canada mystery anthologies. Her essay, *No Beatles Reunion* was published in the Dropped Threads 3: Beyond the Small Circle anthology.

The Unravelling, her debut novel, was a Canadian Book Club Awards finalist. Joanna is proud of her podcast JCVArtStudio - From the Dressing Room and the many artists and authors she's interviewed. Joanna's novels, art and podcast can be found at *jcvartstudio.net*.